SWEET SURRENDER

"Ya may fight me at first, lass," the dashing pirate whispered, "but it won't be lastin' long. I have a most convincin' manner."

Victoria trembled as Dru bent to kiss her. His lips brushed the corner of her mouth, her cheek, then settled warmly on her lips. She felt as if her breath, her will to fight had vanished, a pleasant warmth spreading through her and awakening a long hidden passion she scarcely knew existed.

Dru wondered if the nearness they shared affected her as it did him. He had desired many women, but none had invaded the recesses of his mind as this one had. Logic told him that once he returned this beautiful, delicate creature to her father he would never see her again. Or would he? Was it possible she would return again and again to haunt his dreams, steal into his thoughts, rob his sanity? His head whirled with the fragrance of her, sweet, tantalizing, seductive. He wanted her, wholly. He wanted to tame her. But why? And was he willing to pay the price?

EXCITING BESTSELLERS FROM ZEBRA

STORM TIDE (1230, $3.75)
by Patricia Rae
In a time when it was unladylike to desire one man, defiant, flame-haired Elizabeth desired two! And while she longed to be held in the strong arms of a handsome sea captain, she yearned for the status and wealth that only the genteel doctor could provide—leaving her hopelessly torn amidst passion's raging STORM TIDE. . . .

PASSION'S REIGN (1177, $3.95)
by Karen Harper
Golden-haired Mary Bullen was wealthy, lovely and refined—and lusty King Henry VIII's prize gem! But her passion for the handsome Lord William Stafford put her at odds with the Royal Court. Mary and Stafford lived by a lovers' vow; one day they would be ruled by only the crown of PASSION'S REIGN.

HEIRLOOM (1200, $3.95)
by Eleanora Brownleigh
The surge of desire Thea felt for Charles was powerful enough to convince her that, even though they were strangers and their married was a fake, fate was playing a most subtle trick on them both: Were they on a mission for President Teddy Roosevelt—or on a crusade to realize their own passionate desire?

LOVESTONE (1202, $3.50)
by Deanna James
After just one night of torrid passion and tender need, the dark-haired, rugged lord could not deny that Moira, with her precious beauty, was born to be a princess. But how could he grant her freedom when he himself was a prisoner of her love?

Available wherever paperbacks are sold, or order direct from the Publisher. Send cover price plus 50¢ per copy for mailing and handling to Zebra Books, 475 Park Avenue South, New York, N.Y. 10016. DO NOT SEND CASH.

ECSTASY'S CONQUEST

BY KAY McMAHON

ZEBRA BOOKS
KENSINGTON PUBLISHING CORP.

ZEBRA BOOKS

are published by

Kensington Publishing Corp.
475 Park Avenue South
New York, N.Y. 10016

First printing: September 1984

Printed in the United States of America

*To my own Victoria, Heidi,
and, of course,
my Irish rogue, G.W.*

PROLOGUE

England, January, 1778

An eerie stillness born of night and veiled in a cloak of heavy mist crept along the barren streets, slithering unheeded to encircle the single lamppost, clinging frantically to its golden halo as if to suffocate its beacon. Two figures passed beneath it, stirring up the fog to billow and curl and angrily descend upon the intruders, but to no avail, as they seemed unmindful of the threat. Steps unfaltering, they moved swiftly along the cobblestones, their passage unseen, lost in the midst of haziness as they journied toward the waterfront. The chilling night posed warning to the travelers to seek shelter, its icy fingers reaching out to claim them, hindered by black velvet capes clutched beneath their chins. Neither spoke, each caught up in his own misgivings.

Edwin Neilson cast a glimpse at the woman by his

side from beneath the dark brim of his tricorn. They had argued. 'Twas their custom, it seemed. He for her safety and she for his lack of courage. He sighed resignedly. If she only knew. He affixed his attention on the dark, monstrous shape of the frigate anchored offshore—their destination. He prayed everything would go well.

"Have you decided what to do if he doesn't agree?" Edwin asked, forcing his tone to be light. He stole a glance her way, spying a hint of yellow curl spilling from the protection of her black cape.

"I'll find another," she answered, each word short, crisp.

Edwin's patience escaped him. "But there isn't time. We sail at sunrise, and the conditions were that you have the guarantee of a captain and crew."

She stopped abruptly, the fullness of her skirts billowing out around her to sway into stillness. Sea-green eyes flashed angrily up at him, stealing his breath away as they so often did. Beneath the blanket of velvet, he knew there were a shapely figure, narrow waist, long, tapering limbs, full, tempting breasts, a prize he frequently claimed. And that face! Although Melissa Bensen had seen more than two score years, the passing of time had been kind to her, and Edwin recurrently wondered if as a young maid her beauty could have surpassed what he saw now.

"But it was you who said this captain dared anything. It was you who talked with his crewman, who assured me they only sail under a British flag for a guise. 'These men are pirates,' you said, 'free to go and do anything they want. They're perfect, Melissa.'" Her voice rang with sarcasm. "Are you saying it's different now?''

Edwin held his temper. ''No. I only told you what the mate told me. We were friends a long time past and I know he wouldn't lie. But it's the captain's choice, not his mate's, and since I don't know the captain, I'm not positive he'll agree.''

The corner of her mouth twitched. ''Then we'll find someone else later.'' She started off again.

''I don't know,'' he frowned, not moving.

She spun to face him. ''Don't be such a coward! You knew this venture would be dangerous when you agreed to come along. The others aren't afraid.''

''I'm not afraid,'' he growled. ''I'm simply concerned for your welfare.''

In the shadows of her hood, he could faintly see her smile. ''Then help me with this. You know they only agreed to my idea if I could hire a ship and crew to meet their demands. Do you think they're willing to sail us to America on a promise?''

''And why not? Less than three months ago you more than proved your loyalty by helping the general to establish a disguise for Colonel Kingsley.''

''Yes, but unfortunately, nothing's come of it.''

''That's not your fault,'' he exploded. ''And now you're willing to risk your life for them, and they want more. It doesn't make sense. If I were in your place, I'd tell them—''

Melissa reached out to touch his arm and calm him. ''You don't know the whole of it, Edwin. Don't be too quick to judge.''

''Then tell me, for I swear I'll go mad not understanding.''

Melissa smiled secretively. Why couldn't all men

9

adore her as Edwin did? "Do you remember my partnership with Colonel Truman Wingate?"

Edwin nodded.

"Fifty-fifty on a shipping line. I paid half for the brigantine but borrowed against the future profits to supply it."

"Yes, I know. A wise business deal, Melissa. It will make you wealthy," Edwin assured her, gently patting the hand resting on his sleeve.

"It got caught in gale winds last week and sank," she replied flatly.

"What?"

"And Wingate wants what I owe him. Of course, I didn't have it so he threatened to put me in debtor's prison. That's when I came up with this plan. But Wingate said it wasn't enough, my word was no good. He told me I must hire a ship, as well. If I don't, I'll go to prison." Melissa slipped her arm into his and slowly started off down the pier. "But I decided that the amount I owe in exchange for my possible capture and death wasn't equal. Thus my reward when England wins the war. Now do you understand the need to speak with this pirate captain?"

"Yes, of course. However, there's still one problem."

Stopping, she let go of him and turned to listen.

"What will you do if this pirate doesn't agree?"

Melissa's shoulders drooped, her patience thin. "We can always find someone else."

"Where?"

"Barbados!" she snapped.

"And how will you explain our sudden change in destination?"

Melissa's nostrils flared slightly. "That part of the deal was to prove my honesty on such a scheme by sailing to Bardados. I don't know! I'll think of something!"

"It won't work," Edwin stated objectively.

Her knotted fist found its way to her hip. "Do you prefer not to come? I'm sure I can manage without you."

He stared at her for several moments as if her suggestion held merit, then extended his hand. "That one," he said softly, pointing to a lone frigate anchored far out in the bay.

Standing at the bow of his ship, the captain and two of his crew guardedly watched the couple approach in a longboat, climb on board and start across the deck, their dark cloaks floating about them as if demons of the fallen angel had descended upon the vessel. The gray mist serpentined their figures, adding still another facet of foreboding. Yet the captain and his men held steady, listening to the gentle moans and creaking of the ship beneath them, their eyes unblinking as they silently contemplated the purpose of the meeting.

Once the strangers stood before the circle of men, the heady aroma of perfume attacked the captain's senses, setting him back momentarily. In all his years he had never been summoned by a woman to barter out a deal. In the darkness he studied the smaller figure, hoping to catch a glimpse of the refined breeding the scent implied.

"May I assume one of you is the captain?" she asked, the whiteness of her hand illumined against the ebony curtain of her cape when she reached up to read-

11

just the hood. A bejeweled finger caught the captain's eye. He raised an interested brow.

"Aye. And what is it ya be wantin' of me?"

"I have come to offer riches for your services." The velvet cloth enveloping her beauty wrinkled into soft folds when she quickly glanced around them. "But I must insist on privacy, captain. Your cabin, perhaps?"

The illusion shattered—for would a woman of quality seek to be alone with a pirate?—the captain retreated a step and leaned against the railing, his arms folded over his chest. "I hold no secrets from me men, lass. So be on with whatever ya've come ta say."

"But, captain, what if someone else should hear and try to take away your profits?"

Even in the misty gloom, Melissa saw a flash of white teeth.

"Ya come ta deal with thieves and worry about another's dishonesty?" His head moved as if he gazed over the ocean's surface. "Ya be makin' me wonder how sound this offer might be."

A hateful snarl curled her lip. Men! They were so stupid. Always wanting to prove how superior they were. She squared her shoulders and lifted her chin slightly. If only she had another option to choose. "All right," she conceded, her contempt for the man radiated in the bite of her words, "then we shall talk here, if that's what you wish." She moved to stand beside him, her hands resting on the balustrade. She would show this scoundrel that men weren't the only ones with enough intelligence to think out a plan that required skill and brilliance. "I am in need of a ship and crew to sail the American coastline, a privateer to attack all ships aiding the colonists in the war. Your reward will be whatever you take from these ships and enough silver to fill your pockets for the exchange of each vessel's captain. Dead or alive.'' She smiled in the protection of the shadows. That should take him down a notch.

Turning to face her, he leaned an elbow against the railing to support his upper torso. He cocked his head to peer beneath the hood of her cape. ''And why would I be agreein' ta such a thing? If we be wantin', we can be doin' it without your permission.''

A smile wrinkled the corner of her mouth. ''With one big difference. You'd be under British protection. And where would you receive extra silver for a dead ship captain? Any supplies you need will be furnished, and if your ship is damaged or sunk, we'll get you another. Where can you get a deal like this?'' Melissa could sense the way his gaze traveled the length of her, setting her nerves on edge, her heart pounding.

''And your reward be half of mine?'' he stated more than asked.

Her head jerked toward him. ''No! Mine will be the selection of any plantation I choose once England wins the war.'' She withdrew sharply and stared out at sea once more. Damn him! It wasn't any of his business.

The captain smiled at his men. ''And what must ya be doin' ta claim such a profit? Hirin' a ship is hardly a fare exchange. But then, what more could a lass like yourself be doin'?''

The son of a cretin! She had more courage than the lot of them! The edges of her cape grasped in an angry hold, she twirled to face him. And she would prove it. ''I am sailing for Quebec in the morning. From there I will go to New York. It will be my job to feed any information I can about the colonists to my contact in Quebec and verify your part in this. I must say, captain, what I must do will be far more dangerous."

"Aye, that it will," he agreed. He stood erect and started for the aft of the ship. "Since I have no intention of acceptin' your proposal."

"What?" Melissa exploded.

Several feet away, he turned back. "Aye, ya heard. I be havin' no desire ta aid in the war whether for England or the colonies. So I be suggestin' ya find yourself someone else. Now, if ya will be excusin' me—" He took a low mocking bow, turned on his heel, and walked away, his men close behind.

"I told you, Melissa," Edwin shrugged, watching the swirling mist engulf the pirates.

She glared at him, nostrils flared, a single word to denounce his claim escaping her. "Oh—oh—" she stammered, "just *shut up!*" In a whirl of petticoats, she bolted past him and disappeared into the darkness.

ONE

March 1778

Dark, ominous clouds, densely interwoven, blackened the skies and harbored a multitude of blinding flashes of light, followed by piercing cracks and volleys of thunder, intense enough to weaken even the bravest of hearts. The air, thick with moisture, closed in around the prey of the forthcoming tempest with an eerie stillness, oddly comforting, while masking the uncertain violence of the storm. Although the hour neared only ten bells, the darkness of the impending downpour transformed day into night in the minds of all those who witnessed it, save one small form that stood challengingly at the rail of the *La Belle Fleur*.

Staring out across the bow of the ship sailing for Paris, Victoria Remington studied the horizon where black met the opaque green of the sea, praying the small dot of land they had expected to see three days earlier would materialize. Although no one on board spoke of the possibility, Victoria, certain everyone else felt the same, feared they were lost, voyaging aimlessly about the ocean's surface, their supply of food and water dwindling rapidly as was their hope. She looked skyward, wondering now why she had ever pressed her mother and father into allowing her to sail the sea, intent as she had been on stilling the restlessness that stirred within her. A month past, Victoria had thrilled at the thought of a school for young ladies in Paris, a place her mother had never seen and her father praised. A tear pooled in the corner of her eye, moistening the band of thick, sooty lashes adorning it as she fought to control the sudden flow of trepidation that threatened to shatter her calm reserve. How foolish she had been to think a young woman who had spent her entire life on a plantation near Williamsburg, Virginia, could readily accept the daring adventure of a sea voyage. Having listened to her father talk of war and bloodshed in the colonies, escaping to the hardships of a long, grueling journey by land to New Orleans, where she booked passage on a sympathetic French ship, she had felt nothing could be as horrifying. How wrong she had been.

Trembling fingers fanned out to comb the dark mass of curls from her brow as she glanced up once more to watch the lightning dance about the sky. Hardly more than a child, her eighteenth birthday still to celebrate, Victoria's tiny frame had already blossomed into womanhood, a fact she knew and used to her advantage. Many a male admirer had come to Raven Oaks to claim her, only to be turned away disheartened. The

16

young heiress of the great plantation had yet to find the man she loved, dismissing all those who pledged their undying admiration of her as stumbling boobs, thinking the one to capture her heart would be of the mold from which her father, Beau, was made. He had not come by the title The Hawk falsely.

Dark brown eyes flecked with golden lights reflected the anxiety Victoria felt contemplating the storm. Many said she had inherited the beauty of her mother, Alanna—high cheekbones, delicate, straight nose, a soft arch of dark brows that shaded the thick, black lashes she used repeatedly to entice her suitors. Now all they aroused in those who observed her was sympathy. She feared the storm, and worse, she feared a lonely death at sea without the chance to send word of her love to Beau and Alanna Remington.

Off port, Victoria thought she heard a low rumble of thunder, too low, however, to have come from the clouds overhead. Clutching her shawl tightly about her shoulders to shield herself from the precipitous bite of the wind howling around her, she set her eyes on the foreboding shadows of the horizon, the erratic pounding of her heart quickening. A ship! White sails flashed out against the murky backdrop as the craft glided effortlessly toward the *La Belle Fleur,* bringing an amorphous twist to Victoria's otherwise flawless features. What caused the muted noise that drew her attention to the cryptic vessel? The question had little time to form in her worried mind before a white puff of smoke belched forth from the side of the brigantine, its explosive thunder obliterating it for the moment in the moisture-laden formations above her. A spray of heavy droplets showered over the *La Belle Fleur,* the cannonball having whizzed just off the prow. A warning shot, intended to be harmless but enough to bring the ship to compromise.

Fingers securely gripped around the railing, Victoria watched, unmoving, as the intruder sailed closer, her dark, sultry eyes growing wide when the flag bearing a skull and crossbones inched its way up the main mast in short, jerky movements, flapping boldly in the turbulent wind. Pirates! Panic rose within her, starting in her toes to spread wildly upward, constricting the muscles of her chest and squeezing the very breath from her, the name of Edward Teach surfacing in her mind. Even though he had died three score years ago, stories of his fierce rampage lived on, handed down from sailor to sailor in distorted verse, more bloodcurdling than the original legends. Word of the holocaust he had inaugurated reached even the ears of townsfolk planning a journey by sea, revived by those unfortunate enough to have witnessed the destruction he had caused. Many of the indentured servants living at Raven Oaks spoke of the stories their ancestors had told about the man, and Victoria would sit captivated for hours, listening and wondering about Blackbeard.

Knowing this militant ship could not possibly be captained by the fierce pirate, except perhaps his ghost, Victoria found her breath again, short-lived as visions of her doom filled her mind. This ship on which she stood, devoid of cannons of its own, stood little chance of fight against the invader closing in on them, announcing her fate in uncertain terms. What could she do to save herself? No corner in the hold or trunk within a cabin would serve to hide her from the searching, ruthless seizure by the enemy.

Shouts rang out as pirate ship and *La Belle Fleur* moved closer, a warning by the former to lay down arms and surrender peacefully, false promises of immunity if they would do as they were told. Chances were no one on board would escape unharmed and Victoria summoned the courage to flee the deck for safety in her own cabin, if only temporarily. She needed time to devise a plan that would insure her good health and leave her maidenhood intact, knowing the threat of her father's wrath would do little but bring a flood of laughter from her molesters.

The crack of musket fire filled the air, bringing with it a startled and frightened whimper from the raven-haired woman below decks and an urgency to see her masquerade fulfilled in utmost haste. Frantically, she scanned the small confines of the cubicle in search of a hiding place, shaking off the fatuousness of the idea with a toss of her dark curls. A pistol, perhaps? No, only one would fall victim, many to take his place when her gun fell silent. Her jewels and monies? But, of course, they would have them too before abusing her. Tears sprang to her eyes. How could she possibly stop them? If only she had been born a boy. A calculating smile twisted the corners of her mouth upward, a scheme coming to mind and flooding her with hope. But she must work quickly.

Down the narrow corridor from her cabin, she had, a morning past, discovered the cabin boy clumsily stepping from a door rubbing sleep from his eyes, and could only assume it to be the quarters he shared with the crew. Thinking he must possess more than one day's change of clothes, she hurriedly left her shelter, determined to borrow what she had to to accomplish her goal. Without knocking, certain he would be topside and not really caring if he wasn't, she hurried into the cabin, stopping abruptly at the sight of befouled untidiness. How could anyone live in such disorder and grime? Surely they could perish in the mess and naught be found for weeks. With a dismissing click of her tongue, she set about to find a shirt and breeches, acquiring both within a few moments, and proceeded to abandon her own red velvet gown and considerable layers of white ruffled petticoats, which fell into a discarded heap on the floor. Her nimble fingers untied the cords of her corset, and pitched the garment to rest with the others. Having hiked up the breeches to her waist and secured their position with a piece of twine, she slipped her arms into the sleeves of the shirt, displeased with the effect the simple garb projected as the homespun cloth clung revealingly across her bosom. They would know in an instant the charade she played. A nervous grip repossessed the rejected petticoat from the pyramid of clothing, swiftly ripping off a quarter section, with which she tightly bound her firm, round breasts, producing the illusion she desired, the underdeveloped shape of youth. With one final task to seal her guise, she scooped up her bundle of clothing and raced to the portal. Tossing the only clues to womanhood out the starboard side, she felt a twinge of sadness as she watched the exquisitely made velvet gown billow out, its skirt capturing the sea air as it drifted downward. Within moments its scarlet hue turned blood red, and the waters of the ocean claimed the expensive cloth. She squeezed her eyes closed, blocking out the vision.

Beads of perspiration dampened her brow. Wiping it dry with the heel of one hand, she discovered yet another problem as her fingertips became entangled in her waist-length mane. Her slim shoulders drooped dismay, then stiffened instantly at the sounds of angry voices and barrage of hurried footsteps thundering on the deck above her. No time to cut her great lengths of hair. Procuring a red bandana from the mound of the foresaken gear of a seafaring lad, she feverishly donned it, entwining the long strands of hair beneath it and securing a knot at one temple as she had seen most of the sailors do. With any kind of luck, it would see her through.

A shrill scream perforated the gloom from somewhere down the passageway. The splintering of wood from doors thrown open and the uproarious, venomous laughter crescendoed with each beat of Victoria's heart, telegraphing the advance of the victors and chilling her to the very bone. Would her disguise conceal her identity, disguise the truth hidden beneath the simple rags? Once more shaky fingers touched the scarf in a noncommittal gesture, lightly brushing the fairness of her cheek. Dear God! The costume would serve to veil her form, but what of the purity reflected in the smoothness of her skin, the innocence of her eyes?

The heavy thudding of thick-soled boots hit the deck outside the cabin. Her heart beat faster, anticipation of discovery greatly overwhelming her. She must find a substance to darken her face, grime to soil her cheeks. The interior of the residence rendered disarray, but as unkempt as it was, she could find no muck to serve her purpose. Time had run out as the door of the cabin was viciously torn from its hinges and came crashing down.

The shape that filled the framework appeared as if to tower three times her size and width, and Victoria cringed, certain her life was about to end as he stepped into the cabin. His black knee-high boots, their toes grayed and heels unlevel from years of wear, clung tightly to thick calves and disappeared beneath the balloon of his soiled breeches. A bright orange sash adorned his waist and clashed offensively with the dirt-smudged lavender shirt. A huge tricorn sat snugly upon his head, it, too, worn and dirty, its large plume in various stripes of brown hanging broken at the tip and pointing earthward. Beneath its large extremities, round, pudgy cheeks darkened with several days' growth of stubble, placid bloodshot brown eyes, and narrow, unsmiling lips delineated the face of a man unknown to her, but obviously a threat. The mere sight of him sent shivers through her. Then the stench that haloed his obese form reached out to engulf her. She gagged, retreating several steps to trip over a pile of debris and fall unceremoniously to the wooden deck.

"Get yeself topside, boy!"

The voice thundered disapproval and Victoria eagerly scrambled to her feet, fearful of even a moment's time alone with the man, her bare foot touching the first rung of the ladder before she realized how he had addressed her. A fleeting smile, an emotion stemming from hope for her survival, dashed across her face and vanished. Maybe, just maybe—

A state of violent disorder ruled the main deck. Of those men who were not thrown heartlessly overboard, the remaining were shot and left to bleed to death in disfigured, twisted shapes on the deck, their own puddles of blood encircling them. Terror filled Victoria once she witnessed the cruelty, but her heart ached when she heard the pained squeal of a woman and watched as it seemed every one of them was forcibly held down while each member of the pirate ship took his turn. Her stomach convulsed, certain at any moment it would spill forth the small acount of food she had eaten earlier, and she forced herself to look away, sucking in a score of breaths, the salt air burning her nostrils, to lessen the uncontrollable trembling of her limbs.

An hour passed, and all the while the tiny shape masked in boy's clothing stood by helplessly watching the pirate crew rip apart the once orderly and guiltless ship, until they had sated their avaricious hunger for riches, loading their own vessel with crates of ill-begotten gains.

"Set a torch to her!"

The voice loomed above the den of desolation and a new fear gripped the youth dressed in tattered rags. Victoria's thin face reflected horror as she observed the reddened tongue of fire quickly lap up its feast, spreading wildly across the deck, destroying everything in its path.

"Do ya intend to stand there until it burns the breeches off that skinny arse of yours?"

Victoria quaked in silence, her head lifting slowly to look upon the man who spoke. With trembling courage, she shook her head.

"Then board our ship and be quick about it, or I'll leave ya where ya stand."

Strong, steely fingers purchased the thin cloth covering her shoulder, hoisting her to the railing and the plank balanced precariously from one craft to the other. If she fell, she would drown, but, glancing back at the inferno racing to claim her, knowing life was more important to her no matter how bleak the prospect, she commanded her feet to move. The swirling waters below her, slapping one ship then the other defiantly, reached up long, wet fingers, beckoning her to join the cold uncertainty of the current. Her throat constricted, her breath labored, her lungs filled with smoke as she started across, suddenly lifted from her feet by a strong arm clamped around her waist. The rancid odor gagged her once more.

"If I wait for you, my backside would be singed. Cause me any more trouble and I'll throw ya to the fish!" As if to verify the threat, the meaty pirate made to drop her, bringing a fearful squeal from the slight burden propped on his hip. His loud, throaty laughter overruled the smell of him. "Ya feel like a woman and ya act like one," he added acidly, throwing Victoria to the deck of the pirate ship.

Pain bolted through every limb, summoning tears to her eyes, but knowing she must see the pretense through, she forced herself to endure the aching numbness of her knees and elbows and gallantly lifted herself up to face the man.

"I ain't no woman," she hollered, her voice cracking. "And don't you call me that!" She doubled up a fist as if to strike him, praying not to anger him overmuch, for him to see the humor of her innocuous warning.

At first his bulk stiffened in surprise, the knuckles of each hand buried deeply in the flabby tissue of his hips, his head tilted to one side, contemplating her from the corner of his eye. He scanned the length of her, toes to bandana, his brows furrowing in such a way Victoria knew not whether he might strike her or simply toss her overboard. A pudgy finger reached up to stroke his chin.

"How old are ya, boy?"

His voice, low and sure, proclaimed a threat not to test him further, but knowing she must not let him think her weak lest he abuse her for the mere sport of it, she squared her shoulders and stood her ground.

"Fourteen, soon," she told him, the lie tripping across her tongue. She watched him intently until dark, broken teeth appeared between tenuous lips, causing her to shudder, certain she had been found out.

"Soon, ya say? How soon? Nearly four seasons, I'll wager." A massive hand reached out to claim the collar of her shirt, its seams straining against the misuse it sustained. "Ya know what we do with liars? We feed 'em to the rats!"

"R-rats?" Her question spilled forth without a thought to consequence, her feet stumbling as the pirate dragged her across the deck. "W-where are you taking me?"

Distracted, the grubby man heartily kicked a sailor from their path, the wily beggar's ill-timed journey placing him before them and stirring the pirate's foul temper to the fullest. When they reached the ladder leading below decks, he spun Victoria around.

"Down. Before I throw ya down!"

Without pausing for the slightest moment, she hastily descended the sum of footrests until she reached the half deck, glancing back up at her captor, the vision of his face faint in the gray cloud of smoke spiraling upward a reminder of what her fate could have been. In the next instant, he stood at her side, her left ear pinched tightly between a thumb and finger. She had little choice but to go where he directed.

Standing before a door on the half deck, he released her only long enough to open the hinged covering, exposing the darkened aperture of the cargo hold. Victoria stared, wide-eyed, mouth agape, her mind searching for the right words to win her pardon, when, all at once, she experienced a stinging blow to her shoulder that sent her tumbling, falling to the deck below.

TWO

A groan cut through the stillness. In her half-conscious state, Victoria could not determine from where the plea had come. Her shoulder ached, her mind was foggy. She opened her eyes. Or had she? Blackness still surrounded her. She bolted upright, remembering. The cargo hold! Lifting her attention to the hatch overhead, she witnessed a narrow band of light meeting at four corners and showing the way out. She stood, her knees weak and nearly spilling her to the wooden planks again, to discover that even on tiptoes her fingertips failed to reach high enough to free her. Her spirits dampened, she plopped back down on the deck to rest her aching limbs and lull the throbbing in her temples.

A rustling broke the gloom of prison, a noise from within the space she occupied. Was she alone? She thought so, but the scratching came again. From two directions. Squinting, she studied the blackness until a movement drew her attention to the square outline of light staining the deck. She gasped, watching a fawn-colored fur coat, four feet with clicking nails, a long, pointed nose, and thin, black tail scurry across the yellow beam of light, unwittingly attracting an audience of two black, beady eyes. She shuddered, a chill running through her, her confidence to see the nightmare through shaken a degree. She retreated a step, the furry beast appearing to follow her, and she shrieked when another furry rodent darted across her bare foot.

"Papa," she heard herself whine, seeking comfort now as she had as a small child awakened suddenly in the night by a frightening dream.

A thudding solo of footsteps crossed the deck above her and quieted just outside the hatch. Her gaze, still affixed to the creatures brazeningly advancing as if seeking their next meal, refused to wander, instead locked in absolute observation of the foe. Her heart raced, praying the barrier to freedom would open and send a stream of light flooding over the inmates of the hold, chasing the aggressors to darker recesses, saving her sanity. Then, as if her thoughts were heard above the unearthly silence of the tomb, the eerie creaking of wood pervaded the void engulfing her. The beacon of light divided the ebony curtain, and a voice loomed loud and commanding.

"You there! Look alive!"

Her adversaries forgotten, their presence of lesser importance at the moment, she looked up. "Yes, sir," she managed to reply courageously.

The shadowed form disappeared for an instant, replaced by the uncoiling of a rope ladder thrown into the hold to bounce then dangle within her reach. Although either choice left much to be desired, she decided that at least topside she might be able to sate the hunger that now oddly knotted her belly. How she could think of food at a time such as this, she could not fathom, but knowing without it she would grow weak and be unable to save herself, she justified the yearning and lifted a tiny hand to pull her up the ladder.

"Now, ya little guttersnipe, how old will ya be?"

With his question, a knot tightened her throat, making it difficult to swallow. If she stuck to her story, she might land headfirst in the hold again. Even if she agreed with his speculation the result could be the same. But, by either option, she knew she played the game well. Be it thirteen or one more, the pirate had no idea of her true identity.

"Th-thirteen, sir, for months to come. I only wish to be older." Her voice shook in undeniable fear; of the dread of what was to come, but the pirate heard it with the mistaken assumption that the young lad had gained respect from threat of punishment.

"That's better," he growled triumphantly, reaching out to seize her lean arm in a strong, painful grip and send her off in the opposite direction. "You'll spend your time in the galley, washin' dishes. Until you're a man, you'll do women's chores."

Little did the blackguard know, his punishment of her for lying had been a blessing to Victoria. She had no knowledge of the sea or the manning of a ship, and the truth would have been found out the moment she was ordered to tie a simple knot of rope. Masking a smile of gratitude, she easily allowed him to guide her to her new confinement.

To her surprise, as Victoria found out later, she had spent the entire day, the evening's meal, and most of the night alone in the hold before the foul-smelling sailor had freed her. From the lump on her head above her right ear, she deduced the reason why time had escaped her during her imprisonment. Now, with supper finished long ago, the tin plates washed and stacked away behind secured cupboard doors, she realized she would have to wait until morning to satisfy the hungry rumblings in her stomach. That was, of course, unless she could coax a small morsel of food from the round-bellied, gray-haired man she learned was the ship's cook. She doubted it. From the moment she had stepped into the galley, the man never looked at her, only grunted angrily whenever she trespassed on his attention by stepping in his way, being seated in the chair beside the table that he had intended to occupy or absently clearing her throat when nothing else could dispel her boredom. Not having the vaguest inkling how long she would be forced to stay on board this pirate ship, she mustered enough fortitude to attempt to mold an ally from this reticent, indifferent little man.

"My name is Vic—Victor. My—ma always called me Vic. Y-ya can if ya want," Victoria hastily amended. Her head lowered as if humbled, she carefully scrutinized the cook from the corner of her eye, hoping he had not noticed her near slip of the tongue. "What's your name?"

A weathered face with gray penetrating eyes moved to study her. "I don't need help. I told 'im so. Next port we dock, you get off."

Victoria prayed the smile she felt inside did not reflect in her eyes. Whether he needed help or not, she had no intention of staying with the pirate ship. Somehow, some way, she would free herself from them and send a message home.

She spent the next two hours gazing out the porthole in an effort to occupy her mind rather than watch the cook grow increasingly drunk from the liberal amount of rum he consumed. The only sound that conquered the silence enveloping them both was the periodic belch her companion felt compelled to let out. When the belches seemed to grow in volume and frequency, Victoria forced herself to study the darkening horizon, trying to coax the vision of a rescue ship out of the gathering gloom, her depression and state of hopelessness deepening.

Stifling a yawn, Victoria glanced back at the man, wondering if he, too, felt the burden of a long, trying day, her eyes widening in surprise to find she was alone. When had he left and why hadn't she heard him? But did it really matter? She relaxed with the comfort of being alone, to let down her guard and give vent to the anxiety that seemed to rule her isolated existence, her uncharted plans for survival weak and unnerving.

Settling herself in a chair, she crossed her arms over the wooden surface of the table and rested her head in the crook of one arm, vowing only to close her eyes for a moment lest her offensive friend enter quietly with thoughts of some greater torture for her than that of the hold. Soothed by the gentle lapping of the ocean's water against the ship and the occasional creaking of wood in the cabin, her mind wandered, recalling the adventure her mother had described to her. There had been a storm at sea much like the one Victoria had experienced, and, although alone, a prisoner of pirates as

Victoria now was, Alanna Remington had sailed through it, never faltering, and emerging stronger than before. They had kidnapped her in Williamsburg and whisked her off to New Orleans, an act paid for and devised by a certain Melissa Bensen, a woman who despised Alanna. Her mother had never told every detail of the wretchedness she had endured during her capture, and Victoria could only assume that it was simply too painful for her to relive, even to sympathetic ears. Her father knew, but when pressed on the issue, he strongly suggested she let it lie, and, since Mistress Bensen had a long time past left Williamsburg, Victoria knew of no one else to question to satisfy her curiosity. The only part she understood in full concerned her mother's betrothed, Radford Chamberlain, a man who had died trying to save her from the pirate captain, Dillon Gallagher. Beau and Alanna spoke of Radford as if he were a saint, and, had he not died, Beau would now be only a neighbor, rather than her own beloved father. Indeed, she would not have been born. A smile played with the corners of her mouth. She was glad things had worked out as they had.

A chorus of impetuous voices volleyed Victoria from her retreat on the chair, her eyes wide and alert and devouring the space that surrounded her. The cries sounded urgent, and, dashing to the porthole, Victoria could only hope their warning meant favorable tidings. The blind nothingness of a starless night malevolently greeted her, the only thing staring back at her was her reflection in the glass. She turned away disheartened, then heard the muffled voices in the passageway just outside the galley and moved to listen. Her heart beat faster. The voices were discussing the divvying up of the spoils of their siege and suggesting that they should all be gone from the ship in record time to squander their shares in the manners of their choosing. To leave the brigantine could only suggest that the pirate ship had dropped anchor. Dear God! Let it be so!

Pressing an ear to the hatch, Victoria waited until their mumblings faded, lingering a moment longer to make sure the men had really departed before lifting the latch and venturing outside the galley. Finding no one about to question her presence, she quietly moved for the companionway, pausing briefly to make sure she was alone and giving herself time to think. If she could make it topside without a detour, she was certain once she reached the railing she could jump overboard and swim to shore. What awaited her there surely must be more rewarding than what could happen to her in the hands of these pirates. After one last fleeting glance around her, Victoria swiftly climbed the ladder to the main deck and a chance at her freedom.

"Where ya think you're goin', boy?"

Victoria felt the cloth of her shirt across her shoulders tighten as the sailor grabbed a fistful at the nape of her neck and lifted her from the deck.

"Ah, Kelsey, let 'im be," another voice suggested with a moan. "We's got better things ta do than watch some snot-nosed brat. Turn 'im loose and let's go."

"Yes, and if I do, he'll be far gone when we get back. No," he added, giving her a bone-rattling shake, "I'll take 'im with me so's I can keep an eye on 'im. I'll make a pirate out o' 'im. Besides, we can use someone to fetch our rum for us."

A disgruntled curse trailed from the other man's lips, followed by a dismissing wave of one hand at Kelsey's insistence at having the adolescent tag along. Without further speculation on the subject, the sailor hurriedly walked away.

"Ever been in a pub?" Kelsey grinned corrosively.

"No-er-yes!" Victoria exclaimed, fighting to free herself of his hold. She must persuade his sordid mind into thinking that she lied again, and, to prove her wrong, take her with him. A pub meant civilization, and among the crowd there must be someone she could trust. "I've had my share of rum."

"About as many times as ya've had a woman, ya lying cur. But I like your spirit." With a hearty shove, he sent her stumbling to the rope ladder and a rowboat. "It's about time ya learn what it's like ta be a man."

A hand clamped securely on Victoria's shoulder dispelled any thoughts she had of fleeing the pirate's company before they reached the pub. He didn't trust her any further than he could row the brigantine out to sea, and she realized that unless he got staggering drunk he would watch every move she made. She would have to remain alert at all times, and the moment his attention was drawn away she would quickly and unobserved depart his ill-intended hospitality.

They walked a few hundred yards down the waterfront, meeting several grubby seamen who didn't even bother to look up at them, and stopped outside a small building. The absence of windows prevented them from viewing the interior, but the chorus of noisy voices suggested the drunkenness inside. In an instant, Victoria found herself slammed against the swinging doors leading inside as the pirate exploited her shoulders and head to open the way.

"Give me a tankard of rum," he bellowed to the barkeep, shoving Victoria into a chair. "And bring one for my friend. Tonight he'll become a man."

A rally of whistles and cheers filled the room, all eyes centered on the slight form crouched beside the table, and, although she never lifted her gaze, she knew everyone studied her. She hoped the heat of embarrassment hadn't stained her cheeks enough for anyone to notice, else the laughter and hurrahs would begin again, forcing her to slouch even further. Above all else, she wanted no one to watch her.

"Here ya go, boy," the besotted pirate offered, banging down the pewter mug before Victoria. "Drink up. I wanna see how much ya can hold."

Her tremulous fingers wrapped around the cup, she raised the liquor to her lips, its heady aroma descending upon her and filling her with doubts about her sanity for ever having gone this far. She glanced up at Kelsey, then back at the drink she held, knowing of no way out of her predicament other than forcing the rum down her throat. She intended only to sip it, but with the mug to her lips, Kelsey suddenly leaned in and raised the bottom in the air with the tip of one finger, spilling most of the rum down Victoria's chin, neck, and shirt.

"See there!" he wailed. "I knew ya couldn't hold your rum!"

Again the room brimmed with mocking laughter, and for a moment Victoria entertained the thought that the fate of *La Belle Fleur* was more appealing that what she was experiencing now.

"Where'd ya get him, honey?"

Soprano tones pierced the gaiety, filling Victoria with hope that God had sent a friend. She looked up, her face reflecting that hope, her thoughts immediately

35

shattered when her gaze met a disapproving look. With her arm draped over Kelsey's huge shoulder, a woman Victoria guessed to be nearly two times her own age smiled disdainfully down at her. Her bright yellow hair, pulled tightly back into a knot on top of her head and streaked with silver above each ear, failed to add color to her already milk-white complexion. Her scarlet-painted lips, pinched with unkind years, sneered over yellowing teeth, and Victoria knew in an instant she would find no support from this creature. She went back to squeezing rum from her saturated clothing, centering her attention anywhere but on the conversation the two held.

"I brung 'im along ta show how a man enjoys hisself. Thought maybe you could teach 'im."

"Not me," the woman shrieked, pulling away. Kelsey caught her wrist.

"I didn't mean you and 'im. I meant he could watch."

Appalled by his words, Victoria's entire being seemed to lose all animation. Her empty stomach knotted, her limbs trembled, and she fought an overpowering urge to scream disapproval.

"Why you ol' devil," the woman crooned insidiously. "You like that sorta thing?"

A wide grin broke the line of his mouth. "Better yet, I like to have two women in my bed."

Victoria closed her eyes, feeling the convulsive tremor spread throughout her, knowing that if she was to be saved it would be by her own words. Her mind raced for a solution.

"Look at 'im. Sittin' there daydreamin' about it."

Her eyes flew open. "I ain't neither," she barked

36

somewhat nervously. "I just don't think it's fair I gotta watch. 'Sides, what makes you think you're so good you could teach me better'n anybody else in this place?"

Several disgruntled agreements droned in the densely smoke-laden room, building Victoria's courage. She glanced about, noting nearly every eye trained on her. She smiled to herself.

"I'll wager none of these men do."

His pride injured, Kelsey bent down to strike her. "You son of a whoremonger." Before the blow landed, she squirmed from his reach. "Come back here!"

"Yeah, go ahead and hit me," she baited courageously, carefully positioning herself behind a chair far enough away where his meaty fist could not connect with her jaw. "Show 'em how big a man you are to hit children."

"Yes, Kelsey, show us!" a voice called from the multitude of jeering laughter.

His round face darkened in rage, abashed by the goading of his comrades. He cast them all an evil glare, silently challenging any one of them to step forward and prove the contrary. Then, with a swiftness of his boot, he viciously kicked away the chair shielding Victoria, a movement that did not register until the vibrating of splintering wood against the wall filled her ears. He stormed on her, seizing her arm just above the elbow in a painful grip, then hurling her to the floor.

"Mock me, will you!" he roared, his voice echoing throughout the hall.

Fear overruling her, Victoria covered her head with her arms when she thought he would strike her, feeling instead cruel fingers bite the flesh of her arm as he lifted her to her feet and painfully shoved her across the room toward the stairs that disappeared into a long corridor. Pleadingly, she looked back to the faceless occupants of the tavern. No one moved.

"Come wench," he ordered loudly. "I have need of you to warm my bed."

The misbegotten trio climbed the stairs in silence, the delicate form that led the caravan praying somehow that her next breath would be her last.

THREE

For nearly an hour Victoria quailed in the corner where Kelsey had ordered her to stay. He had stripped himself of only his breeches, stockings, and shoes, hungrily torn at the flimsy dress of his whore, and tumbled heavily into bed with her, there to grope clumsily at her thin buttocks and thighs while suffocating her with wet, rum-scented kisses, grunting the entire time like some boar in a mating ritual. Victoria forced herself to stare blankly ahead, as if watching them, while actually conjuring up visions of her beloved home, Raven Oaks. Its black trees filled the front lawn shading the enormous white-pillared house, a place where she had spent endless hours playing. How could she have possibly grown bored with it all?

She drew in a weary breath, the stench of the room awakening her senses, her stomach churning with the origin of its cause. She had overheard two male servants of her father's discuss a woman like the one who now lay in the bed, but she had failed to understand the disparaging remarks they made until this moment. How could a woman, any woman, lower herself even to associate with such a man, much less lie with him? She touched her brow with the back of her hand, feeling the fever that seemed to possess her entire body. How much longer?

Canvas bed-straps, straining against the weight of the bodies they supported, creaked one final time as Kelsey lifted himself from the bed. "Well, boy. Ya learn anything?" He jerked on his breeches, sending Victoria a salacious grin and lift of one brow, something she failed to see since she had chosen to cover a yawn of mocked boredom with one hand.

Only how much you disgust me, she thought, then smiled. "Certainly did," she said aloud, hoping her hatred of the man had not tinged the deliverance of her words.

"And I'll wager your skinny little arse is jealous," he boasted loudly. "Ain't never seen a man as big as me, have ya? Or you," he laughed, whirling around and throwing himself across the bed and the woman buried deeply in the covers. She expelled an accumulation of giggles that seemed to bounce off every knot in Victoria's spine.

"Ya know what I'd really like ta learn?" Victoria purposely interrupted, since she wished not to have to view an encore of the past hour's bestial activities.

An irritated snort rumbled from the direction of the straw mattress.

"I'd like ta learn brag. I ain't got no money now, but if ya teach me how to play, and I work for a couple of

40

twopence, I might win more."

A round, dark head with dirty ruffled hair peeked out over the edge of the bed. "You?" Kelsey chuckled opposingly.

"Yes, me. Don't ya think ya can?"

Piqued by the stab at his dexerity, he lifted himself higher. "My skill at teachin' ain't what worries me. I wonder if a runt like you has the brains to learn."

"I can learn. I just need a *good* teacher."

Kelsey rested back on one elbow, his other hand gently stroking his bedmate's thigh. "All right. We'll just see if ya can. But remember this," he added, pointing a warning finger at her, "ya watch with your mouth closed. Ya don't even raise a brow. Got it? One little twitch will tell 'em what I got in my hand and I could lose it all. If I do, and I find out it's 'cause of you, I'll beat the hell outa ya."

Unaware he had given Victoria a grand idea, he bent down, kissed the bare breast partly hidden beneath the graying sheets, and rolled from the whore's side. "Well, come on, if you're going!"

The next hour Victoria found herself acting barmaid more often than watching the round of hands dealt out. Since she knew the game well from watching her father and grandfather play, she had no real desire to join in, and welcomed the opportunity to refill Kelsey's mug. The more he drank, the more intoxicated he would become, and the greater would be her possibilities of quietly slipping from the tavern.

"Where'd ya get this squirt, Kelsey?" one of the men at the table laughed when Victoria tripped over an outstretched foot and fell headlong on the floor, dumping the tray of rum-filled mugs she carried.

41

"That's *my* money you're throwin' away," Kelsey roared, spinning in his chair to place the heel of his boot to Victoria's backside. She lay spreadeagled, hearing the room explode into laughter. "I found 'im sneakin' around this French ship we jumped."

Slowly Victoria stood up, dusting off her breeches and wincing when her hand touched a sore buttock.

"Ya shoulda been with us. Best damn ship we got in a long time."

"Carryin' lots of furs and jewels, was it?"

"Naw. Somethin' better."

"What could be better'n that?"

"Women. I never had me so many woman in one time for as long as I can remember!" Kelsey chortled wickedly.

Victoria closed her eyes, hiding the remorse that tore at her and the gratitude that she had been spared. At least, she was still alive and untouched, and if God would grant her one thing, she would be gone from this pirate before the sun rose again.

"Well, just don't stand there. Get more rum, you idiot!"

Victoria snapped to attention, listening to the snickers and lascivious speculations on the destiny of the passengers on board *La Belle Fleur,* her heart aching with the cold, insensitive hardness of the men. When she returned to the table, mugs refilled, Kelsey pointed to an empty chair.

"Slide that over here and sit down. You mess up one more time and I'll lay your head open. You understand?"

Victoria nodded respectfully and studied her hands folded over one knee, not daring to look up until everyone's attention had been drawn back to the table and the large stack of coins lying in the center. At first her interest lay elsewhere, until she noticed Kelsey's turn of bad luck. His pile of silver dwindled rapidly, and, with an inward glee at seeing him without a twopence, Victoria watched intently. With every loss of the cards, he downed another mug of rum, his temper smoldering. Another round dealt and all the wagering done, only two men remained holding cards. Studying him, Kelsey's face reflected nothing Victoria could define as hope or failure.

"Show me what ya got," the stone-faced pirate demanded.

Victoria's heart sank. His voice, sure and calm, rang with victory.

"If ya be seein' me cards, laddie, ya will have to be meetin' the wager." A lean, sun-darkened hand shoved a stack of coins into the already heaping pile.

Victoria's eyes widened, knowing the sum was more than Kelsey possessed.

"But—but—" he stammered, frantically searching his pockets. "I ain't—"

The clinking of silver scooped across the table brought a panic-striken bellow from the man. "Wait! A note. I'll give ya a note. A promise ta pay."

Victoria quickly looked to her lap, biting the inside of her lower lip to hide her delight. Be it small, this downfall chimed with justice.

"Sorry, me friend. I can't be spendin' a promise."

"Then you name it! Anything! Anything I got against the cards."

Victoria played with the dirty cuff of one sleeve, sensing the pain Kelsey experienced and loving every

43

minute of it. She only wished—

"The lad."

Victoria stopped in her musings, the words the stranger spoke taking precedence. What lad? Had a secret this man knew in Kelsey's past come to haunt him? Slowly, her eyes lifted to look at Kelsey, discovering the same bewilderment she felt contorting his face.

"What lad?" he asked, befuddled.

"The one ya be kickin' about. Scrawny though he is, I be havin' need of him and think his worth the same as ya be needin' ta see me hand."

Every tiny hair on the back of her neck stood out, marking the sudden and powerful fear that bolted through her as quickly as a flash of lightning in a storm-darkened sky. Now what was she to do? And how long could she hide the truth? Although Kelsey was no prize, she had already learned how to bait him into doing what she needed. But what of the stranger? Slowly, so as not to let him know, she turned to appraise the gambler. The thick smoke of many cheroots mixed with the dimness of the room hung heavily in the air and partly obscured her vision of the man, but not enough for her not to instantly feel a bolt of mystifying attraction charge through her. Raven-colored hair, wildly tossed and much shorter than fashion allowed curled gently around his sun-darkened face, bronze in complexion as she imagined a Greek god would be. He had a strong brow, wide cheekbones, and a straight nose, which seemed to accentuate the square jaw and full, almost sensuous mouth, now slightly lifted in a mocking smile, deepening the dimple in one cheek. She gulped, feeling her heart flutter at his handsomeness, and quickly met his gaze. Steel-blue eyes stared back at her, seeming to touch her everywhere, undressing her, discovering her secret. Did he know already? She watched in paralyzing fear as the stranger lifted his mug in the air in a silent salute. She strained to breathe.

"This brat? Hardly weaned from 'is mother's teat? Ya want 'im?" Kelsey's mirth vanished. "It's a deal."

Cradling his cards in both hands, Kelsey fanned them out methodically, savoring their touch, their sight, their promise of wealth, his eyes peering over the tops to stare across the table at the man who had made the wager. The crowded room full of ruffians quieted, every one of them breathless and waiting and paying no heed to the slight form quaking in the chair at the end of the table.

The stranger, shadowed in the gray curtain of smoke, smiled confidently, laying down one, then another, until all of his cards rested on the table face up. His eyes never broke their hold on the stunned face of the man who, in an instant, knew he had lost everything.

"Aarrrgh!" Kelsey roared, catapulting from his chair and knocking it noisily to the floor. With an angry swipe, he seized the pewter mug before him, gulped down the rum, and stormed from the tavern, hurling the empty tankard at the barkeep before he passed through the door.

Staring wide-eyed, fingers gripped around the back of her chair, Victoria felt her doom close in around her as she watched the night swallow up Kelsey's huge frame. She glanced back across the table, saw the stranger scooping his winnings into a small leather pouch, and sought the opportunity to escape. Flying from the chair, she raced for the door.

"Sean!"

Another dark figure stepped out in front of her, barring her way out and blocking her entire vision as the huge frame of the man filled the doorway. She looked up into the smiling face of the intruder, as different from the first as night is to day, with blond, sun-lightened hair pulled back sleekly at the nape of his neck and tied with a red ribbon. Sandy-colored brows shaded his blue eyes, but his grin was more a challenge than one of friendship.

"I wouldn't be thinkin' ya'd want to go with the likes of him, lad. It appears he spends more time kickin' ya about."

Frantic, Victoria glanced back at the gambler to find he had downed his mug of ale and made to rise, filling her with an urgency to run. But her feet refused to move as she watched his long, lean frame unfold to a greater height than that of the one called Sean. The plain white shirt he wore clung to his wide shoulders and fell open to the breastbone, exposing a thick mass of dark curls and taut muscles darkened by hours spent in the sun. But what mainly caught her eye was the narrowness of his waist, in comparison to his broad upper torso, and the well-shaped thighs revealed beneath the tightness of his cotton breeches. Her mind failed to register whether he wore stockings and shoes, for her eyes lingered on and held the fabric which stretched across his manhood, an observation that raised a strange curiosity in her. She blinked suddenly with the realization of where her thoughts had wandered, embarrassment scorching her cheeks, and she spun around, doubling up a fist, intending to land a blow to Sean's belly. If the mere sight of this dark, handsome man shattered her

46

steeled reserve, she knew she must never be alone with him for long. She must escape and now! Her arm drawn back to launch the attack, she discovered instead the strong capture of her wrist in another's viselike grip, not hurting but impossible to break. She didn't have to look up to know her captor's identity.

"Let go of me!" she screeched, striking out at the hand that held her.

"Are ya deaf as well, laddie?" The deep baritone of his voice sent an alien tremor through her. "I wagered good money against your oversized friend because I be needin' ya. Now it wouldn't make sense ta be lettin' ya go."

Of a sudden, Victoria found herself shoved into the other man's arms.

"Now let's try it again, Sean."

The trio left the tavern and guffaws that drummed in Victoria's ears, her arm clamped securely in an unyielding grasp. They headed for the shoreline in silence, and with each step they took Victoria's heart beat faster. Who were these men? Friend or foe? If they knew the truth about her would they laugh at her venture, then each have his way with her? They were certainly no gentlemen, for no one of class would elect to patronize an unsavory establishment such as the one they had left behind. Were they different from Kelsey or of the same mold? She decided to listen, to observe them, and make a judgment then on which of the two to trust. Stealing a secretive glance at the one who squeezed her arm, she noticed in the dim lights of the street that he frowned. Was he angry with her? Or at his partner? Could she possibly win the friendship of one and turn him against the other? But which should it be? She covertly looked at the second man, the one who "owned" her, and her pulse quickened. Even in the muted light, his rugged features and forceful profile projected a stubbornness that made her doubt that anyone could sway him in any direction other than the one he chose. Finding little comfort there, she nominated the other one, Sean, as her target, and returned her gaze to the path they took.

When they had traveled a safe distance from eavesdroppers, Sean slowed his pace, pivoting Victoria to his other side and placing him next to his friend. "I know ya always have good reason for what ya do, but for the life of me, I can't be figurin' out what ya need with another cabin boy. Has your heart gone soft and ya felt pity for the lad's abuse?"

A low chuckle brightened the void of their ebony surroundings. "And have ya not always trusted me, Sean?"

"Of course! But ya usually let me in on what ya plan before ya do it."

"I couldn't. Not without lettin' everyone know."

"Well, we be alone now."

"Be patient, cousin. As soon as we board the ship—"

"No-o-o!" A wail cut the stillness, and in the next instance Sean found himself victim of a futile attack. A fist struck his chest and shoulder, a bare foot kicked his shin, all causing the assailant more discomfort than Sean himself.

"Ya little outlaw!" Sean exploded, swiftly grabbing the youth with both arms around her waist and clamping her own to her sides, her feet dangling in midair. He glanced at his friend. "Now I know why ya be

48

takin' me along," he grunted. "Ya figured I could be handlin' this. Someday, Dru, I'll be gettin' even." He gave his delicate baggage a rough shake. "Now straighten up, lad, or ya'll be knowin' me fist to your jaw!"

Fearing certain doom if taken to their ship, Victoria fought harder, falling limp when Sean squeezed all the more. "You're hurting me," she moaned breathlessly.

"And what ya think ya be doin' ta me?" Sean argued. "I be a gentle-raised lad. Not used to wrestlin' with some half-grown beggar."

"Then put me down."

"And do I have your word ta behave?"

A moment passed before an affirmative mumble answered him.

"What? Ya need ta talk louder so I'll be sure of what ya say," Sean baited playfully.

"Yes!" she barked, squirming in his hold.

In the next moment, Victoria found herself painfully sprawled in the sand, Sean's merry laughter bruising her ego. She glared up at him.

"Now will ya be walkin' like a good little lad or do I drop your breeches and give ya the thrashin' ya deserve?"

"I-I'll walk," Victoria quickly guaranteed, finding her feet in a hurry. "Just point the way."

His thumb jutted northward, and, without another word, the group started off again, Victoria a crisp three yards ahead of the men.

"You'll be havin' nothin' but trouble from that one, Dru," Sean whispered, watching the determined gait of their new seaman plodding through the mounds of sandy beach.

"I not be thinkin' so."

"And what makes ya so sure? Ya can't be keepin' an eye on him all the time, and threatenin' ta redden his bottomside won't work for long. He's got a strong will and one you'll be testin' quite regular." He looked up at his companion, noting a smile on the man's face. "Ya be knowin' somethin' I don't, Dru, me boy?"

"Aye. Watch the way he walks."

Fixing his gaze on the youngster again, Sean squinted in the shadows, studying the delicate step the boy took, stumbling over sticks, tripping in dried seaweed, and all the while maintaining an almost seductive sway to his hips.

"He walks down right sissified. Hardly the swagger of a seagoing lad."

"Me point exactly, cousin."

"And what ya be makin' of it?"

"How did he feel when ya held him?"

Thoughtfully quiet a moment, a fingertip scratching his temple, Sean resignedly shrugged one shoulder. "Scrawny for a lad. Even a young one. Almost soft, I'd say."

"Near soft as a woman?"

"Aye. Soft as a—" He stopped sharply, catching the crook of Dru's arm in his hand. "Ya don't mean— The lad ain't— Oh, Dru, we can't be takin' a woman on board. The men will each have their turn at her and we'll have nothin' ta do ta stop them."

"If she fooled her big friend, I'm sure she'll fool our crew. For a while, anyway. I only be wantin' ta find out her plans and who she is. I'll wager me winnin's she's the daughter of a man who could fatten our purse."

"Ah-h-h. I see what ya be after," Sean grinned, a

silver beam of moonlight sparkling in his eyes. "But tell me. How did ya know? What gave her away?"

"I started wonderin' when Kelsey decided to take the lad upstairs ta watch him roll in the bed with his woman. Very few young lads wouldn't be curious. This one was horrified. I could see it in his face. I kinda shrugged it off, but when Kelsey talked about the women he had on the ship they took, the lad turned nearly green. And then, of course, his hands." Dru slowed a bit, retrieved a stick from the sand, and started off again, whirling the twig out across the gentle rolling tide to watch it splash then float back to shore again.

"What about his—er—her hands?"

"There's not a callous or sore on them. In fact, they be the prettiest hands I've seen in a long time." Draping a long, lean arm across Sean's shoulders, Dru leaned closer. "That's why, me dear cousin, I think we be havin' a treasure in front of our own eyes."

"And bein' the sort I am, Dru, I'll be more than willin' ta care for the lass. She can stay in me cabin and I'll string up a hammock for meself. I wouldn't want ta see our captain's good nature tested."

Dru's grip tightened around his cousin's neck. "A saint ya are. But since it was me own money and me who found her out, I be thinkin' she can stay in the captain's quarters. If she came this far untouched, I'd hate ta have *you* be the one ta force yourself on her."

"Dru," Sean moaned, feigning injured pride, "I have never forced meself on a woman in me life."

"Aye, that ya haven't. Not so's they say, anyway. But a reliable source has told me how your words talked her into doin' somethin' she never would have thought

51

of without your help.''

Sean chuckled lightly. ''And what can be the harm if it's done with their consent?''

Dru glanced back up at the thin shape hopping along the shoreline on one foot, the other held up awkwardly to brush away a pebble that threatened to do damage. ''I doubt you could find the words to soften that one, cousin.''

''And would ya care ta put a piece of silver on it? A friendly wager, I be askin'. Ta see who can tame her first, you or me.''

The suntanned cheek wrinkled with amusement. ''A great feat for a great prize.''

''Any amount ya be wantin'. Name it.''

Tapping a fingertip against his lower lip for a moment, Dru contemplated the price. ''Your share of the next ship we take.''

''*All* of it?''

''Are ya doubtin' your charm, Sean?''

''Ah—no. But since I've not had the lass, I be wonderin' if she be worth that much.''

''The wager is whether or not you're man enough ta have her in your bed. Not whether you'll like it once she is. That is, *if* she ever is.''

''If?'' Sean howled, arching a tawny brow. ''Then I'll take ya on, me cocky friend, just ta prove ya wrong. But ya must be givin' me a sportin' chance. Ya are ta promise not ta take advantage of the lass while she's sleepin' in your bunk.''

Dru shook his head sadly. ''Me poor aunt was right.''

''Me mother?''

''Aye. She raised a fool.''

Sean knotted his fist, raised it to Dru's jaw, and paused a moment before a wide grin broke free. "A fool, maybe. But a damned good-lookin' one."

"And conceited as well," Dru added, ducking out of the way of Sean's playfully thrown punch, still laughing when he spotted the young girl wandering toward a grove of trees. "Over here, lad."

Victoria wondered if they were to walk the entire length of beach for lack of something better to do. As close as she could determine, the sun would rise soon, and she had not slept a wink since the morning past. Every bone in her body ached, her muscles were bruised, and now, walking through the thick sand full of sticks and rocks, she felt certain her bare feet could take little more. If only she knew she could outrun them—for escape offered a better reward than trusting strangers—she'd race for the cover of trees some few hundred feet away. But then again, what did she have to lose? Fixing her gaze on a likely spot, she swallowed hard and took a deep breath, when all at once a hard, stinging slap caught the seat of her breeches.

"Me sainted mother, are ya deaf?"

Victoria spun around, outraged. "How dare you!" she demanded, all sign of impish, untrained youngster gone.

Resting his weight on one foot, his other knee bent slightly and arms folded across his chest, Dru silently contemplated the affront, unable to keep a wide grin from parting his lips or the dimple from appearing at the corner of his mouth. "I dare anythin', me boy. I paid for the privilege."

Victoria's face flushed with color, but in the darkness it went unseen. "Yes, sir," she mumbled obediently, looking to the sand that nearly covered her feet and praying her outburst had not given her away.

"Now come along. Our longboat is tied off over here," he instructed with a short nod of his dark head.

Mutely, Victoria led the way, stepping into the warm saltwater of the shoreline and wincing at the stinging bite of it in the cuts and sores of her feet. Would she ever be comfortable again? She sat quietly in the back of the boat, watching the diffused orange flickerings of lamplight grow dim and wondering if she was destined for a life as a cabin boy.

FOUR

"Would ya be carin' for a drink of me fine Irish whiskey before turnin' in, Sean?" Dru askcd as the trio climbed on board the *Defiance*.

"I'll be passin', cousin. Me bones are tellin' me I be needin' a bunk more. Take care of the lad," he threw back over his shoulder as he disappeared across the main deck on his way to his cabin.

"And how 'bout you, lad? Would ya care to sample me whiskey?" Dru asked, turning on the silent figure beside him, a soft smile playing on his lips.

"I don't drink," Victoria mumbled, then stiffened with her near slip. "Whiskey, I mean."

"And what do ya favor? Milk?"

"To be quite honest, sir," she returned, twisting out of the way of an arm about to rest around her shoulders, "I don't find favor in any drink."

"Don't ya now? Well, that will all change. Ta be a

good pirate, ya must drink.''

"Pirate? I don't intend to become a pirate," she said most emphatically.

"No? And what would a scrawny lad like yourself be wantin' ta do? Own a plantation in the colonies?"

Her heart fluttered. "No. I guess I haven't thought much about it. Would it be too much to ask that you show me a place to sleep? I'm not used to being up all night."

Dru hid his smile, nodded, and started for the passageway, listening to the soft slap of bare feet following him. When they reached a hatch at the end, he opened it and went inside, waiting until Victoria had entered before closing it and turning the key in the lock. The click it echoed spun her around.

"But this is *your* cabin."

"Aye, that it is. On the morrow, I'll be findin' a hammock ya can use, but for tonight ya can share me bunk." He crossed to the large desk sitting in one corner, pulled the small bag from inside his shirt and tossed it on top, proceeding to undo the buttons of his garment as he studied her intently. "Just sleep in your breeches if ya be wantin'." His hands slipped to the brightly colored sash at his waist. "I prefer sleepin' without."

Victoria's heart seemed to race to her throat, strangling the breath from her. Quickly, she centered her attention on the wall lined with numerous paned portholes, the blackness of night painted on them. If only their darkness would spill into the cabin and cover everything. If only this was a dream—

"Somethin' be troublin' ya, lad?" she heard the deep voice ask.

56

She swallowed, the beating of her heart pounding in her chest as if it would tear itself from her. She opened her mouth to assure him of no great need, finding instead, no voice to utter the words. A weak, trembling smile lifted one corner of her lips and, forgetting why she had looked away, turned back to face him, her eyes growing into wide circles. Her mind swirled, the lights of the cabin swiftly blending into one, her breath leaving her. A thudding pounded in her ears, and without warning Victoria slumped, unconscious, to the deck.

The gentle sway of the ship bobbing in the waters off-shore lulled everyone on board to sleep. But for Victoria, it played with her, teased her, and brought a harsh reality racing to her half-conscious state. Her eyelids fluttered, then flew open. She bolted upright, discovering the soft cushion beneath her was his bunk. She rapidly scanned the room, relaxing only slightly when she realized she was alone. Where had he gone? Would he return? She scooted off the large velvet-covered bunk and hurried to the hatch, there to test the lock. The latch would not move in her hand. Dejected, she turned away, her mind filling with various plans to see her through. She glanced back at the closed hatch. Its lock forbade her to leave, but possibly she could bar the way for anyone to enter. Glancing about, she spied a huge, graying trunk sitting in one corner of the cabin. With one handle held securely in her grip, she struggled with the trunk's weight until she had inched it across the deck and placed it before the hatch. Satisfied, she expelled a long sigh. At least now she would be able to refresh herself without worry of intrusion.

Tightening the thin rope at her waist again, Victoria's spirits sank with a new thought. What of her womanly curse? She could hide her curves and the length of her hair, but the first would cause great difficulty. She fought tears, telling herself the problem would not occur, for as soon as she could, within the day, she would be free of these pirates and on her way home to Raven Oaks. The weight of her troubles pressing down on her, she decided it was best for now to sleep. She must be alert to stay ahead of the man called Dru, for during just the short time she had spent with him, her instincts had warned her that he would not be fooled for long.

Having washed herself with water from a pitcher on the table, she replaced the trunk in the corner, returned to the bunk and lay down, experiencing a chill that cut through her. Slipping beneath the dark blue coverlet, she settled herself comfortably and closed her eyes, praying sleep would come quickly.

The amber glow of lamplight melted darkness and chased away the shadows in the cabin, spilling out across the floor to fall gently, tenderly on the tiny shape nestled beneath the covers of the bunk. Behind the desk, the captain of the vessel poured himself another drink and settled back in the chair, his heels propped on the corner of the dark piece of furniture, his ankles crossed, quietly observing the delicate figure and pondering the reasons he was sharing his cabin and his bunk with this not-so-ordinary woman, if she was indeed a woman.

Dru Chandler raised the glass to his lips, his eyes never moving from the sleeping form, wondering what her true name might be and from where she hailed. But as the whiskey warmed his weary body and relaxed his muscles, he suddenly found himself speculating on the beauty she hid beneath the rags, the ivory-colored skin masked in dirt smudges. A stirring in his loins, he raised one brow curiously, contemplating the age of the child and the possible foolishness of the wager with his cousin. If this youth proved to be just that, a child, a girl, there would be no contest on his part. He sipped his drink once more. Though she was small in stature, a good ten inches shorter than his own six feet, Dru sensed the traits of womanhood, recalling her outrage when he had soundly slapped her bottom. He smiled one-sidedly, a spark of devilment glistening in his gray-blue eyes. He refilled the glass and stood, the thumb of his free hand hooked in the sash of his breeches. And of course the way she had fainted when she turned back to face him and found him standing before her without a single thread of clothing to cover him. His lips parted with his chuckle. A woman of gentle upbringing, for no harlot would have swooned.

The dimple appearing in his well-tanned cheek, he casually strolled the distance to his bunk and gazed down at his sleeping cabinmate as she lay enveloped in blue velvet. Dark, thick lashes rested against the pale complexion of her face. Finely arched brows and a thin, delicate nose, its tip blackened with soot, drew his appraisal to the high cheekbones only briefly, for in her slumber, unaware of his presence, she dreamed of something pleasant, and he noticed the slightly up-turned mouth, lips begging to be kissed. How could Kelsey have been so blind? he mused, lowering himself to the edge of the bunk. But the offensive pirate's fumble had won Dru a great prize. He was sure of it. If only he could see the treasure she fought so bravely to conceal.

Leaning down, he placed his glass on the floor near his feet, then returned his attention to the tiny woman who seemed so vulnerable in the mammoth bunk. When he reached to pull away the dingy bandana hiding her hair, the wrinkles in his brow faded as he compared the size of his hand to the sleeping face, realizing he could crush her skull if he'd wanted to. She stirred in her dreaming, one arm shooting out from beneath the covers to lie across her brow, and Dru fell back, disappointment curling his upper lip, for not only had she spoiled his chance to remove the bandana, but she had exposed the fact that she slept fully clothed.

"Rose," he whispered, his smile returning, "they should have named ya Rose, for ya have the beauty of the flower, lass." He remained a moment longer, then sighed and left her, knowing he would sample her nectar before sending her home again. But for now he must be content with the promise and allow her to tell him her name freely, lest her anger play him false and at every turn seek to slip a blade between his ribs.

A warm breeze touched against Victoria's cheek, its fragrance filled with salt, surprisingly comforting, yet at the same time invigorating. She stirred, rolling to her side before opening her eyes. Lids still heavy with sleep, Victoria struggled to open one eye slightly, thankful she had not yawned or stretched or in any other way announced she had awakened for near the desk with his back to her stood the pirate captain. Drawing courage from his unawareness that she watched, she studied him openly. He was dressed only in his breeches, and she noticed with some surprise the crisscrossing of scars across his broad, muscular back, muscles that rippled with each move he made. His wide, sun-darkened shoulders seemed to accentuate the narrow waist and lean hips, held erect by well-shaped thighs and by the way he stood, his equally tanned calves and feet spread apart as if he expected a sudden swell of whitecaps to rock the ship. His slate-black hair, combed neatly and glistening in the rays of sunlight that stole into the cabin, curled defiantly against his neck, and Victoria smiled, recalling how her father wished to style his hair so, only to be constantly reminded by his wife how the fashion called for it to be tied with a ribbon.

The captain turned to lift a shirt from its place on the back of a chair, presenting Victoria with a striking profile and bringing an accelleration to her already jittery pulse. A thin, straight nose, high cheekbones and the firm set to his jaw—these could also describe her father, except for the eyes. As she recalled the night past, when she had been sitting across the table from him, she realized she had never seen eyes the color of his. Steelblue, reflecting a hardness and indifference. She wondered if they mirrored the inner man.

"So, laddie, ya decided to view the mornin'."

Victoria stiffened instantly, fearful he had seen how she appraised him. She nodded feebly.

"I be thinkin' ya need a good breakfast, seein' as how ya passed out on me the way ya did last night. 'Tis the only reason, isn't it? Or are ya hidin' somethin' from me?" As he spoke, he pulled the white, full-sleeved shirt across his shoulders and walked to the side of the bunk. He reached out a lean brown hand, pressing it to her brow. "Ya not be havin' a fever, so I can't be thinkin' of any other cause." He began fastening the buttons of his shirt, eyeing the young face staring back until he finished the last and made to stuff the shirttail into his breeches. He fought the smile that threatened to reveal his knowledge of the lad's plight when he witnessed the youth turn his head away. After adjusting the collar on the broadcloth garment and fastening the buttons at each wrist, he casually sat down beside his new cabinmate. "I gave it a great deal of thought last night, and because I don't want the rest of me crew to be thinkin' I favor ya, ya will be stayin' in the crew's quarters."

"The crew's quarters?" she stammered.

"Aye. Ya be findin' fault with me choice?"

"No, sir," she mumbled, hoping to repair any damage her nervousness had caused. She studied the rumpled coverlet lying across her lap.

"Well, I could be lettin' ya share me cousin's cabin, but I don't find it fittin' for a young lad. Sean likes to entertain ladies from time to time." Dru stretched back to rest his shoulders against the wall, tucking one arm within the other, and cunningly observed his companion from the corner of his eye. "And ya can't be stayin' with me. Sean and I enjoy the same pastime." He raised a playful, dark brow, watching the flood of color stain the lad's cheek.

"The crew's quarters will do fine," she said quietly, flipping the covers from her. Then the realization that she had slept the night through without awakening once provoked her concern for what had transpired while she lay asleep. "Where—where did you sleep last night?"

"Where?" he asked, looking at her.

She nodded bravely.

"Here," he said with a point of one forefinger to the bunk at Victoria's side. "Ya know. I be thinkin' a voyage with me ship will do ya good. Ya be an awfully soft lad."

Victoria's pulse throbbed at the base of her neck.

"Well—" he announced with a stinging slap to her thigh, "we best be off. I'm sure Sean has been up for hours and more than likely about ta leave us behind." He flashed her a wide, sparkling grin of white teeth and left her side. Reaching the door in three long strides, he stopped and motioned for her. "Look alive, laddie."

Feeling the need to straighten the bandana covering her head and tend to her toiletries, she lingered, hoping her request would neither anger him or be denied. At the moment, she could think of no possible explanation.

"If you don't mind, I'll come topside in a few minutes." She looked away, feeling the heat of her body crawl hotly up her neck to inflame the fairness of her face. "I—I only now woke up."

"Oh, that," Dru said, nodding his head knowingly. "I'll wait."

Victoria's head shot upward, her lips parted in silent perplexity, not knowing what to say or how to avoid the difficulty. She swallowed repeatedly, finding no words to make clear her need for privacy. Then an understanding smile crossed Dru's lips.

"I be gettin' your meanin', lad. A bid modest, ya are. But in time, it won't be botherin' ya any at all." He opened the door and stepped into the passageway, calling back a warning to hurry before securing the door once more. Safely outside where she could not see his gaiety, he paused, his wide shoulders shaking with his tightly held laughter. "Ya are a devil, Dru," he snickered and started off for the main deck.

Topside, he found Sean idly knotting and unknotting a piece of rope, his long, lean frame pressed back against the railing. Looking up at the treading of footsteps in his direction, Dru noticed the worried expression on the man's face.

"Somethin' troublin' ya, cousin?" Dru asked before he reached him.

Gathering Dru closer where no danger of eavesdroppers existed, Sean glanced back over his shoulder constantly in the direction of the captain's quarters. "Now ya be tellin' me true. Do I owe ya me share of our next take?"

Stepping back to better study Sean's face, Dru exhibited an expression of concern. "Sean, me boy, from the looks of ya, I'd say ya haven't slept a wink for worryin'."

"And neither would you if ya knew the lass shared a cabin with me."

"I worry knowin' she shares the same ship."

Sean threw his hands in the air. "Me sainted grandmother. Ya sound as if ya think me a ruttin' stag. Give me a little more thought, cousin. I much prefer to woo a woman that crawl up behind her."

"Then take it from me. I think you'll find yourself crawlin' where this little lass is concerned. I doubt she'll be findin' your charms more appealin' after spendin' a night in me bunk." A wide, suggestive grin parted his lips.

"Ah, Dru," Sean moaned, disappointment marring his features. "Ya didn't even give me a chance."

"The contrary, cousin. I gave meself a chance. Had

you the first move, I would be the one with the long face now.''

''Excuse me, capt'n.''

Dru cooled his attack to face the newcomer, a little man well known for his talents as cook. ''Aye, Thatcher.''

''Will you want me to put the hammock in your cabin now, or do you plan to use it again in the galley?''

An explosive growl filled the air, startling Thatcher into retreating several steps. He quickly glanced from the captain to his cousin, the reason for such an outburst unclear.

''Leave it in the galley for now, Thatcher. I'll be decidin' later.''

''Aye, aye, capt'n,'' Thatcher concurred, thankful for the chance to escape a situation that obviously harbored ill feelings.

''Ya lyin', good-for-nothin'—''

''Uh-unh.'' Dru wiggled a negative finger in the air. ''If ya recall, ya was the one who thought the wager done. I just didn't deny it.''

''Aye. And ya would have taken me money had Thatcher not come when he did I be beginnin' ta think meself a fool for offerin' such an amount. I'll never be sure ya speak the truth.''

''Ah, Sean,'' Dru sang out, reaching over to envelop his cousin within a warm hold, ''don't ya know I enjoy gettin' the better of ya?''

''Aye, since we were youths. I would like ta know your father. Since me aunt was gentle and honest, ya must have gotten the devil from him.''

''And would ya be explainin' where ya come by the same trait?''

"I learned it from you. Always bigger than me, I had to learn quickly just to survive. Ya always pleaded innocence when I tattled to me mother. 'Sean,' she would say," his voice took a higher pitch, " 'now ya know your older cousin wouldn't do that.' Ha! Never where she could hear!"

Laughter rumbled deeply in Dru's chest. "And would ya have it any other way?"

Sean looked away, a momentary agreement curling his upper lip.

"Now, would ya?" Dru gave Sean's shoulders a rough squeeze.

"No, I guess not. But someday I be havin' me turn on you!"

"I won't be doubtin' it."

He stared at his cousin a moment, then smiled. "Well, I don't know about you, but I'm hungry. Will we be standin' here all day or gettin' somethin' ta eat?"

"We'll be goin' just as soon as—" Dru glanced back over his shoulder, spying Victoria as she stepped onto the deck. "Just as soon as our new cabin boy joins us."

"You'll be takin' her with us?" Sean asked in surprise, his voice held to a whisper.

"Aye. What better way for us to be keepin' an eye on her?"

"I be thinkin' ya askin' for trouble."

"Not with Sean Rafferty there to defend her honor," Dru smiled, stepping away and not waiting for a rebuttal. He crossed quickly to Victoria. "Top of the mornin', lad. Feelin' better?"

She smiled weakly, her gaze fixed on the tall figure standing across the deck from them, his arms folded over his chest. He seemed displeased about something.

66

She had no way of knowing from what it stemmed, but somehow she got the feeling it might be because of her. A firm hand on the space between her shoulders started her off in Sean's direction.

"Mornin', lad," he nodded when they reached him. "Hope ya slept well." He cast Dru a sportive look and lifted one golden brow.

"He slept soundly, cousin, but near beat me ta death with his thrashin' about." Dru's face held no hint of falsehood.

Mortified at the thought of such close contact with a man, especially this man, Victoria squeezed her eyes closed, hoping neither of them would notice the impact his words had on her, and in doing so missed the light smile that raced across Sean's face and disappeared.

"A pity. Our captain should not be uncomfortable where he sleeps. Maybe I should be havin' the lad sleep with me, so's ya be fresh in the mornin'. We can't be havin' ya mannin' the helm with your eyes closed."

"Aye, 'tis true, and the very reason I be havin' Thatcher string up a hammock for the lad. Now I be suggestin' we be on our way before we be eatin' two meals at one time." He took Victoria's wrist in a firm hold and guided her to a longboat tied to the side of the ship.

Her bare toes sunk deeply in the warm sand as she waited for her companions to secure the longboat to the stump of a decayed tree, Victoria considered the small town laid out before her, an awful realization coursing through her. What was spread out in front of her was no common village, with no inhabitants sympathetic to her quandary, and Victoria experienced a tightening in her throat. The *La Belle Fleur* had not been at sea long enough for them to reach the shoreline of France, and she wondered if this could possibly be a small island near the mainland. Shaking off the likelihood, she recalled no foreign words spoken in the tavern where she had encountered her new owners.

"What ya be thinkin', lad?"

She looked up, discovering both men had joined her without a sound.

"I was wondering where we are," she dared ask, training her eyes on the scene ahead and failing to notice the exchange of knowing glances between the cousins.

" 'Tis an island called Barbados, a good distance from North America," Sean volunteered. "Why ya be askin'?"

Her small shoulders jutted upward. "Just curious. How far from America?"

"Too far ta be swimmin', if that be your meanin'."

"Oh, no. I only wished to find out how far I had come before—before Kelsey—"

"And where did ya set sail, lad?" Dru cut in, sensing the discomfort the cabin boy felt at remembering the ordeal.

"New Orleans."

"Were ya a stole-away? 'Tis apparent ya not sailed before." His gaze shifted to Sean.

"Uh—no. I was kidnapped." Although the actual kidnapping had taken place many weeks later, she thought it best to alter the time. If these men were at all congenial, she might be able to convince them to return her home.

"Kidnapped, is it? Then your family will not be knowin' where ya are?"

68

"No, sir," she said hopefully, turning to face the captain. "And if you'll send word to them, I'm sure they'll pay you back the money you lost at the card game."

Dru settled his weight on one foot, cupped one elbow in his hand, and tapped the thumb of his other hand to his lower lip, all the while slowly evaluating the slight form from head to toe. "From the looks of ya, I can't be figurin' how they could afford the price. And if what ya say is true, why didn't ya offer a deal ta Kelsey instead of lettin' the man beat ya about?"

"I thought I could run from him. As I thought I could run from you." Glancing back across the shoreline, she added, "But I see that would be a useless thing to do since this is only an island and I have no money to buy my passage home."

"And where would that be, lad?"

Victoria looked from one to the other, praying she was about to make the right decision. "Williamsburg, Virginia, in the colonies."

"Virgin—. What were ya doin' so far from home, lad, to find yourself in New Orleans?"

Victoria's face flushed. "Uh—my father and I had sailed there on business. He's a ship merchant, among all the other things he does, and decided it was time for me to go along to learn the trade." Even if they agreed to take her home, she knew she couldn't expose the fact that she was a woman. Her words flowed easier telling the lie. "We had gone on shore to shop the stores for a gift for my mother and we got separated. The next thing I knew, I woke up on a ship heading for France."

"Well, lad, I be sympathetic to your needs, but Virginia is too far for us to be sailin' for the price of a card game.'' He brushed past her on his way to the village, Sean falling into step with his long, easy gait, and Victoria dashed by them both to block their path.

"Then you name the price. My father can well afford any amount you name."

"Can he now?" Dru smiled.

She nodded vigorously.

He studied her a moment. "I'm truly sorry, lad, but no amount would be enough. Your homeland is at war with England, and we be treadin' dangerous waters." He sent Sean a playful smirk, one Victoria missed as her greatest hope for returning home came crashing down around her. They started off again, leaving her to stand in quiet agony.

Suddenly a new idea struck her and she spun around to chase after them. "Then send a note to him. Tell him where he can find me and the price you want for seeing to my safety. There would be no risk in that. In Florida, perhaps. It's not too far from here."

Dru feigned consideration of the proposal. "I be thinkin' about it," he finally said, stepping past her again only to feel her small hand firmly grasp his arm.

"His name is Beau Remington of Raven Oaks, a plantation near Williamsburg. Everyone there knows of him. It wouldn't be hard to see a note is given to him. If you want, I'll write it myself so he won't think it's a trick."

Dru glanced down at the hand resting against his sleeve, noticing the delicate bones and the color of its flesh only a shade darker than his shirt. A hand not accustomed to work, he mused. He looked to the face staring hopefully back at him. Dark brown eyes, the darkest he had ever seen, flecked with the sunlight dancing in them, mirrored her conviction that she had won his confidence. Absently reaching up to pull away the bandana and reveal the color of the hair hidden beneath it, he caught himself in time, tapping the end of her nose with his fingertip instead.

"I think better when me stomach is full."

Watching the two figures stride away from her, Victoria's face broke into a wide grin, relief and hopefulness flooding through her. Although she couldn't trust them fully, she knew that at least with them she stood a better chance of returning home than with Kelsey. Kicking at the sand beneath her feet lightheartedly, she skipped off after them.

They selected a small inn a good distance from the beach, a building not quite as depressing as the one in which the card game had taken place, but one that still left much to be desired. The small room just inside the front door bulged with an over abundance of tables, as if it expected a large crowd of hungry customers to storm the place at any minute. They settled themselves in the far corner away from the only entrance to the room, and Victoria noticed how both men elected to place their backs to the wall. Obviously, they both were accustomed to unexpected danger, no matter what time of the day. She sat down across from them and silently waited for the thick-girthed woman, the one who had eyed them intently from the moment they entered the inn, to approach.

"Well, boys, what will ya be havin'?"

Victoria's stomach knotted, a knot that rose to her throat and threatened to gag her. The stench of the woman killed any desire she had for food.

"We'll be havin' the same as we always do, Milly.

71

And bring enough for the lad," Dru grinned, reaching out to pat the woman's pudgy rump and bring a squeal of delighted laughter from her.

Victoria watched the woman wobble away, wondering how she would be able to force down any food knowing such a creature had prepared it.

Having leaned back in his chair, his legs stretched out before him under the table and his arms folded across his chest, Dru scrutinized the slight shape sitting before him, a vague smile curling his lips and forcing the dimple in his cheek to appear. Chances were she had never ventured any further from a sheltered life on a plantation than to a grand ball at a neighbor's or into Williamsburg, with her father hovering over her. How such a gentle soul had made it this far sparked his admiration. Although the price Beau Remington would pay to have his daughter in his protection again would be high, Dru oddly regretted the day it would happen. He had had many women in his past, but none that interested him more than the woman-child in his company now. His mother had told him that some day the lass would enter his life who would change it, one who would steal into his thoughts and into his heart, one who would rule his being and force him to give up his life at sea. He chuckled quietly, doubting it to be so, yet wondering what a life spent with this woman would be like. Truly it would be a trial each and every day.

A disturbance at the door of the inn broke his concentration, and he glanced up, watching a small caravan of oddly matched customers enter. Three neatly dressed men led the way, selecting a table that would accommodate them all, then one of them pulled out a chair and waited until the second of them motioned back outside for someone to enter.

Victoria watched in awe as the doorway shadowed with the shapely figure of a very beautiful woman, a new and better hope exploding in her mind.

FIVE

Their appetites appeased, Sean and Dru acquired themselves a tankard of ale, leaving Victoria to sit alone at the table while they engaged in a friendly game of darts in one corner of the room. Dru had noticed the attention the young woman dressed in boy's attire had given the latest newcomers to the inn, and guardedly watched her appraise them, wondering just what might be going through her head. He and his cousin were not strangers to the island, knowing nearly every inhabitant by name or someone else who could furnish it, and after evaluating the foursome who sat quietly to themselves, he discovered their identity would require a little research.

"Have ya noticed the lass's interest in our friends over there?" Dru whispered, tossing another brightly colored dart, its point burrowing deeply into the target on the wall.

Sean cast a seemingly apathetic glance Victoria's way, cognizant of the fact she had slid her chair about to better view the party. He raised a sun-lightened brow. "Aye. I wonder what she be about."

"No doubt to rid herself of us." He flicked another dart in the air, thumping when it hit the board, closer to the center than its predecessor. "Have ya an idea who they might be?"

Sean shifted his gaze to the circle of people, carefully studying each one, his attention lingering on the richly fashioned woman who held everyone's eyes. Her bright yellow hair, styled in an abundance of soft ringlets about her face and neck, dangled beneath the enormous hat she wore, its brightly colored ribbon holding it in place with a knot below one ear, and huge plumes showering out from the crown, dancing about in the breeze each time she bent her head coyly in response to something one of the men said. Although a multitude of folds of cloth covered her bosom in the shawl draped about her shoulders, Sean doubted half the sum of cotton was needed to hide her slender figure. The chair on which she sat all but disappeared beneath the yards of fabric, and, resting stoutly against her thigh, a fringed parasol waited patiently for her hand to possess it once more.

"I can't be imaginin' one lass I failed to woo, but this one, dear cousin, is new to me. If ya be wantin' another share of ale, I'll be only too willin' to fill both our mugs, and slip Milly an extra coin for any knowledge she be havin' of the woman."

The dimple in Dru's cheek appeared. "Aye. If anyone be knowin' of the lass, Milly would. I fear the poor trollop is jealous of anyone who might be treadin' on

75

her territory, and she'll not waste a moment findin' a way to rid herself of the threat.''

Sean contemplated both women. ''Aye, and this be most certainly a threat.'' He chuckled. ''I be wonderin' what Milly would be thinkin' if she knew our little cabin boy's secret? Even dressed as she is, the lass is far more appealin' than ol' Milly.''

Both men glanced back to Victoria just as the delicately fashioned parasol slipped from its perch and plunked on the floor. Bolting from her chair, Victoria hurried to retrieve the defiant article. Sean busied himself with studying the mugs in his hands, Dru the tip of one dart, while both secretively watched Victoria's seemingly good intentions, certain this had been the moment for which she waited.

''Excuse me, madam,'' Victoria whispered, handing back the parasol and carefully avoiding a glance toward her captors. ''I am in dire need of your help.''

A gloved hand accepted the proffered item while sea-green eyes critically appraised the youngster. A full, sensuous mouth, slightly marred by wrinkles denoting her age, gave no acknowledgment of Victoria's pleas.

''I am being held against my will by the men playing darts,'' she bravely continued, the woman's gaze lifting slightly. ''No, please don't look at them. They are pirates and I am truly a woman. My name is Victoria Remington from Williamsburg, Virginia, in the colonies. I dress this way to save myself from them. They have no idea that I am anything but what I appear to be.''

Suddenly, Victoria's shirt tightened cruelly about her neck, brutally yanking her upward. She cringed, knowing the hand that held her must belong to one of the cousins.

"I be beggin' your forgiveness, dear lady, but me cabin boy seems to have forgotten his manners."

"On the contrary, sir. I find the youngster refreshing," the woman smiled, the soft tones of her voice soothing Victoria's stress a little.

Dru grinned playfully down at Victoria. "Aye. He is a lovable little thing. Don't know what I be doin' without him."

Victoria's shoulder shot up, trying unsuccessfully to free her garment of his hold, until the pressure on her earlobe being squeezed unrelentingly between a thumb and forefinger dissolved any desire to move.

"Now will ya be holdin' still, lad?"

With a somewhat sympathic look, the woman rose and leaned forward to envelop Victoria within her arm, thus freeing the painful entrapment of her left ear.

"Please, sir, I do so detest undue violence," she smiled brightly, "and the boy meant no harm, only to aid my need, as I pray you will do also."

Dru flashed Sean a suspicous look, quickly masking his cautiousness with a wide grin and a deep bow. "And what could a poor lad like meself be able ta do for a lady as grand as yourself?"

"I have only just recently acquired a ship of my own, and, not wise to the life at sea, I now find myself in rather an upsetting predicament." She smiled warmly at Victoria, then back to Dru. "I, too, have need of a cabin boy, and I am most willing to pay whatever price you see fit for the boy."

Victoria's heart pounded beneath the baggy shirt, her knees weak, and a smile breaking free on the dirt-smudged face. Until this very moment, she feared the

77

woman had not believed her story, had been intending to return her to the pirates and a future of uncertainty.

"I truly be understandin' of your need, but this lad is not the one ya be wantin'. He has been at sea no longer than yourself. I don't be thinkin' he'd be much help ta ya. And besides"—he reached up to smooth the wrinkles of his brow—"I wouldn't be knowin' where I could lay me hands on another cabin boy right now." He reached out to take Victoria's arm, hearing the click of a pistol warn him away. He froze, his eyes finding the source of the message. Off to one side stood one of the three gentlemen, the long barrel of his gun pointed at Dru's chest.

"As I said before, I detest undue violence, so why don't you just name a figure and we'll be on our way," the woman suggested, a vague smile of triumph revealing a sliver of white teeth. "As you can see, one way or another, I intend to have the boy, and it would only be wise of you to accept the money rather than go away without anything."

Devilment sparkled in Dru's steel-blue eyes. "On that, I would be agreein'. However, I be thinkin' you ta be the one who will lose."

The woman's fine brow lifted slightly beneath the wide brim of her hat.

"Before the night is over, ya'll find the lad not much of a cabin boy," Dru added, disguising his true meaning.

From the doorway of the inn, Sean and Dru observed the group of strangers, Victoria in their midst, board a carriage and pull away to disappear within a few minutes. Having forced himself to remain quiet the entire time the ownership of the cabin boy exchanged

78

hands, Sean suddenly turned on his cousin, an unusual black scowl marring his normally merry features.

"Would ya be explainin' ta me why we let them take the lass?" His eyes bounced up and down, watching Dru toss the bag of coins in the air repeatedly, until, losing his patience, he made an easy grab for the reward. "It seems ta me, you be the one who thought ta make our fortune by sellin' her back ta her father."

"Aye, and that we will," Dru told him, casually turning about to reenter the inn, Sean following closely behind.

"And just how can we, if the lass is no longer with us?"

Dru stopped abruptly and gave Sean a heretical look, holding out his hands, palms upward. "And did ya expect me ta argue with them? I didn't see ya stepping between the man's gun and meself."

"But I never saw ya back down before!"

His sun-darkened hand slapped his chest as Dru feigned injury to his heart. "And now ya think me a coward. Surely no good will come ta me if me own cousin has lost faith." He stared blankly at Sean until the corners of his mouth twisted, and, unable to contain himself, laughed loudly. "I simply saw no point in arguin'. As soon as the lass's new owner hears her tale, the grand lady be doin' the same as us. Let them keep an eye on the lass for a while."

Sean looked sheepishly to the floor. "And what if she doesn't?" He looked up, drawing courage from his thoughts. "What if the woman *is* a true lady and only be wantin' ta see the lass home safely? What then, me smart cousin?"

"They won't be havin' the lass long enough to do

that,'' Dru replied, returning to their table and his tankard of ale. "As soon as I be finishin' me game of darts, we'll think about reclaimin' our property.'' He saluted Sean with his mug, placing it to his lips, and drained the contents, observing the wide grin that covered Sean's face.

Victoria fell back happily against the thick cushion of the seat, dreamily closing her eyes and thinking of how good it would be to return home. Caught up in her own thoughts, she failed to hear the conversation of the other inhibitants of the carriage until the heady aroma of the woman's perfume filled her nostrils. Jumping upright, her mouth forming the words of apology, she smiled weakly at the woman sitting across from her.

"I wish to express my sincere thanks for helping me to escape those awful men,'' she began, falling silent when the woman raised a hand.

"No need, my dear. Besides, I suspect you will have a change of heart." The feathers of her hat bounced severely when the woman turned her head to stare outside.

"But—''

Cold sea-green eyes found hers again. "My name is Melissa Bensen.''

Every muscle in her frame cramped, starting in her toes and shooting upward, until her very breath seemed difficult to draw. How could this be? Of all the places in the world, all the people she could meet, how could destiny have brought her to this woman? Was she to reenact the part her mother had played so many years ago, to enable this woman to have her revenge after all? Frantically, she glanced about her, finding no escape, as the men who accompanied Melissa sat on either side of her, barring her way from the carriage.

"Bind and gag her," Melissa instructed harshly. "I have no need to hear her scream." Uncaringly, she looked outside again.

The ropes cutting into her wrists brought tears to Victoria's eyes, but the lump at the base of her neck stemmed from a different source. The others who had held her captive had nurtured no hatred of her, but the one who ruled her existence now would not hesitate to kill her, nor would she feel even an ounce of remorse for the deed. Trapped in a web of her own making, Victoria's spirits, moments before gay and hopeful, plummeted to the deepest recesses of her imagination.

The carriage came to an abrupt stop, the man at Melissa's side quickly stepping down into the street to assist her down. Readjusting the fullness of her skirts, she refused to look back at those still in the carriage. Fidgeting with an already perfect curl, she spoke in a hushed tone.

"Charles, you're in charge of seeing that she doesn't get away. I don't care where you keep her, and rather prefer not to know, but she must be carefully hidden from the gentlemen at the inn. I have the feeling they will try to acquire their 'cabin boy' again, no matter what the expense. Do you understand?"

"Yes'm," came the curt reply.

"Good. When you've finished, meet me back here."

Moisture-laden eyes watched the hostile figure walk away, never once looking back or reflecting any sign of sympathy. Victoria blinked, a tear spilling over the black rim of her lashes to trail down her cheek and hide itself in the white lace handkerchief that veiled her trembling lips.

"Keep a close eye on her while I talk with Bonita," Charles told his companion as he climbed from the carriage, carefully surveying their surroundings for any unwanted interloper. A smile broke the line on his clean-shaven face. "We might as well earn a little money for ourselves."

A low rumble of laughter filled the carriage, and a pair of brown eyes dartingly looked to its origin. Who is Bonita? Victoria thought fearfully, and what did Charles mean about earning money for themselves? No doubt it boded ill, for the man at her side grinned viciously, and since both he and Charles were cohorts of Melissa Bensen, the longtime villainess of her mother's past, no good could come from their plans. She tugged at the ropes on her wrists, praying somehow they would loosen and set her free, only to have them bury themselves more deeply into her flesh. She cringed in silent agony. Alone with one man now, Charles having disappeared into the back entrance of a two-story, freshly painted building, she noticed from the corner of her eye that her keeper elected to watch a stray mongrel rummage through the garbage and debris piled haphazardly in the street, allowing her to calculate her next move. Would she have time to throw open the carriage door and run before he knew what she was about? Suspecting that at any minute Charles would return, she gave up on all caution and broke for the door. Her feet, barely feeling the warm sand beneath them, had no chance to carry her away as two meaty fists latched on to her clothing, spinning her around. Her muffled gasp was absorbed into the gag about her mouth as a hand came up to strike her.

"No, Dunstan, don't hit her!"

"But she tried to get away," the man pouted boyishly, slowly lowering his hand. "It made me angry."

"I know, I know," Charles soothed him, turning back to the woman beside him. "I realize she'll probably be troublesome, but if you lock her in, and don't feed her for a few days, I'm sure she'll settle down. What do you think?"

The woman stepped forward, rubbing a thin finger against her chin. "She looks more like a boy. I doubt she'll bring a good price."

"But look at her face. Clean her up a bit and dress her in a gown, I'm sure you'll have no trouble finding customers." Charles excitedly moved in next to Victoria, reaching up for the soiled bandana. "Here, take a better look." With one quick movement, he freed Victoria's great lengths of hair to tumble seductively about her shoulders and waist in rumpled disarray. All three business partners gasped, knowing the island of Barbados had never seen such beauty.

"I want half of everything she brings in," Charles quickly announced, "and you furnish her clothes."

"Half?" the woman argued.

"Half of something is better'n nothing and without me bringing her to you, you wouldn't have that much. Now is it a deal, or do I take her someplace else?"

A disgruntled expression pursed the woman's thin lips. "A deal," she said quietly, bringing a wide, satisfied grin to Charles's face.

"Dunstan, take our little lady anywhere Bonita wants."

Having been thrown roughly over his wide shoulder, Victoria, uncomfortably jostled about with each step, a bony shoulder cutting into her stomach, could not see the area through which they traveled, only the small space of floor beneath her as she dangled helplessly, precariously high. They climbed a set of stairs, each tread squeezing the wind from her as she bounced against Dunstan. Her pleading moan, distorted by the gag, went unheard, and she closed her eyes, praying their journey would end soon.

"In here," Bonita instructed, opening a door and preceding the men.

Agilely, Dunstan slipped Victoria from his shoulder to stand in the center of the room, the only way out barred by the three menacing figures. She trembled, watching Bonita walk to the window and push open the shutters.

"Just so you don't get any ideas," she said, looking back at Victoria, "It's a long drop to the woodpile below. I'm sure a woman as fragile as you could not endure the fall." She nodded to Dunstan. "Untie her. The little lady and I have things to discuss. Come back in two days and I'll tell you whether or not she'll cooperate."

Having done as ordered, the men moved for the door, Charles pausing when they reached it. "If she escapes you, it will be your neck that is slit, not mine," he warned dangerously, no hint of jest in his eyes.

Bonita nodded. "Do not fear, my friend. What we have here can bring a fortune to both of us." Slipping a fingertip under the hem of her skirt, Bonita lifted it high enough to reveal the dagger strapped to her thigh. The weapon held tightly in her hand, she smiled evilly at Victoria, and spoke to the men. "I'm certain the lady wouldn't want an ugly scar to mar her face."

The chorus of cruel laughter rang in Victoria's ears as she watched the men depart the room, closing the door behind them, and leaving her alone with Bonita. Slowly, so as not to cause Bonita to think she sought to steal the knife away, Victoria rubbed her raw and tender wrists, bringing back the circulation to them.

"What's your name?" the woman barked.

"Victoria." Her voice sounded strained. "Victoria Remington."

Easing herself onto the edge of the bed, Bonita picked dirt from her nails with the tip of the knife blade, digesting the title. "Hmmm. Too classy." She thought a while. "Louise will do better." She rose and went to the door. "I'll have water heated for a bath and bring a change of clothes. And wash your hair. I intend to demand a good price for my new girl."

Puzzlement knotted Victoria's smooth brow. "What do you mean?"

Bonita laughed heartlessly. "Very good, my dear. They love a slut that pretends to be innocent."

"S-slut?" Victoria's voice cracked.

A strange expression changed the shape of Bonita's face. "You really don't know, do you? You're in a whorehouse, my dear, and with luck you'll be my main attraction." A callous sneer appeared on the woman's face before she turned and made her exit.

Victoria slumped to her knees, burying her face in the crook of her arm resting on the bed. Dear God, now what was she to do? Her secret gone, she had no other way to protect herself. And what of Melissa Bensen? What were her plans? Could they be any worse than her immediate future? She doubted it. Nothing could be as horrible as the fate she had witnessed her shipmates endure. *Oh, Papa, bring me home again!*

A loud crashing downstairs startled Victoria, jerking her head up to listen better. Wiping away the sudden appearance of new tears from her cheeks with the knot of her fist, she stood up and crossed to the door. With an ear pressed against it, she relaxed a bit, not hearing anyone on the stairs to this room. She straightened, taking a deep breath and deciding that even this test would not defeat her. She had come this far on sheer determination and strong will of her own, and she would not be beaten down by one more obstacle. She would carry the name Remington proudly and with dignity, and even if it was the death of her, she would never let any of them forget who she was.

Going to the window, she looked out to confirm Bonita's warning. Twenty feet straight down a pile of kindling wood and logs greeted her, forbidding an escape in this direction. Perchance she could trick whoever brought the water for her bath, and slip by them as they filled the tub. Seeing no other solution at the moment, she returned to the bed and sat down. Of the business establishment she had patronized so far on this island, this room at least failed to make her skin tingle with the need to cleanse herself. The walls and floors, freshly scrubbed, shone with their new coats of wax. The dressing table held a pewter candleholder with a single white taper, and a pearl-handled comb and matching hand mirror. The coverlet on which she sat smelled freshly laundered, and suddenly a desire to wash away her own dirt threatened to spoil her scheme. Shaking off the longing, she leaned back against the brass headboard, crossed her arms and waited.

Only a few minutes passed before she heard the sharp words Bonita spoke, hotly demanding her companions to hurry and complaining that the sun would disappear into the sea long before they reached the hallway. Heavy footsteps trudged outside Victoria's door and in the next instant a parade of bucket-toting waterbearers filled her room. A large brass tub appeared in the center of the floor, carried by four servant girls, eager to hold a perfume-scented bath and perform a luxury few of them ever experienced. Victoria sat in awe of the exhibit until only Bonita and one young girl remained, frightfully aware that her chance to run had passed. Not disheartened, and certain she would find another opportunity, she braced herself for whatever Bonita might do.

"I think this gown will do you justice," Bonita said, spreading out a simple blue cotton dress on the bed. "Your beauty should not be hidden by too many frills."

Studying her new attire, Victoria shuddered, noticing the transparency of the cloth. She gulped, vowing no one else other than the two women in the room with her would ever be allowed to make a judgment on how well it suited her figure.

"I'll leave Ellamay to see to your needs. She manages quite well with hair, and I suggest you have it knotted upon your head. Some of our customers have a tendency to get a little rough. With all that hair hanging about your shoulders, it would be an open invitation to drag you about by it."

Victoria's stomach fluttered, then settled when she forced such thoughts from her mind.

"We usually work until nearly sunrise. You may want to take a nap. I'm sure you'll have a full night's work ahead of you once the word's out that Bonita has a new girl. Especially with a face like yours." She started for the door. "I'll leave you two alone. But do hurry, Ellamay. I have need of your services."

Victoria listened to the latch catch, fighting down the urgency to vomit, a new tremor overtaking her. Glancing up, she found the young face of Ellamay staring back at her, and, finding no sympathy in the round blue eyes, decided she could afford the extravagance of a warm bath before testing the girl's loyalty. She easily shed the rags that had been her only possession for the past two days, and slipped beneath the surface of bubbles. Fragrant water swirled around her, massaging her tired limbs and bringing new life to her aching muscles. Closing her eyes, she relaxed, thinking of Daphne, her maid back home, and how wonderful it felt to soak in a brass tub. So calmed was she by her bath, she failed to hear any movement in the room until the door thudded closed for a second time. She sat upright with a start and surveyed the room to discover that Ellamay had left her, taking with her the tattered remnants of the cabin boy.

"No, wait!" Victoria screamed, scrambling from the tub in hopes of reclaiming the clothes. "I want what is mine."

"Miss Bonita told me to burn these," the distant voice coldly informed her. "When you're finished with your bath, I'll come back to do your hair."

Several hours had passed since Victoria had forced herself to don the blue gown. Sitting cross-legged on the

88

bed, the spread torn from it and wrapped tightly about her, Victoria quaked in spite of the heavy quilt and the warm night air. Nearly a quarter of an hour before, she had heard men's laughter below in the parlor and she was certain that at any moment one of them would be shown to her room. Her courage and desire to see this through rapidly left her, leaving in its wake a frightened and tearful child. Her lower lip protruded as she fought to contain her sobs, tears trailing down her cheeks and tasting salty in the corners of her mouth. Then she heard them. The thumping of boots on the stairs, footsteps that brought their owner closer and stopped just outside her door. She abandoned the bed and coverlet to race to the windowsill and stare outside, praying that somehow the woodpile had disappeared and been replaced by a haystack. But even in the darkness she could see the odd shapes and pointed edges of kindling, daring her to throw herself upon them. The latch clicked behind her and she spun around to face the enemy.

SIX

Melissa Bensen stood by the window of the small room they had rented in a rundown inn, staring out at the graying shadows of early evening and recalling the last time she had waited for Dillon Gallagher, an Irish pirate with a reputation equaled by few others. She had hired him many years ago to kidnap a young woman by the name of Alanna Bainbridge, betrothed to Radford Chamberlain, and take her to New Orleans to sell her to a brothel in the hopes she would never return to Williamsburg, Virginia.

The young Melissa had fallen in love with the unapproachable Beau Remington of Raven Oaks, a relationship that was doomed from the start, for he had little love for any woman in his heart. In an effort to spark a flame of jealousy, certain he cared more for her than he claimed, she had set out to trap his best friend, Radford, into asking for her hand in marriage, positive that once Beau heard of it, he would come to her on bended knee, begging for her love. But then a young and beautiful indentured servant had arrived at Raven Oaks, a woman neither man could ignore.

Even though Beau had seduced the young Alanna and left her heavy with child, Radford still wanted her, paying off Alanna's debt when Beau refused to marry her and totally shunning Melissa's pleas for reconciliation. Jealousy had flared high in Melissa, and she had vowed that Alanna would have neither man. Thus her evil plot was born. She would send Alanna away and Radford would be hers again to use. But the success of her plan had shattered when Beau and Radford joined together in finding Alanna, ending in Radford's death by Gallagher's hand and the marriage of Beau and Alanna. Disowned by her father, Melissa had fled Virginia for England, swearing revenge against the woman who had destroyed everything in her life, a vengeance that still poisoned her mind and had turned her heart to stone after twenty years.

With the sudden appearance of the Remington brat, something Melissa had never dreamed would happen, a new twist in her strategy formed, one that brought a rare smile to her lips. She had decided years ago that if she could not have Beau Remington she would take his land instead, leave him penniless with his whorish wife. But now she would add fear to her plan, something that would cut deeply into a mother's heart: the threat of death to her only child if Melissa's demands were not met. A sinister sneer crossed her mouth as she studied the silhouettes of the ships anchored offshore. After all these years of waiting it was only a matter of time now, for once England won the war, Raven Oaks would be

91

hers. She would revel in the Remingtons' look of horror when they found out who came to claim their land!

A frown deepened the faint line in Melissa's brow. To succeed, she needed one more thing. She needed Dillon Gallagher's help or her deal with England would fall void. Her prior worry that he would not come to Barbados surfaced abruptly, and she nervously paced the floor of the room once more, clutching the emerald brooch at her neckline, tugging at the bright yellow curl bobbing against her bosom.

Charles and Dunstan had returned to the inn hours before with their guarantee that Victoria had been safely tucked away where no pirate would ever think of looking for a cabin boy. But this little bit of information had only slightly pacified her, and she had waved them off with an agitated flip of her bejeweled hand. She had resumed her pacing, and nothing either of the men could say would satisfy her.

"Where's Edwin?" Charles inquired when Melissa finally elected to sit down and sip the glass of wine he offered. He had noticed the man's absence when he and Dunstan entered Melissa's room, but until now had had little chance to voice the question. To his dismay, the woman, ten years his senior, restlessly left the tattered high-backed chair to walk the floor again.

"I sent him out to learn if anyone has arrived looking for me."

"Aren't you a bit overanxious? It could take several months for the message to reach him. That pirate could be anywhere."

Melissa shot him an evil glare over the rim of her glass, draining its contents, and held out the goblet to him. "I don't recall asking for your opinion."

92

Sheepishly, Charles took the stemware from her outstretched hand, placed it on the table, and glanced at Dunstan. The oversized man sat quietly, playing with the string attached to the hem of his shirt cuff, oblivious to his surroundings and obviously content. Charles's lip curled. What he needed was an ally, not some half-wit who jumped with every command. He shrugged. Oh well, he had to admit the huge dummy did come in handy. He settled himself in the chair Melissa had chosen to vacate, crossed his knees, and quietly waited. For what, he wasn't sure, but thoughts of the money Victoria most certainly would be earning at this moment for him soothed his bruised ego. This was one venture he had undertaken without Melissa's guidance, one he was certain was foolproof, with a tasty reward he would not share with anyone.

A few taps against the door of the room brought Charles to his feet immediately, but not quickly enough to answer the summons before Melissa. Opening the door, she allowed Edwin Neilson to enter.

"Well?" she asked eagerly.

Edwin, a man closer to Melissa's age than Charles, shook his graying head. "Nothing. I'll try again in the morning."

"Damn," Melissa muttered bitterly, swinging the door closed with a bang.

"Don't worry," Edwin soothed. "He'll come. I'm sure he will. The promise of money always entices a man of his caliber."

Melissa sent him a doubtful glance. "I suppose, but everything hinges on him. I know of no other. He's my last hope."

"How long do you plan to wait for him?"

Marching from one side of the room to the other again, Melissa absently toyed with a ring on her forefinger. "A week. If he's not here in a week than he can rot in hell for all I care. I'll find someone else."

Edwin smiled softly, knowing the task would be greater than she implied it would be. Edwin had met Melissa close to ten years ago. He had fallen deeply and hopelessly in love with her, a love she never returned. She was driven by her desire for revenge, by a vengeance that he suspected had turned a sweet, innocent young woman into a hate-filled, spiteful old maid. Although he still did not know every detail of her past, the moment the young woman dressed in boy's clothing had announced her true identity, he knew Melissa's opportunity to gain her desired justice had drawn nearer. She would use Victoria Remington to seek some sort of satisfaction. Thinking of their hostage, he poured himself a glass of wine and waited for Melissa to look at him again.

"What do you plan to do with the girl?" he asked as Melissa captured his drink in her long, slender fingers. "And take it easy on that, will you?"

"Don't tell me what to do!" she barked, taking a big swallow as if to defy him. Resuming her trek across the room, she continued sipping at the wine until she had drained the glass, returning to the table that held the decanter and a refill. "Her father doesn't know it yet, but he is going to aid England in the war."

"And how do you plan to achieve that?" Edwin asked, watching her hold up the ruby-colored drink before her eyes to study it.

"Quite simply, dear Edwin. If Beau wishes to see his daughter alive, he will find some way to provide us with

94

information on the number of armed men the colonies have, when and where they plan their next attack, or any other facts which might help.''

"You mean spy against his own country? He'll never do it!''

Melissa whirled angrily on him. ''Even at the cost of his own daughter's life? No man has that much loyalty.''

"And what if he refuses? What then?''

Melissa shrugged dispassionately. ''Then he'll never see his darling daughter again.''

"You mean you'd have her killed?''

A vicious laughter cut the tenseness in the air. ''Oh really, Edwin. You more than anyone else know I'm responsible for several—shall we say—untimely deaths.'' Her eyes narrowed. ''And this time I will truly enjoy it.''

Lazily, Edwin pulled a pipe from his pocket. ''I've heard others talk of Beau Remington before. He'd have you—all of us—hunted down. If you kill his daughter, our lives wouldn't be worth a twopence.''

"This is what I've waited for all these years! Don't you understand? He took Radford from me, he and that slut-wife of his. I don't care what happens to me, just as long as I've seen justice done.'' Angrily, she stalked to the window, several droplets of wine spilling from her glass as a tremor of rage shook her. Glaring at the shoreline, she shouted, ''Damn you, Gallagher. Where are you?''

Standing at the window of the room, her knees shaking, Victoria glanced back at the bed to see the discarded quilt lying upon it. Thinking there was enough time to retrieve the cloth and cover herself, she made a dash for it, hearing the pained squeal of the door opening as she reached the bed. Swirling the coverlet about her, her throat tightened against the whimper she fought to control, knowing tears would not sway any man who had paid the price to enter this room. A trembling fist raised to her mouth, she bit the first knuckle of her hand, commanding herself to gain control and think clearly. A quick wit filled with convenient lies to suit her needs, an art she'd practiced often, had brought her this far, and with luck she might be able to talk her way out of what Bonita had planned. She swallowed hard and stood erect, praying her fear did not show on her face.

"Well, what's this I got? You ain't—ah, hell, I never can remember her name. 'Sides, I don't care if ya got one, just's long as you're good in bed."

Victoria felt the tremor in her bones begin anew with the revulsion of the sight before her. Staggering to keep himself upright, Kelsey fell against the door frame.

"Well, just don't stand there. Get them clothes off."

He took a wobbly step forward and Victoria retreated too, suddenly aware of the limited space she had in which to stay at arm's length from the man and praying somehow she could lure him away from the door long enough to give herself time to flee. Glancing first at Kelsey, then the door, she forced herself to smile.

"Why don't you sit on the bed while I disrobe?" Her voice shook nearly as badly as her chin. She gulped and tried again. "I thought maybe you'd like to watch me."

His glazed eyes fought to focus on her, one hand lifting to rub his jaw. "Not a bad idea. I think I will."

96

Stumbling forward, he nearly collapsed before reaching the brass footboard, a dirt-covered hand with blackened nails shooting outward to catch himself and prop his oversized load in a vertical stance. He laughed. "Did ya see that, dearie? Nearly fell on my arse. Why don't you come 'ere and help ol' Kelsey?"

Lunging for her, he lost his balance, a meaty hand shooting out to seize the folds of her skirts and tumble them both to the floor. Astuteness silenced the scream that tore at her throat, certain the act would only excite this sort of barbarian and reveal her true desire to have nothing to do with him. *She* must be the one to guide, to instruct them in their moves to allow her the advantage, a chance to slip from his probing hands and flee the scene. She forced herself to laugh.

"Surely, you'd rather use the bed," she smiled weakly, feeling the bile rise in her throat with the stench of him. "Here, let me help you up." Fighting to wiggle from beneath him, a shriek opposed her plan when a thick hand and agile fingers slid beneath the skirt of her gown to claim her bare thigh.

"Oh, I—I don't mind the floor," he drooled, " 'Sides, it saves time." With a quickness that belied his drunken state, Kelsey threw himself on top of her, crushing her tiny form, her breath leaving her in a rush.

His mouth covered hers, gagging her. She clamped her teeth shut, fighting off the intrusion of his tongue as it prodded and searched for the sweetness of her kiss. She wanted to scream, to scratch his eyes out with her nails, but knew she mustn't lest she arouse him more, anger him, ignite the villainous pirate she had watched abuse the woman on *La Belle Fleur*. Then suddenly, he lifted from her to rest back on his heels, red-rimmed eyes devouring the sight of her, saliva dripping from the corner of his mouth. He licked his lips and reached out for the neckline of her gown.

"No! Wait!" she shrieked, then forced a smile at his disapproving scowl. "It's the only gown I have. You mustn't ruin it." She fought to rise up on her elbows, her efforts useless as Kelsey's weight trapped her gown beneath his knees, disallowing movement of any kind when the cloth strained at the bodice and threatened to rip. "I—I'll take it off for you." He swayed left and right, and Victoria worried he would topple forward and crush her once more. She smiled again, gently tugging at the skirts caught beneath him. Without a word, he staggered to his feet, his expression dark and foreboding as he watched her rise from the floor. Fluttering her lashes as coquettishly as she could manage, she moved toward the door. "I'll just make sure the key is turned first so no one will disturb us." Her back to him, she let out a long, quiet sigh, knowing that within a moment she would be free of him and racing for her life and a place to hide until she could sort out her plans. Once she reached the door, she turned back again to mask her true intent, her eyes flying wide, her mouth agape when she viewed the pirate stagger free of his boots and drop his breeches to the floor.

"Oh—my—God!" Victoria exclaimed, her limbs frozen where she stood, too horrified to move.

"Whatsa matter? Ain't ya never seen a man like me before, ya sweet thing?" Kelsey grinned lopsidedly, tottering a step forward.

The stink of him reached out to engulf Victoria long before he traveled close enough to touch her, snapping her back to reality and the urgent need to escape. She spun around, but before she had taken a step, the mammoth pirate tripped over the garb entangled around his feet and fell headlong, his huge fingers fanning out to catch the hem of her gown as he landed on the floor.

"Come here, ya saucy wench," he groaned, yanking on the skirt, the strength behind the move enough to pull her closer. He reached up, grabbed a trim ankle and knocked her to the floor. His hungry lust to sample the treasure he held commanded his moves, and in an instant he rolled on top of her, his wet mouth capturing her lips as his hands explored the shapely curves of her breasts, pinching and kneading before moving to her hips and the gown that covered them from view.

His weight pressing down on her nearly more than she could endure, Victoria merely fought to breathe until she felt the rough calluses of his palm against her bare thigh moving upward to claim her buttocks. Terror flooded over her. With both her hands clamped on a fistful of his hair, its greasy texture sending a tremor of replusion through her, she broke free of his kisses, her stomach churning, her mind whirling with pleas to make him stop. She opened her mouth to voice disapproval, finding the effort more than she could accomplish when his obese form nearly crushed her, a simple moan all she could achieve.

Mistaking the sound of his companion to mean pleasure at his gropings, Kelsey eagerly nibbled at the smooth flesh of her neck, his knee parting her rigid thighs. The fingers of one hand pulled at the neckline of her gown to free the firm mound of her breast. His mouth came down hard upon it, his teeth biting the tender peak. Victoria cried out in pain, a sudden surge

99

of strength to fend off the attack allowing her to push him from her. He rolled to his back, his mind swirling from his immoderate consumption of rum to lie wide-eyed and confused, for he truly failed to understand what had happened.

Scrambling to her feet, Victoria readjusted her clothing and bolted for the door, halting in her tracks when she spotted Bonita barring the way, a displeased look on her face.

"Kelsey, what are you doing here?" she demanded irritably.

Incoherent gibberish floated up from the slow-moving form on the floor.

"Well, get out. This isn't where you're supposed to be and you know it." Bonita waited, and when it seemed Kelsey intended to stay where he was, she marched over to him and soundly kicked his thigh. "Get up, you good for nothing scum, before I have you thrown out of here. You hear me?"

Rubbing the area Bonita had attacked, he rolled over to his knees, his nose flattened against the floor. "Yeah, yeah, I hear ya, ya old whore." Struggling to his feet, his eyes half open, he concentrated on the location of the door and set off in its direction, taking two steps forward, one sideways, and one backward before his weight hurled him ahead again. Bumping against the door frame, he fell into the hallway, his enormous frame leaving little room for anyone to step by. Annoyed, Bonita tiptoed between his arm and leg, the palms of her hands against each wall on either side of her for support. Standing near his head, she bent down and grabbed a handful of his hair.

"If you don't get up right now, I'll send Jack after

you. And you know how he likes to use his knife."

Grunting a word Victoria had never heard before, Kelsey raised himself up with both hands pressed to the floor, swaying when he reached his full height. "I promised to pay you just as soon as I could," he said, his lower lip protruding in an uncustomary pout.

"And I agreed because you're a good customer, but it doesn't give you the right to pick any girl you want. Now get moving before I change my mind." She gave Kelsey a shove, watched him amble down the hallway a few steps, and decided he'd never make it alone. A disgusted sigh heaved her thin shoulders before she glanced back to someone standing in the hall just out of Victoria's view. "You can go in now," she smiled, turning around to latch on to Kelsey's large bicep and escort him away.

Victoria's frame shook uncontrollably and tears threatened to race down her face. There would be no escape this time. Running to the window, she decided falling to her death would be less painful than the one she imagined at the hands of one of Bonita's customers. Tossing off the coverlet to free her arms, she awkwardly opened the window and lifted one leg to the sill.

"Whoa, there lass. Ya wouldn't be thinkin' of jumpin' this far, would ya?"

Surprised by the familiarity of his voice, Victoria eased her foot back to the floor and slowly turned to verify her suspicion. Lounging boldly in the doorway, the captain's tall frame stood unmoving, his steel-blue eyes raking over her, touching her everywhere and bringing a chill to her spine. He seemed more handsome than the first time she had seen him, or when she had watched him dress that morning. He had donned

101

fresh clothes though they were similar to those he wore earlier, his blue shirt and darker breeches blending well with the color of his eyes. The fullness of the shirt-sleeves stressed the broadness of his chest and shoulders, the strings interlacing the front falling open to remind her of the well-formed muscles beneath the dark curls and contrasting with the soft hue of the cloth. His dark hair glistened in the candlelight as if still damp from his bath, a distinct dissimilarity with the crapulous pirate of a moment ago. Of the two, impulse told her that she would be safest with the captain, but when she forced her eyes to meet his, her confidence fled, for he grinned back at her with an implication that was hardly casual. A chill suddenly overcame her and she quickly bent down to snatch the quilt from the floor and hide the view on which his gaze so hungrily feasted.

"That's better," he smiled softly, stepping into the room, and closing the door behind him. "Me name is Dru Chandler. Would I be knowin' yours?"

Knowing he blocked her exit, her only other way out the pile of kindling wood, she hugged her arms to herself, hoping to still their trembling, and looked up at him. "Victoria."

His dark brow, tipped golden by the rays of sunlight, arched approvingly. "A lovely name, it is, and for a lovely lass." He moved closer. "And I be seein' why Bonita robbed me purse. I am the first, aren't I?" Standing before her now, he slowly reached out to entwine one of her dark curls about his finger. Victoria quickly wiggled away from him, his words having given her an idea. She could only hope her tone didn't betray the nervousness she felt inside.

"There has never been another. And if you help to

102

see it remains that way, I can promise you a reward three times what you paid to be here.''

''Can ya now? And what would ya be sayin' if I told ya I be thinkin' me money well spent?''

A new flood of tears burned her eyes and she blinked repeatedly to hide them. ''But with the amount you could have, you could buy the companionship of many women, not just one.''

Dru eased himself onto the bed, hooking the toe of one boot to the heel of the other and slid if from his foot. ''An interestin' thought, lass. But one I be thinkin' to turn down. I'm not here lookin' for money, if ya get me meanin'.''

Victoria's eyes widened. ''Then take another woman and have the money too. Please Captain Chandler, I beg you.''

''Captain, is it? And how would ya be knowin' what I do for me livin'?'' he asked, untying the strings of his shirt after removing his second boot.

Panic overruled her will to see a satisfactory end, waiting until he lifted his shirt, its folds of cloth covering his face, and she dropped the coverlet and ran for the door, jerking it open only to have it slammed shut again by a hand that came from behind her. She spun around and pressed her body against the door, her head tilted back to stare at him eye to eye.

''Ya not be tryin' ta cheat me out of me money, are ya?'' he whispered, leaning closer, his breath falling warm against her face.

A lump formed in her throat, choking off her reply. Uneasy under his penetrating stare, she started past him, his free hand shooting up to press against the door and trap her between his arms. His manly scent beguiled her, filled her mind and dulled her wit. She dropped her gaze, unable to look at his handsome face or endure the flashing white smile he bestowed upon her. Of all those who had courted her or sought an audience, none had aroused this strange enchantment, the tingling that touched every fiber of her being. It frightened her, for she thought of him as an ally to Kelsey, a man of few morals, a rogue, and she had vowed early on to find the prince of her dreams, a gentleman, a noble man like her father. How could her body forsake her so? The blue of her gown caught her attention as she absently compared its hue to that of his attire, and her breath seemed to leave her in a rush as she remembered the thinness of the cloth and the view it presented, since Bonita had forbidden her to wear a camisole. Her arms flew to her bosom, crossed against the décolletage of the dress in an effort to ease her modesty, her body trembling when his laughter rumbled in her ears.

"Aye, 'tis plain ta see I am the first," he mocked, one hand moving to the long column of her neck, fingers fanned out, his thumb beneath her chin to lift her gaze to his. "I will not be hurtin' ya, lass."

Victoria squeezed her eyes closed, unable to will her body to do anything else, fruitlessly praying he would disappear, and foolishly thinking he meant to leave her untouched. But in the next instant, his lips found hers, warm, moist, tender, kissing her as no other man had ever done before. Her mind reeled, the taste of him intoxicating her, and she relaxed, her knees weak, slightly aware of the arm that gently encircled her waist, pulling her closer. His hand slid to the back of her head, fingers entangled within the thick mass of silken tresses, guiding her, and without realizing what she had done, she accepted his kiss, her body hanging limp in his arms. Wondering if heaven could make so sweet a claim, she vaguely felt his mouth twist across hers, lips parted, until his tongue began to tease, tempt and coax her own lips to open in delicious ecstasy. She unfolded her arms, oddly wanting to hold him tenderly as he held her, but the moment her sparsely covered breasts touched the rock-hard muscles of his bare chest, some sanity returned and she wiggled to break the embrace, fear rising in the pit of her stomach when he failed to oblige. Instead, he crushed her to him, his tongue darting inside her mouth. Her eyes flew open at his boldness and she fought in earnest to free herself, his firm grip forbidding her to end the kiss. In desperation, she reached up to rake her nails across his face, shock bolting through her at the lightning speed he displayed in securing her wrist with the hand that had before gently cradled her chin. But in saving himself injury, he allowed her the freedom of twisting her face away and screaming as though her very life was in danger.

"Hush, lass," he scowled, quickly clamping a hand over her mouth and pressing her back against the door to still her struggles. "Would ya be wantin' Bonita ta come ta make sure I'm not damagin' her property?"

Fearful brown eyes stared back at him, no hint of an answer shining in them.

"As I said before, I'll not be hurtin' ya as long as ya cooperate. Now, will ya be promisin' not ta scream if I take me hand away? We've a wee bit of a matter ta discuss."

Victoria's mind raced with various subjects, all returning to the fact that he intended to get what he had paid for—a woman in his bed. And by his own word, he pledged to use strength if she didn't give in freely. Well, damn him! He could threaten all he wanted. She would not relent. Doubling up a tiny fist, she struck him in the rib cage with every ounce of vigor she could manage, surprising him enough to force him to let go of her. She shot past him and raced to the far side of the room. Her body trembling, the echo of her pounding heart hammering in her ears, she watched wide-eyed as he turned slowly to face her.

Rubbing his injured side, he studied her a while, his blue eyes twinkling with a mirth not on his lips before he relaxed and leaned back against the door, arms folded over the wide expanse of his chest. He had suspected the beauty she possessed but realized the moment he saw her that his estimations had fallen short. Her ebony hair, the color of the blackest night, shone its brilliance in the soft glow of candlelight haloed around the most innocent face he had ever seen. Yet gleaming in the dark depths of her eyes he recognized the spirit of a she-wolf, cunning, swift, and bent on revenge should he advance a step. The pale blue gown she wore did little to hide the curves of womanhood, in fact, sparked a burning in his loins. Her ivory-colored skin washed clean of dirt seemed paler than he had imagined it to be, and when he had slipped an arm around her small waist he had been pleasantly surprised to find that she was not restricted by a corset. His gaze traveled from the daring look on her face down the long, slender neck to the full breasts straining against the thin cloth. With little imagination he envisioned her standing naked before him, and suddenly he found it difficult to draw a breath, wondering what rapture would claim his soul if she were to open her arms and welcome him.

"Take the pins from your hair," he spoke softly.

Victoria's knees trembled. "Captain Chandler," she began, forcing her voice to sound calm, "I think you fail to realize just who I am and what I can do for you."

The dimple appeared in his cheek. "Oh, but I do. Take the pins from your hair."

The tremor raced to her thighs. "No—no, I don't mean—Captain, my name is Victoria Remington."

"Is it, now?" he mocked. "A lovely name." The smile disappeared. "Be takin' down your hair, lass. I be wantin' ta see it hang free."

Victoria's entire body quaked. "And—and if I do, will you listen to me then?"

He nodded slightly.

Shaky fingers found the pins and quickly undid Ellamay's work, the long black curls cascading earthward to reach Victoria's knees. She shook her head, pulling the silky mane over both shoulders to cunningly hide the view he so obviously enjoyed. She took a breath and began again. "My name is Remington. My father is Beau Remington from Williamsburg, Virginia in the colonies."

Dru's gaze followed the thick mass of ebony hair as it fell across her shoulders, breasts, down the trim waistline to her thighs and finally to her knees, appraising the soft curls at the end. The uneasiness in his loins grew evident, and he pictured himself blanketed in the smooth flowing locks.

"Captain?"

He blinked, forcing his eyes to met hers. "Aye,

lass.''

"Do you remember the name?"

"Nay, lass. I never met your father." The corners of his mouth twitched, suppressing a smile. "But I be knowin' your brother."

A frown flitted across Victoria's brow. "My brother?"

"Aye. He's me new cabin boy. Might ya be twins? Ya look a great deal alike."

Victoria could not hold back a chuckle. "No, captain. *I* was your cabin boy."

"The devil, ya say," he quipped. "Now why would ya be dressin' like a boy? Are ya sure?"

The thought of how he had ever managed to become the captain of a ship raced through her mind. "I wore a red bandana to cover my hair and you won me in a card game against that clod who was just here. You have a cousin by the name of Sean. How would I know all that if it hadn't been I disguised as a boy? And my offer still stands. If you'll see me safely back home, my father will pay you whatever you feel necessary."

A playful grin teased the dimple in his cheek. "The money is temptin', but then, so are you."

Her heart lurched when she saw him straighten and start toward her. "Sir, I promise you, my father would have you killed if he knew you had violated me," she threatened, certain it would do little to sway him.

"Violated? What a hard word ya be usin'. I like ta think of it as love." He stood casually before her, reaching up to touch her chin with a fingertip, but she quickly ducked under his arm and crossed the room.

"I doubt you know the true meaning of the word," she spat, her temper rising.

"A long and lastin' one? Can't say I've ever had the experience. Except with me mother. Is that what ya mean?"

Victoria closed her eyes. *I can understand why,* she thought, looking back at him again. "Do we have an agreement or not, captain?"

"And if I be sayin' no, what will ya be doin' then?"

Stepping to the window, she looked down at the ground below. "I will take my chances on the woodpile."

"Ah, but I don't thank ya could throw yourself from the sill faster than I could be reachin' ya."

"Would you care to try?" she challenged carelessly.

"And if I win?"

Victoria's foolishness hit her like a cold blast of winter wind. Her pounding heart threatened to explode, realizing the point he made.

"I don't think ya be in a position ta barter, lass. What I decide ta do is how it will be and I be suggestin' ya not play your hand to the last card. Do exactly as I be tellin' ya, or we be finishin' what I came here ta do. Ya understand me meanin'?"

Humbled, she looked to the bare toes sticking out from beneath her gown, noticing its flimsiness again. Without lifting her eyes to him, she scooped the quilt from the floor and draped it about her shoulders. "Then we have a deal? You'll return me to my father unharmed?"

"Aye. Unharmed," he agreed. *But definitely not untouched,* he mused with a devilish grin. He went to the bed, tugged on his boots, and slipped into his shirt before coming to stand at her side. "If ya would be so kind as ta stand over there," he nodded toward the

109

door, "I'll be findin' a way out of here."

He waited until she did as he instructed then turned to the window and leaned out, placing his thumb and forefinger to his lips. A shrill whistle pierced the still air, and a moment passed before he straightened and stepped back. A knotted loop of rope sailed through the window and landed on the floor with a thud, bringing a startled shock of reality to Victoria. Skillfully tying the end to the brass spindles of the headboard, he tested its strength before smiling back at her, the dimple in his cheek disappearing when he noticed the slight flare to her nostrils. He cocked his head to one side. "Somethin' ailin' ya, lass?"

"You knew," she said through clenched teeth.

He reached up to scratch one temple. "And what is it I be knowin'?"

"That I was here. You knew all along."

"How ya be figurin' that, may I ask?"

Her shaky finger pointed to the rope dangling out the window.

"Ah, but you're wrong, lass. A pirate can never be takin' a chance ta be caught where he can't escape. As I'm sure you've already decided, I'm not an upstandin' citizen, if ya know what I mean, and there are many who would like to see justice brought down on me head." With a nod and a lift of his brows, he extended his hand as an invitation for her to be the first to climb down the rope. "Unless ya be wantin' Bonita to find us disfigurin' her furniture, I be suggestin' we be on our way."

Unable to challenge his honesty without real proof, and truly wishing to be free of her surroundings, Victoria kept her thoughts to herself, approaching the win-

110

dowsill to peer over the edge. The rope appeared to narrow to the size of a thread, and for an instant she wondered if she had the courage or the strength to descend it.

"Don't be worryin', lass. The knots in the rope will give ya a better grip, but I'm afraid ya will have ta do without the blanket."

Craving the desire to do anything other than what the captain suggested, she hesitated before pulling the coverlet from her shoulders. Glancing back outside, she rolled the spread into a ball and tossed it to the ground below.

"I'll be needin' it later," she mimicked, lifting a foot to the sill.

"Aye, that ya will. It gets cold sleepin' in the crew's quarters."

Astraddle the window frame, Victoria stiffened apprehensively. "You can't mean that. I might as well stay here if you do."

He smiled broadly and Victoria suddenly knew her wit would never match his. Flexing the muscle in her cheek in suppressed retaliation, she glared at him a moment, then began her perilous journey down the rope.

Lowering herself one knotted length at a time, she thought she would never reach the end, the muscles of her arms weakening with each new hold, the hemp biting into the palms of her hands, and chafing the insides of her legs wrapped around the rope. She couldn't bring herself to look down, knowing the sight of the distance to the ground would surely cause her head to spin and in turn loosen her hold. Instead, she chose to periodically look up at the captain, finding an encouraging smile on his handsome face. But little did he know that the very sight of him urged her to continue, that once her feet touched the ground she would repossess the quilt and run from him, positive there had to be one person on the island sympathetic to her dilemma.

"You're nearly there, lass. You can do it," Dru called down to her.

A smile broke free on her face at his words, certain her freedom was only a few seconds away. Then two strong hands clamped around her waist, pulling her from the rope, and she screamed.

"Hush, lass," Sean warned. "Ya be wantin' everyone ta know what we're doin'?"

Twisting away from him, she hurriedly gathered up the coverlet. "What are you doing here?"

"Well, did ya think the rope just flew up there all by itself?" He cast her a disapproving look before lifting his gaze to watch his cousin agilely climb from the window and descend their makeshift escape route.

Halfway to his goal, Dru looked down. "Sean! The lass!"

Spinning around, Sean caught only the glimpse of Victoria's blue skirt as she raced down the alleyway and disappeared between two buildings. "Sometimes I be thinkin' you're more trouble than you're worth," he muttered, starting off after her.

Although he'd lost sight of her, her footprints in the wet sand led the way and he stopped just as abruptly as they did. Surveying the area in which he stood, he momentarily failed to understand what had happened. It was as if she had taken flight. A knowing smile crossed his lips. Studying the crescent shape of the broken rail barrel near where her tracks ended, only his eyes

112

moved upward to the small balcony above him. Huddled in the corner, Victoria stared back fearfully. "Now will ya be comin' down or do I have ta come up and get ya?"

"Go away!" she screamed.

"Now ya know I can't be doin' that. Me cousin would hang me from the yardarm."

"Then tell him you couldn't find me. Please, just go away."

"I'm afraid ya not be knowin' the dangers for a lass like yourself ta be runnin' about this island alone."

"And you think I'd be any safer in the company of the likes of you and your cousin? I am not a fool, Sean whatever-your-name-is."

"Rafferty, lass, Sean Rafferty at your service." He took a slow mocking bow, and raised up to be met with a faceful of Victoria's coverlet. Fighting to free his vision of the numerous yards of cloth, he lost his sense of direction, stumbling about before he managed to toss the item from him, and found himself facing the rotted, sun-faded siding of the building on the opposite side of the alley. Whirling about, he saw Victoria dashing back down the narrow street in the direction from which they had come, rounding a bend, and disappearing again. His amusement at the lass's distress shattered and he raced after her, sliding to a stop as he, too, rounded the corner and found that Dru blocked her departure. They squared off, each standing their ground and daring the other to make the first move.

"Can ya be seein' how hopeless it all is, lass?" Sean implored. "And it be too hot to be runnin' about the island this way. Give it up and come with us." With each word he moved closer.

113

Crouching low, ready to spring should either of them try anything, she retreated slowly, unaware of the trap in which she would soon place herself, for behind her a solid wall with no windows or boxes to climb barred her escape. Bumping into it with her backside, she jumped with a start, carelessly glancing over her shoulder to recognize the error of her imperceptiveness and allowing Sean time to move in on her. But before he could reach her, his movement drew her attention, and she swiftly bent down, scooped up a handful of sand and tossed it in his face.

"Aarrrrgh!" he bellowed, spitting particles from his mouth, snorting some from his nose, and wildly clawing at his eyes to regain his vision. "The wench has blinded me."

Dru's amused chortle filled the void of Sean's momentary slightless state. Shaking his head and letting his tears cleanse his eyes, a moment passed before he could focus on either Victoria or the man who tried ineffectively to mask his smile with a sudden clearing of his throat and rubbing of his thumb to his lower lip.

"Oh, go ahead and laugh, dear cousin. But ya wouldn't be thinkin' it so funny if ya be standin' in me place." He brushed the sand from his shoulders and chest with short, angry swipes.

"And I be askin' your forgiveness, Sean, but ya must agree how amusin' it is ta see a lass not half your size cuttin' ya ta meet hers. Knowing ya as I do, I'm certain ya'd be laughin' as hard as me if I was the one spittin' sand."

As they bantered back and forth, Victoria inched her way past Sean, for although he blocked her path, his neglecting to guard her tempted her to run. Failing to realize Dru still watched, she waited until Sean looked down to dust away the granules from his sleeve and hurriedly took a step toward her assured freedom, not noticing the slight nod of the captain in her direction. A strong hand came up to claim a fistful of her hair. She screamed at the painful tug of black mane at the nape of her neck, spinning around on her heels to land a stinging blow to Sean's ear.

"Yeeeooow!" Sean's caterwaul seemed to shake the ground. Thinking his injured extremity of more importance, he let go of Victoria, clamping onto his ear, wincing in pain. "Ya little hellcat. You'll be raisin' a lump the size of me fist." Wishing to bestow his most berating glower on her, he looked up to discover that she had not only not heard him, but had started off down the alley at a breakneck speed. He raised a hand to his cousin. "I'll be thankin' ya to let me be the one to catch her."

His step belied the weight his feet carried as Sean swiftly raced after Victoria, closing the distance quickly. Contrary to his gentle nature, assuring himself the lass had it coming to her, he hurled himself into midair, grasping her just above the knees and crashing them both to the ground in a painful tumble. He rolled, then stood, having clamped onto her wrist, and, spotting the rain barrel that had begun the whole run around, he dragged her to it, bracing one foot to its weathered side and throwing Victoria across his knee.

"As me mother always told me, 'This will be hurtin' ya more than it will be hurtin' me.' "

"Noooo!" Victoria wailed, kicking wildly, her skirts flying erratically as she struggled to free herself. A painful wallop landed on her backside, bringing tears to her eyes instantly. "My father will have you shot!"

Another stinging slap found its mark and another, the donor never faltering in his effort or swayed by the empty promise.

Her threats turned to silence, vowing he would never break her, until, certain she would never sit comfortably again, she pleaded with her assailant to bring an end to the unwarranted thrashing. Standing straight quite abruptly, he purposely allowed her to fall to the sand, causing her to cry out in pain when her tender backside connected with the ground. Through tearful eyes, she glared heatedly up at him, and awkwardly found her feet in a hurry.

"You'll regret the day you did this," she hissed, brushing dirt from her arms and the skirt of her gown.

One of Sean's brows lifted doubtfully. "I don't think I be livin' that long."

"Not if I can help it," she mumbled, examining the small cut on her hand.

Sean stepped forward. "You're bleedin', lass. Let me take a look at it."

"A lot you care!" she stormed, hugging her hand to her chest. "You nearly beat me to death and now you're worried over a tiny gash. I'll thank you to stay away from me."

The corner of his mouth curled disgustedly, and, having noticed Dru's presence, he thrust out a hand to seize her wrist and hurl her in his direction, angrily shoving her into Dru's arms. "Since it be your idea ta be sharin' in her father's wealth, *you* can be takin' care of her.'' Irritably rubbing his bruised ear, Sean stalked off in the direction of the beach.

''I think ya hurt me cousin's feelin's, lass,'' Dru whispered playfully in her ear, easily holding her struggling form to his chest.

Pricked by his sportive words, Victoria vowed to set him straight and satisfy her need to return Sean's favor. ''You should worry more about yourself, captain,'' she spat, giving full rein to her inventive nature, a trait she had used often as a child. ''Before you caught up with us, he told me how he'd take *all* my father's money and leave you to drift about the sea in a rowboat.'' She quieted and gave him one of her most convincing looks, a ploy she had many times bestowed upon her father to aid her in having her way.

''Did he now?'' Dru returned, no hint of a smile brightening his eyes.

Victoria tasted triumph. ''Yes,'' she nodded.

''Then I be thinkin' him a heartless man. One who would be tempted to do more than just redden your backside.'' He leaned down to glare at her. ''And since we be of the same blood, I be suggestin' ya curb your lyin' tongue and return ta me ship without another word. Neither of us looks fondly on one who tries ta set us apart and I'm truly tempted ta have ya repeat your claim ta him.''

Her dark brown eyes widened in fear, knowing she had not fooled this man. Only one other person in her life had recognized her game—her grandfather. But he had loved her and played along, gently amending her tales when the time was right. But what of this man? A tingling crept over her flesh and she lowered her eyes.

"Now will ya come along peaceable? Or do I finish what me cousin started?" he asked with a raised brow, watching her spin about and head off toward the ship. A wide grin broke the lines of his mouth.

SEVEN

Inquisitive stares followed the dissimilar trio as they boarded the *Defiance,* most shrugging off their curiosity, since it was not uncommon for their captain to bring a wench to his cabin. However, the first mate's agitated walk and gruffness in response to their greetings lifted a few brows, for his reputation as a firm yet carefree leader made this a very unusual mood for him.

They parted company when they stepped nearer the captain's quarters, Sean stalking off toward his own while Dru adamantly grasped Victoria's elbow, leading her down the short passageway to his cabin. As soon as his cousin's temper cooled and his pride was restored, Dru would send for him and together they would decide what course to take in reference to their new shipmate. Locking the door behind him, Dru crossed to his desk and tossed the key on top. He would hide it later when her curious eyes looked elsewhere.

Sitting down behind the desk, he pulled open the top drawer and rumaged through it until he found an unused piece of paper, taking the quill from its resting place to idly brush its feathered tip against his cheek while deep in thought. A few moments passed before he began to make hurried scratchings on its yellowed surface, pausing periodically to gaze upward for the words that seemed to evade him. Finally a pleased smile curled the corners of his mouth and he fell back in his chair, his gaze resting on the silent figure across the room.

"Would ya be carin' ta add anythin' to it?" he asked, nodding to the item that lay before him. "Or would ya be havin' the talents ta read?"

"Of course, I can read, you idiot," she spat, closing the distance between them in quick, nettled steps. Irately, she snatched the document from the desk. Her gaze briskly scanned its surface until she read the amount it would cost to free her, her eyes widening, her mouth agape. "You can't demand this much!"

A playful twinkle gleamed in his eye as he rested an elbow on the desk, his chin in his hand, and studied her over the curl of his fist. "Are ya sayin' ya not be worth it?"

Her face reddened in outrage. "Ooooh," she wailed, flipping the paper back at him. Turning, she stomped across the room and plopped down on his bunk, jumping up sharply as the sudden contact painfully reminded her of the encounter with Sean. Gently rubbing her bruised flesh, she cast him an evil glare before going to the porthole to stare outside.

Smiling openly, he settled himself comfortably in his chair, arms folded across his chest, and contemplated the slight form opposite him. Trim ankles peeked from beneath the hem of the blue gown, its transparency outlining shapely limbs before the thick, dark mass of hair hid the rest from view. He remembered the fear that had darkly enhanced Victoria's round, tear-filled eyes, gnawing at the soft spot in his heart when he first saw her until his gaze had traveled downward to spy the full, tempting breasts that threatened to spill from the gown with each labored breath she took. He sighed, recalling the difficulty he had had in stilling the desire that burned in his loins since time would not allow him the pleasure for which he had paid. And he was certain his cabin boy would not give him that pleasure. Yet when he had kissed her—

A ray of sunlight from the porthole at his back shot across the cabin as if guided by some celestial being to shimmer reflectively against the ebony curls cascading down the narrow shoulders, back, and waist. He watched its gentle sway, hypnotized by its beauty as it reached full length just below her backside, teasing the upper thigh as if daring him to try. He shook off the idea. He had something more important to do at the moment.

"Are ya hungry, lass?" His gaze fell upon the full swell of her breasts when she turned to answer.

"I am not in as great a need of food as I am of something respectful with which to clothe myself," she snapped, having seen where his attention lingered, her arms crossed to hide his view. "I demand you find me a gown more suitable to my needs."

"Demand, ya be sayin'?" Laughter mixed with his words. "Ya not be in much of a position to be demandin' anythin'. If nothin' else, ya should be

121

showin' your gratitude for me savin' ya from the hands of the likes of Kelsey.''

"Gratitude? You think I should be grateful that you took me from Kelsey and gave me to your cousin so he could—could—touch me like he did?''

One brow wrinkled derisively. "And from the way ya be talkin' it must have been the first time anyone, includin' your father, ever raised a hand ta ya. I be findin' it very hard to understand why I felt pity on such a small lass.''

"Captain Chandler,'' she began, biting off each word, "I didn't choose to be here. I was on my way to France when our ship was attacked by Kelsey and his men. I didn't beg you to wager for me at the card game or rescue me from that—that place, so don't expect me to thank you for anything!''

"And if I hadn't, what do ya suppose you'd be doin' now?''

"The same as I'm doing right here. Fighting off the crude looks of some *pirate*.''

"Aye. But I be thinkin' that wouldn't be all you'd be fightin'. Now if ya be half as smart as I be guessin' ya ta be, you'll count yourself lucky so far and learn ta keep your mouth shut. Ya've cost me considerable and given nothin' in return. If ya be wishin' ta keep it that way, I be suggestin' ya stop tryin' me patience.''

A quiver of apprehension raced through her veins, stealing Victoria's words and implanting a seed of caution to move slowly where this man was concerned, for she saw the hardening of his steel-blue eyes with his warning and knew him not to be the sort to be played a fool.

"Now, I'll be askin' one more time, are ya hungry?''

122

The stinging bite of his reprimand still tingling in her ears, she lowered her head modestly. "Yes."

"Then I'll leave ya a bit ta see what I can be findin' in the galley this time of night." He rose and went to the sea chest sitting on the floor near his bunk. Twisting the key already protruding from the lock, he lifted the lid and looked inside, sifting things about until he pulled out a shirt very similar to the one he wore. "If this be taming that tongue of yours, ya be welcome to wear it until somethin' else comes along." Tossing it on the bunk, he went back to the desk, picked up the brass key and headed for the door. Without looking back, he left her, only the sound of the lock turning to mark his exit.

Stepping into the captain's galley a few moments later, he pulled up short when he recognized Sean's lean frame crouched in a chair by the table. "Would ya be feelin' better, cousin?" he asked, sitting down next to him.

Sean's grunt brought a fresh smile to Dru's lips.

"I penned the ransom note we can be sendin' to the lass's father. If ya agree, I be thinkin' it best ta stay here until we receive his answer. I heard McGuire and his crew will be settin' sail for Savannah in a few days ta meet with his brother and thought maybe we could be sendin' it with him." He leaned forward to peer at Sean's sullen face. "Are ya hearin' me, lad?"

"Aye, I be hearin' ya." He took a long swallow from the mug held tightly in his hands. "And ya can do whatever ya want with the lass. It be makin' no difference ta me."

Repeatedly rubbing his forefinger across the tip of his nose to hide his mirth, Dru waited a moment before

123

he spoke, wishing not to rile Sean further by even a trace of laughter in his words. "Would ya care to tell me what troubles ya? I be thinkin' the devil be findin' it hard ta play his games with ya."

Sean's pale blue eyes darkened in anger flashed up at him. "Can't there be one day I be actin' the contrary without ya makin' somethin' of it? I see no humor about me."

"There never is unless ya be makin' it."

"Is that why ya laughed at me?" Sean barked, leaving the table, mug in hand, to go to the porthole and stare out at the gently rolling tide.

Dru's chair squeaked with his weight suddenly pressed back against it. "So it be me you're angry with."

"I'm not angry," Sean growled, flashing him a blackened scowl, "I'm—I'm—hurt."

"Hurt? You're hurt because I laughed?"

"At me! You were laughin' at me."

"Ah, Sean," Dru moaned ruefully, leaving his place at the table to walk dejectedly toward his cousin, "ya always be makin' me laugh. Has it hurt ya before?"

Sean's golden hair shimmered with his denial.

"Then why would it be botherin' ya now?" Leaning a shoulder against the bulkhead, he tilted his head to better see Sean's face. "Would it be because of the lass?"

The blue eyes found his before looking away again, an affirmative gleam mirrored in them.

"Sean, the lass was too busy with her own troubles to be worryin' about yours. I got a feelin' she's never been away from her home before this. Ya be knowin' her father owns a great deal, and, from the way she be behavin', I be thinkin' he gave her everythin' she wanted. And look at the way we found her, dressed in dirty clothes, beat about by that obnoxious scum, carted off to a whorehouse—If ya be embarrassed by the way she treated ya, think how the lass must have felt.''

Studying the mug in his hands, Sean chewed on his lower lip, trying to hide the grin that tugged at the corners of his mouth.

''And I wasn't laughin' at ya, I laughed at the way a big, gentle man tried his damnest to control a slip of a lass without hurtin' her. If ya had acted any other way, I would have stepped between ya.''

''But I did. I spanked her,'' Sean contradicted.

''And rightly so. A man can only take so much.'' Dru waited until Sean looked up, presented him with a wide, sparkling grin, and clutched his cousin's shirt collar in his hand, pulling him into a warm embrace. He stiffened suddenly, his gaze closely scrutinizing Sean's ear.

''What is it ya be lookin' at?'' he demanded, pushing away.

''Are ya in need of a bath or is that a bruise I be seein'?''

Sean's shoulders drooped in surrender. ''Thank God she didn't scar me or I'd be fightin' off your words 'til the day I die.'' Moving closer, he playfully doubled up a fist beneath Dru's nose, and added, ''And if ya don't want one ta match, I be suggestin' ya forget about it.''

Both hands raised in compromise, Dru backed away mockingly, a smile appearing on his face again. ''Does this mean you'll be holdin' no grudges?''

''Some day, cousin, I'll be forgettin' our mothers

were sisters and me fist will be findin' its way to your jaw."

"Wouldn't be the first time," Dru said, the dimple appearing in his cheek.

"Nor the last," Sean laughed.

"And as captain of this ship, I order ya to go ashore and get drunk."

"But I haven't even had me supper yet. Why would ya be wantin' me to do that?"

"As the only man I can trust with me life, I can't be havin' ya full of doubts about me love for ya. If ya get blind drunk, ya'll wake up in the mornin' thinkin' it was all a bad dream." He nodded over his shoulder at the door. "Now get goin'. I've got ta be findin' somethin' ta feed the scrawny rat takin' up part of me cabin space. I can't have her father chasin' after us thinkin' we neglected her. Oh, and Sean," he added, delaying his cousin's exit, "while ya be enjoyin' yourself, try ta find McGuire. The sooner we send off the letter, the sooner we be gettin' rid of the lass."

Sean presented him with a sportive click of his heels and rigid salute. "Aye, aye, capt'n," he said most stiffly, but the twinkle in his eye betrayed the honesty of his gesture, and Dru conceded Sean the last word, waving him out of the cabin without comment.

Alone, he set about gathering a small loaf of bread and tin of jam the cook tried repeatedly to hide from the crew, smiling at the ingenious spot the man had chosen this time. The bread and jam were cradled inside a large, empty tin, shoved to the back of the cupboard. He'd remember the man's talents the next time they had gems to conceal. Lifting a jug of rum from the table, he started for his cabin, spying the cook's ham-

126

mock hanging enticingly in the corner. A devious smile pursed his lips.

Having awkwardly unlocked the door, he nudged it open with his toe and glanced back down the passageway one more time to make certain no one had seen what he carried. Even in port, some of the crew disliked having a woman on board for very long, and the extra sleeping gear rolled up and tucked beneath his arm would surely raise a few questions. Not to mention their speculations on why the captain chose not to share his bunk with a wench. How would he convince them she only slept there, since he had never enjoyed anyone's company in his bunk when he needed a good night's rest? And right now he wasn't in the mood to tame a shrew anyway. Satisfied his secret was safe for the time being, he quietly entered the cabin.

"I'm afraid I couldn't find much to fill our bellies," he told Victoria, his concentration centered on finding an adequate resting place for his goods. His hands empty, he glanced up at her, his gaze devouring the entire length of her shapely form clothed only in his shirt, its tail covering her knees. His pulse quickened. "I be thinkin' ya need more than that to cover yourself," he said thickly, walking to his sea chest once more. Foraging through the trunk again, he withdrew a pair of his breeches and handed them to her, carefully abstaining from the temptation to feast his eyes upon her curvaceous limbs. Though her tongue could slice him open with her spiteful words, a match he wished to avoid at present, the sight of her tempted his courage to try, the promise of sweeter reward most evident. He frowned. Maybe later. Right now he was hungry and the idea of sleep interested him more.

"You can turn around now."

Startled by her intrusion upon his thoughts, he jumped, waving off the movement with a flip of his hand as he walked to the hatch and turned the key. "Just so we won't be surprised durin' our meal," he said, glancing over his shoulder at her. His breath caught in his throat.

The breeches nearly reached her ankles, but they were not nearly as troublesome as the shirt she had tucked down inside them. Being virtually three times to large for her, the opening at the neck plunged to the valley between her breasts, barely hiding the firm mounds of flesh beneath it.

"This won't be workin'. Maybe ya should be puttin' it on the other way around," he muttered softly.

"What?"

He straightened sharply. "I said ya should be lacin' up the—the—" He wiggled a directive finger at her neckline, then marched to the table and the food he had brought them. Sliding out a chair, he prudently focused his attention on tearing off two sections of bread and covering each with jam. " 'Tisn't much, but it will have to do," he said, placing the meager offering on a tin plate. He poured himself a drink, listening to her bare feet pad across the deck to join him. A moment passed before he could bring himself to look at her, her dark, flowing hair draped over one shoulder.

"I'm sorry for being so much trouble," she spoke softly, her eyes reflecting the smile on her lips.

A piece of bread lodged in his throat. He gulped.

"I thought about what you said before, and I want to apologize for my behavior. I hope you can understand why I acted like I did."

His gaze moved to the strings entwined through the holes in the shirt front, mentally counting each loop. He stuffed another piece of bread in his mouth, followed by a hearty swig of rum.

"Whatever amount you feel necessary to see me safely home is all right with me. Or if your travels take you to France, you could leave me there and I would see to it that you are paid for my passage."

He only glanced at her this time before hurriedly leaving his chair to go to the corner of the room where he had thrown down the hammock. Quietly, he unrolled the mass of thin ropes, eyeing a likely spot in which to hang it, all the while knowing Victoria watched.

"Ya must be tired," he finally said after stringing up the hammock, "and I be havin' a lot of plannin' ta do. After ya eat, ya might want ta rest." He crossed to his desk, sat down, and pulled out a large book. Unfolding a map, he picked up a quill from the well, and made several entries in the ledger.

Nearly half an hour passed while he forced himself to fix his attention on the papers before him, acutely aware of the movements his cabinmate made finishing her meal, then awkwardly climbing into the hammock. Hoping by now she had fallen asleep, he stole a secretive glance her direction, slumping in his chair when he noticed how seductively her entire backside molded into the gentle curve of the crisscrossing ropes. Of a sudden, he found it difficult to breathe, the stirring in his loins growing evident. Then, angry that a wee mite like this could cause him so much unrest, he slammed the quill down on the desk, hurriedly left his chair, and stormed the hatch.

"Captain?"

The soft soprano tones of her voice paralyzed him.

"Is something troubling you?"

Laughter nearly found its way to his throat. "Aye, lass. But I be goin' ta a place than can cure me." Courageously, he set out to still the aching in his loins.

Cool night air bathed Dru's flushed cheeks as he marched across the sandy beach on his way to the nearest pub and the first willing woman he could find. His step never wavered, determined as he was to satisfy the craving that burned within him. But the frown that marred his brow stemmed from another cause. Never had any woman affected him in the way this one did. Could it be that she was the first *real* lady he had ever met? Not some practiced whore with skills at lovemaking, but a woman with the sweet innocence of a virgin. He swallowed the knot in his throat and hurried his step. This woman-child wore no low-cut gowns, nor did she paint her lips blood-red to entice a man. In fact, she did nothing to purposely encourage him. But the simple way she dressed, combed her hair and sweetly smiled, unaware of the vision she created, stirred a desire in him of which she had no knowledge, one that bothered him deeply. Could it be because he knew a woman of her breeding was unobtainable? That a pirate could only look at such a treasure and never gather it in his arms? Was she the challenge he knew in his heart that he could never seek to conquer?

The dim lights of the tavern a few yards ahead urged him onward. He must put her from his mind, forget the churning in the pit of his stomach that only she aroused. He was a man, a loner, a sort who needed no woman except to satisfy the burning lust of his loins. And he certainly needed one now.

His lean hand pressed to the swinging door of the tavern, Dru entered the building in a rush, his gaze quickly scanning the inhabitants for the one he sought. Paying the crowd of men no heed, he crossed the room toward the barmaid serving drinks at one table, caught the crook of her arm in a firm hold, and set the tray she carried on the bar as they passed by.

"What's the matter, mate?" a voice called out from the group who watched. "Been at sea a long while?"

Hearty guffaws followed this observation, and had his need not been so great, Dru would have returned the banter twofold as he had always done before, paused a moment to chide his friends, and share a mug of rum to set his mood. But he had no time for games, only a lustful appetite to sate, a sovereign cause.

They traveled in silence down the short distance of the hallway that led to several rooms used for such purposes. Without pausing, Dru lifted the latch of the first and ushered his companion inside, closing the door quietly and hooking the back of a chair beneath the knob. He turned to face her, a satisfied smile deepening the dimple in his cheek.

"Is somethin' wrong, Dru Chandler?" the pretty brunette asked, her fists resting on her hips.

Of all the women he had known, none other had sparked his interest as much as Brenna. He had oftentimes wondered if it might be the fact that she too hailed from Ireland, or simply because she understood his moods and never made demands of him, satisfied to share one night or, on occasion, only a few words. And yet her skill at reading his thoughts unnerved him.

131

"And why would ya be thinkin' somethin' troubles me, lass?" he asked lightly.

She raised a thin, finely arched brow. "Have I ever been wrong about ya before? Of all the times ya sought me out, not once have ya done so as ya did just now."

" 'Tis only that I be impatient ta hold ya," he grinned devilishly, stepping forward to encircle her tiny waist with his arms. He snuggled closer, breathing in the scent of her hair as he nibbled at her earlobe.

"Impatient, is it?" she mocked. "And am I ta think ya might care about me more than a single night's time can bring?"

"Ah, Brenna, ya be knowin' in me heart, there is no other like you."

Brenna laughed happily. "Now I be knowin' somethin's wrong." Gently, she pushed back from him. "Would ya be carin' ta talk about it?"

Trailing a fingertip along her jaw, down the slim throat to the full curve of her breast, he whispered, "Talkin' wasn't what I had in mind, sweet Brenna."

"It seldom is," she smiled knowingly, reaching up to unfasten the strings of her blouse and expose the treasure he pursued. Warm, hungry kisses pressed against her throat, his hand gently fondling the firm mound of her bare flesh, a thumb stroking the rose-hued peak. "If only the others would hold me as ya do, Dru Chandler," she whispered. "Would make our partin' less painful."

Without a word or any sound to give evidence he heard, his lips found hers, his tongue parting them to slip inside for the sweetness of her kiss. As though rehearsed a hundred times, both slid from their shoes, the

132

rest of their clothes to follow as they moved slowly toward the bed. Their naked bodies pressed as one, the words they spoke forgotten, they fell together on the straw mattress, oblivious to any world but their own, when visions of another exploded in his mind—dark, sultry eyes, thick lashes, full, sensuous mouth, a flowing ebony mane. He groaned, his life's blood burning through his veins, setting him on fire.

"Go away," he whispered, his voice thick, almost a strangled cry of inaudible words.

"Who?"

The honey-smooth tone of Brenna's question pierced his cocoon.

"Are ya meanin' me, Dru?"

His head shot upward. "What?"

Brenna wiggled from beneath him, rising up on one elbow, the thin coverlet held to her bosom. "Ya said, 'Go away.' Who did ya mean?"

"Did I?" he lied, grinning half-heartedly. "I—er—well—"

"Dru, me love, ya may fool others, but never me. Now tell me what troubles ya."

He rolled to his back and fell against the pillow beside her. "I don't think ya really want ta know."

Brenna smiled sweetly. "Why? 'Tis another woman?"

His gray-blue eyes moved to look at her, a sheepish grin parting his lips.

"I thought so. Now let me guess. The lass wants nothin' ta do with ya and it bruised your poor ego."

Dru's cheek wrinkled in disgust and he folded his

arms in back of his head, staring up at the ceiling. "I can have her any time I be wantin'."

"Can ya now? Then why are ya here when ya obviously don't want ta be?"

"Because she has a tongue sharper than any blade I've carried."

Brenna laughed playfully. "And since when has that stopped ya?"

"Don't tease, lass," he warned, his eyes darkening with the threat.

"Dru Chandler, of all the men I've known, there's never been one who could sweep me off me feet like you. Ya make love ta me before me head's had time ta stop spinnin'. Don't ya think ya can do the same ta her?"

" 'Tisn't the problem," he mumbled. "She's— different."

"Ya mean she isn't a whore and won't give in freely."

Dru closed his eyes with a shake of his dark head, a grin stretching his lips. "Ya know, Brenna, sometimes I think ya are a witch. Ya know what I'm thinkin' without me sayin' a word."

"Ah, not a witch, Dru Chandler," she laughed, leaning over to kiss the tip of his nose. "I'm selfish. I want ya ta get this lass out of your blood so you'll be comin' back ta me clear-headed. I don't mind sharin' ya but not while you're suppose ta be makin' love ta me." She sat up, soundly slapped his hip and left the bed. "Now get out of here. I've got ta get dressed and back ta work." She moved to the pile of clothing they had discarded, pausing when he failed to get up. "Go on. Prove me wrong."

He smiled warmly at her from the haven of their bed, knowing she was right, yet somehow sensing that only one night spent in Victoria Remington's arms would never sate his desire completely.

EIGHT

"You imbecile! How could you be so stupid?" Melissa's wrath filled the room, forcing an involuntary shutter to jolt Charles's frame. Her nose only inches from his, she seethed, "I should have you gelded for what you've done."

"Take it easy, Melissa," Edwin lulled, lightly touching her arm. She yanked violently from his hold. "We'll find her. She couldn't have gone far."

"Out of my sight is too far," she stormed. "I had plans for her. Plans. Do you hear me?" Pacing the floor, she failed to notice Edwin nod toward the cause of her unrest, sucking in an agitated breath when she saw him move toward the door. "Where do you think you're going?"

Frantic, Charles looked to Edwin.

"I thought it best he start searching for her now. He can take Dunstan with him. There's nothing else we can do and you haven't had a thing to eat since this morning.''

Her eyes narrowed dangerously. "How can you think of food at a time like this?"

"I'm not thinking of food, I'm thinking of you." Noticing the paleness of the knuckles of her hand clenched about her wineglass, he covered her hand with his and waited until she reluctantly allowed him to take it from her. "You must eat to keep up your strength. It won't do to have you swooning on us just when we need you most." She half-heartedly tried to pull away from him, but he easily caught her chin in a delicate hold, lifting her gaze to meet his. "You know I'm right, don't you?"

Studying the soft brown eyes of the only face she had grown to trust, she relaxed a degree. "Yes. As always.''

"Good. Then while you and I dine, these two can search every corner of Barbados until they find her. Otherwise, we'll do as you suggested and geld them both." He looked threateningly over his shoulder at the pair. "Now get going and see to it that you don't bungle it this time."

Clubbing his huge companion harmlessly in the belly, Charles motioned them out of the room, never taking a breath until they were safely in the hallway, the door closed firmly behind them. "The bitch," he growled. "Who does she think she is?"

"You shouldn't talk about Mistress Bensen that way, Charles," Dunstan argued, his lower lip sagging, round blue eyes glistening. "She's always been nice to us."

"Nice? She wouldn't give you a crumb off her plate

137

if you hadn't earned it. I doubt that woman has ever been nice to anyone. Or don't you mind being gelded?"

Dunstan stood cleaning the dirt from his thumbnail, sheepishly looking up at Charles, then back to his hand.

"Well, so do I. And when I find the little harlot, she'll pay for this insult." Angry footfalls clicked against the wooden stairs, his hand irately slapping the balustrade as Charles started down the staircase, Dunstan on his heels.

"But where we gonna look, Charles? Miss Bonita said after the girl's first customer, she just disappeared."

"She couldn't have just disappeared," Charles rallied, his steps hurrying. "You saw the room Bonita kept her in. She had to have had help. Or sprouted wings."

"Maybe she slipped by Miss Bonita when she wasn't lookin, just like Miss Bonita said."

Charles stopped midway down the staircase and glared back up at Dunstan. "You're as stupid as she. If the girl has enough money to interest Melissa, she bought her way out. We just have to figure out who agreed to take her money." He started down the stairs again. "And since I'm hungry, we'll ask questions in the inn's dining hall while I eat."

"But you heard Miss Melissa. Her and Edwin are gonna eat, too. What if they see us?"

"Not here, you idiot. We'll go to Milly's where we first found the girl. If we're lucky and Melissa was right, it might have been the pirates we took her from who came to get her back." An odd smile curled the corner of his mouth. "I can just imagine the surprise on their faces when they discovered their little cabin boy was really a very beautiful woman." He sobered. "Now hurry up, will you?"

"Hello, Milly," Sean crooned, sliding into a chair located at a table near the back of the hall. "Have ya got somethin' good ta be feedin' me? I'm afraid me appetite could outdo any man's here."

"Sure do, honey. Fresh caught fish this afternoon," she said, trying her level best to present him with a seductive smile.

"Good. And bring me a mug of ale. I'll be tryin' me damnest to get drunk soon after."

Pressing a pudgy hand on the table top, she leaned in, allowing full view of her ample bosom straining against the bodice of her gown. "Ya think maybe you'll have time for me later?"

Amused by the offer, he veiled his mirth with downcast eyes. "Well, I don't know, Milly. What might ya be havin' in mind?" he teased.

"You know damn well, Sean Rafferty," she barked. "There ain't a bigger stud on the island than you. Except maybe that cousin of yours. And it's been a long time since I had me a real man."

"Now Milly. I be findin' that hard ta believe. Ya've got ta be the most beautiful woman on Barbados. Surely they're beatin' down the door ta your room."

She straightened with the compliment, and a soft red hue mingled with the pockmarks on her cheeks. She lifted short, stubby fingers to caress the curls dangling at her neckline.

"But if ya don't bring me food, I won't be findin' the strength to wait me turn in line."

Giggles exploded from the round figure standing before him. He smiled back, a forced smile, watching her amble away, the muscles of his cheeks tiring from the abuse, and waggled the fingers of one hand in her direction when she smiled toothlessly back at him. *I be doubtin' ya find enough ale in the place for me ta be wantin' ta meet with ya later, Milly, ol' girl,* he mused, praying some other besotted pirate would catch her eye long before she forced him to make excuses. He settled back comfortably in his chair to wait, spying two familiar figures enter the inn, and instantly realized the error in his choice of eating places. But knowing there was little he could do to correct the problem, he folded his arms across his chest and watched.

Charles and Dunstan, unaware they were being observed, took a table a good distance from Sean, motioning for Milly to see to their desires. They engaged in a rather lengthy conversation with her, and Sean safely studied the trio from his corner of the room until Milly inadvertently glanced his way, bringing the attention of the men to him. The smaller of the two stiffened immediately, thumped his partner on the shoulder with the back of his hand, and stood. With little movement to give away his intent, Sean rested his fingertips against the butt of the pistol tucked in his breeches and watched as they approached his table.

"Excuse me, sir," Charles said, his huge companion standing two paces behind him and off to one side, "but aren't you the gentleman with whom we did business earlier?"

Sean cocked a honey-blond brow. "I be doin' a lot of business while anchored in Barbados."

"Yes, I'm sure you do," Charles admitted, pulling

out a chair and sitting down across from Sean. "Allow me to introduce myself and refresh your memory. My name is Charles Murphy and my friend here is Dunstan Crag."

Sean's eyes lifted to take in the huge form shadowing the table. Dunstan remained motionless.

"We purchased your cabin boy this morning and now find ourselves in a bit of a problem."

Sean's face reflected no interest. Charles cleared his throat to begin again, knowing this task would be more difficult than he'd anticipated, and leaned forward on the table to fold his hands.

"Yes, well, it seems we've misplaced the boy and wondered if you might know where he is? Needless to say, our mistress was quite angry to find him gone after paying good money for his services."

"As I be recallin', me mate warned the lass that she might be havin' trouble with him."

A smile slowly made its way across Charles's face. "Yes, so he did. And since it was my responsibility to watch after the child, I now must find him or face the consequences."

Sean silently considered the man, a twinkle sparkling in his eyes. "I'm sorry I can't be helpin' ya, but after the lad left with ya, I ain't been seein' him again."

Charles suppressed his anger, the corner of his mouth twitching, and Sean noticed how the man purposely covered his lips with the back of his hand and pressed them to stop the twitch. He glanced irritably up at Dunstan, dismissing him with a nod.

"Well, I'd appreciate it if you'd keep me in mind should you ever see the boy," Charles said, rising from the chair. "There's money in it for you if you do." He waited for Sean to offer more, but when Sean only declined his head slightly, Charles grew rigid, his nostrils flared. Then, turning sharply on his heel, he stalked away.

Sean finished his meal under the uncomfortable scrunity of the two men. Each time he looked up, either Charles or his companion glared at him, and Sean realized they hadn't believed his story. Deciding it was better he look elsewhere for his enjoyment, he swallowed the remainder of his ale and left the inn.

Darkness shadowed his movements along the narrow streets as he headed for another establishment and the young maid by the name of Prissilla. He had taken a fancy to the young girl the last time they were in port, and, being in dire need of a female companion who wouldn't beat him about, he hurried his step in her direction. Crossing to the row of buildings on the other side, he glanced back out of habit and spotted a movement a few hundred yards away. Pretending not to notice, he kept his pace even until he passed an alleyway, ducking swiftly into its protection to wait. His body pressed against the building, he listened for footsteps, a distant chorus of laughter penetrating the stillness. A few moments passed, time enough for those who followed to catch up to him, but the street intersecting with his hiding place remained empty. Disillusioned, he made a foolish error, one his instincts would have warned against had his desire to see Prissilla not been so great. Running his fingers through his hair in an effort to smooth it, he stepped out into the open. He was caught off guard. A huge hand easily came up to commandeer his shoulder and spin him around. His eyes failed to recognize the figure that lifted a fist before a

142

stunning backhand struck his jaw, catapulting him backward against the building. He withered to his knees. This time, fingers locked in a handful of his hair, raising his chin to connect with the knee brought up in a bone-cracking blow. Blurred figures hovered over him.

"Now, my good friend," a menacing voice implored, "let's try my question again. Where have you taken Victoria Remington?"

His pain-filled eyes fought to focus on the man looming above him. "I can't be sayin' I've had the honor of knowin' the lass," Sean muttered through clenched teeth, certain they had broken his jaw.

Charles nodded to Dunstan. "Maybe Mr. Crag can jar your memory a bit."

With the command, Dunstan effortlessly lifted Sean to his feet by strong hands clamped onto his shirt. Bracing the Irishman with fingers pressed against his chest, Dunstan pulled back, then unleashed a smashing blow to the bridge of Sean's nose, hurling him into a stack of boxes to roll, then tumble to the ground, blood pouring from the gash below his eye. Vainly, Sean tried to push himself up, the pounding in his temples crescendoing to unbearable heights before blackness came to claim him and force him to the ground again.

"Dunstan, you halfwit. Look what you've done. He's no good to us now," Charles snapped. "He could be out for hours."

"But you told me to hit him, Charles. I only did what you told me to do," Dunstan objected, rubbing the fresh bruises on his knuckles.

"I didn't mean hard enough to knock him out, you fool. Now we're right back where we started. Unless—"

"Unless what?"

"Unless we're fortunate enough to find his friend. Come on, we've wasted enough time."

"But what about him?" Dunstan asked, pointing to the quiet body.

"Leave him. By the time he comes around, we'll be long gone."

Glancing up and down the street to secure their safety from witnesses, Charles took the lead, the big bulk of a man following closely behind.

Having never slept in a hammock before in her life, Victoria found the experience trying, indeed almost impossible. After the captain left she tested every position she could think of, none of which satisfied her. Only lying on her back brought any comfort whatsoever, and even that proved uncompromising when she awoke a few minutes later, her left arm numb. Deciding the possibility of lying on the floor, cushioned by a blanket, would offer a more suitable rest, she slipped one leg over the edge and started to climb down. Losing her balance, she hopped on one foot, trying frantically to unhook the toe of the other from the delicate webbing of her makeshift bed, and in so doing forced the hammock to rock to and fro. Unable to catch herself, Victoria toppled to the floor. Anger overruling any pain she felt, she scrambled to her feet, taking a swing at the hammock, determined to see justice done. Instead, her small fist slipped between the ropes as if the hammock had teeth and wished to swallow her up.

"Ooooh," she howled, jerking free and involuntarily spinning herself around to come face to face with the captain, who stood lounging in the doorway, a wide smile on his handsome face. Her cheeks pinkened immediately.

"Havin' a wee bit of trouble, lass?" he bantered carelessly.

Forgetting his earlier warnings, she stiffened instantly. "Yes, I am. And if you were a gentleman, you'd offer your bed to me instead of that—that—" She waved disgustedly in the direction of the object that had caused her unrest.

"Hammock, lass, hammock." He stepped further into the room and closed the door behind him, twisting the key in the lock. He leaned back against the portal, arms crossed and a suggestive gleam in his eye. "Funny ya should be mentionin' it. I'd already thought the same," he said calmly.

While he had walked all the back to his ship, slowly at first as he digested Brenna's advice, then quickening his steps when the huge vessel came into view, he had contemplated the strange events in his life since meeting this beautiful young wildcat. He had never had trouble making love to a woman, and especially not because of another's haunting his mind. He sailed from woman to woman as he did port to port, and not one remained in his memory. So why now? And he had only kissed her! Maybe Brenna was right. The anticipation was what blinded him, occupied his thoughts and ruined his desire for another. Well, he'd put an end to that and right now. He straightened, unfolded his arms and started across the cabin, certain this night would fill him with a bliss never before imagined.

Victoria's breath caught in her throat, her heart suddenly pounding in her ears, for there was no mistaking the meaning of his words or the darkening of his steel-blue eyes. Absently, she reached up for the collar of the shirt she wore, clasping it tightly closed as if that would make a difference. He came closer and she quickly side-stepped him, surprised when he didn't follow but continued on until he reached the hammock, which still swayed gently from her earlier assault. He began unfastening the knots that held it in place.

"W-What are you doing?" Her voice cracked but she managed to hold her head high as if unaffected.

"Takin' it down, lass," he replied over his shoulder. "We won't be needin' it anymore."

"W-We won't?" Her lip trembled.

"Nay, lass," he grinned, freeing the last piece of twisted rope. The hammock fell to the floor with a thump, and he turned around to look at her. "We'll be sharin' me bunk from now on."

Victoria felt every muscle in her small frame tighten. Surely, he didn't mean—he wasn't suggesting— She laughed weakly but she didn't know why. "Oh, I really couldn't put you out—"

"Ya won't," he answered quickly.

She swallowed hard. "The hammock isn't that bad. I mean, once I get used to it, I'm sure—"

He stepped closer. She moved away.

"Did you send the letter to my father?" She forced a smile, backing up further when he continued to advance. "You have a very nice cabin, captain. Who cleans it for you?" A tremor raced through her at his smile, jumping with a start when she backed into the corner of his desk. She hurried around it, placing it between them. But unaffected, he followed. "Captain, I think we should talk this over."

146

He continued to grin, each step he took bringing him closer, until all he had to do was reach out for her. A brief moment of curiosity flitted through her mind, wondering why he chose not to, when all of a sudden, the back of her knees bumped against the long wooden bench built beneath the numerous rows of leaded glass windows at the aft of the ship. Caught off balance, she plopped down on the seat, bouncing up immediately, and hurried past him. It was blatantly obvious that he had no intention of discussing the matter, so she rushed to the door of the cabin, a small whimper trailing from her lips when she found the door locked. She spun around, pressing herself back against the wood surface.

"Captain, we had a deal," she argued, tears choking off her words. "Unharmed, you said. You agreed."

"Aye," he nodded, his fingers unlooping the strings at the opening of his shirt. "Unharmed. I gave me word. But we never spoke of untouched." He slid the garment over his head and tossed it away.

"No-o-o!" she cried. "You—you can't! I'm—I've never known a man—" Frantic, determined to save herself, she spied his pearl-handled dagger lying on the desk, racing to it in an instant. Clasping it tightly in her hand, she confronted him, tears flowing down her face. "Don't make me use this, captain. I really don't want to kill you, but if you come near me, I will."

Dru relaxed, resting his weight on one foot, the fingers of both hands interlaced and dangling at ease in front of him. The dimple showed in his cheek. "I have no doubt you'll try ta cut me open, lass, but I must be warnin' ya of two things. Me cousin would not take kindly ta your spillin' me blood and his revenge could prove ta be more mortifyin' than what ya imagine this

147

ta be.'' He looked down at his feet, swaying slightly on his heels. ''But ya won't have the chance ta try.'' Before his declaration reached its end, he lunged for her, easily knocking the blade from her hand, clamping his own securely around her wrist.

She tried to pull away as he dragged her effortlessly toward the bunk. ''No-o-o. Please, captain, don't do this!'' She tore at the strong fingers entrapping her arm. Some courage returned. ''My father will have you shot,'' she proclaimed adamantly. ''I'll tell him everything. I swear I will!'' She jerked backward, hoping to break his hold, only to witness the muscles of his forearm flex slightly. He had the strength of a lion, and he was just as sleek, powerful, and cunning in stalking his prey. Visions of the women on the *La Belle Fleur* exploded in her mind, their screams, pain, humiliation. Tears welled up in her eyes again. ''What must I do to sway you?'' They stopped at the edge of the bunk and she yanked back again, her only reward the burning of her flesh where he held her. ''You're hurting me,'' she whimpered.

''Only because ya be wantin' it this way,'' he answered quietly.

Dark brown eyes, glistening with tears shot up to glare at him. ''*I* want— I don't want anything to do with you!''

''Ya have no choice,'' he said, quite matter-of-factly.

''Do you expect me to just strip myself for you and eagerly climb in—in—'' —she waved a hand at his bunk— ''there?''

He grinned. ''No. I'd rather be undressin' ya meself.''

''Oh-h-h,'' she moaned fearfully, pulling frantically

148

at his grip, oblivious to the discomfort it caused. She stretched away as far as possible, bare feet sliding against the wooden planks beneath her when he facilely drew her toward him. "Anything. I'll see you have anything you want, if you'll only—"

"Aye, 'tis what I intend ta have." He held her by one arm pressed against the lean, hard muscles of his chest.

The warmth of his body seared her flesh and Victoria felt certain she would swoon from the minor contact. Could she endure an ounce more? Logic nullified her panic and she swallowed hard, willing her lips to move with her question. "Why? Why do you want me when you could have anyone else?"

He smiled down at her, his dark features bathed in the warm glow of candlelight, his flashing white grin unnerving. "Because all the others are willin', lass. And I plan ta show ya *why* they are."

Victoria stiffened. "You conceited lout! If there were no men left on earth but you, you would never find me willing. I would rather remain unmarried."

His grin widened. "Who said anythin' about marriage?"

The query struck a major blow and gave Victoria an idea. "Well, it's something you should consider, sir captain of pirates. If my father doesn't shoot you first, he will most assuredly force you to marry me!"

The dimple in his cheek deepened. "And why would I be wantin' ta marry ya when I can have all the benefits without?"

A devious smile of her own parted her lips. "One distinct difference. Married to you, I would accept my fate and share your bed willingly. As it is now, I will fight you all the way."

His laughter stung her ears and sent a shiver of doubt up her spine. "Ya may fight me at first, lass," —he caught her other arm with lightning speed— "but it won't be lastin' long. I have a most convincin' manner." The hand that held her wrist twisted her arm in back of her, painlessly but unyielding, and he pulled her to him, forcing her back to arch and her eyes to meet his. "As I said before, I won't be hurtin' ya, lass."

When he released her other arm to cradle her chin in his large hand, she tried to push away, her fingers pressed against his chest. The feel of soft curls cushioned the taut muscles there and sent an electrifying charge through her whole body. She squirmed, but the firmness of his grasp forbade it, drawing her face to his. His kiss brushed the corner of her mouth, her cheek, and nose, then settled warmly on her lips. Victoria felt as if her breath, her will to fight, had vanished as quickly as her words, a pleasant warmth spreading through her and awakened a long hidden passion she had scarcely known existed. His mouth twisted across hers, his tongue parting her lips to lightly touch her own. He tasted of rum, and she found it oddly pleasing, filling her mind with a different intoxication. Consciously, she relaxed, her fingers gently discovering the shape and firmness of the muscles beneath her hand as it rested on his chest, surprised to find the dark curls covering it soft, as near soft as down. It excited her, and she could not fathom why.

He released his claim on her wrist to stroke the long strands of her hair, allowing her the freedom to encircle his huge frame with her arms. Her fingertips touched the scars on his back, caressing them as though wanting to ease the pain they had caused so long ago. His hand slid to her tiny waist, pulling her closer, their bodies touching full length. The cotton shirt and breeches she wore did little to mask the contact or stop the sudden flash of heat that shot through her. Her mind whirled and she wondered briefly why his kiss, his touch, *his* caress did not repluse her as Kelsey's had. She had expected such bliss from the man she would marry, and could not understand how this pirate, this rogue, could spark these motions. Had he somehow awakened wanton desires in her?

He broke their kiss, his hands moving to tenderly clasp her face between them, his lips lightly touching her brow, closed eyelids, and the tip of her nose before returning to her trembling mouth once more. He wondered if the nearness they shared affected her as it did him—or would she at any moment lash out at him? He had kissed many women, held them in his arms, desired them, but none had invaded the recesses of his mind as this one did. Once more he contemplated the possibility that it was only because he knew he could never have her, that once he returned this beautiful, delicate creature to her father he would never see her again. Or would he? Was it possible she would return again and again to haunt his dreams, steal into his thoughts, rob his sanity? His head whirled with the fragrance of her—sweet, tantalizing, seductive. He wanted her, wholly. He wanted to tame her. But why? And was he willing to pay the price? Her hands moved softly across the width of his back, roaming with a tenderness to his shoulders as he kissed her. But what really melted him was the fact that she returned his advances, seeming to be as lost in the moment as he. A prickling of worry caught him. How far would she allow him to go? Would the tigress show her claws if he trespassed further? The lust burning in his loins diminished his need for caution. It didn't matter. He would endure all, whether tiny fists against his chest or bitter words ringing in his ears, for the promise of this treasure seemed well worth the risk.

When his lips grazed her cheek to nibble on her earlobe, Victoria suddenly noticed the heat that scorched her cheeks, for his own seemed cool against her flesh. Was this the way it was meant to be? Could any man send a tremor through her as this pirate captain had? She tilted her head back, allowing his kisses to trail down her long neck, unaware of the agile fingers that unfastened the strings of the shirt she wore or the origin of the sensation that raced through her when his knuckle brushed against the smoothness of her breast. Caught up in the wave of pleasure, she even failed to realize he had slipped the garment from her or untied the narrow rope that held the breeches in place, letting them glide easily from her slender hips, leaving her naked in his embrace. Cool night air touched her flesh, and she waited impatiently for him to shed his own clothes, wanting to hold him close to her and chase away the chill.

With tender ease, Dru lifted her, their lips meeting, holding, searching, discovering, oblivious to anything but the moment. He carried her to the bunk, bending a knee upon it, and gently fell upon the velvet coverlet. He rolled beneath her, the long, black tresses blanketing them both, and Dru thought his mind would explode with desire. He kissed her chin, her neck and shoulder, vaguely hearing her moan of pleasure. His heart racing, his passion mounting, he eagerly curled her beneath him, wanting desperately to taste every inch of her. His lips touched her throat, the hollow at the base where her pulse beat wildly, then the valley between her breasts, savoring each delicious nibble. His own heart pounding, he abandoned his want to move slowly, his open mouth, hot and wet, capturing the delicate peak of her breast, gently biting, sucking, his tongue sampling the sweetness of her flesh. He moved lower, white teeth threatening to devour the slim waist and silken skin of her belly.

Eyes closed, Victoria lay breathless, panting, her woman's body eager to welcome each and every move he made, damning the consequences and living for the moment he would take her. In her wildest dreams, she had never imagined a man's touch, his caress, could unleash the passion that burned within her, sending her reeling, destroying her virtuous thoughts.

Dru raised above her, his eyes dark with lust, and lowered his weight upon her, parting her thighs. Victoria moved to welcome him, instinctively guiding him, opening her eyes when he hesitated and found him frowning. Failing to understand his reason, worried he had had a change of heart, she reached out to pull him closer until his manly hardness touched the soft flesh of womanhood and she heard him moan. He came to her then, his first thrust sending a wave of pain through her, wondering if his boldness had torn her apart. But as he moved deeper, faster, the fear subsided, replaced with an explosive tremor that consumed her, lifted her to dizzying heights and filled her mind and body with a magic ecstasy. They moved as one, bodies clinging, desires running free. Time seemed a heavenly void as they explored, searched, conquered, and finally reached a height neither imagined.

Some time passed before Dru eased himself from her. He lay at her side, his head propped up on one fist, his other hand brushing a silky strand of hair from her brow. His features softened as he studied her beauty in the soft glow of candlelight, wondering what words to speak, if any. She seemed content to snuggle, toying with the numerous dark curls on his chest, one fingertip following the path they made in a narrow line down his belly. He held his breath, letting it out in a rush when he heard her giggle.

"I never would have thought I could cause you any pain, my pirate captain," she smiled up at him.

"More than ya'll ever be knowin', little flower."

Victoria pushed back to better see his face. "Flower?"

"Aye," he grinned. "Only a flower can be as delicate and beautiful, enough ta catch me eye."

One dark brow lifted challengingly. "And what of your heart, fierce captain? Will anything ever capture it?"

He ran a fingertip between her breasts, noticing how pale her complexion was compared to his sun-darkened hand, his gaze distant. "Aye, the sea and her uncertainty." He blinked. "And where might you find beauty?"

Victoria looked up at the ceiling above them, deep in thought, and at ease with their nakedness. "Raven Oaks," she said after a moment.

"Raven what?"

"Raven Oaks. My father's plantation."

Dru noticed how her eyes took on a special look of yearning and love at the mere mention of home, and realized how very little he knew of her. Sitting up, he swung his legs over the edge of the bunk and stood, pulling his breeches up over his lean hips. "So, tell me about Raven Oaks," he urged, crossing to the desk. He opened a bottom drawer and took out a bottle of wine, grinning when he saw her frown. "I've always kept it here, just in case I be entertainin' a lady." He held it high for her to examine. "As ya can see, I haven't opened it—until now."

Laughing, Victoria pulled the quilt around her as she sat up against the headboard of his bunk. "Yes, I don't imagine too many ladies find their way here."

He poured two glasses full of the dark red wine and returned to the bunk. Sitting down next to her, he held one out for her to take. "Had there been, Victoria, none could compare ta the one I have now."

She took the glass from him, her hand trembling slightly at his compliment, and wondered if he truly meant what he said. She mentally shrugged it off, for she doubted she would ever know for certain. Taking a sip of wine, she relaxed, feeling its warmth spread through her.

"Would there be any more like you at Raven Oaks?" he asked casually, stretching his long legs out in front of him, one arm behind his head as a cushion.

Her throat tightened at the thought. "I had a younger brother, but he died shortly after birth." She studied the glass in her hands. "We buried him next to my grandfather."

"Must have been a lonely life for ya, growin' up without another your own age," he speculated, observing her from the corner of his eye.

"Oh, no. Quite the contrary." She smiled warmly. "I had many servants with whom to play."

Odd how the candlelight seemed to add golden streaks to her hair. He blinked. "Servants?" A chuckle escaped him. "Me poor mother never knew such a luxury. In fact, she be the one doin' other's work."

"You mean you were poor?"

The dimple appeared in his cheek. "Aye. That we were. But don't be condemnin' me for it. Me mother and I were very happy."

"What about your father?"

The wrinkle in his cheek vanished. "He be thinkin' the ways of the sea more important than raisin' a son."

"How awful," Victoria moaned, feeling a twinge of compassion for this man. She sat up, looking at him. "Didn't he ever come home?"

Dru shook his head. "And me mother never talked about him, although I be suspectin' she loved him very much."

"And you didn't have any brothers or sisters?"

"Only me cousin, Sean. And you be knowin' him." He grinned at the anger he saw clouding her eyes before she turned her head away and fell back against the headboard. "Now don't go thinkin' bad of him. He's a lovable sort, once ya get ta know him."

"I think I know him as well as I care to," she muttered, bringing a renewed smile to Dru's lips.

"Would your mother be as beautiful as you, Victoria?" he asked suddenly.

Surprised by the question, she glanced up at him, watching the slow manner in which he drank his wine. "She's—she's very beautiful. I'm afraid there's no

156

comparison.''

"If that be the case, it be no surprise your father married her. But I be wonderin' about you. Isn't there a lad wishin' ta take the vows?''

An embarrassed smile played with the corners of her mouth as she nervously fidgeted with the rim of her glass. "Maybe. But none I would have.''

"None fittin' your needs, I suspect.''

"They only wish to please my father. I want a husband who will love me for what I am. One who has a mind of his own and will not be molded by my father to suit his wants.''

"It be soundin' as if ya not love your father, lass.''

"Oh, but I do. In fact, I want a husband very much like my father. He's strong and wise and loving. He worships my mother and would do anything in the world for her.'' She sighed, looking up at the ceiling again. "I fear there is no man alive like that for me.''

"One will be comin' along, lass. Never fear. You are meant ta be married.''

She smiled, peering coyly over at him. "And what of you, Captain Chandler? Aren't you ready to give up your life at sea?''

One dark brow lifted mockingly. "Ah, but there's no need. I *am* married and still sail the seas.''

Victoria's tiny chin sagged, the blood draining from her face. She turned away quickly, staring straight ahead and straining to breathe, feeling as if her heart had been torn from her. *Married! He belonged to another!* Her tears tightened her throat and threatened to spill from her eyes. How could he be so casual about it? How could he make love to her while pretending no other woman existed in his life? How could *she* be so

157

stupid? She lifted the glass to her lips with both hands shaking, hoping he would not notice. She forced down a swallow of wine, praying it would soothe her trembling body, a thousand reasons exploding in her mind to justify her actions, each swirling. But not one came to surface and put her guilt to rest. Shame overruled all else, and she vowed to never let this man touch her again.

She swallowed hard before she spoke, pledging not to let him know how his declaration hurt her so. "When did you fall in love with her?"

Caught up in memories, Dru failed to see the silvery droplet of her tear trail to her chin before she brushed it away. "A long time ago, lass. Probably the first time I saw her. She has a strange attraction. Even me cousin felt it." He smiled, sitting up as if he meant to turn and look at Victoria. But urgent rappings at the cabin door interrupted him, and he left the bunk to answer the summons.

"Excuse me, capt'n," Donovan McKenzie apologized once Dru unlocked and swung the portal open. He fought to keep his attention on Dru, but, at the angle in which he stood, it proved too difficult, for his eyes glanced past the man and spotted the tiny figure huddled beneath the covers in the captain's wide bunk. "I didn't mean too intrude, but 'tis important." He studied the deck at his feet.

Confused by his friend's behavior, Dru looked in the direction where Donovan's gaze had drifted, smiling when he saw Victoria staring back at McKenzie. "Ya didn't. We were only sharin' a drink. Now what's so important that it finds ya knockin' on me cabin door instead of wooin' some poor lass on shore?"

158

" 'Tis your cousin, Dru."

The humor of the moment vanishing, Dru stiffened. "What about him?"

"He'll be all right after he rests a few days—"

Anger pouring over him, Dru roughly seized the mate's shirt front. "What's happened, Donovan?"

Donovan McKenzie had grown up with Sean Rafferty and Dru Chandler in a little town in Ireland. They had shared secrets, sorrows, and a lifetime of adventure. Donovan knew the cousins well and thought of them as brothers, neither man's anger ever disturbing him, and Dru's had little effect on him now. He reached out to gently squeeze his captain's arm. "I was on me way back ta the ship and found him lying in an alleyway. He's been beaten."

"Damn!" Dru howled. "Where is he?"

"In his cabin. He's conscious and been askin' for ya." He stepped aside to allow Dru to pass, catching the man's arm before he had traveled three steps. "Don't expect much outta him, capt'n. He's in bad shape."

Dru's features relaxed slightly with his vague smile as he touched Donovan's shoulder. "Thank ya, me friend," he said quietly, then turned and headed down the passageway toward the first mate's cabin, Donovan close on his heels.

The door to the room stood open and the men quickly entered, crossing to the bunk where their friend lay. As he stared down at the unmoving form, the knot in Dru's belly tightened when Sean groaned, turning his head in their direction, for the lamplight fell on the bruised and swollen face. Blackened, puffy skin sealed his right eye closed, a gash across the bridge of his nose still oozing blood. Another wound, caked brown, covered one corner of his mouth and most of his chin. The once straight line of his jaw was now disfigured by a lump the size of a hen's egg.

"Bring cool water," he commanded of the mate standing at his side. "And whiskey."

"Aye, aye, capt'n," McKenzie nodded, and hurriedly left to do as bade.

"Sean," Dru coaxed, kneeling down by his side. "Sean, can ya be hearin' me?"

One eye opened ever so slowly, followed by a slight nod of his head.

"Would ya be knowin' who did this?"

His eye closed. "Aye," came the weak reply.

"Then we'll be seein' that he pays," Dru growled.

"Them," Sean whispered, "the men who bought the lass from us."

"The ones at Milly's?"

"Mmmm. They wanted her."

"Enough ta beat ya like this?" Dru hissed, his ire growing rapidly. Steel-blue eyes suddenly darkened. "Why?" he howled. "Why would they be wantin' her this badly? What lies did she tell 'em?"

"None. I told them nothing."

Dru's head jerked around to find Victoria standing in the doorway, dressed in the shirt and breeches he had given her.

"It was Melissa. She sent them after your cousin."

"Melissa? Who might she be?"

"An enemy of my parents. She was the woman at Milly's. The one I left with. I didn't know who she was until it was too late. Please, captain, you must believe me."

160

Dru slowly came to his feet, the same dark scowl hooding his eyes. "What would the woman be doin' on this island? No one but pirates come here."

"I don't know. Really I don't," Victoria answered bravely, for at the moment she feared he didn't believe her and might strike her for the lie.

Glancing back down at the quiet man in the bunk, his nostrils flaring, Dru snarled, "Then I guess I be findin' out for meself."

NINE

When Donovan McKenzie returned to Sean's cabin with the supplies his captain had requested, Victoria stubbornly took them from him and knelt at the side of the bunk. She felt responsible for the man's injuries and hoped to ease her guilt by tending to his wounds, even though the sight of such abuse to another turned her stomach. Dipping a cloth in the cool water, she gently applied the compress to the dried blood on his chin, slowly massaging the dark crust away. She worked quickly, tenderly, cleansing the area with soap, then folding a clean, dampened rag to the swelling.

"Keep this here," she instructed, glancing up at Donovan who had observed the process in silence. "See it remains cool and moist. It will help."

"Aye, lass," Donovan answered, bending down next to her.

"And when he wakes, give him whiskey. It will ease

the pain.'' She studied the wound on Sean's nose. ''I don't think it's broken, but if it doesn't stop bleeding soon, he may have to have stitches. If he does, send someone for me. But get him drunk first. I want him unconscious. It will make my work easier.''

''Aye, lass,'' Donovan nodded, watching her rise and dry her hands on a towel. ''Thank ya. 'Twas kind of ya ta help.''

''Kind?'' she rallied. ''It was my duty, since it happened because of me.''

''Ya can't be certain of that, lass. No one will be until the captain talks with the men who did this.''

''*I'm* sure, Mr. McKenzie.'' She started for the door. ''And I must stop the captain from looking for them right now. As angry as he is, he could do something stupid.''

''Ah, lass, ya mustn't worry about the capt'n. He can be takin' care of himself.''

''Not where Melissa Bensen is concerned,'' she said decidedly, and left the cabin before McKenzie could respond.

Victoria hurriedly made her way back down the narrow passageway to the captain's quarters, knowing she must talk him out of his foolish ambition to see Sean avenged, simply because no good could come of it, and because of the fact that he could very well expose her hiding place. Maybe if he knew more about Melissa he would understand to what lengths she would go to seek revenge because of a hate many years old.

Tapping softly on the cabin door, she waited for him to acknowledge her summons before opening it and going in. Standing near his bunk, he was checking the barrel of the pistol in his hand, another similar weapon tucked in his breeches.

"Captain, I'd like to talk with you a moment before you go."

"It will have ta be waitin'. I've more important things ta do right now." Pulling back the hammer, he pinched one eye closed to examine the long muzzle once more.

"But what I must tell you is equally important. If you go after these men not knowing what you're getting into, you could put us all in danger."

Carefully releasing the hammer, he dropped the pistol at his side, his steel-blue eyes glaring at her. Victoria's heart pounded.

"Apparently havin' ya here on me ship has done that."

"I—I know. But if I tell you about Melissa Bensen first, maybe you won't make a careless mistake." She could feel the brave lift to her chin falter a degree at the hardening of his stare.

"And maybe if ya do, I might be tempted ta turn ya over ta her."

Victoria wondered at the sanity of her good intentions. "A chance I must take, I guess. Now will you listen or shall I prepare a bunk for you when McKenzie carries *you* back all broken and bruised?"

The dimple flickered in his cheek. Sweeping out his arm, he silently invited her to sit down in the chair near his desk, waiting until she had done so before leaning against his mahogany desk.

"I be listenin'," he said quietly, the menacing pistol still clutched in the hand draped over his knee.

Her attention fixed to the weapon, her voice trembled when she spoke. "Must you hold that thing? It makes me nervous.''

Casually tilting it from side to side, he examined the workmanship. '' 'Tisn't loaded.'' It clunked, hitting the desktop. ''But if it be makin' ya nervous—''

''Thank you,'' she mumbled, closing her eyes. Why couldn't she still be at home sitting before a fire with her mother, merrily stitching a new quilt together? She beckoned the strength to continue. ''Melissa Bensen and her parents lived on a plantation near Raven Oaks. She was engaged to Radford Chamberlain, another neighbor and close friend of my father's until my mother came to live at Raven Oaks as a servant. Radford fell in love with my mother and asked her to marry him. She accepted, and needless to say Melissa was furious. She sought revenge and a way to steal Radford back by hiring this rogue, an insensitive cur of an Irish pir—'' Her words seemed to hang in midair.

''Pirate,'' he finished.

Stealing a timid glance at him to find his expression unchanged, she lowered her eyes to study the wrinkle in the knee of her breeches, then continued weakly. ''Yes. By hiring this pirate to kidnap my mother. But because Radford loved her so much, my father and he set out to find her. They sailed to New Orleans, where they caught up with the—the pir—Captain Gallagher—''

''Dillon Gallagher?''

Startled eyes flashed up at him. ''Yes, sir. Do you know him?''

''There aren't many in Ireland who don't. Go on.''

''Well, my father and Radford confronted him, and during an argument Dillon shot and killed Radford. So you see, Melissa not only lost Radford, she was responsible for his death. If she hadn't had my mother kidnapped, Radford never would have gone to New Orleans or met Dillon Gallagher.''

"Was she held responsible for the lad's death?''

"No. Papa thought letting her live with what she'd done was enough punishment. And shortly after my parents married, she sailed to England. I never met the woman until this morning at Milly's. I told her my name, and then she bought me from you. In the carriage she told me who she was and threatened me.''

Thoughtfully quiet for a moment, he rubbed his thumbnail along the day's stubble of beard on his jaw. "I still not be understandin' why she's here on Barbados. And what were her plans with you?''

Victoria shrugged. "Maybe she thought to blackmail my father. She's always hated him, from what my grandfather used to tell me.''

Chewing on his lower lip a while, he rose slowly to pace the floor, his arms crossed behind his back. He continued for what seemed to Victoria an endless amount of time, until, crossing to the door of the cabin and leaning out into the passageway, he summoned McKenzie to join them. Only a short moment passed before McKenzie arrived.

"Yes, capt'n?''

"There be a woman on the island—Melissa Bensen—that I be wantin' ta learn more about. Take two of the crew and find out what ya can about her. I be wantin' ta know why she's here.'' He went to his desk, picked up a piece of paper and handed it to McKenzie. "And give this to McGuire if ya be seein' him. Tell him I'd be appreciatin' it if he'd see it reaches the colonies as soon as possible.''

"Aye, aye, capt'n.'' The mate saluted, turning

about and disappearing as quickly as he had responded.

"If they be lookin' for Sean, and he gave them no answers, I would be supposin' it's me they're after next." He turned a smile on Victoria. "You were right, lass. It wasn't a good idea for me ta be goin' ashore just yet." The look in his eyes grew distant. "Not for a while, anyway."

"Captain," Victoria said, noticing how the lines of his face deepened as if he shared every ounce of Sean's pain, "if you'd like, I'll stay with your cousin tonight. In case he needs anything."

"Thanks, lass. But I would be likin' it better if ya stay here. You can be havin' the use of me bunk. I'll stay with Sean." Lifting a bottle of rum and the key from his desk, he strode from the cabin.

Morning light stole in across the cabin, pressing heavily against Victoria's eyelids, beckoning her to wake while bathing her face in warm sunshine. She stirred, stretched, and came fully awake almost instantly, scanning her surroundings for some recognition, a clue to her whereabouts. Rubbing her eyes, she focused on the desk across the cabin from her, relief flooding through her when she realized who usually sat behind it. Skidding off the bed, she went to the portholes filling one entire wall of the cabin, wondering how late she had slept, and squinting when the sunlight seemed to blind her. An unexpected yawn caught her offguard, and, pressing the back of her hand to her lips to cover it, she turned back, swallowing her sleepiness almost immediately when her gaze fell on the gown draped over the desk side chair. Looking about the room once more to make certain of her solitude, she hurried over and lifted the gown from its resting place, spying the camisole hidden beneath it on the chair seat. Although it was nothing more than a plain beige cotton dress, she smiled appreciatively, knowing the captain had gone out of his way to acquire the garments for her. A frown flitted across her brow and vanished. Oh, well, she truly didn't care how he managed to get such items, and he probably wouldn't reveal his sources if she asked. Slipping from the breeches and shirt, she quickly covered herself in a fashion more becoming a lady and looped the buttons up the front of the gown, leaving the last two undone for comfort in the already warm morning air.

Smoothing the coverlet on his bunk, Victoria came abruptly to attention with the click of the key in the lock. She turned to face the intruder, knowing it would be the captain, and hurriedly straightened the bodice of her new gown with a tug, fluffed a dark curl hanging over her shoulder, and waited.

Still dressed in the shirt and breeches of yesterday, a dark growth of beard shadowing his face, and his hair ruffled from lack of care, she knew immediately that the captain had slept little the night past. However, his eyes took on a sparkle when he glanced up and saw her.

"Top of the mornin', lass."

"Good morning, captain. How's your cousin?"

Stretching out of his shirt as he came to her, he said, "He'll not be wooin' the lasses for a few days." He grinned, not aware that his simple act of discarding a soiled garment had affected her. He paused beside her, appraising her from head to toe. "You're lookin' grand in the dress."

One corner of her mouth turned upward. "Thank you," she mumbled, stepping away. His nearness made her uncomfortable, and she knew all too well the reason why.

"If ya be done with me bunk, I'll be takin' a nap." He pressed a fist to the small of his back, stretching again, and failed to notice the relief shining on Victoria's face. "Couldn't rest well sittin' in a chair." He sat down on the bunk and removed his shoes and stockings.

"Has McKenzie returned with any news?" she asked, carefully averting her eyes to something less stimulating than the muscles of his wide shoulders. Her thoughts returned to Melissa.

"It may be takin' a while. McKenzie is thorough, and not one ta make mistakes by bein' hasty." He smiled up at her, then lifted a brow wonderingly when he saw the troubled look on her face. "Somethin' botherin' ya, lass?"

A feeble laugh trailed from her lips. "Selfish thoughts, that's all."

"Selfish or worried?" he asked, silently thinking how strong the lass had been. Any other would by now be showing the weaker traits of a gently raised woman. But not Victoria Remington. It would be interesting to meet her parents, he mused.

She looked down. "I know I have no right to ask anything of you, but I fear for my life should Mistress Bensen find me."

"Then rest with your worries, lass. Besides me cousin, John McGuire and Donovan McKenzie are the only men I would be trustin' with me life. We come from the same village, the same streets of Ireland, and

169

share a lifetime friendship, never questionin' the other's reasons, only doin' as he asks. McKenzie will not even tell a shipmate of your presence unless I be tellin' him to.'' He noticed the lines of her brow soften. ''But for your own safety, I be suggestin' ya stay here, in me cabin. The crew may be knowin' you're on board, but they be thinkin' ya only a whore from the island.'' His mood lightened. ''Of course, should one of the men be comin' ta me cabin ta speak with me, you'll have ta play the part.''

The color drained from Victoria's face at the impact of his words. ''What do you mean?''

''Well, how would it be lookin' if they found me in me bunk alone?'' he asked lightly, the need for sleep suddenly gone.

''Sir, you ask too much. I'm no man's whore!'' she exclaimed, clutching the neckline of her gown and backing into the desk with her hip. Stunned, she scurried around to the other side.

''Aye, that I do. Maybe if ya only kissed me,'' he amended, tapping a finger to his chin. ''Ya do know how ta kiss a man, don't ya, lass? I mean without any help from me.''

Victoria's face burned a vivid scarlet. ''Of course, I do. But I'll not prove it to you.''

''Ah, Victoria. Ya don't have ta be hidin' the truth from me. I'm not the sort ta be tellin' anyone.''

''I'm not. I've kissed many men.''

''Many, lass?''

Her nostrils flared. ''Well—well—not many. But enough to know how.''

''Surely you're not thinkin' a father's kiss the same?''

170

"I've kissed others besides my father—"

"And how old might ya be? Seventeen? Eighteen?"

"Almost, but—"

"Well, then the men ya be kissin' were hardly more than children themselves. Not much of a teacher," he said with a shake of his head. "I wouldn't be enjoyin' it, anyway. I prefer a woman's kiss."

Anger cutting short her breath, Victoria failed to see his ploy. She rounded the desk and stomped over to him. "I'm not a child, Captain Chandler. I'm a woman. I'm old enough to marry."

"Are ya now? Would that be meanin' you're truly a woman, or is a child hidin' inside?"

The rogue! How dare he stand there and insult her this way? Why she was probably more of a woman than he had ever met in his lifetime, and she'd show him. Standing on tiptoes, she reached up, draped her arms about his neck, and pulled him closer, raising parted lips to meet his. He didn't move, his arms still at his sides, the muscles of his neck and back rigid, as if she failed to excite him. Piqued by his lack of emotion, she pressed forward until her breasts rested against his chest, her lips moving slowly, warmly against his, discovering in a shocking wave the error of her determination. His arms suddenly locked around her, pulling her hips against him as he crushed her in his embrace. She fought to pull away, damning her foolishness and the warm sensation that raced through her with his kiss. He belonged to another. He had admitted it. He didn't care about her, and she wouldn't fall victim to his charms. She wouldn't! She hated what he did to her, how a simple kiss could stir such fires in her. Any man could affect her so. Couldn't they? Not meaning to, she relaxed, savoring the passion he aroused in her until his hand boldly rested against her buttock. She grew taut with outrage. With no other means to free herself, she lifted a foot and brought it down to crush her heel to his toe.

"Yeeoouch!" he bellowed, letting go of her and falling to the bunk, his injured toe clamped in both hands.

"You knave," she hissed. "You tricked me. Who do you think you are to treat me thus? At least the men," —she used the term he scorned— "who sought to steal a kiss from me were gentlemen."

A pained scowl fixed the dark brows shading his eyes as he studied his wound. "And did they too find no lady waitin'?"

Lifting her skirts to score another blow to the foot still resting on the floor, she hissed, "To you I shall never act a lady." But at the moment she thought to succeed, he realized her intent and snatched his foot away, her own thumping painfully to the wooden planks beneath her. Tears sprang to her eyes.

"And if ya not be actin' the lady, I'll not be treatin' ya as one," he grated out.

With a swiftness that failed to register in her muddled state, Dru reached out, grasped her wrists, and pulled her screaming to the bunk with him before she could wiggle from his hold. He crushed her to him, then rolled and pinned her beneath him, his lips a shadow's depth from hers.

"I welcome the promise, lass," he whispered, caught up in the fragrance of her long silken tresses flowing out around her, filling his senses and driving all caution from him. He pressed in, hearing the soft whimper trailing from her lips. "A lady, Victoria. Ya bc the first lady I ever kissed.''

His lips found hers again, warm and gentle. He kissed the corner of her mouth, her cheek, her earlobe, then found the long column of her neck and felt the rapid pulse in the hollow of it. He sighed raggedly, knowing no other woman in his life had stirred the strange passion that threatened to possess him. He opened his eyes and found her watching, fear shining brightly in the ebony darkness of her stare. He raised up on one elbow.

''I'll never hurt ya, lass,'' he pledged, ''not for the life of me.'' To seal his oath, he lowered his head to kiss her chin, cheek, the tip of her nose, before he captured her lips once more in a gentle, tender expression of his faith.

The thinness of her gown did little to mask the womanly curves it concealed, her firm, round breasts pressed against his bare chest. His heart pounded. Or was it hers? Slipping an arm beneath her, he rolled to his back, taking her with him, the long dark curls falling over them. If heaven be nearly as wonderful, then he vowed to die this instant, as nothing else would ever be as sweet. The fingers of his left hand entangled with the soft strands of hair at the nape of her neck, he held their embrace, his other slowly caressing her spine to linger on the slim curvature of her hip. The flames of passion fanned upward, and he kissed her hungrily, unaware of how she returned the kiss.

Cupping her face in his hands, he whispered her name softly against her lips, his growing desire to have her, to make love to her, spiraling him to heights unobtainable any other way. Pulling her beneath him again, his fingers quickly undid the buttons of her gown, his

173

lips trailing burning kisses down her neck to the fullness of her breast partially concealed beneath her camisole. He lifted to stare at her, a silent plea for consent to consummate the mutual ardor they so obviously shared. Finding no cause to change his mind when she simply returned the look, her lips parted, her gaze shifting to his as if to seek another tender kiss, he moved to fulfill their need. Then he heard, much to his chagrin, a soft rapping at the door of his cabin.

"Damn," he fumed, his passion vanishing as he easily lifted them both from the bunk. "Who is it?"

"McKenzie, capt'n. I'm sorry to bother ya, but I have news of the woman."

Glancing back at Victoria to find her cheeks tinted a soft shade of pink, he inwardly cursed his own turn of bad luck. If only they had had a few more minutes. He mentally shook off the temptation to continue. Had he not declared a moment before that she was the first lady he had ever kissed, made love to? It would be degrading to allow her the embarrassment of having others know what they did. Combing his fingers through his hair, he went to his desk and picked up the key.

"Well, what did ya learn?" he snapped, after letting McKenzie in.

Donovan McKenzie stood nearly a head shorter than his captain, prematurely bald, with a slight belly straining the seams of his shirt front. Yet the manner in which he carried himself and the stocky muscular shape of his form suggested that he was a man who would not easily bend—to any man—including his captain. His eyes darted from Victoria to Dru to Victoria again, flustered by his untimely intrusion. The ruffled bedcovers, the flush to the lass's face, and the gruff, unusual

174

greeting he received from his captain proclaimed sweeter things than casual conversation.

"I can be comin' back later, capt'n," he half whispered, rocking on his heels, his gaze glued to the deck.

Staggered by his mate's quick comprehension of the situation, Dru felt a rush of fever to his own cheeks. Odd. It had never bothered him before. He cleared his throat.

"Now will be as good a time as any." His gaze briefly swept over Victoria standing with her back to them as she stared out the porthole. He sighed. Until he returned her to her father, there would be many more trying situations for him. Slowly, his attention focused on McKenzie, a smile on the mate's lips he tried to hide with a finger rubbing the side of his nose. "What are ya grinnin' at?" he demanded.

McKenzie snapped to attention. "Nothin', sir. Nothin'."

"Then sit down and tell me what ya learned," Dru said loudly.

From the chair beside the captain's desk, Donovan covertly studied Dru, noticing the man's uneasiness, thinking it to be the first time in his affairs with women that he'd ever behaved this way. The tiny lass standing across the room from them acted the same, and from what he had gathered in his travels through the village, there really was a need for apprehension.

"McGuire sails this mornin', capt'n. Says if the winds are right, he'll have your letter to the colonies within the week."

Dru glanced up and nodded. "What else?"

"It seems Melissa Bensen is waitin' for someone. Her men check every mornin' ta see who docked durin' the night. McGuire said he talked with one of them yesterday. They're waitin' for Gallagher, capt'n. Dillon Gallagher.''

A whirl of skirts brought both men's attention to Victoria. ''Here? Dillon Gallagher is coming here?''

McKenzie's hazel eyes appraised the young woman, then glanced to the captain and back again. ''Aye, lass. At least Mistress Bensen is countin' on it. Why would ya be askin'?''

Visions of the pirate of whom her grandfather had spoken materialized before her eyes in exaggerated form. Bright orange hair, cold, insensitive eyes, a scar running the side of his face, all purple and grossly distorting, and in both hands pistols, cocked and ready. She squeezed her eyes closed. Not here. Not on the same island! The childish promise she had made to her grandfather rang in her ears.

''I'll kill him Grandpa, if I ever meet him,'' she had declared. ''I'll do it for Papa and his friend, Mr. Chamberlain.''

''Now, Victoria,'' her grandfather had cooed, ''don't talk like that. Besides, you'll never see that man.''

''Maybe. But if I do, I'll shoot him. Just like he did Papa's friend.''

For days afterward the young child, not quite ten years old, had lain awake long after her bedtime scheming of ways to kill the fierce pirate, never fearing that one day she might actually meet him face to face.

''Victoria?''

She blinked, knowing her thoughts had wandered.

''Are ya all right, lass?''

''Yes, Captain Chandler. I'm fine.'' She moved closer to the men, her gaze set on the mate. ''And has

176

he docked, Mr. McKenzie?''

"No, lass. But I left two of the crew behind to warn us when he does.''

Curious, Dru watched her for a moment. The faraway gleam that appeared briefly in her dark brown eyes had hinted at something he failed to understand. He looked to McKenzie. "Anythin' else?''

"No, capt'n. They be keepin' closed mouths about why he's comin'. But the men were told ta report anythin' they hear. If one of her men let it slip, we'll be knowin' about it.''

"Thanks, Donovan. Ya be a great help.''

"Just doin' me job, capt'n.''

Dru waited until the mate had gone and he had locked the door again before turning back to Victoria. She stared out the porthole again.

"He'll not be gettin' near ya, lass, if that be your worry.''

Her tiny shoulders trembled with her sigh. "That isn't what bothers me.''

"And would ya care to explain? Or would it be none of me business? Maybe if I be knowin', I can put an end to your troubles.''

A light smile teased the corners of her mouth, one he failed to see. How ironic. A childhood pledge had come to haunt her, an oath to see a pirate dead. And now another scoundrel, one she felt certain shared the same qualities of ruthlessness and inclemency, spoke words of pity and selflessness. Would he truly aid her if the need arose? To what end? To own her, possess her, steal into her thoughts as he did now? Or was that his intent? Would he vow to see her free of threat and worry, win her trust, her heart, then woo her into his bed as he had done already without a promise of love? Of marriage? The absurdity of it all! *A fool,* she proclaimed herself, *you are a romantic fool.* Had he not already confessed he belonged to another? She felt an aching beneath her breast. In two short days she had fallen victim to the very thing she promised never to succumb to. She had listened to her heart, not the logic of her mind. And yet, was this feeling that stirred within her truly what she sought? Or merely fascination? Yes, of course. Fascination.

"Thank you, captain, but you've done enough already," she whispered.

TEN

Standing at the helm gazing out across the bow, Dru studied the fleet of ships anchored offshore, his concentration so great he did not hear his name on his cousin's lips, twice called before he blinked and smiled recognition. Fondly, he watched Sean's buoyant gait, silently thanking the man's guardian angel for taking care of him in Dru's absence. The beating he had taken several weeks ago had nearly killed him and had left a scar beneath his eye to remind them both that one careless moment could be costly.

"Where might your thoughts be, dear cousin, that ya didn't hear me call to ya? Has sharin' your cabin dulled your wit?" The scar wrinkled slightly with his lopsided grin.

"Not a bit. But if you're not careful of your words, I be givin' ya another scar to mar that handsome face of yours."

Gingerly, Sean traced the inch-long welt with his fingertip. "Ya know, I be thinkin' it gives me character. The pirates back away from me and the lasses swoon." He glanced over his shoulder, an impish gleam in his eye. "I can be hardly waitin' ta see what the lass thinks of it. Ya've had more than enough time ta win our wager, so I think it's time we saw it done. Apparently ya haven't the charm ya used to."

A cheerless smile pursed Dru's lips, his thoughts reliving the past several days. Every night since Mc-Kenzie had returned with information of Gallagher's expected arrival, Victoria had slept on the bench beneath the portholes of the cabin, insisting on it when Dru offered his bunk in exchange. They shared meals in silence, and now that he thought about it, he realized the lass very seldom even looked at him. Their tense existence had driven him topside when it seemed he would explode with her cool indifference of him. If only he could figure out what troubled her.

"There ya go again," Sean hummed playfully.

Snapping to, Dru experienced a tingling that crept up the flesh of his neck and across his face. Discreetly, he rubbed his finger beneath his nose to hide any telltale signs of his uneasiness. "I was just wonderin' about Gallagher."

"Were ya now? And what did ya decide?"

"Nothin'. That's what troubles me. I can't be figurin' out for the life of me what connection he might have to Miss Bensen."

"No good, I'll wager," Sean hissed, remembering the days that had passed before he could chew solid food again, thanks to the woman's hoodlums.

"Aye. That goes without sayin', but I'm curious

180

what it might be.'' Dru again looked out at the ships bobbing in the water. ''The lass told me Miss Bensen sailed to England before she was born.''

''So?''

''I just think it strange the woman would desert her homeland to live with its enemies.''

''They weren't enemies then.''

''Aye. But they are now. Ya'd think her loyalty would lie with the States. Unless—''

''Unless what?''

''Unless there be somethin' in it for her.''

''Like what?''

Dru scratched the back of his head. ''That's what I can't be figurin' out.''

''Capt'n Chandler?''

Both men turned simultaneously in the direction of the summons and waited until McKenzie joined them at the railing away from ears that weren't meant to hear whatever the man had to say.

''Aye, McKenzie?''

''I got some news about Gallagher and Mistress Bensen. Not much to make sense, but I thought ya should know.''

''Out with it man,'' Dru urged, pulling McKenzie in closer with a tug to his elbow.

''Flanagan overheard the one called Murphy braggin' ta a whore he bought a drink about how rich he'd be once he sailed for New York.''

''New York?''

''Aye, capt'n. Don't really mean much. Not ta me anyway, but I be thinkin' they will be sailin' just as soon as they meet with Gallagher.''

Dru's dark head nodded agreement while his lips

181

held a faint smile.

"What are ya thinkin', Dru?" Sean asked, one tawny brow lifted slightly.

A lean, sun-tanned arm enveloped Sean around his neck, pulling him closer into the group. "That we not be havin' ta wait for Mr. Gallagher ta find out his reason for her bein' here."

"And how do ya mean ta manage it if Donovan here couldn't?"

Dru's grin widened. "I plan ta have a chat with Mistress Bensen."

"What?" Sean flared, his lanky frame stiff. "Ya seem ta forget she be knowin' your face as well as mine and her men wouldn't hesitate to rearrange it. You're crazy, man."

His hand pressed to his chest, Dru pouted playfully. "Sean, me boy, please. Give your poor cousin a wee bit more credit. I don't intend ta let her men see me."

"And how will ya go about that? She's never alone."

"I'll be payin' her a visit before the sun rises."

Sean relaxed, his arms crossed and one hand stroking his chin. "Ahhh. Ya plan ta woo her. 'Tis a good thing ya'll already have her in bed since your charms aren't what they use ta be." He exploded into laughter.

Dru twisted his face into a one-sided smile, his head bobbing up and down. "Ya be treadin' on dangerous waters, cousin. Like I be sayin' before, if ya not be careful, I'll blackenin' your other eye."

Donovan's own smile tugged at the corners of his mouth listening to the banter of his captain and first mate, and knowing no harm would ever come of it. Since the time they had all carried wooden swords and climbed the rocky landscape of their homeland as boys,

Dru and his cousin had never argued over anything, not to the point where blows landed. The bastard son of Sean's mother's sister, Dru had grown up without knowing the love of a father, and Donovan suspected that Dru's gentle nature stemmed from the teachings of his mother alone. She had taught him patience and kindness, and to never let hatred twist his thinking. Katherine Chandler would be proud of her son if she could see him now.

"Capt'n, Sean's right in thinkin' it dangerous ya go there alone. The lass may not share her bed, but ya can count on her men not bein' too far away. I'll be willin' ta travel with ya."

"Thank ya, Donovan. I'd be honored ta have ya accompany me." Dru glared back at Sean, failing to hide the sportive gleam in his eyes. "I'd be fearin' me life if I took this one along. He lets the skirts of a lass cloud his mind while he should be watching the shadows."

"I was outnumbered," Sean rallied. "Even you wouldn't have stood a chance."

"Two ta one? I wouldn't call that outnumbered. I've seen ya take on twice that many and walk away without a scratch. Are ya gettin' old, Sean?"

Two fists raised in front of him. "Never too old ta take ya on," Sean quipped, bouncing from one foot to the other, his fists casting harmless blows Dru's direction.

Dru rolled his eyes. "Saints preserve us. The beatin' he took ta his head did more damage that I thought."

"Capt'n?"

Dru's attention fell away from his cousin's buffoonery to rest on the mate at his side, his smile fading at the nod of Donovan's head toward the half deck. At the railing stood Victoria, her hands clasped around the balustrade as she gazed out across the sea, the gentle breeze tossing about her dark hair, the delicate lines of her brow reflecting an urgency and longing.

"Excuse me, mates," Dru responded softly, stepping past the men to the ladder.

Boredom had finally taken its toll on Victoria, driving her from the cramped space she was forced to share with the captain. She had too much time alone, too much time to think about her surroundings, her future, her home and her parents. She longed to return to Raven Oaks and resume her life the way it was meant to be, to dress in the finest of cloth, to coyly fend off the attention of gentlemen callers, not hide herself in a pirate's cabin, never certain when he might come to her, touch her, kiss her— She closed her eyes, feeling a twinge of homesickness stab at her heart and bring tears to her eyes. She rubbed her finger across the lower ridge of lashes, knowing this was only part of her distress.

Captain Chandler's presence disturbed her. Although they seldom spoke, she found herself watching his every move, while he ate, donned a clean shirt, or made entries in the large book at his desk. There had been several nights when sleep would not come when she had left the vexation of her bed to sit in a chair across the cabin from him and study him in his slumber. And in the early light of dawn, she covertly viewed his waking from half-closed eyes, seeing him stretch, the muscles of his shoulders, back, and waist flexing with the movement. She observed the way water from a washbowl glistened in his dark, ruffled hair, and the bright, flashing smile he cast her when he caught her staring. Even now as she stood on deck, she could feel the heat rise in her cheeks. She must leave the ship, this island, Captain Chandler—before it was too late.

"Ya shouldn't have come topside, lass."

Victoria jumped at the sound of his intrusion. Could she never find any peace?

"The cabin grew stuffy," she announced, her voice oddly stiff, her words more sharp than she intended.

Dru leaned back against the railing, studying the intricate webbing of the riggings overhead. "And small," he added. "I be appreciatin' how ya feel, lass, but for your own safety, ya shouldn't be seen on deck. A lass with your beauty is rarely found on this island, and word of your presence will spread quickly, and to the wrong ears, I might be addin'."

Victoria glanced up at him. "Melissa?"

"Aye, Melissa."

"I guess I wasn't thinking."

He smiled. "If ya be needin' variety, I could let ya go to the captain's galley from time ta time. Do ya cook?"

"A little," she admitted sheepishly. "It was never one of my stronger interests."

"So what do you want to do?"

Feeling as though a thousand eyes stared down on them, she lowered her head. "To return to your cabin."

Laughter rumbled deeply in his chest. "Aye. A wise choice. And since I be havin' a need ta return meself, I'd be honored ta walk ya back."

A feeble smile twitched one corner of her mouth.

"How long have you been a pirate?" she asked casually once they had returned below decks and Dru had closed the cabin door behind them.

"All of me life, it seems," he half smiled, going to the sea chest near his bunk. "Me father was a pirate."

"Was? Is he dead?" Victoria asked, her interest aroused.

His broad shoulders raised briefly. "Don't know. I never met the man."

"Never met—" She wished she could return the words to her mouth, but they seemed not to bother the captain as he glanced up and smiled.

"Aye, lass. I'm a bastard."

Every inch of Victoria's flesh tingled with embarrassment. "I didn't mean to pry," she whispered, fixing her attention on the floor.

" 'Tisn't a secret, lass. And I can't be doin' anythin' ta change the fact."

"Don't you hate him? I mean for never coming back to claim you."

"Hate him? How could I be hatin' someone I don't even know? And there's always the chance he never knew about me." Lifting the lid of the sea chest, he knelt down and rummaged through it.

"Didn't your mother tell him?"

Pulling out a red bandana, he examined it for only a moment and laid it aside. "Could have, I guess. But I have no way of knowin'. Me mother never talked about him."

"You mean you don't even know who your father is?"

His white teeth sparkled between sun-darkened lips. "Does it matter?"

"But, of course! Everyone should know who their parents are. It's only right."

186

"Why?"

"Because—because—"

"He doesn't owe me anythin', lass, nor I him. It's the way I like it."

"You owe him your life," she argued hotly.

"I owe him me beginnin'. Nothin' more."

"But he should have helped in raising you. He took the liberty of siring a son, it was his duty."

Dru rested back against his heels. "Why are ya so upset over me upbringin'?"

Victoria opened her mouth to respond but when her words failed her, she snapped it closed again to ponder her reason. "I'm not sure. I guess because it angers me to think a man could be so unfeeling about his own flesh and blood."

"If he be knowin' it."

"But that's what I mean. Before a man lies with a woman, he should consider the—" Victoria's mind flashed back to the moments Dru had held her in his arms. "Consequences," she finished quietly, turning away.

Suspecting the reason for her hesitation, Dru cocked his head to one side. "Maybe it just happened. Before he or me mother had time ta think."

She whirled on him. "But he should have! He had no right to assume he could leave her with child. He should have offered marriage before ever considering making love to her."

"Marriage?" he laughed. "In exchange for a kiss?"

"How would he know it would stop with a kiss?"

His smile lingered. "Obviously, it didn't. Or I wouldn't be here now, would I?" He watched the sudden darkening to her cheeks. "Will ya marry me, Victoria?''

Certain the pounding in her ears would deafen her, Victoria fought to breathe. Had he really offered marriage? Or had her befuddled mind played tricks on her? And how could he offer marriage to anyone when he had already admitted he belonged to another?

''M-marry?'' she choked out.

''Aye. I have this overpowerin' urge ta kiss ya.''

Victoria's lip curled, knowing he played her for a fool. She drew her shoulders back and lifted her chin slightly. ''Thank you for the offer, captain, but the answer is no. I find the idea of marriage to you, like your kiss, something I can do without.''

''Can ya now?'' he rallied, coming to his feet.

Spying a pistol laying on the desk, she turned, picked it up, and half-heartedly pointed it at him. ''Yes, I can. And so can you, I might add,'' she smiled, daring him to move.

Dru cocked his head to one side. ''Do ya know how ta use it, lass?''

''Care to find out?''

Thinking to sway her, he said, ''Are ya sure it's even loaded?''

Calmly, Victoria flipped the pistol in the air, catching it by the muzzle. ''If it isn't, I can always use it as a club.''

The muscles in Dru's chest tightened watching the pistol flounder in the air before she caught it, the ebony cylinder pointing at her midsection. ''And if it is, lass, ya might well be puttin' a ball in your stomach. Any man's kiss is worth more.''

''And that, dear captain, is your opinion.''

Sensing he had lost the argument and worrying she

might do herself harm unintentionally, he nodded the moment's defeat and returned to the sea chest, praying she would lay aside the pistol.

Enjoying her sense of power over the pirate, Victoria straightened even more, waving the pistol in mock authority at his back, her lips moving in silent demands as she acted out the roll of aggressor. *And furthermore, Mr. Chandler,* she said to herself, *you shall sleep on the floor and I shall have the bunk. After all, I am the captain here.* For stress, she pointed the weapon in the air above her head, and, believing it to be empty as Dru had implied, squeezed the trigger. The powder exploded in her ear.

Had there been a spot where Dru could have crawled, he would have moled himself into it. As it was, he could only fall flat on the floor, waiting for the blood of his wound to saturate his shirt, certain she had sought revenge against his pranks. Silence closed in around him, save the pounding of his heart in his ears, and when he felt no pain, he glanced back over his shoulder at Victoria.

Even on the day when Kelsey had suggested she watch him have sex with the woman at the tavern, her expression of shock had not surpassed the contortions Dru witnessed now. The whites of her eyes shone clearly around the circumference of dark brown orbs, her face devoid of color, her chest unmoving as she stood paralyzed, the pistol still held in the air.

Regaining the discipline to hide his emotions, Dru pushed himself up with both hands, springing to his feet with little effort. His long, lean fingers fanned out on each hip as he braced his hands against them, his eyes settled on Victoria.

"I—I didn't—think—"

"Exactly. Now be puttin' down the pistol before I take ya across me knee like me cousin Sean."

Obediently, Victoria returned the gun to the desk, a visible tremble of her hand causing the pistol to clatter against its resting place.

"If ya don't mind, I'd appreciate it if ya'd sit down and not move again until I leave the cabin."

A burst of hurried footsteps echoed in the passageway, the door to the captain's quarters hurling open as two figures, pistols drawn, filled the doorway. Dru raised a reassuring hand.

" 'Tis all right, mates. 'Twas only an accident."

"Accident?" Sean countered, the darkness of his frown shadowing his brow, a similar mask covering Donovan's face.

"Aye. The lass didn't know there was a ball in me pistol."

Their weapons lowered slowly, an impish grin returning to Sean's lips as he gave his partner a knowing jab to the rib cage. "And what was I tellin' ya, Donovan, me friend? Me cousin has lost his charm and the lasses have taken ta violence ta fend him off. And he really thinks ta be wooin' the information he needs from Mistress Bensen." A mischievous laughter filled the cabin, until Sean noticed the startled look on Victoria's face.

"What is he saying, Captain Chandler?"

Dru shot Sean an irked glance. "It be meanin' me troublesome cousin talks too much."

"But he said you plan to see Mistress Bensen. Is that true?"

"Aye, lass," he said, turning his back on the trio to return to the sea chest. He knelt down again and continued his search.

"Why?" Victoria breathed, moving closer.

He glanced up at her. "You're not me wife, Victoria, so don't go thinkin' I'm bein' disloyal."

Her frame stiffened. "I don't care how many wenches you bed, you pompous ass. I mean to know the reason."

Dru's eyes took on a playful gleam. "The reason? And must I embarrass ya ta be explainin' me need ta have a woman?"

"Ohhh!" Victoria growled. "That's not the reason I mean and you know it! What do you hope to learn?"

Finding the item for which he searched, Dru picked up the bandana from the floor and crossed to the portholes. Knotting the scarf around his head to cover his dark hair, his back to the group, he lifted the second item to his face and turned around, slumping as he did.

" 'Ow do I look, matey?" he graveled.

"Ridiculous," Victoria spat, appraising the black eye patch. "Why not wait a couple of weeks and grow a beard, too? I sincerely doubt Melissa will let you near her looking like that. I know I wouldn't."

"Aye, but gettin' to her is me problem. Once I'm past her men, I'll shed me disguise." One brow wiggled, hintingly. "And maybe somethin' more."

"You're disgusting," Victoria hissed, turning away.

"Aye, that I am, lass." He moved for the door. "And don't be waitin' up for me. If me luck has changed, I might be takin' all night."

He followed Sean and McKenzie from the cabin, pausing in the passageway when he heard Victoria call his name. He waved the others on ahead and looked back at her.

Toying with the nail of her thumb, Victoria found it nearly impossible to meet his questioning eyes. "Be—be careful. Melissa was responsible for one man's death. She wouldn't hesitate to raise the mark."

Dru quietly came to her, lifting her chin in the air with a fingertip. "I know," he said softly. " 'Tis the reason I wear the patch, so she won't be knowin' who I am until I have her alone. I intend ta find out why Gallagher is comin'." Leaning in, he placed a kiss to her forehead. "Thank ya for the warnin'," he whispered, turning away. When he reached the door again, he stopped and looked back, nearly knocked from his feet when Victoria ran to him and threw herself into his arms. He held her to him without question, feeling her body tremble.

Victoria's mind whirled with a mixture of emotions, but fear overrode them all, fear that she would never see him again, that Melissa Bensen would send him to his grave as she had done Radford Chamberlain. Was it guilt that caused her to fear for his life, that should he die it would be because of her? Or the simple fact that he had stolen her heart? Tears streamed down her face, and she wanted to beg him not to go, to stay with her, to keep her by his side forever. And at the same time she cursed herself for not being brave, for letting him know how much he really meant to her, certain that once he tired of her, he would send her home and return to his wife. That was, *if* he came out of this alive.

A sob escaped her and she felt him tighten his arms around her, brush away the dark strands of hair from her cheek. She lifted her face to gaze into his eyes and found the devilish twinkle that always made a showing suddenly gone. She saw a tenderness in them, as if he understood without hearing her say the words. He smiled softly, and it seemed all the doubts, worries, and shame she had felt vanished. Of her own free will, she slipped her arms around his neck and pulled him closer, raising parted lips to meet his. She kissed him hungrily, urgently, and with wild abandonment. She forgot all the gentle upbringing she had been taught, all the vows she had made to find and save herself for the one man with whom she would live out her life. At this moment nothing else mattered, except that, for this short span of time, she would be his in body, heart, and soul.

Dru bent to lift her in his arms, kicking the door closed with the heel of his boot. His mission could wait. He had sensed her worry over his plan, but failed to understand why she clung to him so fiercely. Had this enemy of her family instilled such terror that Victoria could only find comfort wrapped in his embrace—in anyone's arms? Surely that must be the cause. Hadn't days, weeks passed without the slightest glance his way? And yet it wasn't fear that forced her to kiss him, draw him close, allow him to lay her gently on the bunk. She wanted him for another reason. But what? And why did the mere sight of her, the fragrance of her hair, the smooth touch of her cheek excite him, chase away all logic, cloud his mind with thoughts of her and nothing else? Hadn't others before her always caused the same unnerving repercussion? No, not a single one. Then what evoked this sensation in his heart, his loins? He lay down beside her, resting on one elbow, his free hand tracing the delicate line of her jaw with the knuckle of his thumb. What was it about this tiny female that so infected his mind, ate away at the protective shell around his heart and tamed his spirit? Could it be love? No. Love was for fools. The frown that hooded his eyes softened when Victoria looked at him, and his wonder and confusion vanished, replaced by the desire to hold her, kiss her, make love to her.

Her ebony tresses fanned out against the pillow, haloing the fairness of her skin, enhancing the darkness of her eyes, the soft blush of her cheeks and the full, sensuous mouth, the red lips begging to be kissed. He leaned in, pressing his own lips against her throat, smelling the sweetness of her hair and flesh, drunk with their mystifying power. A witch, an enchantress to affect him thus! Yet, in his heart, he wanted to pull away, to leave her, for he truly doubted that what she was doing was anything but an act of desperation. And to have her want him, come to him freely, he selfishly needed to know no other motive controlled her decision. Pulling back, he gazed into her eyes, searching, praying for the answer he sought. But the beauty, the innocence of her face cast its hypnotic spell, overshadowing his mind with thoughts of pleasure, and fanned the embers of his passion, driving all reason, worry, or need for denials from his head.

He touched the back of his fingertips to her cheek, tenderly tracing the fragile outline of her jaw, one knuckle beneath her chin to raise her parted lips to his. He kissed her warmly, softly, fearing she would break and shatter his dream, the illusion of his desire. Caught up in the fragrance of her hair, his heart pounded, his passion heightening, and he reveled in his delirium. If only he could spend eternity locked in her embrace! He kissed her temple, her brow, savoring the scent, the taste of her, his hands moving to the buttons of her gown. One by one they fell loose, and with no resistance from her he slid the garment off her. His kisses trailed blazing paths down her chin and neck, sampling the fullness of her breast pressed against the constrictions of the camisole. Nimbly his fingers worked the strings free and revealed the ripe fruits of her breasts. His gaze devoured the sight, his pulse racing, and he lowered his head, his opened mouth covering the rose-hued peak, his tongue teasing. He heard her moan, his own song of joy caught in his throat. He nibbled gently at her breasts, at the valley between them, and quickly snatched the camisole from her. Caressing her body with his hands while he kissed her once more, he vaguely felt her pull his shirt free of the breeches. Her tiny hands traced the sinewy ripples up his back until she returned his ardor equally and his lust forbade him to move slowly.

He left the bunk to disrobe, their gazes holding fast, and, a moment later, he pressed his weight against her, their naked bodies touching full length while they basked in the glow of their embrace.

"Make love to me, my fierce pirate captain," Victoria whispered, the dark depths of her eyes reflecting her desire before she pulled him to her, parting her thighs to welcome his thrust. She arched her hips invitingly, her kisses hungry, warm, and wanting.

The dangers of the world outside the cabin melted into oblivion, for, clasped in each other's arms, nothing else seemed of major importance, and a long while passed before they lay breathless, sated in the comfort of their love nest. No other words were spoken as each sensed the other's thoughts, and Victoria snuggled against the warmth of him, her finger curling a dark lock of his hair around the tip, hating the moment he would leave her, but knowing he must.

For Dru, it seemed time hung suspended, that for once in his life he had found peace and knew the meaning of love. His blue eyes darkened with the discovery, for until this moment he had denied he would ever allow himself the pleasure. And now that he had, what would he do? Pressing closer, he kissed her temple lightly and forced himself to rise. Right now, he wouldn't think of it. He had more important matters to solve, and, since he doubted she shared the feeling, he saw no reason to ponder it. Once dressed again, he stopped at the door and looked back, no words upon his lips, only a sadness in his eyes.

"Are ya sure ya got the right room, Donovan?" Dru asked as the two men stood in the shadows of the alleyway.

"Aye, capt'n. I saw her go in. Near as I can figure, it be that window there." He singled out the second-story aperture with the point of one finger.

"Near as ya can figure?" Dru parroted. "Would ya have me crawl inta bed with one of her men?"

"Well, it be kinda hard ta tell what window on the outside belongs ta what door on the inside. As near as I can figure, it's that one!" Donovan stressed his uncertainty with a jab of his index finger upward again.

Dru's lip curled into a snarl. "I swear you're me cousin's brother, Donovan," he mumbled, rearranging the stack of boxes at the side of the building to suit his needs. Standing back to evaluate the job, he realized they fell short by nearly two feet. He shrugged. "Can I be countin' on ya ta catch me when I fall, Donovan?"

"And since when has the great lover had trouble sneakin' in a lass's room?"

Dru cast the man a weary grin. "Contrary to what Sean's been tellin' ya, I usually don't have ta sneak. The lasses open their doors and their arms willin'ly."

"Aye, capt'n," Donovan smiled, a smile Dru missed since he had already begun to climb his makeshift ladder.

Donovan McKenzie and Sean both suspected what had transpired in Dru's quarters once they heard the door slam shut. Neither man spoke of it, but Donovan sensed his friend's uneasiness when Sean failed to stand in one spot for any length of time, finally electing to go below decks for something to eat—or so he claimed. It was a common occurrence where the captain was concerned, but somehow Donovan worried that Dru Chandler had lost more than a little time by staying with the raven-haired beauty sharing his cabin. He smiled again as he watched his friend, certain that if the young lass had stolen Dru's heart, it would be good for him.

The boxes creaked and moaned with Dru's weight upon them, but stood secure as he moved higher. At the top, he calculated the distance between his outstretched arms and the windowsill, glancing back down at his partner, crossed fingers raised in the air. Looking back, his eyes trained on his goal, he took a deep breath and lunged for the framework.

Damn, I pray she be a sound sleeper, he thought, hearing his boots thud against the building as he dug his toes into any crevice that might hold him in place.

"Mmeeeoww!"

The screech riddled his nerves and he glanced down

at McKenzie. Seeing the wide smile part the man's lips, Dru wondered if a single cat in the entire world sounded the same. He grinned, then centered his attention on his purpose as he found himself dangling against the side of a building. Flexing his muscles, he pulled himself noiselessly up the remainder of the way, perching a hip to the sill as he guardedly annalyzed the situation before him. No light brightened the room save the small stream stealing in around him from the window, but it was enough to see a figure lying in bed, the covers drawn nearly over it. Except for the steady breathing of slumber no other human noise greeted him, and he felt safe in slipping his feet over the window frame and onto the floor. Before disappearing inside, he formed a circle with his thumb and forefinger that he waved to the man waiting below.

A candle's glow pressed against Melissa's eyelids. She stirred, pulling the coverlet over her head.

"Edwin, put out the candle and go to bed," she mumbled. "We'll talk about it in the morning. I'm tired."

Silence poured over her. She irritably flipped the covers down, seeing the candlelight flutter against the ceiling over her.

"Did you hear me?" she persisted, closing her eyes.

"Aye, lass, I did."

Melissa bolted upright in bed, the coverlet clutched beneath her chin as she cowered in the corner on the far side. Lounging comfortably in a chair opposite her sat a fierce-looking pirate with one eye hidden beneath a circle of cloth.

"Who—how did you—"

"The window, lass," he smiled. "And I be here

198

about Gallagher.''

"Dillon? Is he here? Why did he send you and not come himself?''

"I'm here ta find out why ya sent for him. He isn't one ta let himself be fooled easily. 'Specially by a lass.''

It was now a score and three years since the day Melissa had sat opposite Dillon Gallagher in her carriage on Williamsburg's waterfront. But even now she could feel the tremor of fear his presence had instilled in her the first time she saw him. His dark brown eyes, his face haloed by flaming red hair, had pierced through her callous exterior and chilled her to the very bone. Of course, Melissa had felt its cause to be simply her youth, but now, sharing the small space of her room with a pirate who was merely a messenger of Dillon's, she knew the falsity of her assumption. Her heart thumped against her arms crossed to her chest.

"May—may I put—on a robe, sir, and pour us both a glass of wine?'' She waited for the nod of his head before cautiously leaving the shelter of her warm blankets, plucking her robe from the footboard of her bed and crossing to the table and the wine.

"I have a job for Captain Gallagher,'' she said, watching lean, tan fingers wrap around the glass she held out, lingering a moment when they touched hers and sending a shiver up her spine. She looked at his face, something oddly familiar about the firm set of his jaw, the gleam in his eye, pricking her security. "I've been hired by the Crown to spy for them, and I need Captain Gallagher's help.''

"He's a pirate, lass, not a spy.''

"Yes. I know. What I need him to do requires the skill of a pirate. And since he is the best, I will pay handsomely for his services.''

''And how will he know ya be tellin' the truth?''

''We've had dealings before. Didn't he tell you?'' she asked, suspicion marked in her tone.

A bright smile flashed her way. ''I'm not supposed ta know everythin', lass. That's why I'm here.''

''When can I meet with him?''

''He be wantin' ta know first if it's worth it. Ya nearly got him killed the last time.''

''I had nothing to do with that. And if he wants to know, he'll have to meet with me.'' Her temper flared. ''I'll not tell some errand boy my plans.''

He heard her rapid intake of breath as he rose and set down his glass. ''Then there be no deal, lass.'' He turned for the window.

''No, wait!'' she called, panic rising in her voice. She chewed at her lower lip, her gaze darting from the pirate to the floor and back again. ''I—I need his guarantee to attack ships belonging to France and the colonies along the American coast.''

No visible sign of interest moved the lines of his face. He needed more convincing, and she knew it, but, pricked by a sense of foreboding, she hesitated to tell everything. She would rather explain to Dillon himself. He moved to exit.

''All right! All right,'' she surrendered, waiting for him to face her again. ''I'll sail for Quebec in the morning. I'm to set up a contact there and then travel to New York. Any information I receive will be forwarded to him.''

''Doesn't sound like ya be needin' the help of Captain Gallagher ta do that,'' he said flatly.

''I don't,'' she ground out through clenched teeth.

"But in order to warrant the payment I require for my services, the Crown needs additional guarantee. That's where the captain comes in."

In the soft flickerings of candlelight, Melissa failed to notice the gleam of recognition in the man's eyes. "And what price might that be?"

An evil smile distorted her lips. "When England wins the war, I'll be the richest plantation owner in Virginia."

"And let me be guessin' which one. Raven Oaks, near Williamsburg."

Melissa's face paled, her mouth agape. "H-How could you possibly know that?"

He smiled, leaning back against the window frame. "Captain Gallagher is not the first you asked to help, lass. But I turned ya down because I prefer stayin' out of the war."

"But—but I only talked with one other. In England. The captain of the ship. You're simply—"

Without a word, Dru pulled the bandana from his head and removed the eye patch. "I be simply Captain Dru Chandler of the *Definace*. And the answer is still 'no,' so I be proposin' ya ask Captain Gallagher." Slipping one leg over the windowsill, he added, "If or whenever he arrives in Barbados." He touched his fingertip to his brow in a mock salute and quietly disappeared into the darkness.

ELEVEN

"Seems the lass has held a grudge for a long time."

Dru watched the unmoving form by the portholes, sensing the thoughts going through her mind. If the States failed in their bid for independence and England again ruled the colonies and their rebels, it would mean Melissa Bensen would be free to claim what she felt fair payment for her help in their quest. And in doing so, Victoria's parents, as well as she, would be left homeless. He truly doubted the young lass would not fare well if that should occur, but the fear she experienced now most likely resulted from the sympathy she felt for her parents, imagining their sense of loss if Raven Oaks was taken from them.

"Dru?"

He blinked, bringing his attention back to the men sitting beside him at the table. "Aye. And knowin' that, we be knowin' nothin' will stop her."

"What are ya plannin' ta do?" Sean spoke softly, discerning the cause of the furrowing of his cousin's brow.

Cupping both hands around his mug of rum, Dru studied its contents. "Not much we can be doin'. If we could be stoppin' Gallagher, Mistress Bensen would simply be findin' another ta take his place. Just as she did when we turned her down. We could delay it a bit but not put an end to it." He looked to Victoria. "We can't be takin' on the entire British army."

"Then why not a small portion?"

Dru's questioning gaze met Donovan's confident smile.

"Ya already admitted Mistress Bensen would hire another if we be eliminatin' Gallagher. So why not rid the British of their spy?"

"That's a grand idea," Sean endorsed, slapping Donovan's shoulder. "I'd be more than willin' ta sail the lass and her partners ta the States and hand them over ta the revolutionaries." Sean's mouth crimped into an odd, vengeful smile, his nostrils expanding then contracting with each labored breath he took. He downed a swallow of his rum, staring blankly off into space.

"Aye, Sean. I be agreein' it be soundin' like a grand idea, however, Mistress Bensen and her friends have only committed one crime that we know of." He waited until Sean looked at him. "Talkin', lad. All they've done so far is talk. The revolutionaries won't hang someone for expressin' their dreams."

Sean's features hardened. "Ya think the scar they gave me was talk, Dru? It was real. They meant ta kill me."

"They only wanted the lass. At any price."

"Aye, that they did. And for what reason?"

"Ta blackmail her father, maybe."

"Aye. Then her father would have reason to want ta lay his hands on the woman."

Dru leaned forward, resting his arms against the edge of the table. "True, cousin. As he be wantin' us. Or have ya forgotten? We are askin' for money in return for his daughter, too."

Sean's blue eyes turned dark. "Do ya not care what they did ta me?"

"Of course, I be carin', Sean. But this is not the way ta be gettin' even."

"And what better way do ya have?"

Dru pressed back in his chair, his hands folded and falling between his parted knees. "None, at the moment."

"Then ya be lettin' them go?" Sean's tone took on a higher pitch, one marked with surprise and stress. He stared at Dru a moment, then hurriedly left his chair to pace the floor.

Dru watched him, a twinge of guilt twisting the muscles in his stomach. He looked at Donovan and witnessed the man lift his brows and one shoulder before turning away. Combing the fingers of his left hand through his hair, Dru sighed and rested his chin on a thumb, fist knotted. He waited a moment before dropping both hands, cupped within each other, to the table.

"Sean, ya be me cousin, the only flesh and blood left I can lay claim to. But I also be the captain of this vessel. And I am responsible for the ship and its crew. I can't be askin' the men ta help me seek revenge this

204

way. I have no intention of lettin' the deed go unpunished, but I must be takin' me time at it. I must be doin' it slowly so that I won't be puttin' me men in danger when there be no need."

Sean stopped his pacing, a hopeful gleam in the pale eyes staring at his cousin. "Then ya do have a plan?"

Dru raised both hands, fingers extended skyward. "Not at the moment, but we be knowin' where ta find the lass whenever we decide the time is right. Ya know our supplies are runnin' low and that we be needin' money. So first things first, lad. As soon as McGuire returns with Mr. Remington's answer, we set sail for the States to remedy the problem."

A vague smile appeared on Sean's face. "I guess that's why ya be captain of this ship and not me, dear cousin." He traced the scar beneath his eye. "And why I be wearin' this instead of you." A wide grin followed the proclamation, a smile Dru rewarded with one of his own. "And since ya are the captain, Donovan and I will be leavin' ya alone ta do your plannin'."

With his chin resting against the heel of his hand, Dru blanketed the smile that creased the smooth lines of his cheek as he listened to the two men leave the cabin, a heavy silence quickly closing in on him. He straightened and looked to the row of windows at his right, spying the trim figure fixed to the same spot she had occupied for the past quarter of an hour. Quietly, he rose and walked the short distance to her side.

"When ya return home, lass, ya can be tellin' your father of her plans. Maybe he can do somethin' ta stop her."

Victoria looked sharply up at him. "What? Pray? Even if she fails, it doesn't guarantee England will lose

205

the war. Either way, Melissa Bensen will claim my father's land!'' She looked out at the sprinkling of stars. ''The only way we can be sure that she doesn't appear on our doorstep someday is if she's dead.''

''Ya not be thinkin' foolish thoughts are ya?''

Dark brown eyes, shadowed by an angry frown, glared up at him.

''Ya've no money ta pay anyone on the island ta do the crime and I be doubtin' ya have the heartlessness ta do it yourself.''

''Then you think I should just allow you to take me home without the slightest attempt to stop her? Really, captain. You should realize I have stronger feelings for my parents than you obviously do for your own.'' She looked out at the tiny silver lights dotting the ebony curtain of night. ''I'll find a way,'' she muttered.

''And either get yourself killed or taken hostage again.''

''Why should you care?'' she flared, casting him a derisive scowl. ''I'm nothing to you.''

A strange tingling coursed through him with her decree. Of course she meant something to him. She meant a great deal. But he would never tell her. She must think that the only emotion she managed to spark in him blossomed from the desire to hold her in his arms and make love to her. Just as he would any woman. She must believe that his concern stemmed from the need to secure her safety until he delivered her to the hands of her father and a healthy-sized ransom found its way to his pocket. She must never learn that the aching he experienced touched his heart rather than his loins. He looked at the wooden deck at his feet.

''While ya be on me ship, ya be guaranteed me protection. I extend that privilege ta anyone." Although he meant the words he spoke, they sounded shallow even to him. "And since I be seein' how ya take care of yourself when you're on the island, I can be thinkin' no good will come of it if ya was ta try again. Melissa Bensen will be servin' her rightful payment for the evil she be doin', but not at your hands. She be a powerful woman, one ya can't be takin' on by yourself."

"Then help me," Victoria pleaded, turning to face him. "You managed once to steal into her room, why not a second time?"

"Ah, lass," he moaned, stepping away, but she quickly reached out to trap his arm in a desperate grasp. He froze, feeling that strange sensation stirring in the pit of his stomach. His gaze rested on the delicately boned hand touching his sleeve, then slowly traveled upward until he met her eyes. Mixed with a frown of urgency and beseeching moisture trimmed her lower lashes, and he felt as if his heart had been wrenched from him.

"You must understand why I have to see justice done now. This woman had my mother kidnapped, murdered the man Mama was to marry, and from the impression I get from my father whenever I manage to get him to talk of the past, Melissa Bensen was responsible for several other tragic things forced on my mother." Her voice cracked. "Now she plans to steal their home. Raven Oaks belonged to my grandfather, and someday it will be mine to pass on to my children. Oh, don't you see? The request I make is minor in exchange for what Melissa has done and intends to do. Please, help me."

Dru's lips parted as he made to respond, drawing in

a slow, negative breath to discredit the sanity of her scheme, taken aback when she threw her arms around his neck.

"I'll pay *any* price you ask," she whispered, one tear spilling down her cheek. "I'll be your mistress for as long as you want me."

Dru felt a sudden pain in his heart, as if she had thrust a knife into it. Dear God, she couldn't be serious! After all she'd been through in the past several weeks, fighting to save herself from the abuse of pirates, forced to endure even his advances, only to give herself as his mistress now? The price she put on Melissa's deliverance came high, and although he was a pirate in every sense of the word, he somehow, oddly enough, couldn't bring himself to accept the offer. Firmly, he set her arms away from him.

"She not be worth that much, lass. And ya be lucky ya offered yourself ta *me*. Any other man would have eagerly accepted."

"Then I'll find another. I'm sure there is one among you who isn't a coward!" She jerked free of him.

" 'Tisn't me courage lackin' why I deny ya. Ya be a lady, Victoria, one in distress and not knowin' what ya do."

His words rang truth in Victoria's ears, and for a moment she mentally argued with herself about the wiseness of her obsession. A woman alone could not aid in the war to the degree Melissa seemed to think she could. How could one pirate, one ship, fulfill the demands that would bring about the downfall of a country? And what guarantee was there that Melissa would succeed in New York, that she would be able to acquire the information needed to benefit Gallagher as he sailed the American coast? Determination—that was Melissa's whole secret. After all, hadn't Melissa solely schemed the abduction of her mother and caused Radford Chamberlain's death? Hadn't she nearly gotten away with the evil deed and not paid the price? Victoria looked away from the confident eyes staring down at her. And as for being a lady not knowing what she was doing—to defend something you love, sometimes a woman must sacrific the only thing she has to give, her pride, her self-esteem, her gentle upbringing. Besides, if he agreed to her offer, it would make her no less a lady, not in her heart. It wasn't as if she sold herself to every man who came along. She drew in a deep breath to calm her quaking limbs and set her gaze upon him once more.

"But you're wrong, captain. I know quite well what I'm doing. As you said before, I have no money to buy help. What I offer is all that I have."

"And somethin' ya will be payin' for for the rest of your life. Have ya thought about that? Do ya realize that no man would marry ya knowin' ya had given yourself ta another? Ya'd be nothin' better than a whore, Victoria."

The thumping of her heart almost echoing in her ears, she moved away, swallowing her tears. "It's too late to worry about that," she whispered, recalling how she had eagerly welcomed his touch only hours earlier.

"That was different," he snapped, angry with her for comparing what they had shared to other nights offered as payment.

She glanced up at him suddenly. "Was it? I don't think so."

His dark brows came together in a scowl. "Aye, it

209

was! Ya didn't offer yourself for payment.''

"And now I do," she said calmly.

"And me answer is nay. I do not want ta buy ya!'' For the first time in his life—or so he felt certain—Dru couldn't find the words to express his dislike of their conversation. But what troubled him more was the reason he hesitated. Since when did Dru Chandler turn down a blissful moment with *any* woman?

Her soft voice penetrated his thoughts. "Then you force me to seek out your cousin.''

He snapped to attention. "That fool would be seein' ya both killed.''

"Then you have no choice,'' she smirked, reveling in her sense of power over him and her realization that she had the power to entice any man to her way of thinking.

"Oh, but I do,'' he declared, having made up his mind not to agree. "I'll be lockin' ya in at all times and order me men ta stay clear of me cabin.'' He crossed to the table, refilled his mug with rum, and raised it to his mouth, carefully avoiding her eyes.

Studying his movements, Victoria wondered at the nervous way he held his drink, as if he craved its intoxication to steel his fortitude to hold fast to his decision. Odd, she found herself wishing to share the drink. But did she need its assistance to strengthen her will to see the business transaction met, or to dull her feelings toward the man? For, strangely enough, she discovered in herself a yearning that *this* pirate captain be the one to hold her, not any other man she knew. She shook off the thoughts, crediting them to the fact that he had already lain with her and the deed would seem less shameful. She took a deep breath and braced herself for what she was about to do.

"Then I think, from your tone, that we have a deal," she added, slowly moving up behind him.

He spun around, nearly bumping into her, and quickly retreated two steps. "How do ya figure that?"

She stepped closer, slowly reaching out a finger to entrap one string of his shirt front in a playfully suggestive hold. "Well, you've obviously made your decision, and since I'm well aware of your taste for gambling, I see this proposition as a wager."

Brown passionate eyes, flecked with golden specks, glanced up at him, melting his tough reserve. He felt his knees weaken.

"I wager you cannot restrain yourself, that before this night is over *I* will have made love to *you*."

Her other hand pressed against the muscles of his chest hidden beneath the muslin shirt. His flesh seemed to burn with the contact.

"Your payment for me will be to see Melissa Bensen dead."

He nearly strangled on the knot in his throat. He shook his head. "N-No."

"Captain, the time for arguments has come to a close," she whispered, standing on tiptoes, both hands encircling his neck to force him down to meet her kiss.

His mind exploded. God, he must stop this madness! She could never seduce him unless he allowed it, and he must not permit her to go too far lest she be ashamed once she realized what she had attempted to do. She drew nearer, her lips only inches from his. He lifted his hands to her waist, intent to set her from him, but she mistook the gesture to mean consent and leaned in, her body molded against the entire length of him. Did he hear her whimper with the touch? Dear Lord, no! It trailed from his own lips!

"Victoria—" Her name formed in his mind, but had no chance to reach his lips as she pressed her mouth to his.

Again he tried to put her from him, reaching up to take her arms from around him and forcefully break the embrace. But she clung harder, pressing her body tightly to his. Her lips parted and Dru's eyes flew open when her tongue darted inside. What was she doing? A small hand gently teased the hair at the nape of his neck, and, unable to stop the effects, he relaxed, savoring the kiss.

"Captain?"

His eyes opened slowly to find the dark-haired beauty staring up at him. "W-What?"

"Do you agree to see your part of the wager done should I succeed in making love to you? Or should I seek your cousin?"

The lantern's glow spilled out across the room, softly flickering against her profile, the sultry eyes trimmed with thick lashes, the finely chiseled nose, the full, rose-colored lips, slightly parted and awaiting his answer. His heart pounded in his chest, his loins ached, and although he had no intention of making her his mistress, he vowed no one else would have the chance. His gaze lowered to the full swell of her breasts, rising and falling ever so slowly beneath the cloth of her gown, teasing him, tempting him, *daring* him to possess what she willingly offered.

"Aye," he whispered, enveloping her tiny frame within his arms, his mouth lowering to capture hers in a searing, passionate kiss. The time for games had ended.

In that instant, Victoria wondered at the soundness of her act. He was so different in nature from any man she had met since leaving home that she had honestly felt safe in his presence. But would his gentle manner hold true, or would he brutally claim what she offered? His embrace inflicted no pain, yet she knew she could not break away should she try. Shame threatened to overpower her, force her to call out, to plead a change of mind, but she fought against this in herself. She did it for Raven Oaks, for her mother and father, for her future. Something had to be done to stop Melissa, and this was the only way she knew how. Repeatedly, she told herself there would be no shame, that what she intended to do was vital.

She would have affirmed her momentary guilt when he gently lifted her in his arms had his kiss not stilled her words. He carried her to the edge of his bunk and stood her on her feet again as he trailed kisses down the long column of her neck, his fingers agilely undoing the buttons of her gown. Her breath caught with the contact of his fingers with the flesh beneath it, and she wished somehow she could whisk her mind away, enable herself not to know what they did. The gown fell from her shoulders and pooled at her feet.

"Ah, Victoria," he whispered hoarsely, "ya be a fine beauty. The likes of which I never be seein' before."

She squeezed her eyes closed, waiting for the next move, praying it would all end quickly, for she suddenly feared he would throw her down, cruelly abuse her without a care as she had seen Kelsey do so many times, then rise and abruptly leave her as if she were of no more importance than an empty rum bottle. After all, it wasn't love that brought him here, only his mistress, and she wondered if she could bear his callousness. The sound of her name on his lips pierced her worry. She opened her eyes. The dimple of his cheek made no mark, his brows were drawn tightly together.

"Do ya fear me, Victoria?" he asked quietly.

Her chin quivered without warning. "No," she answered, knowing the declaration rang false. She lowered her gaze to the floor, only to have him lightly cup her chin in his hand and force her attention to him again.

"Ah, but ya do. I can be seein' it in your eyes. Do ya think me a beast, lass?"

Her tiny shoulder moved upward a slight degree. "I think of you as a pirate. Like Kelsey."

"Ya do me an injustice. Because we share the same way of life, doesn't mean we be treatin' a lady in a like manner. And if I be hurtin' ya, I be knowin' your father would see me hung from the yardarm of me own ship. Let yourself be enjoyin' it, me love."

She found herself tense in his embrace. Somehow this wasn't the same as before. She did it freely, but for a very different reason. And hadn't Dru labeled her a whore if she continued with her plan? Visions of what Kelsey had shared with the woman at the pub raged in her mind, the heartless way he had torn the clothes from her and mounted her barbarically, as if she had no feelings or needs of her own. Dru's body pressed against hers, the heat of his flesh penetrated the thin cloth of her camisole and set her ablaze, forcing an unexpected response from her. It started in the pit of her stomach and shot upward, engulfing her and coaxing her to weaken to the gentle, guiding touch of his hand. *This is only something I do for Raven Oaks, for no other reason,* her mind reeled, although the pledge seemed of secondary importance now. He pressed a kiss to her temple, awakening her senses to the scent of him, the feel of him so close to her. She closed her eyes dreamily. Her arms lifted slowly to encircle his neck and welcome his warm kiss, tender at first until her own passion soared and she met his advances with as much ardor.

Pushing away from her, Victoria feared he had had a change of heart, then was relieved to see him cross to the door of the cabin and turn the key in the lock. He smiled softly, pulling the shirt from his shoulders and kicking the shoes from his feet as he moved toward her again. Her heart pounded wildly. *For Raven Oaks,* she lied. With infinite care, he took the lace straps of her camisole from her shoulders, allowing the garment to fall from her trembling body. He kissed her again, his hands caressing the smooth flesh of her back, lowering to her buttocks, pulling her closer to him until Victoria could feel the hard, manly boldness of him.

Again he put himself from her, this time to shed his stockings and breeches, bending a knee to the bunk to pull her with him as they fell to the velvet coverlet, cool against Victoria's burning flesh. Warm, eager kisses found the hollow at the base of her neck, then moved to claim her firm breasts, proceeding on to the smooth, silken skin of her belly. She moaned, her passion mounting, her now meaningless oath forgotten. Dru lowered his weight upon her, parting her thighs, and pressed deeply into her.

The fiercest of storms hurling its assault upon its victims could not have matched the tempest that raged

215

within the captain's quarters this night. Their bodies, pressed together as one, met in a wild, spiraling ecstasy, reaching a pinnacle neither of them had ever dreamed to experience or wished to end, finally feeling cheated when it had. Dru fell back against the pillow, Victoria tucked within the crook of his arm as she idly played with the dark curls covering his chest. She smiled timidly up at him.

"Tell me true, fierce pirate captain," she teased, "will you soon forget me?"

A low rumble of laughter sounded deeply in his chest. "Never, me little vixon. I fear we both be findin' tonight somethin' that will be bindin' us eternally."

Victoria's head shot upward. Did he mean a child? Dear God, she had never thought of that reward for her well-intended deed. As if reading her thoughts, Dru pressed forward to place a kiss to the tip of her nose.

"Love, Victoria. I be meanin' that we might be bound by the achin' in our hearts."

A pretty pout formed, wrinkling the corners of her mouth. She fell back to the comfort of his arm, certain he only returned her banter. "How can you be loving two women?"

He stretched to look at her. "Two women? What is it ya be meanin', lass?"

Lazily she traced the lean muscles of his chest. "You told me once that you were married and still sailed the seas."

One corner of his mouth lifted playfully. "And does the thought that I be havin' a wife somewhere rub ya the wrong way?"

A sheepish smile distorted her face. "I simply thought I would never share the man I gave myself to, that's all.''

"And the same dream be includin' a seal of wedlock, didn't it now?"

Victoria nodded weakly.

"Well, part of your wish has come true. What I be meanin' was that I be married ta the sea.''

"Married to the sea?'' She thought her heart would explode with joy.

"Aye. Sailin' the oceans of the world is the only thing in life that be holdin' me. I be committed to it, as you be committed ta Raven Oaks.'' He cast her a sideways glance, spotting the frown that wrinkled her brow. "Of course, that will be changin' for ya, Victoria. Someday ya will be findin' a man that will steal your heart from your homeland.'' He felt the gentle nudge of her shoulder against his arm.

"I sometimes wonder. The qualities of the man I will marry must be high, and I have yet to find him.''

"And what would they be, lass?''

"He must love me solely and deeply, as I will love him. He must be strong in his ways and his beliefs, determined, kind, forgiving. And he must love children.'' She looked up at him, a bright smile lighting up her eyes. "I intend to have many.''

"Do ya now? And what if he shouldn't agree?''

Her head fell back against his arm as she stared up at the ceiling. "Then he will not be the one I wed,'' she answered matter-of-factly. "He will be much like my father in his thoughts.'' She raised up on one elbow, firmly setting her gaze on him once more as she added, "You'd like him. The two of you are very much alike.'' The happiness of her smile faded, and she sat up, presenting her back to Dru. "In some ways—but not all.''

217

The fine arch of her brow knotted. She didn't truly mean that. This pirate captain wasn't anything like her father. What he possessed he stole. Her father had worked very hard for what he owned and would defend it to his death. Then why did she think they had anything in common? She felt a gentle hand caress the knots of her spine.

"Ya better be careful, me love," he whispered. "Ya be soundin' as if ya already lost your heart."

Victoria's head snapped around to confront him and deny his words. "No. It isn't that way. If I searched long enough in any man, I would find some similarity between him and my father. 'Twas all I meant."

A sparkling smile flashed her way. "And if there be only one similarity between me and your father, I be takin' it as a great compliment. After all, he must be an exceptional man to have sired such a perfect offspring as yourself."

An embarrassed laugh trickled from her. "And you, sir, are full of the spirits. I am far from perfect."

"Aye, that is true. But I intend ta be makin' ya perfect in the one only fault ya have." He reached up, took her arm in a firm yet tender hold, and pulled her to the bunk beside him, rolling her beneath him as his passion soared again.

"He says ya are ta sail to the shores of Virginia, Dru. But let me be warnin' ya. Me instincts tell me ya should be very careful. He's not a man ta fool with."

"Thank ya, John. For all your troubles," Dru replied, shaking McGuire's hand. "I be seein' ya paid for the inconveniences just as soon as we be havin' his daughter in his hands and our money in our pockets."

218

"I'll not be worryin' about me payment. I be owin' ya more favors than one. I be worryin' about your hide more."

Dru smiled appreciatively in the early light of morning, casting his gaze out to sea.

"When will ya be setting sail?"

Looking back toward his cabin, Dru sighed heavily, knowing his decision would outrage the young woman sleeping in his bunk. "Within the hour."

TWELVE

The murmur of softly spoken voices outside the door of the cabin stirred Victoria from a peaceful slumber. She stretched, spreading out her arms in both directions on the bunk as she lay on her stomach, content in the warmth of the captain's bed. She opened one eye, peering at the wall filled with portholes to view the pastels of early dawn, marred only by a sprinkling of a few clouds. She rolled over on her back, her head cradled in her arms, a smile playing with the delicate features of her face, and stared up at the ceiling above.

She wondered if all mistresses felt as wonderful after a night in their lovers' arms as she did. Or was it because it was Dru and none other? Closing her eyes, his face appeared in her thoughts, warm, passionate, smiling. A shiver darted through her, starting at the base of her neck and ending at her tailbone as she recalled the things he did to her, feeling a rush of blood scorch her cheeks and flood her body. She opened her eyes to stare at the cabin door, oddly wishing he would step through it, that they might begin again. You're shameful, she giggled inwardly, and rolled over to lose herself in the heavy blankets of his bunk, feeling their softness caress her naked flesh.

A foreign sound penetrated her daydream. She sat up, clutching the coverlet beneath her chin. Although she couldn't explain why, a sense of dread simmered in the pit of her stomach. She listened to the voices outside the cabin, recognizing Dru's, but not the other. Wrapping the quilt around her, she slid from the bunk and tiptoed noiselessly across the room to eavesdrop.

"I be needin' your help, John. I must be certain the message gets ta the right hands in New York, and since I not be knowin' who it is, I wondered if you might know."

"Not directly, Dru. But I be knowin' someone who would." He reached up to squeeze Dru's shoulder. "I'll be givin' it to him right away."

"Thank ya, John," Dru sighed, nodding his farewell as he watched his friend walk away.

"And remember me warnin's, Dru. Remington isn't ta be trusted," John called over his shoulder, his foot on the first step of the ladder. "Good sailin'."

Dru sent him a weary smile and a wave of one hand, realizing what a good and trustworthy friend he had in John McGuire. The man had never lied to him, and oftentimes had warned Dru of danger solely by instinct, instinct that had always proven correct. But the circumstances had always been different. There had never been a woman involved, not one for whom he felt something. His gaze moved to the door of his cabin. And now he would have to tell her that he could not fulfill his part of their bargain, knowing she would never understand, nor believe him when he said he would deal with Melissa Bensen later, after he had returned Victoria safely to her father's arms. A frown creased his brow. And taking money for the act turned his stomach, cheapened the night spent lying in her arms. He squeezed his eyes closed, a tightening to his chest cutting short his breath. Why couldn't they have just sailed past Barbados? Gone on to Ireland, as they had planned? Why did he have to get involved? Damn, he muttered to himself with an agitated slap to his thigh. Since when did any woman touch his heart? He lifted a hand to the latch.

The brightly colored rays of sunlight spilled into the room, acting as a beacon to draw his attention to the empty bunk. His brow furrowed briefly, wondering where Victoria might be. He started to call her name, then caught sight of a movement from the corner of his eye. He turned, his wonder resolved when he found her standing beside his desk, clothed only in her camisole, a pistol aimed and cocked and pointing at his midsection. His curiosity changed to alarm.

"You loathsome guttersnipe! You cad! You vile, fatherless son of a whore!" Victoria's ire strained her voice to a high-piercing shriek. "You used me. You had no intention of seeing our wager through. You *are* no different than Kelsey, except you sweeten the rape with fancy words and a gentle touch." Trembling hands clasped the weapon, its narrow black muzzle raising higher to claim Dru's breastbone. "I should have shot you when I had the chance, and seen Melissa

222

dead besides, rather than trust the word of a pirate. No wonder your father deserted you. You're a liar and would have disgraced him.''

Her words sorely pricked his pride, but Dru made no move to stop her.

"Say something, damn you! Or does the fierce pirate captain find himself trembling in his boots?''

"What would ya be havin' me say, Victoria? The truth would only be soundin' false.''

"What you consider truth is always false, you rutting knave! It's a shame my father will not have the honor of seeing you hanged for what you've done. But I'm certain he will justify the loss when he learns it was I who took your worthless life.'' She took an assured step forward. "If you know how, captain, I suggest you pray. Maybe God will forgive you.'' Holding the pistol at arm's length, Victoria braced herself for its loud explosion to crack the stillness of the early morning, closing her eyes involuntarily.

At that moment every muscle in Dru's body tensed. He prayed as she bid, but not for absolution, rather that she find the preciseness of her aim lacking as he faced the fury of her wrath. His life flashed before him, certain the curtain of death would close upon him in the next instant. Could his words sway her? Could he plead for his life? A chance to explain? Would she listen or cut him down before the sentence reached its end? To die for honor, or to spare the life of his cousin seemed justified. But to merely stand here and allow her to take the very breath from his body for payment on a conclusion drawn in error jarred his dignity. He opened his mouth to speak, the words frozen in his throat as he witnessed Victoria's

223

slim finger squeeze the trigger. The click of metal answered him.

Victoria's eyes flew open. What was wrong? She pulled back the hammer and released it again. Nothing. Tears of frustration welled in her eyes. But it worked the last time, her bufuddled mind implored, why not now? All too clearly the reason came to her. No one had reloaded the chamber after her earlier escapade. Overwhelmed by the thoughts that nothing commissioned itself in her favor, she stared at the useless weapon in her hands, tears burning her eyes, her lower lip quivering.

Dru fought to restore his breathing, a cold sweat dampening his brow. He had been close to death before, sword to sword, pistol to pistol, but never had he felt so helpless, life so dear to him as at this moment. His muscles ached, his stomach churned, and he contemplated falling down on his knees to thank whomever might be watching over him for this one more chance to see a sunset redden the waters of the sea. A long, rasping sigh quaked his shoulders and he raised a hand to wipe his brow, his gaze falling on the source of his distress. She stood paralyzed, her eyes lowered to look upon the weapon she held, and he knew an aching in his heart. He *had* betrayed her. But not for the reasons she thought. Compelled to set the matter straight, he moved toward her.

Victoria blinked, sending a stream of tears down her cheeks. How could she have been so stupid? To give what was hers alone to give in exchange for the word of a thief? A sob echoed in her mind, breaking the trance that engulfed her. She glanced up, spying the very man who had stolen the precious gift she had intended for

224

her husband. A throaty growl broke free as Victoria hurled the useless firearm at his head.

Dru easily ducked out of the projectile's way, hearing it thud against the wall, then the floor. He moved closer.

Frantic, wanting nothing more of him than to keep his distance, Victoria fervently scanned the surface of his desk for more objects to rain on him. Spying the brass paperweight, she clutched it in her hand, pulled back, and threw it at him.

The space between them being minimal by now, he tried to step aside in time but failed, catching the item in the shoulder instead. He winced as pain shot through his arm.

"Victoria, listen—"

A silver candlestick whizzed by his ear.

"This can't be meanin' ya don't want ta go home." He stepped back when she threatened to club him with a spyglass. "Ya do want ta see your father again, don't ya?"

"Not until you've paid your part of the wager!"

He flinched, hearing the glass of the eyepiece shatter when it hit the floor. It had cost him a fine jeweled brooch in trade, and had warned him of approaching ships many times. It was something he could not do without. Oh, well, he shrugged, I'll get another. He looked back at Victoria, his eyes widening in alarm. Where had she found the dagger?

Circling the desk, she bravely moved in on him, forcing her victim to withdraw. "I'll cut out your slimy heart and feed it to the fish. Then I'll see to Melissa's justice."

His hands raised in front of him, Dru spoke softly,

"Now be takin' it easy, lass. One of us might be gettin' hurt."

"You're right, captain. One of us will." Lunging forward, Victoria slashed out at his arm, the dagger's blade slicing a hole in the sleeve of his shirt.

Sweat beaded his brow again as he studied the gaping tear, knowing how close she had come to cutting into his flesh. " 'Tisn't a fair fight we be havin', lass. Contrary ta what ya claim, I am a gentle man, not takin' ta fightin' with women."

"Then change your ways or watch yourself bleed to death!"

"Would it be makin' a difference if I told ya I love ya?"

Victoria's nostrils flared, her breathing labored, her eyes narrowing with rage.

"No," he half whispered, "I be seein' it wouldn't. Then would ya be agreein' ta lay down the knife and talk things over?"

The wrinkle of confusion barely made its way to her brow before Dru swiftly knocked the dagger from her hand and planted a blow to her chin with his fist. A multitude of twinkling lights exploded in her head, her knees buckled and she fell into the aiding reach of Dru's arms before she could hit the floor unconscious.

Staring at the closed eyes and watching a small dot of blood appear in the corner of her mouth, Dru shook his head. "I didn't want ta do that, lass, but ya wouldn't listen." Effortlessly, he lifted her limp form in his arms and carried her to his bunk.

The ticking of the small clock sitting on his desk drummed in his ears as Dru sat there studying the unmoving figure across the room from him. Several minutes had passed since he had bound her wrists and ankles with a piece of rope, knowing if he didn't she would only continue her assault when she awakened. The corner of his mouth twitched. Maybe I should be gaggin' her, too, he mused, so I won't be havin' ta listen ta her prattle. He poured himself a stout measure of rum and settled back in his chair, his eyes trained on the long, dark tresses flowing about the sleeping face.

He had sailed the seas for nearly a score of years, only ten and three the first day he had stepped on board a ship with his cousin by his side. He had loved every minute of it, finding it exciting, challenging, profitable, and never stifling. He was free to go as he pleased, never having to answer to anyone except himself. And in all this time, he had never grown weary of sailing from port to port. This was his life, the way he wanted it. His dark brows, their tips bleached by the scorching rays of sunlight, knotted tightly together. Then why did he dread the days to come? The time when he would place Victoria in a longboat and glide her inland to the waiting arms of her father? Was she a new adventure for him? One he could easily put aside when the time came, and take up where he had left off? He watched the rum swirl about in his glass as he tipped it from side to side. No, he couldn't. And why? He sighed heavily and cast his gaze at the ceiling overhead. Because I love the lass, he admitted silently. Downing the remainder of his rum, he set the glass on the desk, rose and wandered to the portholes to watch the sea roll toward the shoreline.

Why couldn't he be as callous as his own father? Why couldn't he just drop her off, collect his money, and sail away? Why? Because his mother had taught him to be kind and loving, to worship the woman who finally steals his heart, to pledge undying loyalty to her, not do as his father had done. The muscle in his jaw flexed repeatedly.

"I be wishin' I know who ya are, Father," Dru whispered. "I'd be askin' ya why ya left me mother like ya did. She loved ya. She needed ya." He paused, sucking in a breath. "*I* needed ya. I need ya now ta tell me what ta do as I always needed ya when I was a boy." His rage mixed heavily with a long hidden resentment and hatred. "Ya coward! Ya ran away, ya spineless cur. Someday I'll find who ya are and kill ya for it!" Realizing his voice had grown louder, Dru took a slow breath to calm himself, raising shaky fingertips to his brow. *The lass was wrong,* he announced inwardly, *it 'was you who disgraced me.*

"Dru?"

He heard his cousin's voice, a welcome intrusion upon his thoughts.

"Dru, are ya in there?"

"Aye, Sean. Come in. The door's unlocked." Dru wiped the moisture from his eyes before his cousin opened the door.

"We're ready ta sail. Shall I be givin' the word?" Sean's eyes sparkled with their usual gaiety even at this early hour, until he spotted Victoria lying in the bunk. One tawny brow raised. "The lass must be tired. She's still—" His eyes widened, having seen the ropes entangled around her limbs. "Me God, Dru. Ya've tied her up. What happened?"

228

"I had ta hit her."

"What?" Sean exploded.

"Aye. She overheard McGuire and meself talkin' in the passageway about takin' her home, and when I came in the cabin, she tried ta kill me. I didn't have much choice."

Sean's mouth opened and closed several times, failing to voice his confusion over the incident.

Dru smiled one-sidedly. "Sit down and I'll explain." A tired walk denoting his agony, Dru returned to his desk and refilled his glass with rum. "She doesn't want ta go home just yet. She wants to see Melissa Bensen dead first."

"Don't we all?" Sean muttered bitterly.

"Right now, I be wishin' it more than any of ya," Dru confessed, perching a hip to the corner of the desk as he sipped the rum.

"Is there somethin' you're not tellin' me, Dru? I got this funny feelin'—" Sean's voice trailed off.

Glancing over at him, Dru realized how much he needed, *wanted* to tell someone. And who could he trust more than his cousin, Sean Rafferty? Rubbing the muscles in the back of his neck, Dru relaxed a bit. He set down his glass and crossed his wrists to one knee. "I promised the lass I would put an end to Mistress Bensen's life in exchange for—" He swallowed hard, wondering about his cousin's reaction. "In exchange for her becomin' me mistress."

"Ya've kissed the blarney stone," Sean rallied. "Ya mean she willin'ly gave herself as payment?"

"Aye," Dru nodded sadly.

"And now because we be settin' sail, she thinks ya cheated her?"

Dru didn't answer.

"No wonder she tried ta kill ya."

"But that's not the half of it, Sean, me boy," Dru added, forcing his tone to be light. "I didn't agree because I wanted payment. I couldn't be lettin' another man touch her as she said she'd do if I refused. I did it because—because I love her."

"Saints preserve us," Sean moaned.

"If John hadn't returned with her father's answer when he did, I would have fulfilled me end of the deal. Maybe. I don't want her harmed, Sean. And bein' here on Barbados leaves little guarantee. I only wanted ta see her safe before venturin' into such a plan. You understand, don't ya?"

"Aye. But I'm not Victoria."

Dru left the desk and went to stare out at the small village nestled in a cove offshore. "No, you're not. And if I tried ta tell her what I've told ya, she'd never be believin' it."

"I'd say ya have a wee bit of a problem, cousin. What do ya plan ta do?"

"Take her home," he said quietly.

"Just like that?"

"What else can I be doin'? I won't give up me ship, and a life at sea isn't fit for a woman." He looked back and smiled softly. "Besides, do ya think she'd say yes if I asked her ta marry me, thinkin' what she does now?"

"But if ya truly love her, how can ya be lettin' her go?"

Dru's broad shoulders trembled with his sigh. He cast his attention to the shapely figure lying quietly in his bunk. "It's because I love her that I must. And ya

230

got ta be promisin' me that you'll never tell her.'' His steel-blue eyes, filled with his sadness, found Sean. ''Promise me, cousin.''

"I promise, Dru. But for the life of me, I don't understand.''

THIRTEEN

If the gentle winds continued, the *Defiance* would reach the coast of Virginia before nightfall, Sean had told Victoria. *Virginia,* she hummed to herself, *home.* It seemed ages ago when she walked the grassy meadows of Raven Oaks, watched the planting of the spring crops, or rode bareback to her father's childhood swimming hole. Sitting on the cushioned bench below the row of portholes in the captain's cabin, she studied the horizon, praying the small dot of land would materialize sooner than Sean expected. Little more than a week had passed since they had set sail from Barbados, but she found herself longing for companionship of any kind. After she had regained consciousness that day, it was Sean who stood beside the bunk, who untied her, and brought her meals. She never spoke to Dru again. Not that she wanted to, for every time she thought of him, shame flooded through her and seared her heart.

He came to his quarters only to sleep, and long after everyone else was abed. He rose before dawn and stole noiselessly from the cabin without awakening her. A discarded shirt and ruffled bedcovers marked the only clue to his presence, save the one evening when sleep would not claim her and she lay awake, hearing him quietly enter the cabin. From half-closed eyes, she peered at him, watching him shed all but his breeches and slip beneath the quilt. She could not understand why he avoided her. Not that it mattered. She truly wanted it that way. But it puzzled her that he did not try at every turn to scorn her, mock her, remind her that he had stolen her innocence and played her for the fool all along. He had obviously never intended to see to Melissa Bensen's demise and had found no difficulty in accepting her proposal. It simply meant it would be easier to get her in his bunk than before. Her throat tightened, tears burning her eyes, and yet there was an aching in her heart she could not fathom.

By midafternoon, Victoria found herself pacing the small confines of the cabin, her patience wearing thin and seclusion threatening to rob her sanity. She took to snooping through the desk drawers, rifling the pages of every book she could find, staring out at the sea time and time again, but to no avail. Then she heard the doorlatch click, and she spun around to welcome the company, her pulse beating wildly when Dru appeared before her. He glanced at her only briefly before going to his desk.

"We'll be droppin' anchor soon," he said, his tone stiff and formal. "I've ordered two of me crew ta go ashore and arrange our meetin'. On *me* terms, I might add, so ya must be knowin' what ta do. Ya don't want

233

ta get your father killed."

"Killed?" she choked.

"Aye. Me plans are ta be followed ta the letter. One wrong move and me men will cut him down."

"Dru, you mustn't. You can't," she said, taking an urgent step toward him.

The hardness in his gray-blue eyes softened for an instant with the familiar use of his name, then changed just as quickly, taking on an air of indifference. "Then be listenin' ta what I have ta say." Avoiding her intense stare, he shuffled through the papers on his desk, not really searching for anything, only wishing to have the matter done with as soon as possible. "He is ta be comin' alone, leave his carriage a hundred yards from the shoreline, and walk to the water's edge. When I'm certain he hasn't been followed we'll row ta shore, you, me, Donovan, and four others. After the exchange, ya are ta stand where ya are until we're out of firin' range. Simple, 'isn't it?"

She nodded weakly and looked to the bare toes sticking out from beneath the hem of her gown.

"Would ya be knowin' how ta swim?"

Puzzlement twisted her brow. "Yes," she replied softly.

"Then I'll be tying your hands. I wouldn't want ya ta jump out of the boat and give your father a chance ta kill us. 'Twould be a stupid thin' ta do, anyway. I'd shoot him down, take the money *and* you."

Victoria's spine stiffened. "Me? Why would you take me?"

A lazy, almost sinister smile crept over his face. "The small amount of time we shared is hardly fair payment for all the trouble ya've caused me." He watched her closely, hoping his threat frightened her enough into doing as she was told. Then, as if it were an afterthought, he added, "And I'd be givin' ya ta me cousin as well. Ya owe him, too. Or any of me crew, for that matter. After all, I always share with me men, and it wouldn't be fair ta keep ya ta meself, now would it?"

Victoria's eyes widened into large circles, her heart thudding in her chest. "I—I'll do whatever you say, captain."

"Good," he grinned triumphantly. "Now, be an obedient little lass and find yourself a place to sit. I've got work ta do and don't need ya botherin' me." He plopped down in the desk chair, pulled open a drawer to acquire the needed items, and centered his concentration on the papers he held.

Backing away from him, Victoria fumbled behind her until she felt the edge of the bench by the portholes touch her leg. Slowly, she sat down in the corner, her eyes never breaking their hold on Dru. Did he truly mean what he had said? Could he use her so callously, then give her to his men for their sport? Her lower lip trembled. She wanted to deny the possibility, tell herself he really cared what happened to her. As he had done until now. What had changed his mind? Had it all been a game played at her expense? A tear pooled in the corner of her eye and she quickly wiped away any trace of it. Maybe he had tricked her. She thought back to their conversation when they had lain in each other's arms. He had warned her that they might share love, as they had shared his bunk. Was that a ruse, too? Could she have been so wrong about him? Her throat tightened and she swallowed repeatedly to abort the torrent of weeping that threatened to claim her. And what of the wager? Had she been wrong there, too? Or had he given in to her not because she pressed him, but because he truly wished to hold her gently in his arms? Yes, she was wrong. Terribly wrong. He thought of her as he did any other woman he bedded, now that the deed was done. The challenge was gone. No need to woo her any longer. He had won. That was why his words were crisp and biting! He no longer desired her. A sweep of embarrassment burned her face, thinking of all the secrets she had shared with him, how she had told him of the qualities she looked for in a husband. How he must have laughed at her! Victoria's body trembled, but not from the grief of a moment ago. She shook with rage. And if there was a way, she would see he paid for his chicanery.

Exactly when Dru left the cabin, Victoria did not know, only that when she looked away from the sandy beaches of her homeland she had found herself alone again. How many hours had passed? Would her father come soon? She sighed impatiently and set her gaze on the shoreline once more, a movement from the edge of the trees several hundred yards inland catching her attention. She leaned forward, straining in an effort to distinguish its form. The dark shadows of foliage camouflaged what she thought she had seen until she spied the four white stocking feet of a mare trotting to an abrupt halt. Behind it she could vaguely make out the silhouette of a carriage. Its door swung open and out stepped the tall, muscular figure of a man. Her heart raced. He moved into the sunlight, its golden rays dissipating any doubt as to his identity.

"Papa," Victoria cried, her throat thick with urgency and longing to be cradled in his arms.

He stood tall and powerful in his black coat and breeches, dark leather boots hugging his muscular legs. Only the sprinkling of gray at his temples denied his youth, and Victoria knew again why she had not met a man to be his equal.

"Oh, Papa," she whispered. "Take care. They watch you closely."

He walked the distance across the beach, his stride sure and demanding. Many feared the man called The Hawk, and even Victoria trembled as she observed him.

She heard the door of the cabin open and Sean's voice telling her it was time to go, but she lingered, afraid that if she took her eyes away from her father's proud figure he would disappear.

"Now, lass. The captain's waitin'," Sean ordered.

Numbly, she rose on shaky limbs and allowed the Irishman topside.

The main deck held every member of the crew, armed and waiting. Victoria's heart labored when she saw them, wondering at the need for such a display against one man. Surely they didn't think he would storm the ship and attempt to rescue her.

"Over here, lass," she heard Sean instruct and felt the gentle squeeze of his hand to her elbow as he led her to the side of the ship. Looking over the edge, she saw a longboat bobbing in the water awaiting its passengers.

"When ya have her on board, tie her wrists," she vaguely heard Sean order, for her attention had returned to the lone figure on shore. He had not moved, his feet planted were squarely beneath him, his arms crossed over his chest, and sitting in the sand next to him, she spotted a dark satchel. The bounty, no doubt.

The ship took on a deathly silence as Victoria, aided by Donovan, climbed down the rope ladder into the longboat where they joined four other crew members. Her arms were bound in back of her, and she sat quietly, staring out to shore.

"Now remember, Sean, should anythin' go wrong, you're ta drop sails and go. I'll not be havin' ya put me ship and crew in danger because of me and a handful of men. Ya understand?"

"Aye, Dru. I only wish we could be anchorin' closer in so ya wouldn't have so far ta row and be out of reach of the ship. I've got a queer feelin' in the pit of me stomach."

Dru's dark blue eyes glanced out at the man waiting for him. "Aye. So do I."

"Ya wouldn't want ta change your mind, would ya? About the lass, I mean. We could be sailin' out of danger in a few min—"

"No, Sean," Dru interrupted, a firmness in his tone. "We do it this way and be done with it. There's no room on board for a woman." He extended his hand to his cousin. "For luck."

"Aye, for luck," Sean agreed, resolutely taking Dru's hand in his. "I'll be expectin' ya back on board within the half hour."

Sitting fore in the small vessel as they navigated their way toward land, Dru didn't center his attention on the man who waited there, but scanned the horizon for any possible signs of trickery. To all appearances, it seemed Beau Remington had followed Dru's orders precisely. But as both Sean and McGuire pointed out, Remington was not to be trusted where his daughter was concerned. The man seemed too calm, too sure of the situation to allow Dru to relax. Was it his imagination or had the native fowl inhabiting the seashore stilled their accustomed chirping?

It took them nearly one quarter of an hour before Dru could swing his legs over the edge of the boat and touch the sand footing below the water's surface. With the aid of the others, they pulled the vessel on shore, a section of its hull resting in the wet sand. Without comment, Dru stepped back into the water and easily lifted Victoria from the wooden seat, her arms still bound securely, and carried her to the beach. The moment her feet touched dry land, she broke free of Dru and ran to the open arms of her father.

"Victoria," he cried out, then put her at arm's length to study her. Her beautiful dark mass of hair lacked its usual luster, her face was pale, thin, her eyes looked exhausted. But through it all, he could see the spirit in her that he loved, admired, and never tried to alter. She was her mother's daughter, a bit untamed perhaps, but with the promise of growing into a fine woman, one of whom he would always be proud. Thank God she was safe. "Are you all right?"

"Yes, Papa," she answered, long-held tears streaming down her face. "Oh, Papa, I'm so glad to be home."

"I know, child. Now hold still while I untie the ropes." Quick and agile fingers freed her, and the two Remingtons embraced once more. "Did he hurt you, Victoria?"

Dru's warning rang in her ears. She mustn't say a word. Not until they were a safe distance apart from the pirate captain and his crew. "No, Papa." Her voice sounded weak and unconvincing, but if her father noticed, he hid it well, for, instead of pressing the issue, he turned his attention to her abductors. His eyes grew dark, hooded by the thick arch of his brow when he frowned.

They stood face to face now, Beau Remington and Dru Chandler, for her father had pushed Victoria behind him. She clung desperately to his arm.

"I have done as you instructed. The sum you requested is here in this satchel. But I must warn you, captain, you have not heard the last of me. No one takes what is mine and goes without paying."

A soft, daring smile played on Dru's lips, the dimple in his cheek appearing. "A fine trait in any man, sir, ta be claimin' what is his and not backin' down." He glanced to the trembling figure behind Beau. "And proud ya should be of her. She's a spirit I've never seen in a lass before." He took a low, sweeping bow. "An honor ta have had ya on me ship, Mistress Victoria." Standing erect, he nodded toward McKenzie, who retrieved the black bag from the sand, and carefully scrutinized the line of dark trees ahead of him before turning for the longboat.

Dru realized the danger surrounding them. Without Victoria beside them, the men were open targets should Beau Remington have thought of a plan. They must return to the ship quickly. While Dru and McKenzie shoved the boat into deeper waters, the four crew members remained on the beach a good distance apart, their pistols drawn and their eyes focused on the trees and bluffs around them. A shrill whistle from Dru instructed the men to join him, and they began their perilous journey to the *Defiance*.

"Papa—" Victoria said as she watched the boat float

further away.

"Hush, child," Beau warned, his eyes narrowed and filled with hatred as he watched the cocky figure of the captain turn back to wave a salute at him. Only a few yards more.

"It went too easily, Dru," Donovan observed.

"Aye, it did, me friend. And in a few more minutes we'll not be able ta fire on him and we'll be too far from the ship for safety. A spot I'll not be likin'."

As he spoke Dru noticed how leisurely Beau Remington turned and walked toward his carriage, Victoria's elbow securely clamped in his hold. Once there, he firmly put her aside, opened the buggy's door, leaned in and picked something up. Turning back, Dru could see the carriage pistol in Beau's hand. But what good would it do him? The ball would never reach this far. Raising the muzzle in the air, Beau returned Dru's mocking salute with one of his own and fired.

"What's he doin', capt'n?" Donovan asked.

But before Dru could speculate on the move, he spotted the figure of a man climbing to the top of a nearby bluff. At the crest, he, too, raised a pistol in the air and fired. The crack of powder sent a tightening fear to Dru's chest.

"Harder, men, row harder," Dru urged.

"What's it mean, Dru?" Donovan asked again.

"It means I should have paid heed ta John's warnin'. I'm afraid we're in for a run of it."

"A signal?"

"Aye. Look over there."

Donovan followed the direction in which Dru pointed, spotting the topmast of a schooner as it moved out from behind a headland to their left. It glided with

241

ease, its sails billowing in the crisp breeze, its prow southbound, aiming to cut them off from the *Defiance*.

Dru looked to his ship, wondering if Sean had seen it, his question answered as he watched the crew ready the cannons. If luck favored them, one hit from the capital ship would maim the foe and give Dru and his men time to escape. But the swiftness of the schooner held the odds high.

As it sailed closer, Dru could see the great number of crew that manned the ship, and wondered what price Beau Remington had paid to have them there. Without cannons of its own, its ease to maneuver swiftly in less shallow waters than a frigate marked its only advantage and left its crew to bear muskets for a close-range skirmish.

Thinking of the man again, Dru glanced back to shore. Beau Remington had moved away from the carriage to stand in the center of the beach, his feet spread apart confidently, his hands clasped behind his back as he watched his well-though-out plan executed. A hint of a smile broke the straight line of Dru's mouth, knowing he had never met a man like this one before.

The explosion of cannon snapped Dru around in time to see the ball miss its mark and splash harmlessly in the water near the aft of the schooner. A second volley thundered, closer to its target but still failing in its attempt. Skillfully, the helmsman of the craft pulled the tiller port then starboard, gliding the vessel in a zigzagging compaign to outsail the attack. Another cannon fired, sending its shot tearing through one of the topsails, unsuccessful in slowing down the affront. As if playing a cat-and-mouse game, the smaller ship cut rapidly through the water, closing in on the distance between it and the longboat full of helpless men.

A fourth explosion filled the air, only distant in its origin. Scanning the waters surrounding them, Dru spotted another capital ship of equal size and weaponry as the *Defiance* sailing toward it.

"Saints preserve us," Donovan shouted above the rallies, "he's hired an entire fleet!"

"Aye," Dru agreed, pulling his pistol when he realized the hopelessness of attempting to outrun the schooner. With each second that passed, it sailed closer. "Draw your weapons, mates. They'll not be takin' us easily."

A barrage of musket fire from the schooner answered their assault, one ball grazing the flesh of Dru's cheek, another hitting one of his men in the head. His lifeless form fell into the sea and disappeared. Swiftly, Dru reloaded. He raised his pistol and fired, hearing the scream of another when he hit his mark.

The second frigate manned its cannons and hailed their salvo against the *Defiance*. The smell of gunpowder, blood and death filled the air, spelling out an urgency to retreat as the crew of the pirate ship took warning. They must withdraw, sail away to safer waters, to do as their captain had ordered.

The schooner whizzed by the longboat, spraying its inhabitants with a fine mist of saltwater and leaving it to bob dangerously in its wake. They came around swiftly and sailed toward them again, this time their prow aimed to hit them broadside.

"They're gonna ram us!" Donovan screamed.

Glancing back to shore, Dru observed the figure standing there. "A steep price I be payin' for carin' for your daughter," he whispered, certain he could see the

243

smile on Beau Remington's lips.

"Capt'n. Capt'n, give the order," Donovan called, his eyes trained on the fast-approaching schooner.

Once more Dru poured gunpowder in the pistol, packing it down and adding the round lead ball. He cocked it and raised it high in front of him. "Swim for it, mates," he hissed, hearing the splash of three bodies hit water.

Clinging to the edge, ready to jump, McKenzie urgently pleaded, "Capt'n. Capt'n, aren't ya comin'? Ya can't be doin' any of us good by layin' down your life."

"Go, Donovan," Dru barked, squeezing one eye closed, the muzzle of the pistol aimed at the figure at the schooner's helm. "I be takin' their captain first." He waited, allowing the schooner to scud closer, insuring he wouldn't miss, when of a sudden Donovan presented him with a stinging slap to his shoulder. Dru toppled from the boat instantly, his silent pistol flying from his hand.

Dark waters swirled around him, burned his eyes and pounded against his temples. Knowing the need to swim away quickly lest he be cut in half by the keel of the schooner, Dru kicked his legs, his arms pulling at the water in powerful strokes. His breath nearly gone, he surfaced, twirling about to view the remains of the longboat floating in a thousand pieces. Where was Donovan? And the rest of his mates? The schooner came around again, heading back in Dru's direction, hoisting several of her sails to slow them. Obviously they intended to take him on board. But not without a struggle, he vowed, a devilish smile deepening the dimple in his cheek. "You'll have ta chase me."

Sucking in a deep breath, he dove under the water,

coming up several yards away. The schooner had sailed closer. He dove again. However, this time when he surfaced, the vessel nearly covered him, and he spotted several of the crew leaning out over the edge with boat hooks in their hands. He ducked under the water when one nearly struck him. He held his breath as long as possible, certain this time he would not get away. There were too many of them, and he grew tired.

He emerged again, unable to swim out of reach in time before one of the crew clubbed him with the long wooden shaft of the boat hook. His vision blurred, his head throbbed, but he managed to stay above water. Excited voices penetrated his fog, and he looked up, seeing the iron tool extend outward, seizing the folds of his wet shirt across his shoulders, tearing into his flesh as the sailors cruelly hoisted him on board. There was a pounding in his temples that seemed a promise to burst his skull, and he barely caught a glimpse of the *Defiance*, its sails unfurled and trapping the hearty breeze in its hold as it headed for open sea before blackness came to claim him.

FOURTEEN

"Dru. Dru, are ya all right?"

The voice sounded distant. He ignored it. It only played in his dreams.

"Dru, wake up!"

He moaned, his eyes fluttering open then closed again. Every muscle in his body ached.

"Capt'n, please," the voice begged, "ya got ta wake up. If we're ta get away, I'll be needin' your help."

He tried to move, but something held his arms in back of him. He rolled his head to one side, trying to focus on the face whose voice had called his name. Distorted figures floated before him, gray and fuzzy. He closed his eyes again, the throbbing of his temples almost unbearable.

"Capt'n, please. 'Tis me, Donovan."

Donovan? he called, but no sound escaped his lips. Blackness surrounded him.

"Open your eyes, capt'n," Donovan instructed, rewarded by two small slits of steel-blue. "That's it. Now listen to me." Hands and feet bound in heavy ropes, his clothing dripping with saltwater, Donovan hastily glanced about them, scooting closer to Dru when he was satisfied no one could hear. The crew of the schooner boisterously celebrated their victory a good distance from the prisoners, leaving only one man to guard them. But he too guzzled his share of rum and sat glassy-eyed several yards away. "Can ya be sittin' up, Dru?" Donovan whispered.

A ragged moan answered him and Donovan winced with the pain he felt certain Dru experienced as he awkwardly pushed himself up.

" 'Twas a hell of a blow ya took mate. I was fearin' they killed ya."

Dru closed his eyes, slowly twisted his head around to stretch the muscles of his neck. "I be wishin' they had. I wouldn't be feelin' so bad."

The creases in McKenzie's cheeks deepened. "Ya can't be meanin' it, capt'n. Ya wouldn't want ta be leavin' the care of your ship ta Sean, now would ya?"

"Right now I not be havin' much of a choice." Dru carefully studied the crew, then strained to see over the edge of the ship for a clue to their whereabouts. "Where they be takin' us?"

"Not sure, but I be guessin' ta meet with the lass's father."

"Mmmm," Dru agreed. "He warned me he wasn't through with me."

"Do ya think you'll be able ta stand? Or run, if we be gettin' the chance?"

"If it means escapin' a father's anger, ya can wager

247

all your gold.''

''Aye. Somehow I be thinkin' I would rather fight the British navy than face that man,'' Donovan conceded. ''But if we be havin' a little of our Irish luck, we might be stealin' away without doin' either.''

''Not unless ya have a knife hidden on ya,'' Dru pointed out as he analyzed the tightly bound knots of rope at his ankles. He twisted, trying to free his hands, feeling the rope cut deeper into his wrists when he did.

''Well, you scurvy son of an Irish fishwife. You're not so cocky now.''

Guardedly, Dru lifted his gaze to meet that of the schooner's captain. He blinked, but made no other move or sound.

''Thought you could kidnap Mr. Remington's daughter and get away with it, didn't you? Well, we'll show you what happens to a pirate who's that damn stupid.'' The shiny silver buckle of the captain's shoe brutally buried itself in Dru's rib cage, knocking Dru to the deck again. Laughter howled in his ears as the captain turned and walked away.

''Dru, Dru, are ya all right, lad?'' Donovan appealed, wanting desperately to free himself and help Dru up again.

''Aye, but I can remember feelin' better.'' Once more, Dru elbowed his way off the deck and carefully leaned back against the bulkhead. He shifted around until he found a comfortable position where he could rest and still keep an eye on the schooner's crew. ''I'm afraid, Donovan, me boy, that we'll have ta be acceptin' their hospitality until Sean returns.''

From his location on the deck, Dru quietly observed the nearby bluffs lined with trees and dense greenery, knowing they sailed close to shore. He could only assume they awaited assurance that the *Defiance* had indeed sailed off and would anchor only when certain it was safe. What he guessed to be the better part of an hour passed before the sails were hoisted and they dropped anchor, and he assumed that before another hour ticked away, he and Donovan would face the man who had devised this master plan.

The crew made ready to dock while Dru and McKenzie looked on. The first of them disappeared down the rope ladder while the captain supervised their departure from his position at the helm. A few more moments exhausted themselves before the captain, anxious to be on his way, summoned his first mate. Several words were spoken between them, none of which either Dru or Donovan could overhear, and, after a nod of the captain's head in the prisoners' direction, the first mate quickly headed toward them. Without a word, the man pulled a knife from the scabbard hanging on his belt and leaned down to cut the bonds around their ankles. Having hauled them to their feet, he gave both Dru and Donovan a hearty shove toward the ladder, then awaited the captain's order. With a cocksure swagger, the captain joined them.

"It's a shame I'll not be able to witness Mr. Remington's punishment for you, but I must leave at once for Boston." He stood with arms crossed behind his back, rocking on his heels as he spoke, an ominous smile twisting his mouth. "However, I'm sure whatever it is will be justified and most painful. I only hope he doesn't have you hanged too soon. You deserve to suffer a long while."

Dru returned the man's smile with one of his own,

mocking yet full of promise. "Pay heed, good captain. Sail quickly for distant shores. Me cousin has a way of not forgettin' how ya tricked him and would likely hunt ya down."

The captain's shoulders stiffened at the forewarning, for though he feared only few men, the tone in which this pirate spoke hinted at a danger even he would take heed of. With a quick jerk of his head, eager to be done with the villains, the captain silently instructed his first mate to see them to the longboat bobbing in the water below them.

"I not be likin' the looks of it, Dru," Donovan whispered as he sat aft of the boat watching the two figures on shore. "I figure we be standin' a better chance without the lass there ta make lies of our words."

Dru's gaze, distant and longing, swept over the trim shape standing beside Beau Remington. He had thought to never see her again, to sail away and leave behind him a part of his life, someone who had stirred desires in him he had never before experienced. He had thought long and hard about abandoning her, knowing it would be best for them both. But seeing her now, he wondered how long he could have stayed away. He loved the sea and its ways, but it didn't love him back, not the way a woman could. He laughed to himself with the thought that Victoria Remington could possibly ever love him. Hadn't she told him of the qualities she looked for in a husband? Hadn't she spoken of a gentleman, scorning a pirate? *Oh, well,* he mused, *'tis for the best.*

"Dru?"

Startled, he glanced at Donovan and smiled when he realized his thoughts were elsewhere. "Aye, Donovan," he hummed, "it will bode us ill ta have the lass stand in judgment. Me only regret is that you'll have ta share me fate and not have had a thing ta do with puttin' yourself there."

Donovan shook his bald head, its top tanned golden by the sun. "Dru, we be friends for as long as I remember. What happens ta you will happen ta me. I'll not be leavin' ya ta save me own hide."

The longboat with its occupants easily glided into shore, its prow buried deeply into the sand. Uncaringly, Dru and Donovan were dragged from its comfort and thrown to their knees before the man who had ordered it done.

A shudder ran through Victoria's tiny frame when Dru's eyes found hers, for the wound to his temple had oozed blood, now dried and caked in a thin stream down his cheek and matted in his black hair, and another marred his cheek. The dark eyes held pain, and she longed to go to him, to soothe him, to tend his cut. How her pulse had raced watching the battle of wits and sheer valor between him and her father. And when the schooner had torn the longboat in two, her heart had pounded, the muscles of her chest cramping until she had to fight for a breath, certain he had been crushed by its keel. She remembered looking to her father, a cry for mercy on her lips until she saw the almost wicked, truly satisfied smile on his handsome features and knew that no amount of words from her would alter the turn of events. Beau Remington would have his revenge.

"Well, Irishman," Remington beckoned malignantly, his hands still clamped behind his back, "what do you have to say now?"

Forcing his eyes to focus on the elder Remington, Dru remained quiet. There was no need to state the obvious. This encounter would be one among many, another soon to follow once his cousin found the aid he sought and sailed once more for the shores of Virginia. A confident, somewhat victorious smile crept over Dru's face, his gaze clashing with the stern, demanding glare of his captor. If only they had met under a different contest, they could have shared their knowledge, for Dru knew he could learn a considerable amount from Beau Remington as well as teach the man the ways of the sea. Sighing softly, he looked away, knowing it could never be, when all of a sudden, the heel of the first mate's shoe struck Dru between the shoulders, sending him to sprawl face down in the sand.

"Answer Mr. Remington, you bloody cur," the sailor spat, "before I lay open your skull and cheat the hangman."

Cruelly, the man grabbed a handful of Dru's hair and yanked him to his knees again. With arms bound behind him, Dru could only submit silently to the abuse, though his patience wore dangerously thin. But, in fact, he knew of no way to stop the sailor from doing whatever pleased him.

A small cry of pity escaped Victoria for the man trapped in the heavy bonds, her delicate hand urgently touching her father's sleeve in silent request to see the mistreatment arrested.

"That will be enough, Higgins," Beau instructed.

"But sir—" the sailor argued, a near pout puckering his lips.

With one hand raised to still Higgin's justification, Beau cut in, "Such a display in front of my daughter is

252

offensive to her gentle nature."

Though his head throbbed, each breath he took painful, laughter rumbled deeply in Dru's chest, for he knew, too well, the other side of this fair maiden's gentle nature.

"You laugh at me, captain?" Beau demanded tersely, the man's glee pricking his tolerance.

"Nay, sir. At what ya be sayin'. If ya would give the lass your pistol, she would finish what your man started without the slightest care or blink of an eye. She's truly heartless when me punishment, as she deems it, is placed within *her* hands, no matter what the crime."

Hot denial flared to boiling over as Victoria took a deep breath. "You *deserve* to die for what you did to me!" She stepped forward, failing to see the startled, questioning look on her father's face. "A gentleman would not have forced himself on me as you did." Not comprehending the warning frown on Dru's handsome face, Victoria raised her nose in the air, daring him to deny her accusation if he could. But when his gaze left her to fall on the man at her side, she knew too late the error of her quick and inane tongue.

"How so did he force himself on you, Victoria?"

Victoria felt as if every muscle in her body were diseased, stiff, unmoving and frozen for eternity as her father's question rang in her ears. She couldn't lie to him, but then again she could never tell him the truth of the matter. He would never understand. Especially now, when her plan had failed. She looked to Dru for help, but found he rested back on his heels, his shoulders slumped, his gaze fixed on the sand in which he knelt, and she judged this trap to be of his making. No doubt he reveled in his workmanship.

"Victoria?"

The name on her father's lips, sharp, demanding, cut through the heavy blanket of silence surrounding them, weaving a casement of doom to engulf her. Bowing her head, she lifted shaky fingers to her mouth to chew on the nail of her thumb and forefinger. She couldn't bring herself to look at her father. He would know in an instant the falseness of her game.

"Now, Victoria. You will tell me now," he bade, reaching out to touch her shoulder.

Startled by the contact, somehow thinking he would strike her even for the thoughts in her head, she jumped, shrinking back when she saw the angry scowl on his face. "He-e-e—" she whimpered, unable to assemble a structure of words any more complex than that of a simpleton.

Remington's towering figure stiffened in rage with her failure to comply, thinking her tribulation too horrifying to voice. He cast his damning glare on Dru. "He abused you?" he finished, his words more statement than question. But before she could affirm or disavow his claim, he continued. "And fed you poorly, from the looks of you."

A tenuous sense of triumph sparked Victoria's courage to aid in her father's denunciation of Dru. But she must be careful with her words, choose them wisely, lest he suspect her cause. "Oh, no, Papa," she said, feigning innocence, "they always fed me supper."

"Supper?" he roared. "And what did you do with the rest of the day? Sleep? As well as all night?"

Victoria hung her head in mock shame. "I-I very seldom was allowed to sleep the night through, Papa," she whispered.

Remington's nostrils flared, his scowl deepened. "*Every* night?" he growled.

"Nearly," came the weak reply. Through lowered lashes, she stole a peek at her father.

He stood rigid, his arms at his sides, fists clamped tightly closed. "What other misfortune did he beset upon you?" he demanded through clenched teeth.

Not truly wishing to upset her father further, she hesitated. "Oh, please, Papa, it is over now. I just want to forget it." She looked to her hands, sheepishly entwining a finger in the loose thread on the bodice of her gown. "If I ever can," she added softly.

"What else?" he howled.

Vocabulary evaded her. She had gone too far, pushed too much, and the implication of her claim tasted bitter in her mouth. She looked to Dru, a glimmer of apology in her dark brown eyes. She hoped he would understand. She couldn't tell her father she had willingly made love with the pirate, no matter how just the cause. Although he had tricked her that night, she knew he had kept her safe from Kelsey and Melissa, and what she had proposed had been her own doing. She couldn't truly blame him for taking advantage of a foolish woman. However, she could not discredit the tale she told her father either, else he would have the truth proclaimed. And, after all, what harm would come of it? Her father did not take to violence. He would not see Dru hanged for returning her home. No, she must continue on with her ploy to seal what seemed to her father the candor of her words and hopefully to save her own beguiled neck. She turned sympathetic eyes to the man who stood in judgment.

"I would have tried to escape, Papa, but he locked

me in his cabin."

The muscle of Remington's cheek twitched. "*His* cabin?"

"He told me that if I tried to get away, he would— would—" She allowed a ragged sob to spice her falsehood. "He would give me to his crew. And he took my clothes away just in case. Oh, Papa," she cried, forcing a tear to trickle down her cheek, "it was awful."

Dropping his gaze to the soiled knees of his breeches, Dru managed to hide his smile. *The little vixen,* he thought. *She'll be havin' me neck before the day is through. And ta be tellin' her father how awful it was, just ta save her own cunning hide. A mistress of illusion, she be, for I rather thought she enjoyed it.* Feeling the humor of her entrapment, though he knew the price for it would be high, he cast his gaze on his companion at his side, to consider whether McKenzie also shared his amusement. To his surprise, he found the man glaring hotly at the teller of tales.

"Go to the carriage and wait there for me, Victoria," her father ordered, his eyes never leaving Dru.

"What will you do, Papa?"

"I shall see he pays for this insult."

Fear suddenly gripped her. "How do you mean?" she asked.

Remington's shrill whistle pierced the stillness on the beach, scattering sea gulls from their loftly perches in the bluffs to wing frantically overhead. The rattling of a wagon followed, plowing its way through the thick sand toward them. Instantly Victoria recognized its driver. Avery Fielding, the overseer from Raven Oaks.

"Papa, where are you taking them?" she asked, her voice urgent.

"To prison, my child."

"Prison?" she repeated.

Having folded his arms across his chest to await Fielding's descent from the wagon and the few steps it took him to reach his side, Remington cast his daughter a sideways glance. "Of course. You didn't think I went to all this expense just to turn them loose again, did you?"

"But, Papa—"

"Victoria, do as you're told and go to the carriage."

Victoria recognized the tone of his voice as one not to be tested, a timber that she had oftentimes heard as a child and knew not to question. Helpless to deter him, she looked pathetically at Dru, chewed numbly on her lower lip, and turned to do as her father bade.

"Dru, ya'll not be sittin' here and let the man think what he does," Donovan whispered, a frown deepening the lines of his brow as he studied the two men exchanging words. "Ya saved the lass from a terrible fate and her father should be knowin' of it. 'Tisn't fare ya take the blame for somethin' that ain't so."

Observing the agitated sway to Victoria's hips as she plodded through the sand on her way to the carriage, Dru quietly responded, "Put yourself in her father's shoes, Donovan, me friend. Whose word would ya be takin'? Your daughter's or that of a pirate?"

A muffled grumble came in return, bringing a soft smile from Dru as he looked to the man who held the reins of his future.

"Well, Irishman," Remington said, glancing briefly over his shoulder toward the carriage, then back again, "now that we're alone what do you have to say in defense of yourself?"

257

Dru's shoulder lifted ever so slightly, refusing the chance to clear the injustice brought against him. It would be better left unsaid, for he doubted Beau Remington would believe a word of it anyway. Instead he might possibly plant a seed of doubt in the man's mind that would grow and blossom into a suspicion of his daughter's honesty. And Dru had no wish to curse the relationship of the two headstrong and proud Remingtons. He smiled to himself. Besides, the lass would more than likely trip over her own verbiage, hint at the truth, and give herself away. He would know his own revenge in time.

"Then does your silence mean guilt, young man?" Remington cocked one brow at him.

Donovan, who had fought not to voice rebuttal, edged his way closer to Dru, nudging him in the side with his elbow. "Well, won't ya say somethin', man?"

"As I said before, Donovan, good friend, the man will only be listenin' ta what he wants ta hear." As he spoke, Dru returned his gaze to Remington.

"But, capt'n!"

"No, Donovan. Not a word."

A vague smile softly made its way across Remington's face. "I might be hard convincing, captain, but I assure you I will listen if you feel the need to deny my daughter's claims."

"I'll not be denyin' what she says is true. A little mixed up in places, but for the whole, a true account on her behalf."

The lightness of the elder man's mood faded with the pirate's remark, sensing something hidden deeper than the words alone would tell. Yet from the brevity of their acquaintance, Beau also suspected that no matter how he persisted in finding the truth, this pirate, humbled to his knees before him, would hold fast to his principles. Or did Beau Remington merely seek to find the tiniest sliver of guilt in the man to ease his own conscience? Although they stood on separate shores, an underlying speck of respect for the pirate's character gnawed at Beau's reserve. And what of his daughter's appearance? No bruises or cuts indicated any abuse. Her wit and tongue were still sharp. Sadly, he recalled the way in which he had found her mother those many years past. A story never told, she too had been misused by pirates, an event that had nearly snapped her mind. Each time he looked upon his daughter he saw the likeness to his wife in strength, character, love, and tenderness. Why then had Victoria not returned to him in a similar state of withdrawal? Had she twisted the truth to suit her needs, as she had always done before? No bold-faced lie, just tinged a mite to satisfy her wonts. He frowned defensively. But no matter. This pirate captain would pay for using his daughter, whether it be in body or in name alone.

"Fielding," he growled, "put them on the wagon and take them to the prison. Mr. Werner awaits you." He turned to glare at the prisoners, the thoughts he wished to speak failing to reach his lips. Angrily, he turned and walked to the carriage.

From within the darkened shelter of her buggy Victoria sat trembling, watching the steady, angry gait of her father trudging toward her. Her careless tongue had nearly cost her the truth, and once they reached the manor, she vowed to hide herself away until the nowness of the affair grew dim. Only then would she feel safe in the solitude of his companionship, when facts were vague and the witness of the deeds imprisoned. A shudder ran through her. What were her father's plans for Dru? Surely he would not order him hanged. A chill not born of the air grasped her tiny frame and she locked her arms around her for what little warmth they offered as the carriage rocked with her father's weight on its step. A sharp command set the vehicle in motion, and Victoria peered out the window for one final glimpse of Dru.

Little more than a few street lamps lit the darkened, eerie streets of the waterfront. Dark shapes, menacing in form, moved along the cobblestones, keenly aware of the others while courageously ignoring them. Dressed solely in black, a high-collared cape pulled up beneath his chin, a tricorn cocked over his brow, a dark stranger made his way to the warehouse at the far end of the street. Each time he passed an ill-clothed wretch, he placed a gloved hand to the tip of his hat, purposely hiding his identity from those who, for a sixpence, would spill the truth of his presence to the ears of those who might foil his plan.

FIFTEEN

Sitting before the dressing table mirror, Melissa lazily stroked the long golden tresses cascading over her shoulder to rest gently against her full bosom. She stared at the dispassionate eyes looking back at her from the mirror, sea-green in hue and framed softly with the light brown arch of her brow. Her high cheekbones still had the delicate shade of pink, an attribute of her youth that had won her many gentlemen callers. Tilting her head to one side, she studied the faint lines marring the corners of her eyes and mouth. She seemed pale, she but cocked one immodest brow in denial of them, thinking that no other woman her age looked as young. An arrogant smile parting her lips, she gracefully left her chair and stepped back to catch her full image in the glass, turning sideways to view her profile in the transparent silk of her nightgown. Long shapely limbs, flat tummy not abused by childbearing, full, round breasts jutting outward—all this brought a smile of satisfaction to her lips. She looked better than any woman who had seen two score and five summers blossom and die. Her nose raised slightly higher. She could have married any man she chose, had she so decided. But none had suited her after Radford Chamberlain. The slight wrinkle to one corner of her mouth deepened. No, not even Radford had ever really pleased her. Beau Remington was the one she sought, the one who stirred any desire in her whatsoever. And he had all but thrown her off Raven Oaks, left her to find comfort and compassion in Radford's arms. Her lip curled in bitter memory. *And that spineless cretin dumped me for a servant, a fortune-seeker, a whore!*

"Damn you, Alanna Remington!" Melissa screamed, the ivory-handled brush flying through midair to crash against the wall. "You shall pay! After all these years, I will see you pay!"

Hatred stiffening her moves, she returned to her place before the mirror. The long strands of gold found their way to a knot on the top of Melissa's head, held securely with pearl-tipped pins thrust deep into the silken mass. A vindictive smile twisted her mouth, her ire easing with a thought.

When England wins the war I shall have all I've waited for these twenty years, dear Alanna. I shall have Raven Oaks, and in time your husband. The land his father worked and died for means more to him than you, and when I offer him the chance to own it again, he will forsake you. And then he will be mine, as he should have been from the very start.

A moist tongue touched to the tip of her third finger, Melissa vainly smoothed one brow to a fine, perfect line. All she had to do was wait. England would win the

262

war, and she would taste sweet revenge.

A soft rapping at the door of her room intruded upon her thoughts. Snatching her rose-colored robe from the foot of the bed, she hastily put it on, pulling the sash snugly around her trim waist and going to the door.

"Who is it?"

"Edwin, Melissa. May I come in? I've good news."

"Is it Gallagher?" she half whispered before the door clicked shut behind him.

"Yes. He's dropped anchor and sent word you are to come to his ship."

"His ship?" Melissa echoed, a slight tremor in her voice betraying her usual genius at hiding her vulnerability.

"Yes. And I must say I don't like it," Edwin admitted, a worried frown twisting his black-flecked-with-silver brows. "He says you are to come alone."

Hugging her arms to her, Melissa tried unsuccessfully to rub the chill from her that had suddenly seized her slight form. She had traveled the seas, visited many countries, seen blood oozing from the gaping wounds of men struck down in duels, but none of this turmoil had induced the trepidation she now experienced. Only one man in her entire life had ever been able to frighten her, and now she must meet him on his ground, alone.

"When?" Her voice came in a hushed whisper.

"Right away. He says if you're not there within the hour, he'll set sail." Reaching out to trap her hands in his, Edwin pulled her closer. "Let's find someone else for the job, my love. I fear for you being alone with a man of his nature."

"And that is the very reason I chose him." She withdrew her hands and went to the armoire, pulling open

263

the door to view its contents as she added, "I will not worry he may cheat me, nor will I run in the face of danger. The man fears nothing." Selecting a dark blue linen gown, she turned to face Edwin. "Now, if you'll excuse me, I must get dressed and keep a very important meeting."

"Please, Melissa, I beg you—" His tone rang more cowardice than concern and Melissa sighed impatiently, her dislike for such emotion evident in the nettled steps she took toward the door.

"Out, Edwin, before I do agree to find another. One with courage to replace *you*."

Pricked by her callousness, Edwin's tall figure stiffened, his mouth open to deny her accusation, then snapped closed again. Damn her! He would not beg again. Let the man do what he might to her. It mattered little! Pulling his dark cape about him for protection against the crisp sea-borne breeze, he moved to make his exit, pausing briefly to glare into her eyes. Didn't she know? Couldn't she see how much he loved her? Her languid eyes returned his stare, hinting at the wish to see him gone. Anger flaring again, he clutched the doorlatch in his hand, flung the portal wide, and stomped from the room.

Standing haloed in its frame, Melissa watched him until he disappeared around the bend in the hallway, an impervious gleam in her eyes. Touching a fingertip to the oak panel of the door, she stepped back and gave it a gentle push, appraising its ease to swing on its hinges and secure her solitude again.

"Capt'n, you sure you wanna do this?" Clayton Parker asked.

Watching the white smoke from his cheroot curl upward, Dillon Gallagher grinned. "And what better things have we ta be doin', Clayton, me boy?"

"None. But I see no reason to do anything *she* wants." Clayton took a swig of his rum and crossed to the wall of the cabin filled with stained glass windows overlooking the small town on Barbados. "I thought—" His statement hung in the air.

Dillon's smile widened. "Ya thought I hated the woman." He leaned forward to rest his elbows against the edge of the desk. "Well, I do. And, I don't trust her. But me curiosity begged me ta find out what's on her evil mind. And besides, maybe it's a deal we can be takin' on. Our hold is gettin' empty, ya know."

Glancing back over his shoulder, anger knotting his brow, Clayton growled, "Not that empty." He looked outside again.

Resting back in his chair, Dillon clamped the short cheroot between his teeth, the finger of one hand tracing the long, purplish scar running from temple to chin. "And might I be askin' why it upsets ya so?"

"I have no love for the woman either. I'd just as soon see ya slit her throat as talk to her."

"Aye, that I be knowin'. Me question is why?" Interlacing the fingers of both hands across his protruding belly, Dillon relaxed, enjoying the game he played with his first mate.

"Ain't none of your business," Clayton snapped, his gaze still fixed on the tiny assortment of twinkling lights dotting the town.

"Why, Clayton, lad. I never be hearin' ya talk ta your captain like that before. Have ya gone mad?"

Whirling, Clayton shouted, "You know damn well

265

why!''

A bronze brow lifted. ''For what she did ta the lass from Williamsburg?''

''Aye. And stop playing with me. You feel the same.''

Dillon reached up to suck on the cheroot, squinting when the smoke burned his eyes. ''I just be wantin' ta hear ya say ya loved the lass, 'twas all.''

Clayton's arms fell to his sides, rum nearly spilling from the tipped mug dangling in his hand. ''How long have you known?''

A smile creased the thick lines of Dillon's unshaven face. ''From the moment ya took it upon yourself ta see ta her care. 'Tisn't nothin' ta be ashamed of, lad.''

''No,'' Clayton agreed, sitting down on the long velvet-covered cushion of the bench below the windows, ''only hopeless. Her love belonged to another.''

''And do ya still carry the longin' in your heart?''

Clayton smiled for the first time since the *Sea Falcon* had anchored offshore of the small island. ''Yes, you nosy old pirate. I do. Now, are you satisfied?''

An amused gleam sparkled in the blueness of the older man's eyes. ''How long ya be sailin' with me, lad?''

''Close to twenty-five years, capt'n.''

Dillon shook his head, red hair glowing in the lantern's light. ''Ya never once told me anythin' about yourself.''

''You never asked.''

A wide grin wrinkled the disfiguring scar on his cheek. ''Maybe that's why you and me get along. We don't bore each other with things only meanin' somethin' ta the one who says it. Ya suppose,

Clayton?"

"Aye, capt'n."

Easing his weighty frame back into his chair, an elbow to its arm to support the chin resting in his hand, Dillon gazed upward. "I wonder what ever became of the lass."

"Don't know, capt'n. The last I heard was that she went back to Virginia with Remington."

"Aye," Dillon hummed, stroking the evidence of a well-placed sword, "Beau Remington. 'Twould be me guess she married the man."

"Why would you say that? She was promised to the chap you killed."

Dillon shrugged a thick shoulder. "Aye, that she was. But it doesn't always mean a lass must love the one she marries."

"Nor does it mean a lass will marry the one she loves."

Angry blue eyes flashed at the first mate, certain the man hinted at what Dillon thought a well-kept secret.

"Aye, Dillon. Just as you knew I held a love in my heart, I know of another who loved you and refused your name."

Heatedly stuffing his cheroot in the gold-trimmed glass ashtray on the desk, Dillon hissed, "Now ya be strainin' our friendship, lad. I be suggestin' ya keep your thoughts to yourself."

"Aye, capt'n," Clayton Parker concurred, feeling the bite of the man's words, but knowing no real danger lay in them. He lifted his nearly empty mug to his lips, frozen before a drop reached his mouth by the timely knock to the cabin door.

"Come!" Dillon bellowed.

Clayton came to his feet and moved to stand opposite his captain when the door swung wide and presented a woman draped in a black, fur-trimmed cape, its hood all but covering her head. No doubt in his mind, they were graced with Melissa Bensen's presence.

"Won't ya come in and take a seat, lass?" Dillon asked, rising from his chair, an outstretched hand pointing the way.

"Thank you, captain," she replied, closing the door behind her.

Only the gentle sway of skirts and petticoats marked her step as she walked to the proffered piece of furniture and sat down. Willfully, she spread out the abundance of cape covering her shapely limbs, reached up to drop the hood of her cape and undo the silk frogs at her neck. The black cape fell against the back of the chair, and Dillon doubted that if the woman lived five score years she would ever lose her beauty. But when she lifted her gaze to meet his, he saw the underlying malice of her nature, the only blemish in an otherwise flawless face.

"The *Sea Falcon* sailed a great distance at your request. I pray it won't be in vain," he said, refilling his mug with rum. He held out the bottle to his guest. "Would ya be carin' for a sip?"

Melissa's nose wrinkled distastefully. "No, thank you, captain."

"Aye," he half laughed, "not truly fittin' for a grand lady like yourself." He slammed the bottle down on the desk, its thud adding to Melissa's already frayed nerves, and heartily swallowed his rum in one gulp. After wiping away a few spilled droplets from his chin with the back of his hand, he set a hard look at her. "Now what is it ya be needin'? Ya plan ta do away with someone?'' he baited, a devilish glint in his eye.

"No, captain,'' she said, withdrawing a lace handkerchief from the sleeve of her gown to dab at the perspiration beading her upper lip. "I work for the Crown and need—''

"England?'' Dillon pealed. "How can ya be workin' against your homeland?''

"I have lived in England for over twenty years now and place my loyalty with it. What I propose is to aid in the war.''

Dillon fell back in his chair, a deep rumble of laughter shaking his belly.

"What do you find so amusing, sir?''

"I can't understand what ya would gain by it. I know ya well enough ta know ya wouldn't do it out of loyalty!'' He laughed again, glancing up at Clayton, who stood in silent observation.

"I will be paid,'' she announced, her gaze traveling from the first mate to Dillon again.

"Can they afford ya now? Your last venture cost a man's life.''

Melissa stiffened instantly. "I didn't kill Radford. You did.''

"Aye. But through your lies, ya put him there.'' He leaned forward on the desk, his arms crossed to support his heavy upper torso. He glared at her.

Melissa cringed under the damning glare, his huge bulk seeming to proliferate as if he was consumed by the devil himself. He radiated contempt for her and she decided to be about her business quickly lest the man burst into flame and take her with him to a fiery grave. She opened her mouth to speak, hearing her teeth rattle instead. She swallowed hard and looked to her hands folded in her lap while she fought to gain control of herself once more. The creaking of his chair abruptly pulled her attention back to the man whose help she so desperately needed. She watched him relight the cheroot and lazily blow the smoke into white, fluffy circles, his gaze never leaving her. Unnerved, she wiggled in her chair to find a more comfortable position.

"Then tell me what ya want, lass. I can't be affordin' ta sit here and relive the past. 'Sides, I know an achin' in me loins I truly wish ta put an end to."

Melissa's face burned at his vulgarity. "And I do not wish to listen to such talk."

An impish grin appeared on Dillon's pudgy face. "Ah, such a lady ya are. Is that why ya travel with three men, to none of whom ya be wed?"

"My private life is none of your concern," she said in outrage.

"Me point exactly. State your business and I be decidin' if I like the odds. Otherwise ya can be returnin' ta your lover." He stuck the cheroot in his mouth and just as quickly withdrew it. "Or lovers," he added, his weighty frame bouncing hilariously with the prod of his scorn.

His laughter was slow to die, and Melissa's spine stiffened more with each note of his revelry. Unable to utter a single syllable in her own defense, she shunned his implication, raised her chin gallantly, and cleared her throat. "If you wish to be on your way, sir, then I suggest we get to the core of my proposal." She waited until the pirate had narrowed his amusement to a vague smile and continued. "I have been authorized by the Crown to hire a captain and his crew to sail the east coast of America and attack all ships aiding the colonists in the war. I chose you. After securing the ships, you are to take the supplies to Quebec for sale and receive payment for your work, as well. If you sink any of the ships, deliver the captain, dead or alive, to the British authorities in Quebec as proof, and you will receive an additional sum. If you find you require the help of another vessel and crew, their earnings will come from your pocket. Are you interested?''

Again Dillon puffed on his cigar, smoke rings filling the air over his head, his eyes trained on her. ''I fail ta see a deal. I be doin' all the work.''

''Not hardly, capt'n. I am to establish a contact in Quebec, then travel to New York. Any information I acquire there will then be sent to him. So you see, I'm actually in more danger than you.''

No hint of a smile moved his mouth. '' 'Tis a risky business for a lass. What be your payment for the deed?'' he asked quietly.

''I don't see where—'' Melissa began but Dillon quickly stilled her rebuttal with a raised finger.

''I be needin' ta know the worth ta ya so I know ya won't be changin' your mind. If ya not be tellin' someone in Quebec to expect us, our riskin' our lives could be for nothin'. If ya not be tellin' me, we have no deal,'' he warned.

Sea-green eyes flashed dangerously, but no argument crossed her lips, only a slight flare to her nostrils marking disapproval. ''The Crown has kindly agreed to my choice of any plantation in the colonies in payment for my help in winning the war.''

Sparkling white teeth contrasted brightly with Dillon's tanned face. "Let me guess which one it will be. Raven Oaks, owned now by Beau and Alanna Remington. Am I wrong?" he asked playfully, watching the woman's gaze fall to her lap.

Only Dillon's eyes moved to look at his first mate, who had remained silent during their statement of terms. Maybe Clayton knew of the lass Dillon had offered marriage, but did Clayton know Dillon still carried a deep and lasting love for the woman they had kidnapped over twenty years before? Dillon had lied when he said he guessed Alanna married Beau Remington, for he had sent a man to watch over her and knew very well every move she made. With Radford's death, she was willed his estate, and the union between her and The Hawk had made their plantations one, the largest in the commonwealth of Virginia. No wonder Melissa Bensen wished to lay claim to it. He popped the cheroot into his mouth again and leaned back in his chair. Two years after their marriage, Alanna had given birth to a daughter, Victoria by name, and his spy declared her beauty equal to her mother's. The gray-blue of Dillon's eyes softened. He wished to verify the fact for himself. Maybe someday when he was too old to sail he would travel to Williamsburg to get a glimpse of her. But not now. He had more important things to accomplish. And one would be to see Melissa Bensen never collected her reward. He would attack the French ships, gather his earnings, but, should England win the war, he would make sure Melissa never lived long enough to set foot on the soil of Raven Oaks.

"One condition and we have a deal," he said. "This will be the one and only time you will be seekin' me out. Ya are not ta find yourself in me company again. I bear an urgent hatred of the mere sight of ya, and, given the chance, I'd likely cut your throat and throw ya overboard ta the sharks. Do ya understand me meanin'?''

The constricting of muscles in her neck and chest prevented Melissa from verbalizing her understanding of the warning. She nodded her head to seal the pact.

"Then be off with ya," he snapped, waving a dismissing hand, "so I can find a worthy wench ta bed rather than be sharin' company with the likes of you."

Had any other spoken the insult, Melissa would have protested, turned her words to play her the favorite, then let him feel the sting of her sharp tongue. But as it was, she held her silence, lifted her cape from the chair, and made a quiet exit.

Melissa sat huddled in the corner of her bunk, a heavy quilt draped around her, and still she could not chase the chill from her. Dillon's conditions for the bargain would be easy for her to meet for Melissa had no desire to ever be in his company again. The soft sea breezes drifted into the cabin from the open portal and she cursed her lack of observation, blaming it for the discomfort that overwhelmed her. Awkwardly finding her feet, she stumbled to the port, her attention drawn to the gray-white sails of a frigate skimming the waters starboard toward the shoreline her ship had just departed. A loathing sneer curled her lip.

"If I hadn't this great need of you, my pirate foe, I

would wish this vessel hunt you down and blow you from the waters!''

A mad laughter filled the cabin.

SIXTEEN

The first day of June held promise of a long, hot summer. Moisture was thick in the air, and even the shade was barely comfortable. Nights were unbearable. Thin cotton sheets seemed to glue themselves to perspiring bodies, disturbing restful slumber before it had begun. Tempers flared unduly in the heat, strained friendships, and set everyone's nerves on edge. To those around Victoria, it seemed the misery struck hardest whenever she walked the halls of Raven Oaks or summoned the stable boy to fetch her saddle horse, Beldon. She had no time for niceties or idle talk with anyone. She stayed to herself, either in her room or riding the meadows of the great plantation, ignoring warnings to stay close should British soldiers be about. Nothing held her attention for long, and it appeared her thoughts were elsewhere. No one was particularly interested in eating, but for Victoria food had no importance at all. Her thinning figure caused her parents great worry.

More than a week had passed since she had returned home and she had cunningly avoided speaking with her father. However, no amount of reading or needlework had occupied her mind enough to rid it of thoughts of the pirate locked away in prison, put there by her lies. But to free him meant she had to tell the truth and surely bring shame upon the eldest Remington—to say nothing of bringing his wrath down upon her ears.

Sitting before the mirror of her dressing table, the heat of midafternoon intensified by the closeness of her room, Victoria wanly brushed her long, thick mane of black hair, her eyes fixed on the stare that looked back at her. So much had happened in the past weeks. She wondered how it had all slipped by so quickly. She had left the manor a child and returned a woman, an experience she could not share with her mother. Dru Chandler wasn't the sort any mother would welcome. Yet, oddly enough, Victoria felt certain her mother would like him if given the chance. He wasn't the usual pirate, not vulgar, filthy, or the type to kill a man in cold blood. He had a tender side, compassionate and gentle. A soft smile played upon her lips, her gaze drifting upward as she recalled the intimate way he had held her, kissed her cheek, her neck, her breast. A healthy glow blossomed in her cheeks, the first in weeks, as visions of her pirate came to mind.

Rising, she crossed to the window of her room to gaze outside, noticing how few workers roamed about in the yard below, and she settled on the sill to study them. Had these men and women experienced the joy she had experienced held tenderly in another's arms?

Had they known the bliss, serenity, contentment? Had they shared moments of discovery, a time of learning about the secrets of another's past? She sighed happily, lifting her eyes to watch the clouds drift aimlessly about the sky, recalling her discovery of a faint scar at the corner of his eye, put there, he had told her, by his cousin as a child. She had gently traced its fine line with her fingertip, finding still another on his jaw below his ear. When asked if he had acquired it in the same manner as the first, he had denied remembering, and Victoria had frowned, certain *she* would remember when and how she had obtained such marks. She thought back to how she had wanted to ask about the numerous markings on his wide back, afraid the tale would be too horrifying to hear. Had a whip torn his flesh as a youth, or as a man full grown, and why? She smiled when she realized what had chased away her musings. Catching a dark strand of her hair, she idly twisted it around her finger. He had kissed the corner of her mouth, his hand gliding down her waist, her hip, her thigh, then slipped beneath her to roll her on top of him, the thick mass of her hair flowing about to cover them. She had propped herself up on his chest to study him, returning his playful smile and feeling the warmth of their naked bodies pressed together. Nothing else at that moment had seemed as important, and she had prayed their scandalous turpitude would go on forever. He had buried his face in her neck, lightly nibbling her flesh and bringing a squeal of delight from her. Then his eyes had darkened, his lips finding hers, and they had shared once more the glory of their passion.

There was an unexpected knock at the door of her room, and Victoria jumped with a start at the intrusion, blood rushing to her cheeks in burning embarrassment. "Who is it?" she called, rushing back to the dressing table where she twisted the long strands of hair into a knot.

"Just me, Daphne, Miss Victoria."

No matter how even her temper, the high-pitched squeak of the young black maid's voice pierced Victoria's good nature. It was a curse from birth, and Daphne could do little to change the tone. But had she known the effect it had this day, she would have sought the aid of another in summoning her mistress.

"What do you want?" Victoria snapped without giving her permission to enter.

"Not me, Miss Victoria. Your papa. Says you is to come down right away."

Was it her imagination or had her face paled at the announcement as she watched herself in the mirror? She had played the game so well, stayed out from underfoot, avoided his presence at all costs, so that not a single breath had been drawn to discuss her treatment on board the *Defiance*. Had the time now come? Did he suspect, and mean to hear the truth? Dear God, she couldn't tell him. Although her memory denied he had ever raised a hand to her, Victoria cringed at the thought. Surely he would thrash her soundly for her wicked behavior.

"Tell him I'm feeling poorly," she replied, her voice thin.

"Yes'm. He knows. That's why he wants you in the parlor. He says you and him is to talk about making you feel better."

Dear Lord, he does know! Tears moistened her eyes, her lower lip trembling, betraying her anxiety. What

278

was she to do now? Could she hold to her story and see it through? Or would the guilt that plagued her bend her will and force the truth to spill forth?

"Miss Victoria? He says I ain't to come down without you."

Panic rising high, she placed both hands to her face, fighting desperately to still the trembling of her chin. She blinked repeatedly to dry her eyes, sucked in a deep breath, and expelled it slowly. She looked at her reflection in the mirror. Would he know by merely gazing at her? Lifting her chin and squaring her shoulders, she drew the fortitude to test him.

"I'm coming," she answered, a noticeable hesitation to her words.

Descending the wide, circling staircase, Daphne several steps behind her, Victoria felt as if she were on her way to the gallows. She drew a ragged breath and wondered if Daphne heard. Time and time again she forced a smile to her lips, practicing concealing her worry behind a smooth front. At the bottom, she paused, then turned to the maid.

"You've done as you were told, Daphne. You may return to your work," she instructed.

"Yes'm," Daphne squeaked, a quick curtsy bending one knee before a hurried step moved her through the foyer and into the adjoining room.

With the maid's departure, some of Victoria's confidence faded also. Her shoulders drooped and a slight tremble raced up her spine. Would she live to see this through? The soft tones of her mother's voice drifted out from the parlor and Victoria relaxed a bit, knowing she would always have an ally. Then a new sense of dread erupted as she heard what Alanna was discussing with her husband. Victoria stepped closer to listen, hidden just outside the door.

"Darling, I don't see where Damon's courting will help. You know Victoria. If she doesn't want to do something, she won't. A trait she inherited from you, I'm afraid."

Damon? Damon? Victoria's mind raced to recall the name.

"Yes, but even you will admit he's handsome," Beau replied. "He's a man of wealth, and it's time she thought of settling down."

"But we know so little of Mr. Rutledge."

Damon Rutledge! Victoria's lips moved but the name made no sound. She fell back against the wall to catch her breath. Surely her father couldn't mean it! The man was more than twice her age. Granted he was handsome, strikingly so, but to pair her off without her consent as he would some breeding mare was unthinkable! Victoria closed her eyes, recalling the first time she had seen Damon Rutledge six months ago. He had just purchased Willow Glen from the auction block and had come to Raven Oaks to introduce himself to his new neighbors. He stood as tall as her father, with slate-black hair and dark eyes, a muscular shape and broad shoulders, the only flaw in his appearance being a terrible limp. His right leg twisted grotesquely and Victoria had doubted he could walk at all without the aid of a cane. She had always wondered if it was an affliction from birth, but no one ever found the courage to ask him. He had a gentle smile that he bestowed on Victoria repeatedly as he shared a brandy with her father in the parlor. His words were sweet and flattering while he compared Victoria's beauty to her mother's, but when he bowed to place a gentle kiss to the fingers of her hand, she felt an urgent need to pull away. She truly couldn't explain her reaction to the man, simply that his presence disturbed her. When his visits grew more frequent, Victoria had found herself making excuses not to be near the house whenever he came to discuss business with her father. Thinking of it now, she wondered if he hadn't been part of the reason she had so strongly wanted to go to Paris. And now what would she do? If her father gave permission for the man to court her, she would be helpless to avoid him. Well, nothing had been agreed on as yet, and she would have a say about it first. She straightened, smoothed the wrinkles from her gown, and stepped into the parlor.

"Did you wish to see me, Papa?" She smiled sweetly.

Beau stood by the tall french doors, gazing outside, a demitasse filled with black coffee in one hand. At the sound of her voice he looked at her, but made no other move. His gaze swept over her, appraising her, taking in the slightness of her form and the dark color beneath her eyes that spoke of little sleep. He glanced at his wife, then back outside.

"I've given my permission for Damon Rutledge to court you," he announced flatly.

"But—" Victoria began, her surprised frown darting from her father to the woman seated on the velvet sofa before the fireplace. "Mo-o-th-er," she whined.

"It was *my* decision, Victoria, so don't blame her. Your mother doesn't quite agree, but in time she'll see I'm right."

"Papa, Mr. Rutledge is too old!" Victoria moaned.

"He's forty. A lot younger than I. And even at my

age, I have trouble understanding you. If I had my way, I'd find someone older.''

''You can't mean that,'' Victoria breathed, moving further into the room. ''I'd be a widow before my time. And what of me? Shouldn't I have a say in my future?''

A black scowl met her. ''It *is* your future I'm thinking of! By your own word you admitted the possibility of your growing heavy with child without the benefit of wedlock.''

The color drained from her face. She glanced at her mother, who had chosen to study the lace handkerchief in her hands, then back at her father. ''But only a possibility. Not fact. Could we not at least be certain before—''

''No!'' he howled. ''You'll not disgrace this family.''

Panic coursing through her, tears sprang to her eyes. ''But maybe Mr. Rutledge would not want me if he knew.''

''He already does.'' Beau looked outside again.

''You told him?'' Victoria sobbed. ''How could you? Must I share my shame with strangers?''

''My point exactly!'' he stormed, turning away from the day's brightness to place his cup on a nearby table. He walked the short distance between them and stopped only inches before her, his heated glare burning into her. ''I will not have you parading about with a fat belly for the world to see! I respect Damon Rutledge, and his wealth will give you all you want.''

''Except love,'' she bravely whispered.

''A sacrifice you must make,'' he growled.

''But you punish me for something I could not—'' the truth of the matter stuck in her throat, ''avoid.''

She lowered her eyes.

"And for that I am sorry. But I will have it no other way." He brushed past her and left the room.

The trap she had innocently, carelessly built around herself seemed to be stifling the very breath in her. A man sat in prison, and she had been given to another—all because of a few thoughtless words. She hung her head and fought the tears that burned her eyes.

"Victoria."

She looked up to find her mother by her side. The years had been kind to Alanna Remington, for not a silver hair marred the dark mane neatly curled and knotted on her head. No wrinkles touched the corners of her eyes and mouth, and her slim frame still attracted the complimentary stares of many gentlemen, young and old. But she had never noticed, for she had total love in her heart for the man she had married over twenty years ago. Even as a child, Victoria had felt the loyalty between her mother and father, and she had vowed to find her own with a man who would return it. A tear raced down her cheek. Now it would never be. Her own tongue had destroyed any chance for it.

"Victoria, do not hate your father for what he's done. He loves you so very much and only does what he thinks is right," Alanna soothed her.

"I know, Mama. And I don't hate him. I never could. It's just—well, I had planned to find a husband I could love as much as you love Papa is all. Now it will never be." She moved away.

"Don't talk as if there is no hope. In time you may grow to respect the things in Damon that your father does," Alanna said.

"I'm certain of that. But respect for a man is not

283

what will make me happy. I wish to welcome his touch, long for it.'' Flashing gray-blue eyes emerged in her memory. She squeezed her own shut, forcing the image to disappear. ''I want to think of no one else. Live to please him as wife and mistress. Bear his children with pride, not because it's expected of me. Take care of him when he's sick, laugh with him when he's happy.'' A sparkling smile intruded. She opened her eyes. ''Don't you understand, Mama?'' she sobbed, turning back. ''I already I—'' Quick fingers pressed against her lips. Dear God, what had she almost said? Not him! She didn't mean she loved the pirate. No!

''Already what, Victoria?'' Alanna asked, her dark eyes soft and sympathetic.

''I—I already know what it is I look for in a husband,'' she answered, unable to meet the sad eyes of her mother. ''I—I just wanted to be the one to choose. Like you did.''

Stung by the irony of her daughter's words, Alanna looked away.

''And how could a man agree to court a woman who may carry another's child? What kind of man is he, Mama?'' Victoria pressed, certain she had won her mother's support.

Tears lining the lower rim of her lashes, Alanna moved toward the french doors, hoping her daughter would not notice. She stared outside in silence. The day Victoria had been born, she and Beau had vowed to hold fast to their secret of the other baby, the one cheated of a life of any length. Had it been a mistake? Would knowing about the infant have helped Victoria understand? A glimmer of longing for the past flashed across Alanna's face. She had carried a child without

284

the benefit of wedlock; Beau's child. But she had promised to wed Radford Chamberlain. She recalled the day she had told Radford of the child and the fear she had experienced, certain he would have a change of heart. But he hadn't. In fact, it seemed to pull them closer together. He had loved her, and had loved Beau as a brother, and had vowed the raising of his friend's child would be an honor. *Oh, Radford,* she sighed inwardly, *you were such a gentle man.* Inspired by her memory of him, she blinked away her tears and turned to face her daughter.

"Damon Rutledge is a gentleman," she stated.

Her shoulders slumping, Victoria moaned, "Oh, Mama."

"Now hear me out," Alanna insisted strongly. "It may sound shallow, but it's true. And a real gentleman, one who respects a friend, would help him out in any way he could."

"Enough to marry?" Victoria raised a skeptical brow.

"In this instance, yes. At the risk of sounding prejudiced, you are an extremely beautiful woman, and a marriage with you can benefit Mr. Rutledge."

"But that's what I mean. The marriage would be empty. Papa doesn't understand. He doesn't care."

Alanna moved to stand next to her daughter, her hand gently touching Victoria's arm. "You're wrong. Your father knows Damon, trusts him, admires him. And it's a great honor that he would give the man something he treasures with his heart. Don't you see," she added, turning Victoria back to wrap her in a warm embrace, "if your father thought you would be unhappy with Damon Rutledge, he never would have

285

given the man his permission to court you."

"But marriage is forever, Mama," Victoria moaned, wanting to say more, to share with her the joy she had felt in the pirate's company. Though she doubted it could be love, he had awakened in her the knowledge that there could be more to share with a man than just his name. But how could she explain that to her mother without telling her the whole of it?

"He hasn't asked for your hand as yet, my child," Alanna smiled impishly. "Who knows? He may find you are not what he looks for in a wife after all."

Confusion wrinkled the younger woman's brow, and she looked at her mother for an answer. Brown eyes flecked golden twinkled back at her, a smile cajoling the corners of her mouth to turn upward.

"Just because your father wishes it, doesn't mean it will be so," Alanna whispered. "But should you say from where that idea came, I'll deny it. I still must share his bed and I rather enjoy the warmth he has to offer."

Her spirits, nearly at their lowest, soared upward, forcing giggles to erupt from Victoria. "Now I see why so many people claim we are alike. Our thoughts run the same path. Thank you, Mother. And I'll try not to be too obvious with Mr. Rutledge."

"One thing more," Alanna added when her daughter made to leave her. "Should what your father fears come true and you are with child, I, too, will urge a marriage, whether it be of your choice or your father's. It is hard enough to raise a child with principles, much less a bastard child whose father would have forsaken it. Do you understand?"

Victoria bowed her head. "Yes, Mama."

"Then go now before your father finds us and wonders what secrets we share." Reaching out, Alanna gently touched her daughter's cheek and smiled. "He knows me well and would guess in an instant by the falseness in my eyes should I tell him none."

Clasping her mother's hand in hers, Victoria placed a kiss to its palms, turned, and left her mother's side.

Victoria spent the next hour alone in her room, the book *The Canterbury Tales* resting on one knee. Though she tried, she could not focus her eyes on a single passage, for her mind was filled with visions of Dru locked away in a prison cell. If only she could free him, the guilt that possessed her, robbed her sleep, would vanish and she could concentrate on matters more urgent.

"Damon Rutledge," she hissed, slamming the book closed and tossing it on the bed. How could her father do this to her? Leaving her chair, she went to the french doors of her room that led out onto the balcony, finding little relief from the intense heat of midday. Lazily, she scanned the yard below her, smiling at the slow movements of men and children alike as they labored in the sun's piercing rays. Even though war raged about them, the fields and meadows had yet to feel its violence, and peace seemed to rule the plantation. Her eyes moved to view each building, freshly painted and spotlessly clean, spying the one that knew her presence most—the kitchen. A glimmer of hope flashed into her mind as she thought of who usually could be found there. Twirling about, she set off to make good her idea.

"Good afternoon, Cinnamon," Victoria smiled a moment later, stepping into the stone building filled with the sweet aromas of fresh-baked bread.

The rounding figure of the plantation's cook straightened from her task at the stove and turned to greet her visitor. Cherry-brown eyes beamed approval at the intrusion, and a wide grin creased the lines in her pudgy cheeks.

"Victoria. I haven't seen you for a couple of days. How are you?"

"Fine," she returned, "and you?"

"Hot," Cinnamon remarked, the back of her hand raised to wipe the sweat from her brow. "What brings you to this hell's kitchen?"

Unable to mask her amusement at the woman's choice of words, Victoria interlaced her fingers behind her and rocked to and fro on her heels, studying the gentle sway of her hemline. Cinnamon Cockrin had lived on Raven Oaks since she was nine years old. She had come to America as an indentured servant to Victoria's father, but once her time had been served she had elected to stay on and function as the manor's cook after Bessy, the former kitchen maid, had died. No one had had to tell Victoria of the friendship between her mother and this woman, it shone clearly in their words and treatment of the other. From birth, Victoria had been cuddled and pampered by Cinnamon, and Victoria loved her as the aunt she never had.

"I became bored in my room, and trying to read in this heat is impossible."

"Trying to do anything in this heat is impossible," Cinnamon agreed, wiping the flour from her hands on the edge of her apron. "Why I always curse the cold drafts of winter in this room, I'll never know. Think this damned old crone will ever be satisfied?"

"You're not an old crone," Victoria argued.

Cinnamon's dark eyes sparkled disagreement. "Take a better look, my little one," she bade, sweeping her ample frame with outstretched hands. "You see here the product of too many years sampling food. Your mother doesn't look like me and she has two more years."

Victoria laughed lovingly at her. "But you're still beautiful, Cimmon," she quibbled, using the pet name she had used as a child of five. "You always were."

"Ha!" Cinnamon exploded. "Even my hair betrays me, with more silver in it than red. Don't know a single man who'd look at me with loving eyes. Or lustful ones for that matter," she giggled.

Perching herself on the stool next to the long trestle table, Victoria happily watched the robust woman sprinkle more flour on its surface, adding a large ball of dough she would knead into a loaf of unbaked bread. A long while passed in silence, and Cinnamon felt instinctively the need to find out the reason for the young girl's visit. Although Victoria's gaze never wandered from the simple task being performed before her, Cinnamon knew the girl's thoughts were far away.

"Well, do I have to pull it from you, or will you tell me on your own?"

Victoria blinked twice and looked up. "What?"

"The real reason you find yourself in this unworthy place," Cinnamon answered boldly, still working. "From your behavior, I would guess you seek a friend. Perhaps someone with whom you may share a secret that cannot be told to a mother. Am I right?"

A laugh more like a sigh escaped Victoria. "Yes," she replied, marveling at the woman's ability to feel her stress. "How did you know?"

Cinnamon shook her head scoffingly. "If you thought I was stupid enough not to guess that much, you wouldn't have come. Now what is it?"

Leaving the stool, Victoria strolled to the window. Resting a shoulder to the coolness of the stone wall, her elbow supported by the sill, she gazed outside, unable to look at Cinnamon. "I'm in trouble," she said quietly and rather matter-of-factly.

"So I heard."

Victoria's head snapped around.

"Your mother told me everything," Cinnamon said curtly. "Does this mean you're with child?"

Victoria shook her head vigorously. "No. I mean, I'm not sure yet, but that's not the problem."

"It's not?" Cinnamon asked sarcastically. "It should be. It's a rather big problem, if you ask me."

"All right, yes, it is. But it's not the *only* problem." She studied the sprinkling of clouds again.

"So tell me about him."

Slowly Victoria turned to face the woman, finding that Cinnamon had sat down on the stool, her hands folded in her lap, her gaze glued to her. "Him?" Victoria questioned apprehensively.

"The pirate. The one who's in prison because of you."

Suddenly a knot formed in Victoria's throat. She looked to her hands and nervously fiddled with one thumbnail. "He's there of his own doing."

A soft laughter stung Victoria's ears.

"Well, he is."

"Oh, most assuredly," Cinnamon agreed with a raised brow. When the young woman failed to respond,

Cinnamon sighed, her unsympathetic mood changing. "Victoria, you know you can trust me, and everyone talks of how ill you look. It's not a disease herbs can cure, it comes from your heart. Tell me about it, and maybe I can help."

"I don't know where to start," Victoria half-sobbed.

"Tell me the truth of what happened between you and the pirate. I've heard and seen a lot in my day, so nothing you can say will singe my ears. Tell every detail and don't lie to make yourself feel better. I suspect your need to look righteous has caused the shadow beneath your eyes."

Once Victoria set to telling the story, her words flowed easily and truly, and not once did Cinnamon stop her or blink an eye accusingly. When Victoria had finished, she sat down in the ladderback chair in one corner of the room to wait, her gaze pinned to the woman she called a friend.

"So, because you told your father that the pirate raped you many times, he is driven to see you wed quickly lest the babe be born before the vows. And since you love the pirate—"

"Wait!" Victoria shouted, leaping from the chair, "I never said I loved Dru."

Cinnamon cocked her head to one side, her face glistening with perspiration. "You didn't have to," she scorned. "I saw it in your eyes when you spoke of him. Now sit down and let me finish."

Mutely, Victoria obeyed.

"Since you love the pirate, you do not wish to marry another. But greater still, you fear he will be hanged, and you know no way to save him unless you tell your father the truth." Cinnamon shook her head in disgust.

"A lovely mess you've gotten yourself into. Not to mention the fact you can't even warn your father of the bitch Melissa's plans. O-o-oh, how I hate that woman!" Angrily, Cinnamon slapped the palm of her hand against the table top, billowing white puffs of flour everywhere. Rising to her feet, she idly paced the room. "It will take some time to figure out what to do, child. But I'm afraid if you told your father now about Melissa Bensen, he would wonder why you waited so long. Well, maybe I can figure out another way."

"But what about Mr. Rutledge?"

Cinnamon stopped her pacing to stare at the wide, tear-filled eyes. "I'm afraid you'll not be able to do anything about him, Victoria, but allow him to court you. Nor can you free the captain unless you decide to stand up to your punishment and tell your father the truth."

Her lower lip quivered. "I can't, Cinnamon."

"Then I can't help you, either," Cinnamon whispered. "Sometimes I think we spoiled you."

Moonlight trickled into the room and fell softly on the floor, spreading outward to trail across the wide four-posted bed and the tiny figure lying there, arms folded behind her head as she stared at the ceiling above her. The hall clock had struck twelve some time ago, but sleep failed to overtake Victoria, leaving her wakeful and troubled. The image of a handsome pirate plagued her thoughts, his gray-blue eyes, flashing white smile, and dark hair. Frustrated, her mouth twisted into an unflattering snarl, wishing somehow she could chase away the illusion. She rolled to her side and glared at the wall, bolting upright in bed when she saw the shadows, silver and black, in vertical strips, her silhouette caught in the middle as if her own ambivalence had trapped her in its prison. *But I do hate him,* she moaned inwardly, collapsing on the mattress again. *He tricked me, played me for a fool. I can't love him!* Tears pooled in the corners of her eyes. And he certainly didn't love her. Did he? Could he? "No-o-o," she cried aloud. Not now. Not after what she'd done to him.

She squeezed her eyes shut, her tears stealing between her lashes, and she hurriedly wiped them away with shaky fingertips. A ragged breath escaped her, and she turned her head to look at the moonlight streaming in through the partially drawn draperies. *A night made for love,* she mused sarcastically. Her lip trembled.

"Oh, Dru, I'm so sorry."

The light in the warehouse fell to darkness with the signal. Its door creaked opened and the tall, cloaked figure stepped inside. Several moments passed and neither man spoke, waiting for the silence surrounding them to ease their nerves. Finally the stranger reached into his pocket and pulled out a piece of paper.

"You'll see this to the right hands, as before?" he asked.

"Yes, colonel."

"Have you any news?"

"Only that General Washington and his men camp near New York. They lack in number to afford an attack against the British army."

"Hmm," the colonel replied, stroking his chin with long, lean fingers. "I had thought as much."

"How goes it with you? Have you any news?" the

sergeant pressed.

"I'm much closer. They trust me completely and I don't think it will be long before I'm asked to join them. Then I will learn what they plan and be able to aid in the cause. Does anyone grow suspicious of you?"

"No, colonel. I do my job and speak little to anyone."

"Good," the other nodded, turning for the door. "I must go now. I'll return in one week. Be careful, sergeant."

"Yes, sir."

The click of the doorlatch echoed in the night.

SEVENTEEN

The *Defiance* with its crew sailed into port brandishing no illeffects from the battle in which it had engaged ten days prior. Only one cannonball had posed a threat when it tore through the top mainsail, missing the mast by inches. But even that laid lie to the deed, as the canvas had been repaired and hoisted before the shore of Barbados had come into view. They had sailed away by the captain's orders, but abandoning him in the arms of the man who wished him harm left a bitter taste in Sean's mouth. He had slept little on their journey back, spending the greatest amount of hours pacing the quarterdeck, hurling orders in short temper to waste no time in find their friend John McGuire, and praying to the Maker that each dawn would be clear and boast a hearty breeze.

Michael O'Brien, a stocky man ten years Sean's senior, took the brunt of the abuse in stride. He had sailed a good number of years with the cousins and knew no stronger kinship than theirs. He, too, sought swiftness in their venture, for the times Captain Chandler had saved his worthless hide had grown in number more than he could count. He owed the man and would do anything to help insure his safety once more.

"Michael!" Sean barked. "Be makin' ready a longboat. You and I are goin' ashore." He stood at the helm overseeing the crew drop anchor, the sails flapping loose as the ship swung around to rest against her chains in the steady undertow. "Cassidy!"

A hulk of a man, his head shaved clean, gold earring dangling from one ear, suddenly appeared before him. "Aye, sir."

"I be leavin' ya in charge. See the ship's supplies are filled and be wastin' no time. As soon as I be findin' McGuire, we'll set sail."

"Aye, sir," the man replied, hurriedly stepping aside to allow Sean to pass.

While Michael O'Brien strained against the pull of the oars, Sean scanned the gathering of ships anchored around them. "Can ya be spottin' McGuire's vessel, lad?" he asked. "I pray to all that's holy it isn't that one." His worried gaze fell upon a frigate, her sails full, her speed sure as it effortlessly glided out to open waters. If only the lass hadn't broken the spyglass, he could tell in a moment whose flag it flew.

"Over there, sir," Michael instructed with a nod of his head toward a lone ship held secure several hundred yards away, not once breaking stride in his steady, brisk rowing.

"Good. Then I be knowin' right where ta find him."

Although the hour neared one past midnight, the

hearty guffaws mixed heavily with muffled oaths, and songs sung slightly off key floated out from the pub to greet Sean and Michael O'Brien. This unkempt, scurvy hole nearly always enticed John McGuire, a fact Sean had never understood but silently thanked at this moment for easing his search.

The dense, smoke-filled room veiled its occupants in a gray curtain, faceless voices looming out to cloud Sean's mind. Would McGuire be here or in one of the back rooms as was his custom? Sean and Michael stepped further inside, both pair of eyes hurriedly scanning the group of sailors for the one they searched.

"Mister Rafferty," a voice called from within the mass. "Over here."

A hand raised high above the bobbing heads waved the direction to the one who beckoned. Elbowing through the crowd, Sean and Michael approached a segregated few engaged in a friendly game of arm wrestling.

"Didn't expect ya back so soon," Owen Kelly smiled.

"We weren't plannin' on it," Sean informed the *Shamrock's* first mate. 'Where's John?''

"The capt'n? Oh, he's back there," Owen nodded over his shoulder, a wide, sententious grin wrinkling the corners of his eyes.

Sean took a step forward, intent to talk with McGuire.

"I wouldn't, if I were you," Owen warned. "He told me he wasn't ta be disturbed. No matter what."

"Well, you're not me, Owen. And I'm sure John will be forgivin' me once I tell him why."

The playful gleam disappeared from Owen's eyes.

"What's happened?" he asked, sensing the man's urgency to speak with his captain.

"Michael can be tellin' ya. And ta save yourself time," Sean added, "I be suggestin' ya round up the crew. You'll be settin' sail 'fore sunrise."

Formalities forgotten, Sean grasped the doorlatch and swung the portal wide, his unannounced presence bringing a string of vile oaths from the man lying naked in the bed.

Incentive fleeing for the moment, Sean relaxed against the door frame, a smile on his lips as he watched the bare bottom of his friend roll from his companion in the bed. A long muscular arm covered with the same reddish brown hair that lay in a thick unruly mass on McGuire's head reached out to seize his pistol from the crude bedside table, not once bothering to gaze upon the intruder. The cocking of the pistol's hammer echoed threateningly long before John's unshod feet touched the floor. He stood, legs apart, pistol raised high, his muscles gleaming with perspiration from his lovemaking, and Sean could not contain the chuckle that erupted from within him.

"Now I be knowin' why the lasses wait their turn at ya," Sean chaffed, his arms folded over his broad chest. "But must ya be paradin' around like that ta shame the rest of us unfortunate others?"

"Ya crazy fool. I could have killed ya!"

"Aye, but it would have been worth seein' ya like ya are," Sean added, laughter straining his words.

Feeling the near fatality of a well-intended prank, John's will to see the humor of it failed to surface. He slowly released the pistol's hammer, returned the weapon to the table, and glared angrily at his friend.

"Well, if ya be that interested, next time ask before poppin' in like that—if ya be the sort ta enjoy watchin'." He noticed how Sean's attention had drifted from him to rest on the wide-eyed young woman huddled beneath the thin, graying sheet. His scowl deepened. "I sincerely doubt the lad is here ta watch, lass, and whatever is so damned important that he risk his fool life, it be a matter we discuss in private. Get yourself dressed and get out!"

Startled by the sudden outburst, the young woman quickly scampered from the bed, acutely aware of how she held the other man's attention. Not the sort to let a good prospect slip through her fingers, and ignoring the possibility she might enrage the first by her actions, she casually lifted a thin robe from the back of a nearby chair, cast Sean a coquettish glance over her shoulder, and slowly covered herself, pulling the sash only slightly to allow full view of the valley between her ample breasts. She smiled seductively to Sean and strolled from the room, pausing just outside the door to bestow upon the man a flutter of lashes before she disappeared from view.

"Contrary ta what I offered, I truly don't enjoy exposin' meself ta others," John growled. "Will ya close the door?"

Quick to favor his request, Sean sealed in their privacy after stealing one quick peek at the shapely figure walking down the hallway, and crossed to the only window of the room to gaze outside and allow his friend the time to dress.

"We've trouble, John," he sighed forlornly.

"What kind? And where's Dru?"

"He's the reason I'm here."

299

Shoes in place, John lifted his shirt from the foot of the bed and stretched into the broadcloth sleeves. "Remington," he hissed.

"Aye. He played us well and won. He's got Dru and Donovan and killed the rest who went along. I be here askin' for your help."

"No need ta ask, Sean. Just be givin' me a moment ta tell Owen—"

"I already have. I figured ya wouldn't turn me down."

"Then we be sailin' within the hour. Have ya any idea where ta look for them?"

Rubbing the muscles in his neck with one hand, the other resting on the butt of his pistol stuck in the sash of his breeches, Sean looked back at McGuire and shook his head. "Not really. But I suppose a gentleman as fine as Mr. Remington wouldn't have the likes of pirates in his house. They probably took Dru and Donovan to prison. I only hope we arrive before they hang them."

"Aye. And we will. Have faith, me boy."

Sean smiled weakly, wondering if faith would be enough.

Stepping out into the night, Sean and McGuire headed toward the beach, a silent agreement to make haste understood between them. But once they reached the sandy shore looking out upon their ships, John nudged his companion's ribs.

"See that one over there, lad?" he asked, pointing to a frigate set apart from the rest. "It belongs ta Gallagher."

"Ya mean he's here? On the island? Ya've seen him?"

300

"Aye, to all your questions. He's a bad sort ta be havin' at your back, so I kept me eye on him."

"How long has he been anchored?"

"Only since sunset. And the funny thing is he never left his ship until an hour ago. After he met with a lass."

Sean turned to face McGuire, grasping the crook of the man's arm in his hands. "What did she look like?"

John frowned. "Couldn't be sayin' for sure. She wore a hooded cape down over her head. But I did catch a glimpse of yellow hair. Why ya be askin'?"

"Ahhh, damn," Sean moaned, letting go of McGuire as he slapped a fist to the palm of one hand. "Did ya watch where she went?"

"No. I saw no need. Why would ya be carin'? And who was she, anyway?"

"Melissa Bensen," Sean hissed, glancing back toward the group of buildings on the dimly lit street. "How long before you're ready ta sail?"

"One hour—at best. But—"

"That will be givin' me enough time," Sean muttered.

"Time for wh—"

Clasping John's shoulder and ignoring the man's questions, Sean begged, "See Michael has me ship ready. If I'm not back before ya weigh anchor, sail without me."

"And what will I be tellin' your cousin when we show up without ya?" John asked irately, one fist perched on his hip as he watched his partner turn to leave.

"That I be makin' even a score," Sean called, the distance between them growing wider.

"With who?" John pealed.

"Melissa Bensen." Sean's figure blended into the shadows of the trees several yards away, only the lone movement of his brisk walk marking his whereabouts.

"Well, ya will be needin' a hell of a lot of luck!"

Only the gentle slapping of the sea rolling into shore cursed the stillness for a while until the apprehensive tones of Sean's voice loomed out to greet John. "Why?"

"Because Owen told me the lass who met with Gallagher sailed with her crew shortly after she met with him."

"What?" Sean roared, stepping out from the cover of foliage.

"She's gone, me boy. Weighed anchor, set sail, drifted off," John's voice grew in volume and irritation. "I fail ta see the urgent need ta find her anyway."

"Because she sails for New York!"

"So?"

"So? I wanted to stop her!"

A heavy sigh trailed from John's lips. "Ya be makin' about as much sense as me little sister, Sean," he said, turning in the direction of his ship.

"She's goin' there ta spy!"

"I be knowin' that."

Instantly Sean's frustration vanished and he hurriedly walked to catch up with his companion, grasping the crook of his arm to spin him about. "How?"

"The day ya set sail for Virginia, Dru gave me a message ta give ta a friend of mine sailin' ta New York. The message told of the lass's plans. She'll be arrested the minute she sets foot in New York."

His shoulders slumping, Sean tilted his head backwards to gaze up at the blackness above them. "Why didn't ya say so before?"

"Do ya think me mother is a witch, Sean Rafferty? How was I ta know what ya be thinkin'?"

"Well, ya could of said somethin'!"

"How? Ya wouldn't give me a chance ta draw a breath, much less say a word. And why would ya be so hell-bent ta even the score? It's the colonists who stand ta lose, not you."

"Ya see this?" Sean asked heatedly, pointing to the scar beneath his eye. "Her men did it. They nearly killed me."

"Then ya should be payin' them back."

"They were lookin' for the Remington lass at Melissa Bensen's order. They didn't care who stood in the way. She's been an enemy of the Remingtons for years, and since Dru loves Victoria, I be thinkin' ta do us both a favor."

John straightened in surprise. "Our Dru is in love with the lass?"

Knowing his carelessness had let slip a secret his cousin wished to share with no one else, Sean anxiously glanced about them, holding his voice to a whisper. "Aye. But ya must promise not ta be tellin' a soul."

"Does the lass know?"

Sean shook his head.

"Does she share the feelin'?"

"How would I be knowin' that? And what difference would it be makin', anyway?"

"Because if she does, she'll be the only thing that might postpone Dru's hangin' should we be findin' unfavorable winds, me boy," John said, reaching out to envelop Sean in his hold. "And I be suggestin' we set a

303

fire under our crews. I be knowin' Dru's charm could sweeten the sourest of lasses, but for some reason I be worryin' he failed this time."

They walked several steps in silence before Sean half whispered, "Thank ya, me friend, for your help. I couldn't be doin' it without ya."

"No need, ya scurvy beggar," John bantered, easing the other's mood. "I would have done it without your permission."

With John's arm already circling Sean's neck, the pirate gave him a squeeze, bringing a choked laughter from his fair-haired friend as they hastily set off for their ships.

EIGHTEEN

Bright lavender flowers delicately rested in the wicker basket Victoria slipped over her arm as she strolled about the gardens in back of the manor. Nearly a week had ground its way by since her conversation with Cinnamon, and Victoria had still to find any peace. Her days and nights were haunted by visions of Dru clamped in shackles, his face bloody and a curse upon his lips. She had done him an injustice and until she made right the disservice brought against him, her every hour would be a burden to her.

Two days past she had decided to avoid the mirror of her dressing table when its reflection heralded unrest in the dark, sultry eyes staring back at her. The color of her cheeks had faded and her gowns hung loosely about her. When her father looked at her suspiciously, she had assured him of no ill health but said she was exhausted from the stifling heat. Only slightly appeased, he had muttered to himself and walked away, leaving with her the worry she could not avoid Damon Rutledge much longer.

Deciding to use the ferns that grew near the front steps of the house to accent her bouquet, Victoria lazily walked in that direction, stopping short when she spied an unfamiliar horse tethered to the brass ring of the hitching post. Curiosity quickened her step when she heard the deep, rich tones of her father's voice drifting out from the open study window, thinking their visitor might be with him. She paused just below it to rearrange the flowers in her basket, something that only a few minutes before she had not thought necessary.

"I've heard the magistrate will be in Williamsburg next week," the visitor stated placidly.

"It truly matters little to me. Either rot in jail or march to the gallows, just as long as he pays for what he's done," Beau's voice roared angrily.

The basket of flowers forgotten on the front steps, Victoria moved to the veranda and stood beside the window, body pressed against the wall to dispel any chance of being seen. The odor of a cheroot floated out to greet her. Who was her father talking to?

"I'm afraid, sir, that if the trial isn't heard soon, there'll be no need."

"What do you mean?"

Victoria heard the dull clicks of leather heels against the wooden floor as someone moved toward the window. She embraced the whitewashed lumber of the house, hands and fingers fanned out. She sucked in a breath and prayed the pounding of her heart wouldn't give her away.

"I mean, sir, that your dislike for the pirate is shared

306

among the townsfolk. From what I've heard, he receives only bread for his belly and water to quench his thirst."

"It's enough to see him through. What more can he need?" Beau growled.

"Some say he needs the herbs and tending of a doctor. Apparently, the jailer finds sport in burning the man's flesh with a hot poker. Of course, I have not seen the captain, but I'm told he does not fare well."

Squeezing muscles in her throat reduced Victoria's breathing. Her eyes flooded with tears. *Dear God, what have I done?* she appealed, her lips moving in silence.

"Are you pleading his case, Damon?" Beau hissed.

A moment of silence passed as the man near the window moved away.

"You misjudge my words, sir," Damon corrected, a lightness to his tone. "I seek to court your daughter and want as much as you to see the man pay for the abuse he has brought down on her."

Beau studied the dark features of the man's face, his own scowl lessening. Snuffing out his cheroot in the ashtray on his desk, he sighed, reaching for the brandy decanter next to it. "Sure you wouldn't care for a drink?" he asked, watching the vague smile dart across Damon's face with a shake of his head. He poured his own, drank it completely in one swallow, and forced a smile to his lips. "I apologize for my—rudeness, young man. But I've had to sit by helplessly watching my daughter's health continually worsen. We never talk of what happened, but I suspect it lives with her every hour. She doesn't eat, sleeps very little, if at all, and wanders around in a flutter. You can understand why every day that passes and the reason for her distress still goes unpunished would tend to set my nerves and good humor on edge. I love her dearly and would do anything to protect her." His frown returned and he strode to the window to look out. "I'm tempted to kill the man myself."

"I'm sure no one would blame you, if you did," Damon said quietly, his own compassion for Beau Remington shining in his dark eyes. The idea of having a father-in-law like this one sat well with him.

A low chuckle escaped the elder of the two as he reached up to pull the lace curtain away to better view the yard. "Yes, I'm sure they wouldn't. In fact I imagine I'd have plenty of help finding a rope." His eyes caught sight of the wicker basket sitting on the steps a few feet away. He bent down and leaned out the window.

"Is something wrong?"

Only the white rocker moved slowly in the gentle breeze kissing the veranda and Beau wondered at his own state of mind. "No," he answered softly, then pulled back to face his guest. "Since we've already discussed business, why not enjoy the company of two very beautiful women? I'll walk you to the parlor and find Alanna and my daughter."

"It would be an honor, sir," Damon smiled, allowing Beau to rest an arm across his shoulders and gently guide them from the room.

"Cinnamon! Cinnamon!" Victoria shouted, bursting into the kitchen.

Startled by the noisy and somewhat unrefined entry of the young girl, the buxom maid straightened sharply, knocking the large clay bowl from the table. It

308

crashed to the floor and shattered into a thousand pieces, its unnecessary destruction causing the woman's temper to flare.

"Victoria Remington! I'm not so old I cannot hear a whisper. Kindly control yourself." She glared hotly at her for a moment, then stooped to collect the brightly colored hand-painted chips lying everywhere.

"I'm sorry, Cimmon, but this *is* important," Victoria whined, bending down to retrieve several fragments that had scooted across the floor to her feet. "It's about Dru."

"Have you told your father?"

Victoria stopped her gatherings. "Why—no."

"Then it's not that important. Honestly, Victoria, sometimes I doubt you'll ever grow up."

Victoria's brows drew together. "I have," she scoffed, feeling the bite of the older woman's upbraiding.

"Oh, really?" Cinnamon retorted, standing erect, her hands full of testimony to the contrary. "Then why didn't you tell your father the truth at the very first? You still play at letting others take the blame for your foolishness."

"I do not!" Victoria shrieked.

One corner of Cinnamon's mouth puckered. "Do you think everyone over a score is stupid? Even I saw past your tomfoolery." Turning her back on Victoria, she went to the hearth, where she tossed the broken bowl into a tin bucket. "Your grandfather wasn't the only one."

Victoria's shoulders drooped. "All right, I used to once in a while—"

The fair face sprinkled with freckles cast her a dis-

309

dainful look.

"All right, all right!" Victoria exploded, "but I'm not here to discuss my faults." Crossing to the hearth, she added her contribution to the bucket. "I've come to ask your help. I overheard Mr. Rutledge—"

"Pooph," Cinnamon declared, "anything that man has to say doesn't interest me." She returned to the table and set about stirring the cake batter in short, angry swirls.

The heat of their argument cooled by curiosity, Victoria followed Cinnamon to her work place, dipping a pointed finger into the creamy yellow mixture, and received a crack to her knuckles with a wooden spoon. She retreated a step, a painted smile to her lips, and recalled how many times such a venture had been rewarded with the same end. And the mingling of sugar, eggs, and flour still tasted good upon her tongue, no matter how much of a welt appeared on the back of her hand.

"Don't you like Mr. Rutledge?" she asked, one brow raised suspiciously.

"I don't hardly know him. I just don't trust him." Cinnamon continued stirring.

"Why?" Victoria pressed, sitting down on a stool opposite the cook.

"Because we don't know nothing about him. One day he just shows up."

"But he purchased Mathew Bensen's place. Why wouldn't he just show up? He's a neighbor."

Cinnamon's lips twisted to one side, then the other. "I don't know. I just got this feelin'—"

"Oh, you and your feelings," Victoria scolded. "How many times have you been right?"

"More than you know," Cinnamon barked. "Now tell me what it is you want or be on your way. I've enough work to do without having to clean up after you."

Bracing her thin frame on the table's edge, Victoria leaned closer. "I overheard Mr. Rutledge tell Papa that Dru isn't fed properly and the jailer abuses him."

"So what do you want me to do? Stand guard or break him out?"

"Cinnamon, I'm serious," Victoria growled.

"So am I. I can't do anything about the way he's treated in prison. Nor can you." She squinted one eye at the angry face. "Except tell your father."

Victoria's lip curled defiantly. "Oh, yes, we can. You're going to visit him."

"What?" Cinnamon exploded, the spoon clunking against the bowl. "I'm doing nothing of the sort."

"Yes, you are."

"Why?"

"Because I want you to take him food and whiskey. And bandages for his wounds." She looked away, pain reflected in the dark depths of her eyes. "I hear he suffers."

"And all because of you," Cinnamon added, casting her a condemning glare down the end of her nose.

"I know that! You don't have to keep reminding me." Tears flooded her eyes, sedating her temper as she looked beseechingly to her friend. "Please, Cimmon. I know I don't deserve it, but do it for Dru. He needs help. I'd go myself, but I'd be recognized and someone would tell my father." She raised a hand quickly when Cinnamon opened her mouth to respond. "If he's to know, at least let it be me who tells him."

311

The soft, pleading eyes that never failed to awaken the tenderness Cinnamon had in her heart for the young woman curbed the reprimand about to be articulated. She looked away with a sigh, knowing that as foolish as the child might be, she still wasn't heartless enough to turn her head and not try in some small way to ease another's suffering.

"All right," she conceded, "but if your father finds out I went there and asks me why, I'll not lie to him."

"I wouldn't ask that much," Victoria smiled happily. She scooted off the stool. "You make up a basket of food and I'll find herbs and bandages. I'll be right back."

Cinnamon stood in the doorway of the stone building watching the buoyant gait of the youngest Remington as she headed off toward the main house. Her stubbornness equaled her beauty, and Cinnamon smiled, realizing she could not have been any other way with Beau and Alanna as parents.

A dark scowl clouded the cherry-brown eyes fixed on the road ahead as Cinnamon grudgingly guided the buggy into Williamsburg. With the excuse of needing some time alone, she had left Raven Oaks unchaperoned, and had been bothered with numerous comments about the foolishness of traveling without benefit of protection. A lone woman on the roads these days invited trouble. But, unable to reveal her real reason for going, she closed her ears to their warnings, knowing in her heart they were right. Thus when the rooftops of the houses on the outskirts of the town came into view, she breathed comfortably for the first time since leaving the safety of her home.

The courthouse stood majestically in the center of town, its whitewashed face beaming out upon its subjects as a constant reminder of justice and truth. Tall, thick colonnades reached the second-story roofline, shadowing the many stately windows overlooking Williamsburg, a flood of steps spreading out to welcome all those who wished to enter. Adjacent to it on the left, and set back several score of feet, an addition had been built several yards after the construction of the main building. But, unlike the first, it lacked warmth and friendliness. It was made of stone, its windows crisscrossed with iron bars, and very few persons had the desire to inspect its interior. Those who did never sought to view it again, for here the jailer ruled and dealt out his own punishment with impunity, until the inmates had their day before the magistrate.

The buggy from Raven Oaks rattled to a stop outside the courthouse, and Cinnamon's plump figure descended hesitantly, a shawl draped over her head and shoulders. Gathering her basket from the rig, she glanced briefly around her to make certain of no familiar faces and started toward the stone building. Her corpulent figure cast little shadow, and she raised her eyes skyward, squinting when she found the sun high overhead. The worried frown disappeared. Her arrival couldn't have been at a better time. Surely the noon hour meant nearly everyone would be seated around the dining table filling their bellies, which would leave her alone to fulfill her errand without disturbance. At this moment, she feared Master Beau's anger more than the jail.

At her entry into the dark, musty smelling hallway, the jailer merely turned sleep-filled eyes her way. He sat back on a chair that rested on two legs, its back balanced on the wall behind him, and Cinnamon wondered how the fragile piece of furniture managed not to break. His obese frame, spilling over both sides, all but enveloped the chair. His beefy arms crossed against a large belly reminded Cinnamon of the two boned hams that were usually hung in the root cellar and served to feed two score of guests. But what intrigued her more was how his chin seemed to disappear into the many folds of his neck. Wishing not to tarry any longer than necessary, she swallowed her contempt for the man and his work, and took a deep breath.

"Excuse me, sir, but I've come to see—"

Before she finished her sentence, the gaoler, eyes closed, a wide yawn separating his thick lips, raised a thumb to point the way.

"Thank you," she whispered, lifting her skirts to tiptoe between the barricade he formed and the opposite wall.

Although torchlight led the way, its flickering flame did little to spread cheerfulness or chase away the dampness that seemed to cling to everything. Tales of the Tower of London had always delighted the freckle-faced child who had sat for hours listening to her father narrate them in exaggerated verse, but when his stories turned to the dungeons hidden deep in the bowels of faraway castles, Cinnamon had never quite believed such places existed. Until now. The distant clanking of chains, a moan or two, the stench of unwashed bodies and human waste made it all too real. Surely no man, young or old, could sustain life and sanity locked behind these prison walls.

Feeling light-headed from the malodorous smell that

burned her nostrils, Cinnamon pressed the hem of her shawl beneath her nose to ease the stomach-wrenching scent. A scratching to the left of her feet warned her to step lightly, and she cast her gaze upon the source, a shriek lodging in her throat when two beady black eyes glared up at her. The twitching nostrils sniffing the air had obviously detected the contents of the wicker basket, and Cinnamon clutched it tightly to her bosom, fearing the rodent would hurl itself upon her to steal a morsel. Then the befoulment of the jail filled her senses once more, and she quickly turned to find the pirate and bring an end to the nightmare of her journey.

Peering in through the narrow window covered with bars, Cinnamon found the small space behind the first of many iron doors held nothing but a straw mattress and a wooden bucket, a slimy substance reaching its rim. She swallowed hard, forcing down the bile that rose to her throat, and moved on. Another cell proved empty and another, until she came to one that housed the shadowed figure of a man crouched upon the bed, knees apart, an open hand raised to cradle his head as his elbow rested on one knee.

"Captain Chandler?" she said, her voice weak.

The man's head shot up. "What ya be wantin' with him?" he growled.

"I—I've brought something for him." Even though thick iron bars divided them, Cinnamon shuddered for fear the man could tear them apart as if they were nothing more than straw.

"Aye. A stone ta throw at him," he hissed, slowly rising to his feet.

Cinnamon stepped back. "No, sir. I've brought food."

Two hands, their knuckles bruised and bloody, reached up to encompass an iron post. "Laced with poison?" he sneered.

"No, sir," she denied, quickly lifting the edge of her shawl again.

"Then why ya be hidin' your face from me?" he asked, pressing closer. "Ya not be wantin' me ta know who ya are, just in case I be gettin' out and seek me revenge on ya."

"No, sir," she quickly offered, dropping the veil, "it's just the smell—" Disapproving eyes glanced about the hallway as the cloth slid from her coppery curls.

"Ya get used to it," the voice snarled. "Who are ya?"

"My name is not important. Only that I find Captain Chandler. I've brought bandages for his wounds." Wishing to convince the man, she hurriedly dug into the basket and withdrew clean white gauze, followed by a silver flask. "And whiskey for his pleasure."

Tilting his head to one side, the man eyed her suspiciously. "Bring it to me," he ordered, his voice low and hinting at harm should he find she lied.

Anxious to be on her way and rid her nostrils of the awful stench, she hesitated only a moment before lifting the flask to the prisoner's outstretched hand. She shrieked when his steely hold encircled her wrist.

"Just makin' sure I can reach ya if I be findin' vinegar in this instead of what ya claim," he grinned dangerously. With his other hand he procured the bottle, pulled the cork with his teeth and spit it to the ground. "To your health," he mocked, lifting the flask in a short salute and gingerly testing its contents. Satisfied it

316

contained nothing but whiskey he raised it high and took a long swallow.

"Correct me if I be wrong, McKenzie, but I thought I heard the lass say the whiskey belonged ta me."

The sudden voice from behind her jerked Cinnamon free of the prisoner's hold as she spun around to discover another inmate smiling out from between the bars of a cell opposite her.

"Aye, that she did, capt'n. I only wanted ta be sure she wasn't playing games, 'twas all."

"Ya knew that with the first drop. Seems ta me your greed got the better of ya."

Cinnamon stood in wide-eyed fear of the two men as they bantered back and forth, the single torch in this section of the hallway dancing across the square opening of the captain's cell door. There was no mistaking this man was Victoria's pirate, for although a heavy growth of dark beard covered his face, and his equally dark hair was in dire need of trimming and brushing, the steel-blueness of his eyes sparked recognition in her mind. Absently, she stepped closer to get a better view. His right cheek just above the beard showed a fresh scar, still healing and bright red as infection hampered the process. His other cheek sported a dark bruise that spread upward to include his eye. And when he spoke, his gaze betrayed the pain he felt inside. Her speculation was that he suffered more from other wounds not possible for her to view.

"Captain Chandler?" she ventured.

A soft smile greeted her and she watched as he stepped back and made a low, sweeping bow. However, he was slow to rise. "At your service, lass," he replied, his hand pressed to the ribs beneath his left arm.

"And who might ya be?"

Glancing back at McKenzie, his face pressed between the bars, it grew humorously obvious how wrong she had been to mistake him for the captain. She guessed them to be nearly the same age, but instead of thick black hair, McKenzie's shiny bald head reflected the dim light of the jail. She turned back.

"It doesn't matter. And I can't be staying any longer. Here—" She began to pull various cloth-covered items from the basket, handing him one at a time between the bars. "Food. And bandages for your cuts," she added, passing another.

"Who sent ya?"

Cinnamon stopped the transfer of gifts. "I've been instructed to keep it a secret. I was simply told to see these things to you, inquire about your health and go. Now do you want the food or not?"

A low rumble of scornful laughter echoed in the cavity of stone. "Me health?" he asked, the amusement gone from his voice. "Step closer, lass, and see for yourself."

Leery of doing as requested, Cinnamon glanced briefly at McKenzie and back to the square opening in the door, surprised to find that the captain had stepped away. Drawing a small measure of courage from this, since she felt certain no harm would come to her when iron bars separated them, she allowed her curiosity to guide her steps. She moved closer and peered into the cell.

A single stream of gray light shot into the space from a small opening in the stone wall, too narrow for anyone to crawl through and too high to reach, should one be inclined to try. The man purposely stood in the stream of light. What had once been a linen shirt hung in tattered shreds from his broad shoulders, shoulders marred by ugly red welts obviously inflicted by the end of a whip. The dark hair across his chest lay matted with dried blood. Cinnamon could feel her stomach churn. His torn breeches barely covered his lean, lank hip, and the scarlet wound on his thigh indicated that a hot iron had indeed been pressed against his flesh. Cinnamon cringed, imagining the pain accompanying such torture and the horrible smell that surely rose in the air.

"I know you suffer, sir," she whispered, tears burning her eyes. "And I will try my damnedest to see it stops." Tossing the remainder of bandages and herbs between the narrow metal shafts, Cinnamon turned and fled the scene.

"I be thinkin' she don't like our humble dwellin's, Donovan, me boy," Dru grinned, pressing a cheek to the cold bars in an effort to catch a glimpse of the woman.

"She's not the only one," McKenzie added with a wrinkle to his nose. "Who ya be supposin' she is?"

Through the thick mass of beard, the deepening of Dru's dimple went unnoticed. "Like she said—who she might be isn't important. Who sent her is."

"Aye," Donovan agreed, "but for the life of me, I can't be figurin' out who that is."

"Oh, I think I can," Dru hummed.

McKenzie straightened sharply, his hands clamped around the thin poles in the opening to the portal of his cell. "Not Miss Victoria!"

"Aye." Dru grinned, his attention still centered on the vacant hallway as if clinging to the shred of life that

319

had come from outside the confines of the jail. Two long, pain-filled weeks had laboriously exhausted themselves since Dru and his companion had been taken prisoner and sentenced to the small stone cells. Days passed like nights, dark and chilly, since no window graced their cubicles except the narrow gaps in the wall where some other forgotten fool had sought to free himself and had chipped away uselessly at the rock, an act of desparation, for many others had tried and failed. For Dru, the simple task of pushing himself up on the straw mattress of his bed proved enough of a feat. The ride into town in the back of the wagon had proven difficult enough for him when his head throbbed from the blow he had received while being taken prisoner, as well as the bruise on his side where the captain's shoe had found its mark. But that had only been the beginning. It seemed the rotund jailkeeper enjoyed the sport of beating a bound man into unconsciousness, and Dru had spent the first day lying on his bunk drifting in and out of sleep.

Although the pain had been unbearable at times, since the jailer continued the abuse, Dru's thoughts had always managed to focus on the raven-haired beauty of his dreams and the promise of seeing her one more time before he set sail for friendlier shores. Standing by his cell door now, straining to see the ample figure with reddish hair on the chance she had lingered, he pleasantly realized Victoria cared more about him than he had begun to think. He doubted she could ever love him, but at least she had proven to have a compassionate side. He chuckled. If only to ease her conscience.

"Ah, Victoria," he whispered, "I wish I could be gettin' me hands on ya." His smile faded, replaced by a longing in his tired eyes, for although he meant to ring her pretty neck, the thoughts of holding her in his arms overruled the need for revenge. Clasping his injured side, he walked the short distance to his bunk and lay down. Staring up at the ceiling overhead, he concentrated on things far lovelier than the stench of his present domain, transposing the dark shadows to a flowing ebony mane and hauntingly beautiful eyes. Recalling the tenderness of their kisses, he envisioned her parted lips, the sweet scent of her, the silken strands of her hair encasing them both, his blood pounding through his veins. He closed his eyes. What torture! To have known such rapture of the soul, only to be denied when he needed it most.

NINETEEN

"Victoria, would you care to join us?"

Startled by the sound of her name, Victoria glanced up at the somewhat irked scowl on her father's face.

"For a glass of wine in the parlor," he directed, noting the confused look she gave him.

The color in her cheeks heightening, she glanced briefly at her mother and Damon who stood in the doorway of the dining room, then quickly found her feet. "Yes, Papa," she muttered, falling into step with the others.

She knew she had paid little attention to the conversation around the dinner table, and, with Damon's presence, she felt certain her actions had been misread by her father. She didn't truly find Mr. Rutledge uninteresting, there were simply other matters more pressing than idle talk. Cinnamon had returned to the plantation earlier in the afternoon, sick at heart with what she had witnessed in the jail. She had spared Victoria no small degree of berating on the subject, and, in fact, had threatened to seek out the master of Raven Oaks if Victoria didn't pledge to see the captain freed of his agony. Having promised to do so, Victoria had fled the irate cook for the safety of her bedchamber, where she could gather her wits and calm the churning in her stomach. But with each tick of the mantel clock above the fireplace, its rhythmic peal had grown louder, driving her from the privacy of her room to seek out anyone who might help divert her thoughts.

She had gone to the study, hoping to share a light-hearted moment with her father, as had been their custom before Victoria had left for Paris, but had instead intruded upon the business meeting he was having with Damon Rutledge. Since she had barged right in without the courtesy of knocking, a situation from which she could not simply disappear, she had forced a smile to her lips and had graciously accepted their guest's compliments on how lovely she looked. A few more words had passed, enough, Victoria had decided, to satisfy politeness, before she had turned to leave, stopped by Remington's instructions to see an extra place set at the dinner table. Damon Rutledge would be joining them.

At first Victoria had cursed having to take dinner in the dining room, especially with company, but she had later decided it might help busy her thoughts away from Dru, a subject she would rather ponder later. But no sooner had they all been seated at the long, lavishly decorated table than her mind began to wander to a meal taken somewhere else, a meager sampling of bread and water.

I must thank you, Mistress Remington, for such a ...ious meal," Damon said as he guided Alanna to ...f the high-back chairs before the fireplace, his ... ...humping against the carpet. "I'm afraid it's been ... while since I ate so well."

I know of someone else who has more right to complain, Victoria thought, a one-sided smile wrinkling her cheek as she half-heartedly acknowledged Damon's compliment when his eyes met hers. She sat down in the chair next to her mother's, hearing a loud crack of thunder dissipate into nothingness. She glanced up at the window to see the disfigured droplets of rain trickle down the glass in zigzag patterns.

"I'll be sure to tell our cook," Alanna nodded, accepting a goblet of wine from her husband. Settling more comfortably in the chair, she waited until the others were served, then continued. "So, how do you like living in Virginia, Mr. Rutledge?"

"Please," Damon interrupted, "Mr. Rutledge sounds so formal. Call me Damon."

"All right, Damon," Alanna smiled warmly. "Do you miss Pennsylvania?"

Looking at the goblet in his hand, he said, "I did at first. I guess maybe because I didn't know anyone here. But now I find it much to my liking." His dark brown eyes glanced up at Victoria, and she squirmed beneath his regard. She took a sip of wine.

"Beau tells me you owned a plantation there."

"That's correct, between Chester and Philadelphia. I still would if the British hadn't decided they needed it," he added, the tone of his words spiced with bitterness.

"What do you mean?"

He limped toward the fireplace, resting the richly polished boot of his good leg to the marble slab as he leaned heavily against the walking stick. "The British had to have a battle headquarters to work from during their attack on the colonists at Philadelphia. And since my plantation seemed to have the best vantage point, they moved in and told me to leave."

Victoria noticed how the muscle in Damon's cheek flexed several times before he took a long swallow of wine, then studied the goblet in his hand without a word. An angry scowl puckered his brow, and it appeared as if he had forgotten their presence while he drifted away in thought, allowing Victoria a moment to consider him. It seemed, now that she thought about it, that Damon Rutledge never wore any color other than black. Black waistcoat, ascot, jacket, breeches, and shoes. Maybe that was what disturbed her about the man. His very manner of dress lacked daring or change, as if he might be content to do whatever anyone else considered normal or practical. He even admitted he had easily given up his home when told to do so, rather than fighting for it. Of course, how could a cripple— She blinked suddenly, mentally scolding herself for condemning the man because of his lameness. She looked away. She knew of another who would fight no matter what the odds, she half argued with herself. Hadn't Dru been outnumbered when her father's army chased him down? Hadn't he continued to struggle even after his longboat had been cut in half and its small crew killed? They had bound his arms in back of him and thrown him to the sand, but the fire in his eyes affirmed even then that his spirit was far from broken. She smiled secretively. Hadn't he laughed at something her father had said, knowing it might possibly award him another blow to his temple? He was no coward! Her eyes darkened when she recalled the bruises and cuts on his handsome face, an image that sent a sharp pain through her heart. If she had told her father how Dru had protected her— Her mind wandered off to the times she had lain enveloped in his arms, his lips warm against her neck, his hand caressing her breast. She remembered the shivers she had experienced watching him undress, the rock-hard muscles of his back and shoulders, his flat belly and well-shaped thighs. She had even discovered a strange attraction, tingling as she observed the dark curls covering the wide expanse of his chest to trail downward to— She stiffened instantly, realizing what picture she had drawn, raising her glass to her lips in hopes no one had seen. Forcing her gaze on the man standing near the fireplace once more, she questioned his ability to spark such blazes as plagued her now. Could his kiss, his touch affect her so? Would she think of him at odd times—or simply find him lacking? She suspected it would be the latter, for no one had filled her thoughts as Dru Chandler, her Irish pirate, had.

"It's happened to others besides you, Damon," she heard her father say as he sat down on the small sofa opposite his family. "And all of us live in fear of losing what is ours should England regain control."

Damon sighed heavily. "Yes, I know. I guess that's why this whole thing upsets me more than most. I chance to lose again."

"Why didn't you stand up to them?" Victoria carelessly blurted out and received a scowling frown from her father. She chose to sip her wine again.

A soft smile played across Damon's face as his eyes drank in the beauty of the youngest Remington. "With a household of slaves who care more about eating than defending their master's home? Either way they knew they had a place to live and food to eat in return for their services."

"You mean you have no family?" Alanna asked.

"What there is of it still lives in England. Both my parents died when I was a young boy, and my aunt raised me. But I hated poverty and came to the colonies about twenty years ago." Purposely, Damon sat his wine goblet on the mantel's edge, a sad expression darkening his eyes as he rested both hands on the pearl-handled cane. "A mistake I found out too late, for with my absence my aunt could not support herself and was thrown in debtors' prison to die."

"How awful for you," Alanna said. "But you mustn't blame yourself. Had you known of it, you would have sent for her."

"Of course," Damon stated, "and that's what fuels this burning hatred I have for England. They could have sent word, but they didn't. Then they suddenly appear on my doorstep and take away everything I worked for. They destroyed the only justification I had for leaving my aunt." Reaching up for the goblet, he pressed it to his lips, threw his head back and swallowed the wine in one angry gulp. Absently spinning the stem of the glass between his thumb and forefinger, he blinked several times, as if fighting to regain control. He glanced up to find a reassuring smile on Alanna's face and his sorrow vanished. "I didn't mean to depress everyone," he smiled.

"You didn't," Remington promised him, rising

from the sofa. "May I get you more wine?"

"Yes, thank you," Damon eagerly nodded, handing Beau his glass.

Crossing to the buffet and the wine decanter, Beau threw back over his shoulder, "Alanna can sympathize better than most with you since she's from England."

"Really?" Damon grinned. "What part?"

"Liverpool. Might we have been neighbors?"

"No. I lived in Bristol. But I went to Liverpool once. Just before I sailed for the colonies. A lovely town. And as I recall, every woman I saw there was just as lovely. Only stands to reason you grew up there." He smiled brightly with a slight nod of his dark head.

"Oh," Alanna laughed, "now you carry your flattery too far."

Having given Damon a fresh drink, Remington came to stand beside his wife's chair, a hand resting on her shoulder. "But none more beautiful. Right Damon?" He smiled down at her as Alanna lovingly patted his hand.

"Mmmm, unless you'd agree to the possibility of one other."

Remington raised one brow questioningly.

"Why, Victoria, of course," he answered. "But then it's understandable, since she favors her mother."

All eyes centered on Victoria, and she felt their penetrating stares, wishing somehow she could force the attention away from her. She smiled weakly and mumbled, "Thank you."

"Of course, I've seen her looking better," Remington grumbled.

"Now, Beau," Alanna soothed. "You promised not to pick at her. She's had a rough time and needs to re-

328

cuperate."

"By locking herself away in her room? She hasn't seen anyone or gone anywhere since she returned. How can she recover if she doesn't try?" Remington inquired firmly, a hint of sarcasm raising the pitch of his voice.

Sensing the likelihood of heated words between the two, Damon quickly interrupted. "If I may be so bold as to suggest—" He waited for them to look at him. "Why not make arrangements to attend the theater in Williamsburg next week? I think we could all use a change of scenery. Perhaps spend several days."

"I think that's a wonderful idea, Beau," Alanna said, smiling across to Victoria. "Don't you, dear?"

A burning sensation seemed to crawl upward from her toes to clamp onto her stomach, tossing and turning it inside out. Anywhere near Williamsburg was the last place she wanted to be. And certainly not with Damon Rutledge. Dear Lord, there would be no escape from him. She just wasn't ready. She swallowed hard and drew in a breath to make her excuses, distracted by her father's movement toward the door.

"An excellent thought, Damon. I have business to attend to in town anyway, and the trip will be more enjoyable with company. Let me know what days would better suit you, and we'll work something out." He cast his daughter a challenging glare. "Now if the ladies will excuse us, I'd like to discuss something with you in the study, unless you have something to add, Victoria."

Feeling as if the entire world had taken sides against her, Victoria quietly resigned herself to make the best of the situation. "No, Papa," she mumbled, looking to the goblet she held in her hands, vaguely aware of the men's departure.

"May I refill your glass?" Remington asked as they entered the study.

"No, thank you. I'm fine," Damon replied, instinctively closing the door behind them. He crossed to the desk and awkwardly sat down in the chair set off to one side while his host settled in the one behind the mahogany structure. "I have a feeling this isn't about the crops we plan to harvest in the fall."

A relaxed smile made its way across Remington's face. "That's what I admire about you, Damon. You're perceptive. To be successful, you must be. And you're right. I didn't bring you here to talk about our plantations." Reaching for a cheroot from the box lying on the desktop, Remington struck a flint to it, inhaling a long breath and settling back in his chair. He quietly observed the man for a moment. "I usually don't take a man into my confidence that I've known only a short time, as I know you, but my instincts tell me I can trust you. I've watched you for several months, listened to you talk, and suspect you have the same feelings for the British as I."

"The British?" Damon barked, abruptly leaving his chair to hobble to the window where he studied the lightning dancing across the sky. He remained quiet, unmoving for several minutes. "I surprised myself a while ago, talking with your wife. I usually become more angry than I did when I'm forced to remember why I live in Virginia." He turned back to face Remington. "I apologize if I was rude."

"Rude?" Remington laughed. "You have every right to be more than rude. You not only lost your home, but your aunt because of the British." Remington leaned forward against the desk. "How would you like to get even?"

"I'd like nothing better," Damon growled, "but I'm only one man. Don't you think I've considered such a thing before? No, I'm afraid there's nothing I can do to settle the score."

"I agree one man stands little chance against an army. But hundreds of men can do something."

"Hundreds?" Damon rejoined.

"Yes, hundreds. A group of men who live in this area have joined together in an effort to aid General Washington. Since Williamsburg sits so close to Chesapeake Bay, we have stationed several men along the shoreline to watch for British ships. As often as possible we meet secretly to discuss any ideas anyone might have to help. In itself, it's small, but we figure any amount is better than nothing. In fact, I received word this morning that a meeting is scheduled for as soon as everyone can get together, and I'm asking if you'd like to come. We can use some new ideas."

"I'd be most eager," Damon said with a slight flare to his nostrils. "As you said, it may be a small part, but at least I would feel as if I tried to seek justice for my aunt's death."

"Good," Remington smiled. "Then if you can manage so quickly, we'll leave day after tomorrow."

"I'm ready now," Damon returned with an angry sigh, his gaze fixed on the knotted fist of his left hand.

TWENTY

A searing fulmination of light followed instantly by a deafening crack of thunder illuminated the sky and rocked the ships dropping anchor off the Virginia coastline. Black, inauspicious clouds promised a beating of raindrops to anyone caught unprotected, but the men on board the *Defiance* and the *Shamrock* cared little about the warnings. In silent urgency, they set to securing their ships and readying the longboats to go ashore. The cover of night had eased their arrival, and, once the landing party had disappeared into the thick covering of trees several hundred yards inland, the frigates would weigh anchor and sail southward several miles to await their return.

A group of five hid in the dense foliage offshore, watching the magestic ships skillfully glide out to sea once more, each silently praying all would go well and return them quickly to their vessels. A bolt of lightning shot across the sky, followed by the jarring vibrations of thunder that seemed to shake the ground. As if torn asunder by a sword's blade, the clouds opened up and hailed the earth and its inhabitants with immense, stinging water droplets, promptly saturating the lot of determined rescuers. Without a word, they scrambled from their retreat and headed further inland.

Noiselessly they made their way along the fencelike row of maples parallel to the riverbank. Williamsburg lay several miles further north, a distance they felt they could travel in a few hours. But with the rain beating against them, turning dry, hard footing into oozing mud, their journey took on new perils as they fought the dangers of slippery knolls that might tumble them downward into the James River and a current swift enough to carry them to the sea. They climbed higher, further into the denseness of the trees, where the rains had yet to fully soak the ground, hoping that with each bolt of lightning they could see the river to their left and know they hadn't traveled in circles. Nearly an hour passed before they paused to rest, certain the town for which they headed lay on the other side of the next hill.

The rain diminished to a drizzle, cold and irritating to all of them, as they felt the anxiety about their undertaking. But none voiced his discomfort, instead they rechecked their weapons for the hundredth time. Alone and away from the others, Sean singled out a dead tree on which to lean. Its branches barren and entangled with those surrounding it, the trunk leaned diagonal to the ground, its decaying roots torn from its covering of earth and exposed to every kind of abuse the elements might impose. Hooking the heel of his shoe in a crevice of rotted wood, he rested forward on one knee, his forearms crossed, hands dangling as he lost himself in thought.

He worried if they would arrive in time or learn that his cousin had already been hanged, the body tossed into an unmarked grave. They had no real plan, only to patronize a local inn and hopefully to learn where they were keeping Dru, if he was still alive. They were fighting not only time, but unfamiliar terrain, the chance meeting with British soldiers who might mistake them for those who spoke out against the Crown, or colonists who might wonder why sailors suddenly appeared in their town so late at night looking eager to be on their way. Sean found himself wishing it was all over, that he and Dru again stood side by side at the helm of the *Defiance,* sailing the open sea, for he truly doubted that people would not suspect the reason for their presence once they noticed the distress in his eyes.

Sailing back from Barbados, they had made good time, but, all the while not knowing Dru's fate, Sean had felt imprisoned on his own ship, and that he had failed his cousin. They had been so easily tricked by a man of whom they knew so little. A powerful man to have had the aid of so many. Would their attempt to free Dru be futile? Once there, would they find themselves outnumbered? He looked at the band of men resting quietly near him. Michael O'Brien, John McGuire, and two of John's crew. They should have brought more, he just knew it! Well, it was too late now. They would have to make the best of it. Rising abruptly from his perch, he silently motioned them to move on.

The lights of Williamsburg dotted the horizon and the rescuers hurried their step, crouching low once they moved into a clearing cut in two by a well-traveled road. They spread out, racing across the opening one at a time. In the distance the rumble of hoofbeats grew louder, and they looked urgently about to seek cover again. The last having joined the others, each found a tree or bush to hide behind as a trio of British soldiers galloped across the pathway.

Studying the shadows into which the riders and their mounts disappeared, Sean noiselessly moved to John's side. "I be thinkin' we should split up," he whispered.

"Aye. The thought crossed me mind, too," John agreed, motioning the others to move out. "But since we don't know what lies ahead, I be thinkin' we can't take the chance to be caught short-handed."

Sean's mouth opened instantly to argue the point, silenced by his companion's raised hand. Clasping the younger man's elbow, John guided them both to their feet, glanced back at the road, then hurriedly set off after the others. When reasonably certain of the distance between them and the British soldiers, he chanced his explanation.

"If we be seen, we stand a better chance with more ta do the fightin'. And I don't know about you, laddie, but I not be likin' the idea of leavin' anyone behind." He ducked beneath a low-hanging tree branch.

"Aye. I agree," Sean sighed. "It's just—"

"Say no more, me friend. We all feel the same."

"Not quite, I'm afraid."

John stopped suddenly, latching onto Sean's arm when he made to walk further. "What is it ya mean, Sean? Surely ya not blame yourself for Dru's misfortune."

Pale blue eyes, slightly moistened with tears, glanced

up at him and then away. "Aye," Sean said softly, then rushed on, leaving his friend to stare after him.

A black velvet sky cushioned the twinkling of stars overhead. The storm had passed, leaving all in its wake freshly cleansed and the weary travelers chilled to the bone. But none would stop, turn back, state defeat. They would find their comrades first.

The main road that led into town proved empty of residents. The men split into two groups; Sean, Michael, and George Arnold, a mate from the *Shamrock,* on one side of the street, John and his trusted mate, Thomas Smith, on the other. Hidden in the alley between the darkened storefronts of a haberdashery and a printer's, Sean and his men watched John and Thomas casually enter an inn opposite them. Certain a while would pass before their return, George and Michael crouched down between the barrels sitting in the alleyway to rest and wait while Sean anxiously eyed the building where his friend had gone. A gentle breeze stirred the sprinkling of leaves and paper on the ground around him, touching his damp attire. Sean clamped his teeth together to silence their rattling.

Minutes passed, a measure of time that seemed an eternity to Sean, and still no sign of the two across the street. Cupping his hands together, he blew into them for what little warmth it would give. A click of a window sash above them. Michael and George scrambled to their feet, bodies pressed against the wall at their backs. Sean drew his pistol, his breath caught in his throat. A moment of quiet, its tempo pounding in Sean's ears. He leaned out a fraction, eyes trained on the window one story higher. In the silvery glow of moonlight he spotted the grayish-white color of a chamberpot dangling percariously over the sill of the window. His eyes widened. He wanted to warn his companions, whose location, unfortunately, lay in the path of the pot owner's intended disposal. But as the cascade of gold fluid poured earthward, Sean could only squeeze his eyes closed, impressed when neither man uttered a sound. He pressed the fist of his left hand beneath his nose, imagining the stench the two must be enduring and realizing there would now be no escape until a change of clothes offered itself.

Turning back to view the street, Sean grew frantic, aware of the click of heels against the wooden sidewalk only a few steps from his retreat. He froze, knowing any movement whatsoever would indicate his presence. The palm of his hand moistened. The finger pressed to the trigger of his pistol trembled. Dear God, he didn't want to sound an alarm. It would bring all of Williamsburg down around their ears. Two more steps thudded closer. He waited. A figure loomed out before him. Unaware of the existence of others nearby, the man paused to relight his pipe. Then, just as he moved to travel on, he sensed someone watching, turned, and stood paralyzed, his mouth agape, his pipe falling to the ground. Without a moment's thought Sean reached out, seized the man's jacket collar in his left hand, and clubbed the nozzle of his pistol to the man's temple, spinning him into the alleyway before he could crumple into an unconscious heap.

"Tie and gag him. If ya must, shred his coat," Sean whispered to his men, looking back across the street at the inn. Now they must hurry. Someone was certain to find the man lying in the alley. A halfwit could figure out what had brought strangers, sailors, in fact, to their town, and double the guard around Dru. He looked at his men briefly and back at the vacant door of the tavern.

"Come on, lad," he droned, bumping a fist repeatedly against the wooden wall at his side.

Michael moved up beside him. "Now what do we do?" he asked, his own worry twisting his brow.

"Nothin'. We gotta wait," came the curt reply.

Michael looked back at the unconscious figure. "Maybe we should be movin' across the street."

"No!"

"But—"

Sean turned on him. "Then John couldn't find us. Now be quiet!"

Realizing the truth of his words, Michael submitted to the order, moving across the alley opposite Sean where he could better view another section of the lamplit street. No one moved about, but the tension in the air seemed to increase the crickets' song tenfold.

Several more minutes ticked away. The entrance to the inn darkened with someone's figure. Sean came to attention immediately, clicking his fingers for George to join them. Pressed together, they watched. But to their dismay, a stranger stepped out onto the sidewalk and quickly set off down the street away from them.

Voices raised in laughter filtered out into the night, a merriment enjoyed within the tavern. It grated on Sean's nerves. Surely it didn't take this long to learn what they wanted to know! Maybe one of the customers suspected. Maybe John and Thomas were being held at gunpoint, forced to be quiet and await their companions' aid. His breath held. He took a step. No. He must wait. He fell back, resting his head against the building, his eyes closed. When this was over he vowed to finish off a whole bottle of rum and sleep for a week.

"Sean!" a harsh whisper called.

His eyes flew open. Michael motioned toward the inn. Focusing on the doorway, Sean could see three men walk out. Two shook hands before one turned and left the others. He wasn't certain, but he thought he recognized John's swagger as the two men headed across the street toward them. He hoped he did, anyway. But until, in his nervous state, he could be sure, he lingered in the shadows, pistol raised. Without hesitation, the first stepped onto the sidewalk, calling Sean's name as he did. A long-held breath whizzed between Sean's lips.

"What did ya learn?" he asked, pulling John into the protection of the alleyway. All gathered round.

"He's bein' held in the prison. It's at the courthouse. End of this street."

"And Donovan?" Michael questioned, pressing closer as he held his voice to a whisper.

"Aye," John answered, half turning toward the man. He straightened suddenly, sniffing the air. "What kind of soap ya be usin'? Or did ya tangle with a skunk in my absence?"

Michael quickly stepped back. "No, sir," he mumbled.

"Well, if ya don't mind, try ta stay downwind, lad."

"Aye, sir," the sailor murmured, absently pulling his damp collar away from his neck.

"How many guard them?" Sean urged, trapping John's sleeve in his hand.

"Only one. Shouldn't be too difficult to overtake

339

him.''

"Good. Then let's be on our way." Sean moved to take a step.

"I must be warnin' ya, me friend," John added, stopping his companion before he traveled an inch. "Dru's been beaten by the jailtender. Hard to say what shape he's in."

Sean's brows furrowed. "Beaten?"

"Aye."

A mask of anger and hatred flawed the fair features of the cousin as he brooded upon the thought. Someone would pay for this. Whether it be the jailer or that Remington blackguard, it mattered little.

Pistols tucked away to hide their obvious threat, the group parted company once more as John and Thomas returned to the opposite side of the street. They passed several darkened storefronts before Sean and his party made their way past the buildings. Even in the darkness, the courthouse loomed out before them, a silent challenge.

Dull thuds of leather heels droned against the sidewalk, light of step, but nonetheless a herald of their presence. Motioning the others to follow, Sean stepped out into the street, the cushion of mud quieting their advance. They hastened their footfalls.

Their destination within a hearty stone's throw, Sean fought the urge to run, frozen in his tracks when he heard the clanging of the town crier's bell behind him.

"Twelve o'clock and all is well," he sang out.

No one moved. If the saints held true, the speaker of the time would continue on without a backward glance. Again the peal rang clear, softer than before.

"Twelve o'clock," —the crier paused to yawn— "and all is well." The shuffling of his feet against the sidewalk marked his departure.

Sean chanced to look back. His long-held breath escaped him in a quiet rush, for the man, lantern held in one hand, bell in the other, moved away. An urgent wave of his arm sent them on. He looked across to John, spying the man's eager nod of his head. All descended upon the jail.

Peering in through the crisscrossing bars of the window on the iron door, Sean spied the sleeping body of the turnkey propped back in his chair against the wall, a single torch flame flickering overhead. His finger raised to his lips to warn the others, Sean quietly lifted the latch, carefully pulling the door wide. A flood of rank air met him, bringing tears to his eyes and a burning in his nose. He gulped, wondering how anyone could stay in a place such as this for any length of time, much less sleep comfortably, as the jailer appeared to be doing. He drew his pistol and stepped in, the rest close behind.

A loud snort exploded from the snoozing man, and no one moved, glued to their spots, watching for any sign of wakefulness. When none came, Sean lingered to appraise the dreamer. Surely this small lad had not been given the task of guarding prisoners. Nor would he be the likely sort to have beaten Dru. His cousin could have overtaken him with ease. He was slight of build, and Sean realized the minimal amount of effect it would take to topple him from his perch, an idea Sean found amusing as well as justified. The young, fair-haired man stretched out, arms folded over him, his chin pressed to his chest. Nodding to his companions to wait, Sean stepped forward, slipped a toe beneath the rung of the chair, and yanked upward, hurling the youth to the floor.

"Holy Mother, Silas," he blurted out, staggering to his feet, his attention focused on the soiled knees of his breeches, "ya didn't have to do that. I wasn't sleep—" He caught sight of the menacing forms standing near. "What—"

A black muzzle pointed at his midsection. "And who might Silas be, lad?" Sean asked.

"Ah—why—ah—he's the jailer." The bony chin trembled, eyes widened.

"And if he be the jailer, who might you be?" The question brought a shudder from the one who viewed the dark mouth of the pistol.

"Anderson, sir. Tommy A-Anderson."

"Not your name. Why are ya here?"

Brown circles encompassed by the opaque white of his eyes darted from one stranger to the next. "Silas went to have a drink. I—I'm watchin' the place. I ain't got no weapon!"

"And the keys ta the cell?"

Tommy's adam's apple bobbed nervously. He pointed to the wall behind the men.

"This Silas, would he be the one ta tend this—this hole?" Sean continued, hearing the clank of brass keys being lifted from the peg.

A quick nod affirmed the fact.

"When do ya expect him back?"

Shoulders jerked upward fearfully.

"When?" the inquiry exploded.

Tommy retreated a step when Sean stiffened in rage, relaxing only slightly when John reached out to touch

Sean's sleeve.

"What difference it be makin', lad? We have the keys and very little time." He looked at the youth trembling before him. "Show us the cell where ya keep the man Remington ordered here."

"Y-yes, sir," Tommy stammered, spinning on his heels to half walk, half run down the dimly lit corridor toward a row of closed iron doors. He paused before one. "Here, sir."

"George," John instructed, "stay here and be watchin' for the jailer. Thomas, bring the torch."

"Aye, capt'n," they chorused.

With Sean leading the way, they quickly joined the youth before the barred portal. Effortlessly, John inserted the key into the lock, hearing a click with the first twist of the instrument.

"Stay where ya are, Tommy, me boy," John ordered as he swung the door open and Sean rushed inside. He tossed the keys to Michael. "Find Donovan and be quick about it. We've got ta be gettin' out of here." He entered the cell, Thomas close behind.

Gold flame flooded the blackened room with light, bringing with it a scurry of clicking nails against the stone floor as other inhabitants of the cell fled for cover. Everyone's breath caught in their throats when the beacon shot across the space to rest on the prisoner who lay quietly, his chest barely moving in slow, labored breaths. His tattered clothes did little to cover him from the chill or hide the numerous bruises and welts on his body.

"Dru?" Sean's voice cracked. He knelt beside the cot. " 'Tis me, Sean."

The arm that covered the man's face lifted gently to

rest across his chest as if it was too difficult to move any further. Dark, pain-filled eyes slowly focused on the figure hovering close to him, an equally lanquid smile parting his swollen lips.

"Ah, Dru," Sean moaned, unfamiliar tears flooding his vision. "You'll be all right now. We've come ta take ya home."

"Capt'n," George called from the entryway. "Someone's comin'!"

"Quick, Sean," John urged. "We've got ta get him out of here."

Silas Werner wiped the droplets of ale from his chin on his sleeve, his red-rimmed eyes drooping half closed. Both elbows pressed against the table top, he slowly moved his head around to stare at the empty doorway of the inn. He had never seen those two men before. He wondered who they were. Lifting a dismissing brow, he wavered back to his mug. Leaning forward, he peered into its darkened depths. Empty! Always empty, it seemed. He raised heavy eyes in the direction of the tavernmaid, indicating the need for another refill.

Pewter mug clenched in his beefy hold, he brought the treasure to his lips, stopping midway once his eyes focused on its golden hue. Yellow. Nearly the shade of one of the strangers' hair. The mug clanked on the table. The only one who spoke. Was the other a mute? A thick shoulder jutted upward. He raised his mug. Seemed awfully damned interested in the way ol' Newton rambled on about the pirate. The cool draught flowed into his mouth. Oh, well, everyone took an interest in him, seein' as how it was Master Remington

344

who had ordered him there. He grinned lopsidedly. And he was entrusted to guard him. Damn good jailer he was, too. Showed that pirate who was master. His blurry gaze traveled to the door again, his brows tightening, and wondered where the strangers had gone. Damned if the mute didn't sway when he walked. Almost the same as that pirate. Silas snorted. Maybe they're kin. The big dummy and the—

All color drained from Silas's face, his befuddled mind clearing. By God, that's just what they were! Kin to the pirate! His eyes caught sight of his drink, and, being the sort never to waste a drop, he lifted the mug, threw back his head, and swallowed the ale in one gulp. Slamming the tankard on the table, he used both hands to push himself up to his feet.

"Aarrrugh!" he bellowed, realizing that only the skinny-arsed Anderson boy was there ta stop 'em. He stumbled from the inn.

Looking up and down the street, he spotted Henry Smiles walking toward him, and stepped in the man's path as the crier paused to ring his bell.

"Where'd they go?" he demanded, the air around him reeking of stale spirits.

Henry retreated a step. "Who?" Even without the evidence of a night spent in the tavern, Silas's odor always offended, and rumor had it that he bathed only once a month.

"Them strangers."

"Didn't see none, Silas. You have a bit too much ale tonight?"

"They was here, right here." He pointed to the inn. "Ya musta seen 'em."

"Sorry, Silas. I saw no one."

A dissatisfied smirk at the man's ignorance curled the jailkeeper's pudgy lip. "Outa my way," he growled, shoving Henry aside. His obese frame waddled down the wooden sidewalk, each board creaking and moaning with the abuse and threatening to break. The crisp bite of night air cleared the cobwebs from his mind, and with each step his ire grew, that someone, *anyone,* would think to violate his prison. His moves quickened. He pulled the pistol from his belt as the lights from inside the gaol came into view. He'd kill the bloody cur and ne'er bat an eye.

Standing before the pathway leading to the prison door, Silas paused to listen. Had they not come as yet? Or gone before he had a chance to stop them? No, surely the Anderson brat would have come crying if they'd succeeded. Hiking up his breeches, head down, he stormed the jail, bursting through the door to frighten Tommy from his sleep. Wide-eyed, the boy scrambled to his feet.

"M-Mr. Werner," he squeaked, nervously wringing his hands. "I-I—"

"Shut up, ya mindless idiot," Silas roared, eyeing the extremities of the room. It wasn't the first time he had caught the milksop dozing, and his guilt only enraged Silas. "Have ya had any visitors?"

"V-visitors, sir? Why n-no, sir."

"Well, ya will." He slammed the door behind him and reached for the keys, not noticing how they swung on the peg. "I'm gonna look at the prisoners."

"B-but sir," Tommy objected, barely moving in time to allow the jailer to pass. As the man ambled down the passageway, the young boy glanced frantically back toward the door, inching his way closer to it until certain the rotund beast could not fling out a crushing fist and reach him. He turned and fled the jail.

Hearing the hurried departure of his assistant, Silas spun around. "Ya spineless cur!" he howled, then spit a long stream of saliva to the floor as if the boy stood in its path. Tommy Anderson had never been known to have much courage, but tonight seemed worse. It was as if— His gaze lifted to the empty peg, recalling the way the keys had rocked to and fro with no gust of wind to aid them. He cocked a suspicious brow and started down the corridor again, listening for the usual sounds of slumber. Silence prevailed, slowing his step to a guarded pace. Reaching the door to the pirate's cell, he paused, looked back down the corridor, then tried the latch. It held secure, bringing a smile to his round face. The wimp had only run out of fear of punishment. The pirate's friends had not yet arrived, and he would be waiting when they did. He set the key in the lock and gave it a twist, pulling the door wide. His smile broadened once he spotted the huddled form on the narrow cot, the golden stream of torchlight from the hall flooding in.

"Ya won't get away from me, ya ill-sired rogue. Not this jailkeeper, Silas Werner," he boasted, stepping closer. "Ya hear, ya scum?" He nudged the sleeping form with the heel of his boot. "Not so cocky now, are ya?"

The quiet of the cell gave the answer until an eerie squeal of rusted hinges swinging shut jerked the man around. In the shadows to the left stood the shape of a man. And to the right! Silas's eyes bulged. He gulped, then braved a look at the man on the cot, who now raised himself up to match Silas's height. Not the pirate captain but his mate, the one he called Mc-Kenzie.

"Not so cocky now, are ya?" the menacing voice beside him mocked. "Ya son of a whore!"

A huge fist raised instantly to smash against Silas's nose. Bright dots twinkled around him. He fell to his knees, only to have the other's fist brought up to crush his chin, snapping his head back and tottering him onto his backside. He sat hunched over, spine curled, head down, arms slack, like a great grizzly bear contemplating naptime. The clicking of a pistol stirred his consciousness, and he shook his head to clear his vision.

"A score of nights I be hearin' ya come ta this cell," the man towering over him hissed, pistol raised high, "and I be helpless ta stop ya. I've killed a man for much less than what ya've done, and won't flinch when I pull the trigger ta end your worthless life."

Silas opened his mouth to take a breath and found it difficult to draw as panic threatened to overcome him. He raised a shaky hand. "P-please d-don't," he begged.

Shoving the muzzle of the gun in Silas's nose, the man crouched down before him. "And can ya be tellin' me one reason why not?"

Every pore in Silas's body flooded with sweat. A seizure of trembling overtook him, tears burning his eyes. "I-I—beg ya," he whimpered.

"Ain't good enough," Donovan growled, jabbing the man's nose a little harder.

"O-o-oh," Silas cried, a mixture of sweat and tears racing down his face.

Even in the shadows Silas could see the flash of white teeth as Donovan's lips twisted into a sneer. "I can be givin' ya one, ya whoremonger." He leaned closer. "The shot would warn the town and bring your friends upon us. Besides I be thinkin' it's too quick an end." Donovan stood, feet apart, his thumb easing the trigger back into place. "I'd rather be leavin' ya bound and gagged ta rot in this cell if luck be holdin' and no one comes ta visit."

Silas's eyes goggled to near bursting as he fearfully watched the man before him raise the pistol high, then thrust it downward to crush against his skull. He saw nothing else as blackness claimed him instantly and slumped him into a motionless heap on the floor beside the bucket filled with human waste.

"Come on, Donovan," John urged from the cell door, "we've got ta be gettin' out of here. The lad will surely go for help."

But Donovan remained, staring at the quiet form at his feet and wishing he had a blade to slip between the man's ribs. Only then, watching this boar's life blood spill upon the floor to mingle with the dirt and slime, would Donovan feel the taste of revenge.

"Come on, lad!"

Startled back to reality, McKenzie spun around, stopping just inside the cell to watch as Sean and Michael carried Dru's unconscious body from the spot Donovan had inhabited for a great number of days. Eyes lifted toward heaven, Donovan paused. Never having been one to frequent a place of worship on the Lord's day, he found it difficult to put his feelings into words, and he could only frown, hoping his silence would be understood.

The group of men swiftly moved out into the night, the only evidence of their passing the jailer's unconscious body in his own prison, the keys to unlock the cell dangling from Donovan's waistband.

TWENTY-ONE

"Thomas," Sean exclaimed, carefully scrutinizing his change of attire. "Where ya gettin' such fine clothes? I swear I look like a real dandy." He gave the lace cuff of his ivory-colored shirt a fluff.

"Aye, Thomas," John agreed, slipping a foot into the black shoe, "Where did ya find such things?"

Studying himself in the small crescent-shaped piece of broken mirror, Thomas finished securing the knotted ribbon in his hair at the nape of his neck. "I borrowed them," he said, then grinned back at the men, "for an indefinite length of time."

"Ya stole them!" Sean howled, sweeping out a hand toward the man. "And you lookin' like such a fine gentleman. What is this world comin' to?"

Hearty guffaws chorused throughout the cabin, each picturing some disheartened man who was a mite poorer after meeting with Thomas Smith. For needs such as this, John had not hesitated a moment when asking the man to come with the small group of rescuers. Thomas had been born in the colonies, and his speech and mannerisms would blend easily with those the band might chance to meet. It was he who would do whatever speaking was necessary. And, next to his first mate, Owen Kelly, John trusted Thomas Smith more than any other man on his ship. From the look of things, his choice had been a good one.

"Well, dear cousin," Sean said once the laughter died away, "when Mistress Remington sees me dressed in all this finery, I be thinkin' ya don't stand a chance." He struck a haughty pose, one fist to his hip, his nose in the air, while he appraised the nails of his other hand. "What do ya think?"

Dru eyed his mocking foe from across the room, his gaze traveling from head to toe. "I be thinkin' the breeches are too tight and give yourself away."

Explosive chortles rallied from the men as Sean straightened sharply, knowing his wit no match for his cousin's. A light hue settled on his face as he glanced from one man to the next, a rebuttal of any sort failing to come to mind. Out of frustration and lack of defense, he lifted the tricorn from a nearby table and sailed it across the room at Dru, who all but crushed it to his chest.

"Since we sent George and Michael back ta the ships ta tell them we'll be joinin' 'em in three days, I be suggestin' we be on our way," Sean said, forcing a frown to his face, which somehow only enhanced the gleam in his eye. It would take a matter of great magnitude to ever make him angry with his cousin and life-long friend.

"He's right, Dru," John agreed, shrugging into his coat. "We best be movin' on. We've pushed our luck stayin' in one spot so long as it is."

"Maybe they haven't found ol' Silas yet," Donovan grinned. "The stench of that jail could hide a number of things."

Rising, Dru reached behind him to tuck his pistol in his breeches, lifted his coat from the chair, and stretched into it. "Aye. I wonder if I'll ever be forgettin' it."

"Just as soon as ya smell the salt air, me friend," Donovan smiled, reaching out to rest an arm across Dru's shoulders and lead the way from the cabin.

During Thomas's travels to acquire the wardrobe fit for any titled English Lord, he had learned that Raven Oaks spread out for leagues, its eastern boundary less than one league away from the cabin they had sought for refuge during Dru's recovery. But what surprised them all even more was the team of horses complete with saddles and bridles tethered to the porch railing once they stepped outside.

"Well," Thomas explained when confronted by the men, "how would it look to find gentlemen like us afoot?"

A hearty round of handshakes, slaps on the backs, and lightly placed fists to his jaw ended in appreciation for Thomas's skills. Only Sean stood back appraising the stallion that awaited his command.

"Somethin' wrong, lad?" Donovan puzzled once he noticed that Sean lingered.

"Aye. Has been a time since I sat on one of these beasts. I much prefer the deck of me ship beneath me."

"Why there's nothin' to it, mate," McGuire grinned. "Just climb on and be lettin' the horse do the rest."

"And do I look as dumb as this nag, me friend?" Sean returned. "I be knowin' enough that without a firm rein this creature will take me back ta the stables."

"Aye, that he will. But knowin' Thomas as I do, ya will probably be findin' yourself in Remington's back yard."

"Nay, captain," Thomas offered, "I'm not that brazen."

"Well, if that be the case," Sean sighed, "I'd better be holdin' on." Slipping a toe into the stirrup, Sean easily threw his other leg over the saddle and spurred the animal into a canter. Without further comment from anyone, the others took Sean's lead, riding off toward Raven Oaks and Victoria Remington.

Three days had elapsed since Dru's friends had freed him from the foul clutches of the jail and secured a vacant cabin in which they could hide and allow Dru time to recover. The warmth of a fire and nourishing food had aided in Dru's physical convalescence, but had failed to heal the ache in his heart or still the thoughts in his mind. Visions of the ebony-haired beauty invaded every waking hour and stole into his dreams. He loved Victoria, and he realized a long while, if ever, would pass before he spent a single night in peaceful slumber without being haunted by memories of her.

Urging his steed on, Dru winced in pain at the faster pace, the muscles of his right side still sore and aching. He would mask his suffering. No one would

354

know the extent of his wounds, for if they did, he felt certain Silas Werner would pay a second time. And the risk his mates had run once in freeing him was all he would ask of them, knowing if they suspected what bad shape he was in they would return again to Williamsburg. He smiled softly, watching the stiff moves of his cousin as he clung to the saddle. It had been under Sean's urgings that the group of misplaced travelers now found themselves heading further inland. Dru could never hide much from his cousin, and his feelings for Victoria had grown evident when in conversations with the quick-witted Irishman. Although Dru admitted to Sean's speculations, he also told him that he intended to sail without the lass at his side. But Sean had wondered about a deeper problem, smiling triumphantly when Dru confessed the guilt that plagued him about the bargain he had failed to fulfill.

"Ya can't be leavin' her with the thoughts ya betrayed her," Sean had surmised, nodding confidentially when Dru had concurred. "Then we be takin' the time ta tell her the truth. Ya can't be takin' command of your ship without a clear mind. And Lord knows what would happen if ya turned over the *Defiance* ta me." As always, Sean's foolery had eased the moment and the two men chorused their glee.

Looking up in thought, Dru watched the streaks of gold and yellow race across the sky, a blinding arc of flame ascending gracefully to warm another day. He would elucidate the reasons for his acts, but proclaim his love? No. To what end? Would be the best to never let her know.

"What is it ya be thinkin, cousin?"

355

Blinking twice in startled surprise, Dru found he now rode beside Sean. He half smiled in embarrassment. "That ya be doin' just fine straddled on that horse," he lied.

Bouncing uncomfortably, Sean argued, "I might be lookin' like it, but me backside tells me different." He chanced a look to his companion. "Can ya be sayin' the same for yourself? I mean, are ya doin' fine? I've seen the way ya hold your ribs."

"Each day helps." He glanced back at the trio behind them. "Just be doin' me a favor and don't let McKenzie know. The man nearly lost his mind bein' unable ta stop Silas from havin' his way."

"Ya know, that's somethin' I don't quite understand. I've seen ya take on three or four and none of them ever laid a hand on ya. How could one man do what those many others couldn't?"

A faint grin turned the corners of Dru's mouth. He relaxed a little, crossing his hands in front of him. "I was delivered to the man bound with me hands behind me. Ya may think me a good fighter, cousin, but I know of none who can be makin' even those odds."

An amused chuckle escaped the light-haired man. "No wonder the cowardly cur quaked in his boots when Donovan took him. He not be likin' the match even, much less findin' himself outnumbered. Would have been fun ta play with him a while." Suddenly a frown appeared to wrinkle Sean's smooth brow. "Uh-oh."

"What is it?" Dru asked, glancing up.

With a nod of his head, Sean motioned toward the bend in the road a few hundred feet ahead. A stately black coach drawn by a pair of dapple-gray mares rolled in their direction, blocking any chance the men had might have had to rein their steeds into the cover of trees unnoticed. Without a word, Dru pulled his horse to a trot, allowing the others to catch up.

"Ride up with Sean, Thomas," Dru instructed, "in case they be stoppin' us."

"Aye, Mr. Chandler," Thomas concurred, spurring his horse ahead.

"Donovan, since we not be knowin' who they might be, I suggest you and I fall to the rear. We don't want anyone ta recognize us," he warned, pulling the black tricorn further down on his brow.

"Aye, capt'n." Donovan, too, shadowed his face with the brim of his hat and allowed John's horse to move to the inside.

The coach rattled nearer, its driver urging the team to move faster. Sean knew they shouldn't have traveled the road, but stayed to the cover of trees. Now they were vulnerable. He sneaked a glance at the one who rode inside next to the window. His breath held. But rather than draw unwanted attention he declined his head as if to practice courtesy while in fact hiding his face, for staring back at him dark, hooded eyes fixed their suspicous glare upon him. Although he had but once seen the man, and then at a good number of yards, the tingling in his stomach and the gold-plated emblem on the carriage door stirred warnings. Even with Thomas's presence to mask their idenity, should the foe call them out, it would take only a moment for Remington to discover who they really were.

The rally of thundering hoofbeats pounded against

Sean's temples. He fought the urge to look back to make certain his cousin's curiosity hadn't pulled his gaze upon the coach. Remington's frown had displayed no recognition, but one look at Dru would bring about their downfall. He listened, certain the coach had not slowed when he heard the driver crack the whip. He wanted to urge his horse faster. The bend in the road offered cover. Without thinking, his chin raised as he turned to look back.

"No, don't," the man at his side warned.

Sean snapped his head forward, his eyes squeezed tightly closed. God, how could he? He worried more for Dru when it was his own carelessness he should fear. Sometimes he wondered why his cousin kept him around.

Once the coach had rounded the curve, they spurred their horses into a gallop, not slowing until they had put a good distance between themselves and the Remington carriage.

"I don't know about the rest of ya, but I be thinkin' I'm too old for this," John half laughed, turning back in his saddle to convince himself they hadn't been followed. "Me heart was poundin' so loud I thought it would be givin' us away. Was that who I be thinkin' it was?" He lifted his tricorn from his head to wipe away the sweat from his brow.

"Ya can wager the *Shamrock* it was," Donovan volunteered. "Did anyone see if he was alone?"

"Even if he isn't, we can still be takin' him," Sean barked, spinning his horse around. "We be owin' it to him."

"Take it easy, Mr. Rafferty," Thomas warned, spurring his steed in the man's way. "We're too close to his plantation. No telling what could happen, and then we'd be outnumbered."

"He's right, Sean," Dru replied quietly, glancing back down the road. "And he wasn't alone. There was a man riding beside him. I only wish I could have seen who sat across from them."

"If you mean his wife and daughter, we'll find that out in a few minutes," Thomas said, pointing ahead of them.

The narrow road divided in two, one to twist and wind through the countryside, the other marking the way down a long line of black oak trees. With trunks bigger than a man's arm could encompass, their leafy branches spread out to entangle with the next and hide what lay beyond them. Reining to a stop at the fork in the road, they waited quietly while Dru appraised the situation.

"What do ya want ta do?" John asked after a moment.

"I think the rest of ya should wait here while Sean and I go in. Just because Remington is gone doesn't mean he hasn't left an army behind. If we're not back in thirty minutes, come lookin'."

"Aye," John agreed, hauling back on the reins as he motioned the others to follow him into the thicket.

Satisfied of their safety, Dru nodded at Sean and together they left the road to travel through the denseness of the trees toward the manor. When they approached the end of the line of oaks, they dismounted and tied the horses to a low-hanging tree limb. Crouching, they studied the movements of the workers and the layout of the buildings. Off to one side of the huge manor and closest to them, they noticed a small stone house, its door open, the sweet fragrances of baking breads drifting out to greet them. Opposite it, the livery and blacksmith. In the center behind the manor towered the mill, its opening bustling with servants. For the most part, it appeared the majority of activity centered around the two-story structure and Dru silently decided on a way to approach the house unseen. Seizing Sean's arm in a light hold, Dru pointed toward the kitchen. Sean nodded, waiting until Dru led the way. They raced across the opening, bent low, and hurried to the protection of the kitchen wall. Resting a moment, they listened for footsteps to warn of anyone near. Suddenly a loud explosion of shattering glass froze them to their spots.

"Damn!" came an outraged cry from inside the stone building. "I swear to all that's holy, it isn't my day. Won't you ever learn, Cinnamon Cockrin?"

Moving along the foundation, Dru paused below the window, then pressed a finger to his lips at Sean and motioned above him. Back to the wall, he raised slowly to carefully peer inside.

Down on hands and knees, the woman presented her backside to Dru as she gathered broken pieces of a bowl. The cook, he observed quietly. Obviously so, from the size of her. He grinned. It had been a long time since he'd seen such an ample bottom. He moved to join his cousin just as the woman straightened, her coppery knot of hair arresting his attention.

Mumbling to herself, Cinnamon crossed to the hearth and deposited the broken pieces of crockery into a bucket. "It never fails," she grumbled aloud. "Whenever I'm in a hurry—damn!" Grabbing the broom that stood in the corner of the room, she angrily twirled about and set to sweeping away the tiny fragments of clay too small to pick up with her fingers. With each stroke of the broom toward the door, her ire grew.

"I haven't time for this!" she stormed, brushing the remnants outside.

Returning the broom to its place, she crossed to the brick oven. Using her apron hem to protect the flesh of her hands against the heat, she carefully opened the door and gingerly removed the hot dish filled with freshly done cherry tarts. Nudging the door with her toes, it thudded closed, and she had just turned around to place the delicacy on the long trestle table when she caught sight of the two figures in the kitchen doorway. She gasped, dropping the dessert to the floor.

"Good mornin', Miss Cockrin," Dru hummed, a smile dancing in his eyes as he leaned against the door frame. Wrists crossed in front of him, his tricorn dangled from his fingertips.

Cinnamon's mouth opened and closed several times, words failing to pass her lips.

"Please be excusin' me cousin and me for not tellin' ya we would be payin' ya a visit." He straightened and stepped inside, Sean close at his heels. "Of course, ya never met me cousin, Sean Rafferty. Sean, this is Cinnamon Cockrin, the bearer of food and bandages and drink to quench me thirst and ease her mistress's mind."

Cinnamon gulped, eyeing the men warily.

"What are ya sayin', Dru?" Sean asked, looking nervously from his cousin to the grounds outside the kitchen.

"Didn't I tell ya?" Dru questioned, his gaze never

leaving the round, full face that stared at him in wide-eyed apprehension. "This good woman paid Donovan and me a visit in the jail ta bring us food and whiskey. I could only guess who sent her when she refused to say. But the minute I saw the fine color of her hair, just now, I knew for certain." He glanced down at the debris at Cinnamon's feet. "I'm sorry if we frightened ya, lass. 'Twas not our intent."

Following with her eyes to where his gaze had traveled, Cinnamon instantly forgot her fear. "Oh-h," she moaned, bending down to rescue any small portion of the tarts she could. Her anger returned. "You got a lot of nerve barging in like that. You could have at least knocked or called out. Now what will I do? They're ruined." A sudden thought struck her and she looked up. "What are you doing here, and how did you get out of the jail?"

Crossing the room, Dru laid aside the tricorn and stooped to assist her. "Me cousin was kind enough ta take care of that, and we've come ta thank Mistress Remington for her kindness."

Cinnamon presented the back of his hand with a stinging slap when he made to lift the dish, spilling another tart to the floor. "If you don't mind," she barked, "I'd rather do without the help."

"Aye, lass," he grinned. Rising once more, he chose to sit down on the stool positioned next to the table to watch. Only after she had cleared away the mess and wiped the sticky sweetness from her fingertips on a damp cloth did she elect to voice her opinion on his ludicrous statement.

"Then you'll have to thank me. Miss Victoria isn't here." She noticed the somewhat disappointed look

362

he gave his cousin. "And she won't be for several days."

When he looked at her again, she spied the dimple in his cheek. "Ya wouldn't be lyin' ta me, lass?"

The slandering of her character stiffened Cinnamon's spine. "If you want to run the risk of being caught sneaking through the main house looking for her, go right ahead. Makes no never mind to me, you blasted fool."

Dru chuckled at her outburst. "Are ya sure you're only the cook and not Mistress Remington's mother? Ya have the same spirit."

"Ha!" Cinnamon exploded, her fists jabbed to her hips. "If I was her mother, I'd have her tell the truth to her father. The little twit. She doesn't know what she wants."

"And what truth might that be?"

"How she lied telling her father you raped her, beat her, and Lord knows what else. She's spoiled rotten, that one." Angrily, she set about wiping the flour from the table top, dusting more to the floor than in her hand.

"Ya shouldn't be so hard on her, lass. She had good reason," he added, enjoying the woman's fit of perplexity.

"Oh-h, yes. She had good reason," Cinnamon snapped, then squinted an eye at him. "She didn't want him to know how she threw herself at you."

"But she didn't," Dru pointed out.

"Didn't what?" Cinnamon barked irately.

"Throw herself at me." He reached over to wipe away the rim of flour piled near the edge of the table. "If anythin', I encouraged her."

"Then you're both idiots," she snapped, briskly rubbing her hands together. A sheet of white powder floated to the floor. "She should have known what a story like that would do to her father."

Dru raised a questioning brow. "What do ya mean, lass?"

"I mean, he's gone and matched her off, that's what!" Turning her back on him, she crossed to the fireplace and filled the kettle with water from the bucket sitting on the hearth. Dru watched her hang it over the fire, waiting for her to look at him again.

"Ya mean she's promised ta marry?" His voice sounded weak.

"Yes, marry. What did you think he'd do, knowing there's even the slightest chance she might carry your child?" The angry lines on her face softened when she noticed the pained look on his handsome features. She glanced at Sean. He, too, seemed troubled as he gave up his vigilance at the door to study the toes of his boots. The heavy sigh that filled the room brought her attention back to Dru.

"As long as she's happy," he murmured.

One corner of Cinnamon's mouth puckered. "There's about as much chance for that as me marryin' the king of England."

A frown darkened his brow. "Ya mean there isn't?"

"With Damon Rutledge?" she bellowed. "Not hardly! And if ya ask me, there's something odd about that man."

He exchanged a curious glance with Sean. "Would ya care to explain?"

Lifting a large copper pan from the peg on the wall, she returned it to the table and clanked it down on the wooden surface. Leaning over it, her hands braced against its rim for support, she said, "Up until six, seven months ago, we didn't know him. He bought the Bensen place and claims to come from Pennsylvania. Says the British run him off. Pooph. He ran all right, the coward. Wouldn't see Master Beau let someone tell *him* what to do."

"Would he be the one with Remington we just met on the road?"

Surprised the man could have been so close to Beau Remington without Beau's realizing it, she glanced somewhat awed to the man at the door, then back at Dru. "In the carriage?"

He nodded.

"Yes. Why?"

An amused smile parted his lips. "From the way ya be talkin', I expected an ugly old man. If his charms be half as good as his looks, he'll win Mistress Remington's heart without much trouble."

Cinnamon's lip curled disgustedly as she stood erect, one fist pressed to her hip. "You're dumber than I thought. How can she love him when she loves you?" The sneer ebbed. Her face paled. She shot a glance at Sean. She swallowed hard, knowing she had betrayed Victoria. Frantic, wanting desperately to retract the words her careless tongue had spilled, she twirled around to go to the fireplace and test the warmth of the water in the kettle.

"I think you're wrong, lass," the quiet voice behind her spoke. "I've done too much to kill the seed of love planted in her heart." A long, silent moment passed. "I not be the one she should love. I be nothin' more than a pirate, a scoundrel. Not good enough to know

365

her love."

"And her mother was nothing more than an indentured servant when Master Beau met *her!*" Cinnamon cried out, spinning back to face him. Though she felt Victoria didn't deserve one ounce of help to ease the trouble she'd created for herself, Cinnamon couldn't bear to see her unhappy. And certainly marrying a man she didn't love would only make it worse. She drew a deep breath, letting it out slowly, and came to stand near the pirate. "If you can find it in your heart, Captain Chandler, don't let her marry Damon Rutledge."

Leaving the stool on which he sat, Dru crossed to the window of the kitchen and looked out. "What can I be doin'? Ask her father for her hand in marriage first? Not a likely prospect. He'd just as soon see me shot down where I be standin'."

"Then don't ask him," Sean chimed in. "Ask the lass instead."

Dru's shoulders slumped. "I already told ya, cousin, she wouldn't be happy married to a pirate."

"How can ya be answerin' for her?" Sean argued hotly. He surveyed the yard outside the cabin from left to right, then stepped further into the room, feeling certain they were safe for a while. "If Miss Cockrin is correct, the love the two of ya share can be overcomin' anythin'."

Dru turned to face him. "Oh?" he asked with raised brows. "And which of us will be givin' up the life we're used to?" He swept a hand down the length of his tall frame. "I might be lookin' natural dressed the way I am, but inside, in me heart, I'll never change. I love the sea, the adventure, the—"

"And Victoria," Sean added quietly.

Steel-blue eyes stared painfully at Sean. Then, reaching up, Dru brushed his fingers through his thick, dark mass of hair. He sighed heavily. "Aye. And Victoria."

Cinnamon stared at Dru, then Sean, and back at Dru, hearing what was said but wondering at the sanity of it. If Victoria loved this man and he loved her, it meant escape for the young mistress of Raven Oaks. She would be free of the arranged marriage. And the babe, if there were indeed a child, would know its true father. But what of Master Beau? Cinnamon shook her head dismissingly. He would be easy to deal with. Alanna would see to that. She studied the handsome captain again. But this one—he would be quite another story. She bit her lower lip in thought, then stepped forward.

"If I may," she announced, drawing both men's attention. "I would like to say that I agree with Mr. Rafferty. You mustn't assume Victoria is willing to allow you to sail off without at least discussing a compromise that would suit both of you."

"Right, lass," Sean heartily concurred. He turned to Dru. "At least be givin' her a say."

"No!" Dru exploded. "Right now she doesn't know the feelin's I have for her and it be makin' it easier for her if she thinks it's only one-sided. I plan ta sail and leave her here. Where she belongs!" Snatching his tricorn from its resting place, he stormed to the door.

"Captain, please," Cinnamon begged, stopping him just inside. Although he did not turn back, she knew he listened by the slight turn of his head in her direction. "At least be sure that Damon Rutledge is the one with whom you want her to live out the rest of her life. Do that much for her.''

Dru stood silently a while, then slammed the tricorn on his head and hurried outside, his cousin close behind. From the doorway Cinnamon watched the two figures race across the yard to be swallowed up by the profusion of trees. She heard a horse whinny, then the gallop of hoofs, and knew they had gone.

TWENTY-TWO

"Beau, darling, what's wrong?"

Realizing his thoughts had wandered, the frown on Remington's brow faded, his apologetic smile taking its place. "I'm afraid I'm not much company, am I?" He leaned forward and patted his wife's hand. "Please forgive me."

"But you've hardly said two words the entire trip, not at the inn last night or today, and we're almost to Williamsburg. You seem—worried," Alanna insisted.

"Nothing you should concern yourself over, my dear," he assured her, absently looking back outside the carriage.

"Would it be the men we passed near the plantation yesterday?"

The frown returned. "Yes, Damon."

"Did you know them?"

Remington shook his head. "No."

"Then why the concern?"

"Just a feeling I had." He looked at the man sitting beside him. "Not much of a reason, is it?" he smiled.

"Instinct, sir," Damon grinned, his hands folded over the end of his cane as it rested on the floor. "Seems you once told me you respected a man's instincts, his ability to be perceptive. In this case, I think they go hand in hand."

Remington shrugged a shoulder. "Maybe. Did you get a look at any of them?"

"A couple."

"Did you know either one?"

"No. But you must remember, I haven't been in this area all that long enough to know everyone who lives around here." Damon tilted his head forward to better view his companion's troubled expression. "So what did your instincts tell you?"

Looking first at Damon, then at the young woman who all but ignored the conversation as she stared thoughtfully out the carriage window, Remington leaned back in the seat with a sigh. "That I better check the jail."

"You don't mean—"

"I don't know what I mean," Remington said, his voice tired. "Living day to day with war raging around us is enough to set any man's sound judgment to the test. Those men back there were obviously gentlemen. Not the sort to be breaking people out of prison." He looked at his daughter again, noticing the vague smile on her lips.

"Well, if that's what they intended to do, why would they be heading away from Williamsburg and further inland?" Damon pointed out.

"That's just it. It really doesn't make any sense."

"But it always pays to be careful, sir," Damon smiled encouragingly.

Remington chuckled. "And it always pays to have a man like you around."

"Me, sir?"

"Yes. To help sort things out. Now I can forget about the strangers and start enjoying the rest of our trip. Right, my dear?" Remington grinned at his wife.

"I hope so. It's been a long time since I've heard you laugh," Alanna scowled playfully.

"See there," Remington said, nudging his companion. "I don't even get sympathy from my wife."

"Ah, but I see a hint of humor in those beautiful dark eyes. Can't you?" Damon teased. "And the way the corners of her mouth fight not to turn upward and spoil the effect of her words."

Unable to fend off the jousting of the pair, Alanna laughed aloud. "Now it is I who cry foul. I am outnumbered and only wished to see my husband's worries put aside for a few days. To listen to you two would make me sound the villain here."

"My deepest apologies, my dear," Remington smiled, touching his fingertips to his breastbone to present a short bow. "What can I do to make it up to you?"

"Careful sir," Damon cut in, "an offer such as that could tend to slim your purse some."

"Mister Rutledge," Alanna quipped, "I would appreciate it if you kept your advice to yourself. I had every intention of spending his coin, and thought to double it until you interfered."

Damon mocked regret. "Then I, too, apologize,

madam. And for my thoughtlessness, allow me to offer that should your husband's funds run low, I would willingly allow you the use of mine.''

''Oh, Damon,'' Remington moaned. ''You have no idea how careless your tongue has gotten.''

A pale blue sky dotted with a sprinkling of fluffy clouds cast the serene backdrop of Victoria's daydream. Tall, spiraling palm trees swayed in the trade winds and on the bleached white shore, a man and a woman strolled aimlessly, arms entwined, faces smiling. Blue waters lapped the sandy beach, rolling inland to swirl about their feet, playing with them, tempting them to shed their clothes and swim the waves, explore the coral reefs below. Warm breezes tossed about their hair and carried the scent of wild flowers, while sea gulls flew above them, their joyful songs raised in chorus. But when her pirate bent to kiss her, she broke away giggling, racing down the seashore, long black hair flying out around her, daring him to chase her, to catch her if he could. She squealed in delight to see him take up the challenge, long, sure strides cutting the distance in half in record speed. Strong arms encircled her waist, lifting her, twirling them both around until they laughed in their dizziness.

Dark brown eyes met steel-blue ones, their passion glowing in their depths. Still held high in his arms, he easily lowered her, their lips touching, bodies pressed tightly together. Bright rays of sunlight warmed them, and her bare feet sank slowly in the sand, her fingers finding the strings of his shirt front, his own the buttons of her gown. Heedless of all around them, they fell naked to the earth, her long, dark hair acting as a blanket. He kissed her trembling mouth, the slim, white neck, the fullness of one breast, sending shivers of delight coursing through her. She moaned, eyes closed, as his kisses traveled further, teeth nibbling at the silken skin across her belly—

Suddenly laughter filled her senses, shattered her illusion, and, cruelly, abruptly, brought Victoria back to reality. Her eyes flew open, a light hue settling in her cheeks when she discovered she was not sharing an island paradise with Dru, but rather the small space of a carriage with her parents and Damon Rutledge. Had they noticed?

Forcing a smile of her own, she looked sheepishly at her mother and asked, "Did I miss something?"

"Not a thing, my dear," Alanna grinned, wiping away a tear from the corner of her eyes. "In fact, you and I will not miss a single shop in all of Williamsburg. We'll come home with more gowns then we could possibly wear in a year."

"But Mama," Victoria protested, "I don't need any new gowns."

"That's beside the point," her mother said, fighting down laughter. "These fine gentlemen have offered all their silver to buy their way into my good graces again, and I intend to spend it all. Won't that be fun?"

"Yes, Mama," Victoria smiled. "I think I would enjoy visiting the shops of Williamsburg. It's been a long while."

"Good. Then just as soon as we take our luggage to our rooms, you and I will leave these two to drown their sorrow in a bottle of wine." Alanna looked at her husband. "I'm sure it is the only thing that will ease the pain."

"Most assuredly, good woman," Remington con-

curred with a slight nod of his head, then smiled resignedly at Damon and caught sight of his daughter from
the corner of his eye. The smile disappeared. Just as
quickly as she had joined their fun, she turned away,
drifting into her private world again.

Guilt overruled Victoria's will to see their journey to
Williamsburg as enjoyable. It meant being much too
near the man who captured her dreams and robbed her
sleep. Located in the center of town, the courthouse
would haunt her vision each time she stepped outside
the inn or visited the shop. If only she hadn't been
forced to come, or had something to divert her attention. Frustrated, she glanced at the floor of the carriage, spotting the tip of Damon's cane resting there.
Discreetly, she followed its length, noticing the lean,
well-formed fingers curled around the minutely carved
pearl handle. She chanced a look at his face, finding
that he stared out at the countryside, his expression relaxed, almost as though he enjoyed a secret. Suddenly
an idea came to her. She would spend as much time as
possible with this man during their stay. Surely he
could fill her thoughts and ease the anxiety of the next
few days. After all, he wasn't anything like she had
imagined. He was polite, soft-spoken, sincere, and by
no means unpleasant to look at. Even the limp bothered
her less than it had before. She never felt challenged or
mocked when she spoke with him. Not like it was
with— Quickly she looked outside again. Yes, that's
what she'd do. She'd fill her hours with thoughts of another. It didn't mean she agreed to the marriage—just
that she accepted his company, his protection, and perhaps even his name, if need be.

The muscle in the elder Remington's cheek twitched.

He had agreed to the trip to Williamsburg in an effort to distract his daughter's thoughts, to allow her the chance to really get to know Damon Rutledge. And all she did was stare out the window. One dark brow lifted. Well, he would see to it she had plenty of time to get acquainted with the young man he had grown to trust and respect.

"Mama's ill?" Victoria frowned worriedly.

"Nothing serious. Just a headache," Remington assured her as he led her further into the sitting room and closed the door behind them. "Are your rooms suitable?"

Staring at the sealed portal leading to her parents' bedchambers, Victoria mumbled, "Yes, fine." She looked anxiously at her father. "Is there anything I can do? Did you summon the doctor?"

"No, to both questions," he smiled softly. "Your mother is sleeping, and I'm sure by this evening she'll be fine again. You know how these things behave. One moment you feel good, the next—"

Victoria looked at the thick oak door again. "Yes, I know. But this one came on so suddenly. She never mentioned it when we talked in the lobby a few minutes ago."

Remington cleared his throat and went to the buffet to pour himself a glass of wine. "Yes, well, you know your mother isn't one to complain."

"Well, are you certain she's all right?"

"I am," he quickly promised with a smile that seemed to sparkle in his eyes. "Would you care for a glass of wine?"

Chewing on her lower lip, she shook her head. "I

guess I'll just return to my rooms and lie down for a while. I am rather tired." She stood, ready to depart his company, when of a sudden he presented her with a glass of wine.

"No, you won't. We so very seldom get a chance to talk, I insist you stay for a while."

She opened her mouth to argue, and he raised a hand.

"Now, I won't take no for an answer. You've done nothing but rest ever since you got home. Please," he smiled, extending a hand toward the sofa again.

Victoria hesitated but realized no way out of the situation other than being rude. And, after all, she had missed the private times she spent with her father. A genuine smile parted her lips.

"I saw Henry Wilkes when we arrived," Remington said, once Victoria had sat down comfortably again.

"Oh? How is he? And his wife?"

"They're good. Henry's thinking of selling the newspaper office."

"Whatever for?" Victoria asked. "He's such an excellent editor."

"Says he's gettin' too old to keep up the pace."

"But if he sells it, what would he and Agnes do?"

Remington sat down in the high-back chair near the fireplace. "That's what I asked him. He said they'd live off what money they got for it."

"But that wouldn't last long."

"I told him that, too. But he said he'd worry about that when the time came."

Victoria thoughtfully studied the contents of her glass. "It's too bad they never had any children. Especially a son. Then he could run it for him and share the profits."

Remington considered his daughter for a quiet moment, until she looked to him and smiled.

"What you are thinking?"

"That if Henry had a daughter like you, he wouldn't need a son."

"Why, thank you, Papa," she replied, a soft pink hue settling in her cheeks. "You don't know how good that makes me feel."

"Why?" Remington half laughed.

Victoria's shoulder jutted upward. "Sometimes I hate myself and expect you to feel the same."

"I could never hate you," he insisted strenuously, sitting forward in the chair. "You're my daughter, the image of your mother. Looking at you is like looking into the past." He relaxed a bit, a hooded scowl darkening his eyes, as if he remembered something of those earlier days. When he spoke again, his voice betrayed the pain he fought to hide. "I merely wish to see that you're always happy."

"I am, Papa," she whispered.

He blinked, looking at her again. "No, you're not. You haven't been the same since—since—"

Suddenly Victoria swallowed the remainder of her wine, gulping for air when it proved too much, and weakly held out her glass. "Might I have more?" she asked, tears pooling in the corners of her eyes.

Remington jumped to attention. "Certainly," he agreed, rising. He took the proffered glass and returned to the buffet, pausing in his mission when a knock at the door interrupted. Glancing nervously at his daughter, then in the direction from which the sound came, he awkwardly set down the decanter and hurried across the room.

"I—I wonder who it is?" he stuttered, something he had never done before.

Victoria frowned suspiciously. For some reason, she knew exactly who would be standing on the other side.

"Damon," Remington sang out, forcing a tone of surprise. "Come in. My daughter and I were just sharing a glass of wine. Won't you join us?" Remington stood aside to allow their guest to enter, closed the door behind him quietly, then looked sheepishly at Victoria. He straightened slowly when he found her smiling warmly at him.

"Good morning, Victoria," Damon nodded, limping toward her. "I trust you're all settled in your rooms?"

"Yes, thank you," she grinned, her attention still fixed on her father. He looked down and cleared his throat.

"How is your mother?" Damon continued, easing himself down next to her with the aid of the pearl-handled cane.

"My mother?" she parried, glancing at him.

"Yes. Your father said she wasn't feeling well."

"Did he?" She looked back at Beau, who now fidgeted with his waistcoat, forcing his eyes to focus anywhere but in his daughter's direction. "Somehow I suspect she'll be fine sooner than any of us could imagine."

A puzzled frown covered Damon's handsome features, then disappeared. "Yes, well, I hope so. Look, since your mother won't be able to accompany you, I thought—"

"I'd be honored, Mr. Rutledge," she broke in.

"What?" he asked, more confused than ever.

"To have you accompany me instead. Unless, of course, Papa objects." Her dark brown eyes took on a devilish gleam as she looked at her father once more.

He swallowed hard and smiled, a gesture that revealed its difficulty. "No, no. I have no objections."

"I didn't think you would," Victoria grinned.

Regaining some of his usual guarded appearance, Remington curtly walked to the buffet and poured another glass of wine. "I'd offer myself, but I have some paperwork to do before dinner." Drinks in hand, he returned to the sofa, giving one glass to Damon. "It's kind of you to make the invitation."

"The pleasure is all mine, I assure you," Damon nodded.

"Not all of it," Victoria speculated.

Damon leaned back in the sofa, one elbow resting on its velvet arm while he looked from Remington to his daughter. "Did I walk in on the middle of a conversation? Somehow I fail to understand a word you say, my dear."

"Oh, it's just a game my father and I like to play." Victoria easily came to her feet, Damon awkwardly following her lead. "And if I'm to have time to visit every dress shop, we'd better be going." Standing on tiptoes, she placed a kiss on her father's cheek. "Don't work too hard."

Wineglass clutched in one hand, fingertips of the other jammed in his waistcoat pocket, Beau watched the door close behind the couple. He failed to hear the footsteps of his wife walk up behind him.

"I told you she'd never believe it," Alanna whispered. "Just as you said, she is the image of her

379

mother, and I'd not be fooled."

"Hmmm." Beau's deep tones attested to knowledge of the fact.

"Would you mind telling me what was going on back there?" Damon asked as they slowly walked down the wide, circular staircase of the Chesterfield House.

"You, kind sir, I'm afraid, were the victim of my father's games," Victoria laughed. "When he told you that my mother had taken ill, didn't you think it was awfully sudden?"

"Well, now that you mention it, I suppose so."

"And then all at once he has paperwork to do, leaving his poor daughter all alone with nothing to do." She looked back over her shoulder at him and fluttered her lashes playfully.

Damon chuckled. "You know, those were nearly his very words."

"I thought so. But what surprises me is how my mother went along with it," she mused, pausing at the bottom of the stairs to brush out the fullness of her skirts.

"Now, don't blame her. Your father can be very persuasive when he wants."

Victoria looked up at him and rolled her eyes. "Yes. I know."

"And since this is his idea and his money, shall we make the best of it? Where would you like to start?"

Damon smiled warmly at her, and Victoria noticed for the first time how truly handsome he was, despite his disability. Nearly a full head taller than she, his height seemed more protective than intimidating. She noticed how neatly his black hair was combed back to a knot at the nape of of his neck and held secure with a dark blue ribbon. Blue, she mused, a color repeated in the rest of his attire. She had never seen him in any color other than black. Maybe there were a lot of things about Damon Rutledge she had yet to learn. Absently she reached up to brush a speck of lint from his lapel. The moment her fingers felt the smoothness of the cloth, she withdrew her hand quickly. Dear Lord, whatever had made her do that? To be so familiar with a man she hardly knew! Her breath caught at the absurdity of the thought. She had been much more intimate with the pirate captain. She looked away, hoping Damon hadn't seen her reaction.

"I think we should start by getting out of here," she said uneasily. "I need some fresh air."

"Certainly," he agreed, presenting his arm for her to take.

She stared at it a moment, wishing not to have to touch him, but knew of no way to avoid it. Reluctantly, she slipped her hand into the crook of his arm, and together they left the inn.

The sidewalks and streets of Williamsburg bustled with people. Many stared openly at the handsome couple coming from the Chesterfield House. Without a doubt, no single woman for miles around matched the beauty or grace of Victoria Remington, except for one, her mother. And yet neither woman seemed aware of it. Now, escorted by the tall, striking man at her side, Victoria seemed doubly beautiful. To each person who greeted her, she smiled warmly in return or paused to inquire about their health. Having watched the dark, curly-haired babe grow to womanhood, the townspeople took pride in what they saw, as if they were in some way responsible. The name of Remington always passed their lips with respect, for Beau had always been fair and honest with everyone, winning their trust and admiration. Should anyone be set against the Remington clan, he would take on the entire town. And if Beau Remington accepted this stranger, Damon Rutledge, then so did they. It seemed only natural that he would be the one to escort Mr. Remington's daughter.

"Oh, look, Damon," Victoria said excitedly as they paused outside the general store. On display in the window sat a delicately painted china doll. "Let's go in. I do so love to hold them."

"Your wish is my command." Damon bowed gallantly as he balanced against the cane, causing her to giggle.

"Really, Damon," she whispered as they walked inside, "you'll have all of Williamsburg thinking you're a buffoon."

"And they'd be correct. Until today, I never had reason to act foolish, nor felt the need. Somehow being with you has changed that." He motioned for the round-bellied man behind the counter, presenting her with a rather exquisite profile. She wondered why she had never noticed him before. He wasn't truly what she had first thought him to be. Her gaze traveled the length of him. His tailor should be complimented. And not even a scuff on the toes of his black shoes. If only he didn't limp—

"Mr. Penbrook," he called, "might we see the doll in the window?"

"Of course, Mr. Rutledge," Penbrook returned. "I'll be right there."

"Don't bother. We'll help ourselves, if that's all

right.''

''Most definitely. Anything I have is at your disposal.''

Damon bowed curtly and turned about, bending low so only Victoria might hear. ''See what money can get you?'' he teased with raised brows. ''As long as they think you'll part with a little of it, they'll do anything for you. I wonder what he'd think,'' he glanced briefly at Penbrook, ''if he found the doll missing.''

''Damon, you wouldn't!''

His eyes sparkled. ''No, but sometimes I'm tempted. Would see a just reward for trusting only those with enough coin to buy it.''

''You have a very odd sense of justice,'' Victoria scolded him lightly with a shake of her head.

''Mmm, just the boy in me, I guess.''

''Well, you're a grown man, and you shouldn't talk like that. Someone might hear.'' She looked about them, hoping it was not already too late.

''You're right, I suppose,'' he replied, scratching his chin. ''I'll forget it. This time.'' He eyed her mockingly, fighting back a smile until they could not refrain themselves any longer and burst into laughter.

''I think I better look at something else,'' she grinned. ''I'd feel so guilty merely holding it now.''

''Whatever is your wish, my dear. And if you'll excuse me, I'll pay Mr. Penbrook what I owe from my last visit.''

''Everything, I hope,'' she whispered.

He straightened as if hurt. ''As much as I can remember of it,'' he rallied. He bowed slightly and turned away, leaving Victoria to watch him.

Although he hobbled noticeably, he carried himself

383

proudly, radiating full command over everything surrounding him. Victoria cocked her head to one side, appraising his wide shoulders, narrow waist, and the way the muscles of his good leg flexed with each step he took. He might be twice her age, but his physical appearance certainly denied it. Steel-blue eyes flashed into her mind. Straightening sharply, she looked around in all directions as though her thoughts had sung the chorus of her musings for everyone to hear. She relaxed only when she found herself alone and forced her attention on the brightly colored ribbons at one of the counters.

A duet of footsteps came along the wooden planks of the sidewalk in front of the store before two well-dressed figures darkened the doorway. Damon glanced up at the sound, nodded politely, and returned to his task of making right the sum he owed Arnold Penbrook. Not the least discouraged by his lack of enthusiasm, Melody Burrows and her twin sister, Maureen, hurried toward him, stopping one on each side of him, and failing to take note of anyone else in the general store.

The entire town talked about the Burrows family and the sudden wealth they had acquired. Thornton Burrow's aunt had died, leaving him with a sizable fortune two years before, turning the candlemaker into one of the richest men in Williamsburg. He forced his family into different circles, debuting his son and daughters as the most eligible catches in town. But all their finery failed to hide their poor upbringing and lack of social graces whenever they opened their mouths.

''Good morning, Mr. Rutledge,'' Melody purred, waiting until he looked at her so she might persent him with a coy smile and a flutter of lashes. "Papa told us you were here."

"Will you be staying a few days?" Maureen chimed in, hoping to draw his attention her way.

His business with Penbrook completed, Damon turned to face them, a lame smile parting his lips. "Yes, a few," he replied softly. "How is your father, ladies?"

Maureen giggled, enjoying the rich, deep tones of his voice.

"Just fine, Mr. Rutledge," Melody offered. "He says if you have time, to stop by and share a glass of wine."

"Well, I-ah—"

"Oh, you must, Mr. Rutledge," Maureen pressed. "Surely you won't have to spend every hour with that Remington bitch."

Victoria's head shot upward.

"I—I beg your pardon?" Damon stumbled, surprised by the attack on his companion.

"Well, we've heard you asked to court her, but it's not like you're engaged or anything, is it?" Maureen continued sarcastically.

"Well, no, but—"

"She's such a spoiled brat," Melody scoffed, "It must bore you to tears to have to be with her for very long." The women exchanged haughty glances. "Now we, on the other hand—"

Damon raised his left hand to hide his smile, and over Melody's head caught Victoria's brittle regard of them. He'd often heard about her temper, which was said to match the eldest Remington's, and he wondered how long it would hold in this case. He had been warned the Burrows sisters sought husbands, but until now had never suspected they would latch on to him. They were pretty enough, but after spending just a short time with Victoria, he knew them to be greatly lacking in comparison.

"Well, Mr. Rutledge?" Maureen coaxed. "Wouldn't you like to spend this evening with us? At dinner, perhaps?"

He blinked, dropping his arm to his side. "Sorry. We're attending the theater tonight," he answered calmly, his mirth at their brazeness infecting his words.

"Oh, that's no problem," Melody cooed. "We can ask our brother Timmy to take *Mistress* Remington."

"Good idea, Melody," Maureen agreed. "After spending all that time with pirates, she can't expect to be too choosy."

Damon's roar of laughter made the girls stop abruptly to stare at him in wide-eyed confusion. What Maureen had said wasn't meant to be funny. In unison, they looked at Mr. Penbrook, spying the beads of nervous perspiration dotting his brow and upper lip. He gulped, then nodded past them. One after another they followed his lead to find themselves beneath Victoria's heated glare. Their jaws sagged, they fought for breath, words vanishing to leave them prey to Victoria's berating.

A slight flare to her nostrils, Victoria otherwise held herself in check as she picked up several ribbons from the counter and walked toward the group. Handing them to Mr. Penbrook, she said with forced sweetness, "Put these on my father's account, Mr. Penbrook." She turned to the twins, a smile parting her lips. "Good morning, Melody, Maureen. Did I understand you to mean you won't be attending the theater tonight? You know, of course, anyone of breeding will be there. But then again, your absence will be understood."

Two noses raised higher in frustrated muteness, any excuse they might have made for not attending deserting them. Their mouths opened and closed repeatedly until, giving way to their loss of face, they lifted their numerous yards of skirts and quickly hurried from the store, knowing their wits to be no match for Victoria Remington's.

"My profound apologies, madam, for being unable to restrain my laughter," Damon chuckled. "But I knew you heard every word and delighted in the way they sank themselves deeper."

Victoria glared at the vacant doorway. "I understand," she admitted. "It just infuriated me to hear them claim *I'm* spoiled. They wouldn't have lasted two days at what I was forced to endure. Not to mention their implications. The mindless twits."

"Forget it, my sweet," Damon soothed, lifting a dark curl from her shoulder. "It will be a long while before they are so free with their words again." Taking the ribbons wrapped in brown paper from Mr. Penbrook, he presented his arm to her. "Shall we visit the dress shop? I think you deserve a new gown."

By the time they reached Mrs. Willowby's establishment, the encounter with the Burrows twins had faded to the back of Victoria's mind. The shop door's bell tinkled loudly as they entered, summoning the gray-haired widow from the back room.

"Miss Victoria," she cried out happily from the doorway. "It's been such a long time. How are you, child?"

"Fine. Thank you," Victoria smiled in return.

Suddenly, Mrs. Willowby's gaze looked past her. "And Mr. Rutledge," she beamed anew. "It's an honor to have you in my shop. My daughter has often spoken of you."

"Your daughter?" Damon began then raised a point finger. "Ah, yes, Claire. I haven't seen her in a while. I trust she's well."

"Yes, thank you. Someday you must join us for tea," Mrs. Willowby invited, with a swoop of her hand to a stray tendril of hair, all but forgetting Victoria's presence.

Victoria pretended not to listen, but in fact marveled at Damon's effect on women. First the Burrows twins, now on Mrs. Willowby and obviously her daughter. Having moved away from the pair to examine a bolt of velvet cloth, she covertly studied Damon again. Yes, of the lot of Williamsburg's bachelors, he certainly was the most acceptable. She returned to her appraisal of the shop's goods.

"Victoria," Damon said, coming to stand next to her. "I'm quite sure you'll find something here to your liking, and since measurements must be taken by Mrs. Willowby, I beg your leave to attend to matters elsewhere. I will return shortly."

"All right, Damon," she nodded politely, watching him slowly make his way outside.

She spent the better part of the next hour selecting several cloths; a blue silk, a pastel yellow cotton, and a mauve muslin, before stepping into the back room where Mrs. Willowby acquired the figures she needed to create a perfectly fit gown. Victoria had just finished brushing the last defiant tendril of her hair into a neatly curled ringlet when the doorbell announced someone's arrival. She looked up to find Damon smiling back at her.

"Ready?" he asked.

She nodded, waved farewell to Mrs. Willowby, and stepped past Damon as he held the door open for her. They visited McNally's Cove for lunch, the millinery shop, where she selected a straw bonnet, another boutique for a new parasol and a bottle of French perfume, and headed back to the Chesterfield House in late afternoon. But as they passed one of the local inns, the sound of loud voices from within drew their attention. Recognizing the sounds as indication of a brawl, Damon took her elbow to hurry their steps. But when they moved past the inn's door, a man flew from the tavern as if he'd sprouted wings and collided with Damon, knocking him into his companion.

"You bloody idiot!" Damon roared dangerously. "Get the hell away."

Having had more than his share of ale, the light-complected man swayed precariously, trying to focus one eye on the tyrant who voiced disapproval. "Well, I c-couldn't help it. And w-who you callin' an idiot, you—you idiot!" He fell back a step, caught himself, and tried to stand erect, failing miserably as he stumbled forward again. His arms shot outward to save himself from disaster, grasping hold of a very shapely figure instead. Victoria screamed when his hand brushed against one breast.

Outraged, Damon jerked the man away and slammed a fist to the drunk's jaw. The stranger's knees buckled, crashing him to the sidewalk. Lifting his cane high above his head, Damon made to strike him with it, bringing a startled cry of protest from Victoria.

"Damon, please! It was an accident. He's drunk," she pleaded frantically.

His entire body trembled with rage, and the ivory scrollwork of the cane quivered dangerously. A long while passed before Damon lowered the walking stick. He glared at the frightened face staring back at him, then seized Victoria's arm painfully and ushered her away as the inhabitants of the inn rushed outside.

"Damn it, John," the blond man said to the man who knelt beside him. "He wasn't supposed to hit me!"

"Aye, laddie," McGuire grinned. "But I think ya got carried away. Ya was only ta get a good look at him. Not introduce yourself."

Thomas gave his captain a sour look, struggled to his feet, and followed McGuire into the alleyway.

TWENTY-THREE

"Mama, you should have seen him," Victoria said enthusiastically. "I never dreamed a cripple would react so. He was marvelous."

Alanna smiled up at her daughter in the reflection of the mirror as she finished coiffuring her hair. "Careful, my child. You sound as if you like him."

All hint of praise for his actions vanished from Victoria's face. She moved away, carefully avoiding her mother's mocking smile. "Well, I guess maybe I do."

"There's nothing wrong with that," Alanna quickly added. "It's just that a few days ago you had made up your mind you never could. I knew that would change as soon as you spent a little time alone with him. Maybe now you can better understand why your father selected him."

Victoria shrugged. "Yes, I suppose." She turned back and went to the bed, sitting down on the edge, a new exuberance taking over. "He was so funny at Mr. Penbrook's this afternoon. He wanted to take a doll from the store without paying for it." She straightened instantly with her mother's frown. "Oh, but he didn't! He only teased. And you should have seen his face when the Burrows sisters flirted with him. Why they couldn't see how much he disliked it is beyond me." She shook her head, smiling with the vision she conjured up, and stood. "Are you ready? I'm sure Papa grows weary waiting in the sitting room for us. And hungrier."

Lifting her shawl from the back of the chair, Alanna stood. "I think so. How do I look?" She whirled to allow a full view, her skirts billowing out from her narrow waistline.

"I don't know," Victoria frowned, then smiled brightly at her mother's worried look. "It's hard to criticize perfection."

"Oh, you—" Alanna laughed, reaching out to pinch the tip of Victoria's nose. "I should know better than to ask you. You're just like your father." Tossing the shawl over her shoulders, she crossed to the door of the bedchamber. "Well, come on, if you're in such a hurry."

Standing outside the Chesterfield House, Sean glanced hesitantly through the leaded glass panes of the door to the lobby. This had to be the place where the Remingtons were staying. He'd tried all the other inns and they weren't registered at any of them. If his luck held, he'd finish his errand and be gone without anyone's really noticing him. He straightened the white lacy ascot at his neck and opened the front door.

The view of the entrance hall captured Sean's attention the moment he stepped inside. A massive chandelier hung proudly in the center of the room, with what seemed thousands of candles and crystal teardrops dangling from each point. Sean smiled to himself as he studied it, wondering how the one who lit it managed to fire every wick before the first candle burned to a stub.

Opposite him, beyond the wide circular staircase leading to the upper level, he spied the registry desk, his destination. Apprehension at crossing to it tickled the hair on the back of his neck, certain every guest casually strolling about the lobby knew his purpose, or at best wondered about it. However, standing mutely in the center of the room would certainly pique their curiosity, and Sean moved to mingle unobserved with the crowd.

A few steps from the full-figured gentleman behind the desk, an explosion of merry laughter hailed Sean's attention. He turned without thought of consequence. Gracefully descending the carpeted stairs was a raven-haired beauty dressed solely in pastel blue silk, a rather striking, almost demanding-looking man at her side. From the angle at which Sean viewed them, they presented only their profiles, one of which he could not recognize. Then his gaze fell on the couple behind them. The second man walked with difficulty, one hand clasped on the balustrade, the other to his cane. But at his side and furthest from Sean, descended Victoria Remington. Worriedly, knowing one glance his way would be devastating, Sean looked at the front door. He took a step. No. His feet could not carry him fast enough to exit the place before the party reached the bottom of the staircase. He glanced over his shoulder. The dining hall! Yes, he would stop inside to wait. In a few moments they would be gone.

"I honestly don't think Henry knew what he said," Beau laughed, "or how it sounded."

"Poor Agnes," Alanna moaned, allowing her husband to gently take her elbow and guide her down the remaining stairs, and then toward the dining hall.

Several steps behind and out of hearing, Damon leaned toward Victoria. "I want you to know how much I enjoy your parents, Victoria. There's nothing false about them. It's no wonder they're so respected in Williamsburg."

Victoria smiled graciously at his compliment. "Thank you. I'm sure they would be pleased to think you feel that way." She paused a moment to allow Damon the chance to switch his cane to the other hand and hold out his arm for her to take. "I never had the opportunity before now to thank you for defending me this afternoon." She felt the muscles of his arm tighten beneath her touch.

"And I must apologize for having lost my temper the way I did. It was unforgivable." He frowned.

"But I quite disagree. The man was rude. You only reacted as a gentleman would."

"Not really. I would have bashed his head in if you hadn't stopped me." He bit off each word.

"I find that difficult to believe."

"But it's true. I nearly killed a man once. In a situation very much like that one. He was drunk, challenged me, and didn't give me a chance to defend myself. He just shot me. In the knee. I was so blinded with rage, I didn't feel the pain. All I remember was someone pulling me off him. He was unconscious for days, and I wound up a cripple."

Victoria noticed the pain in his eyes and wondered if the wounded limb caused it or merely the memories of its happening. She felt a twinge of sympathy for him. They followed the others into the dining hall.

Sean sat down at one of the few vacant tables and ordered a glass of wine to pass away the time until he would feel safe in leaving the dining hall and the inn. At a distance from the doorway, he sat facing it, wondering where the Remington party would spend the evening. Uncomfortable not only in a room of unfriendly strangers but in the tight-fitting clothes that contradicted his way of life, he nervously glanced about the room while he tugged at the collar of his shirt. Then his eyes caught sight of the couples framed in the doorway.

"Damn," he muttered, slinking down in his chair.

Rutledge and Victoria followed her parents to a table a comfortable distance away from Sean and sat down. He relaxed when he noticed that only Victoria had a full view of him. Maybe he could slip out a back way.

"That was one of the most delicious roast ducks I've ever eaten," Damon sighed, pushing his plate further toward the center of the table. "And the wine was superb. Care for a little more, Victoria?" He lifted the decanter in expectation of her approval.

She smiled a nod and watched the clear liquid cascade into her glass. Casually she wrapped her fingers around the stemware but did not lift it to her lips, listening instead to her father.

"Damon, I want you to meet Henry Wilkes. He's one of my closest friends and runs a hell of a newspaper."

"Yes, I know. I've read it."

Remington took a sip of wine. "He's thinking of selling it."

"He is?" Alanna cut in. "I didn't know that."

"Says he's getting old," Remington chuckled. "But I think all we'd have to do is tell him the paper couldn't get along without him a few hundred times and he'd change his mind."

"Beau," Alanna scolded, "Henry's not the type to need compliments continually. You misjudge him."

"Oh?" he smiled. "Then why does he constantly tell me how awful his stories are?"

"Maybe it's an excuse. He wants someone to agree so he can sell the paper and not feel guilty."

"I thought so too once, so I said, 'Yes, I think it needs improvement.' I didn't really, but you should have seen his face!" Remington laughed aloud. "I thought he'd burst!"

Victoria shook her head, a smile parting her lips. "Papa, you're mean to him."

"If you think that's terrible, you should have seen the things he did to your grandfather," Alanna added, the twinkle in her eye negating the stern tone of her words.

"Now I never did anything he didn't deserve," Remington protested.

"Oh? And what about the time you and Radford stole his clothes while he swam in the river, and made him walk home without them?"

"Papa, you didn't!" Victoria exploded.

Remington raised his hands in defense. "I was only a boy then. And besides, it was Radford's idea."

"Oh, yes, blame him," Alanna laughed.

"Well, it was," her husband argued.

Relaxing in the gaiety of the moment, enjoying the laughter and bantering of her parents, Victoria glanced at Damon, who returned her smile, then raised her glass of wine to her lips. Briefly appraising the fine cut of the crystal, she looked out over the end of the goblet, her gaze absently resting on those bright blue eyes staring back at her from across the room, her own widening in disbelief. Hair the color of corn silk, bronze complexion, the devil-may-care twinkle beaming in his eyes, brought instant recognition and a choked gasp from Victoria as she inhaled a drop of wine. Seized with a fit of coughing to clear her lungs, she nearly spilled the remaining wine as she clunked the glass on the table again.

"Are you all right?" Damon's brows knitted in concern as he handed her his napkin.

Gasping for air, tears blurring her vision, she accepted the cloth and covered her mouth, nodding. Several moments passed before she could breathe easily again, and, when she could, she carefully avoided looking in Sean's direction, certain the terror she felt would shine clearly on her face. What in God's name was he

397

doing here? In the dining hall? And if he was in Williamsburg— She closed her eyes, certain that if she glanced to either side of him she'd spot steel-blue eyes glaring back at her. Had he been freed already? Or was this Sean's warning to beware—that within the hour Dru would appear to seek his revenge for her lies? Confusion ruled her inner being, one feeling overlapping the other as early dawn fights to brighten the blackness of night, indistinct, one challenging to overtake the other. Relief to know he would be freed of his torture struggled with her fear that she would pay for her part in causing it.

"Victoria?"

Her eyes flew open.

"Are you all right?" her father asked.

She nodded nervously, fighting the temptation to look at the reason for her discomfort.

"What happened?" He scowled, his dark brows shadowing his eyes.

"I—I laughed when I shouldn't have." She felt herself weaken. She looked to her lap.

"Would you like a glass of water?" Damon offered.

She smiled up at him, shaking off the suggestion, and before she could stop herself looked at Sean again. He raised his glass high in the air in a silent salute. She stiffened and quickly studied the tablecloth. But not before her father had noticed. Wonderingly, he slowly looked from his daughter to across the room where he spotted a lone man casually sipping his wine, his attention centered elsewhere. His brow wrinkled. Where had he seen him before?

"Excuse me, Mr. Remington."

Beau glanced up in startled surprise. Smiling back at

him was Mitchell Clay, the magistrate. "Good evening, Mitchell. What can I do for you?"

"I was wondering if I might have a word with you." He glanced briefly at the others sitting around the table. "Alone."

Sliding his chair back, Remington laid his crumpled napkin next to his plate and stood. "Surely, Mitchell." He looked at the members of his group. "Excuse me a moment," he apologized and followed the man into the lobby. They stopped just outside the doorway.

"Is something wrong, Mitchell?" Remington asked.

Mitchell Clay lived in Richmond. His duties as magistrate forced him to travel the circuit between home, Petersburg, Williamsburg, and all the little towns in between. Because of the distance involved, his visits were few and far between. He had held the office of judge for twenty years, and Beau and he knew each other quite well. And in all those years Beau could never get the man to call him by his first name. Out of respect, Mitchell had claimed. Beau had smiled. If anything, Mitchell Clay was the one who deserved respect.

"You're not gonna like it," Mitchell replied, unable to look at him.

"I can see that," Remington admitted. Mitchell never could hide his emotions, and right now he was downright upset. "So spill it out. No sense in brooding over it."

"Silas Werner was attacked in the jail three or four nights ago. The prisoners escaped with the help of their friends."

His words couldn't have had more effect if Mitchell had doubled up a fist and cuffed Remington alongside his ear. Body trembling with rage, nostrils flared, breathing slowed to long, deeply held breaths that he finally expelled in an angry rush, Beau fought to control his fury. He had known something was amiss! He had sensed it!

"Why wasn't I informed right away?" he bellowed.

"Henry Wilkes was the one who found Silas. He had gone to the jail to do a story on the prisoner. I arrived the following morning. I wanted to send someone out to your place right then, but Henry said you had sent word you'd be in Williamsburg within a few days. So we waited. Wasn't much you could have done anyway. They were long gone by then."

Silas Werner. The town jailer and town drunk. Remington knew he never should have left the captain in Werner's care. He had suspected the pirate's friends would try to break him out, but he had also thought it would take longer. He had assumed the scoundrel would be hanged before any of his mates could— His shoulders dropped. Of course! The men on the road. He should have trusted his instincts. He stiffened, remembering the man at the table. Now he knew why he seemed familair.

His head snapping around, Remington demanded furiously, "Mitchell, arrest that man—" Beau's forefinger pointed damningly at an empty chair.

"Who, Mr. Remington?" Clay visibly trembled in The Hawk's shadow, knowing full well how he had acquired the title.

Slowly, Beau lowered his hand, his narrowed eyes scanning the room for the man. Gone! He had nearly had one of the pirate's accomplices in his hands and didn't know it! His rage began again. Then out of the sea of startled faces staring back at him, Remington's heated glare fell upon his daughter. She knew who he was and had never said a word. Why? Whirling angrily, he clamped Mitchell's shirt front in a steely grasp.

"He's blond, fair, and more than likely Irish! I want him, Mitchell," he hissed through clenched teeth, "and I want him tonight!"

TWENTY-FOUR

Standing just inside the front door of the crowded pub where they had elected to meet, Sean briefly glanced about the room before he spotted Dru, McKenzie, and John at a far table. Removing his tricorn, he quickly crossed to them and sat down.

"Where's Thomas?" he asked, motioning for the barmaid to bring him a mug of ale.

"I sent him back ta the ships. This will be takin' longer than we thought, and I didn't want the crew ta come sailin' in here riskin' their lives when there be no need." Dru leaned forward, resting his arms on the table's edge. "So what did ya find out?"

"They be stayin' at the Chesterfield House," he said.

"Are ya sure?"

A wide grin wrinkled the scar beneath his eye. "That ya can be sure of. Nearly got meself caught findin' out."

"And how did ya manage that, me friend?" John half laughed.

Taking the mug from the dark-haired servant, Sean swallowed a long gulp before answering. "Remington, his wife and daughter, and this Rutledge character came down the stairs just as I was about ta check the register. I couldn't leave without them seein' me so I went in the dinin' hall ta wait. Damn if they didn't follow me in." He took another drink of ale.

"So what happened?" Donovan urged impatiently.

"They sat down a few tables away and ate dinner." He purposely avoided the meaning of McKenzie's question, enjoying the angry look it produced.

"Ya be knowin' what I mean, lad," Donovan warned, his voice low.

As if to contradict him, Sean straightened, a blank look on his face, but the ever present twinkle shining in his eyes.

"After dinner," Donovan enlightened him with a cocked brow.

"Oh," Sean sang out, masterfully hiding a grin. "Well, Miss Victoria saw me, and so did her father. I'm sure he didn't know who I was, but as soon as I could, I snuck out the back."

"Then ya not be knowin' where they are now?" Dru asked.

Sean shook his head, draining his mug and ordering a second. "But I be guessin' from the fine way they be dressed they won't be goin' ta bed."

Dru leaned back in his chair, one arm crossed to support his other elbow while he traced his lower lip with his thumb.

"What is it ya be thinkin', me friend?" John asked after a moment.

"That you are the only one Remington has never seen."

"Aye. So?"

"So I be thinkin' me cousin and Donovan should be the ones goin' ta Pennsylvania."

"Pennsylvania!" Sean exploded. "Why would ya be wantin' us to go there?"

"Ta find out about Mr. Rutledge. All we know is what Cinnamon told us, and no one else around here knows any more. He's suppose ta have owned a plantation there, and if he's what he says he is, you'll be confirmin' that fact. Then we can be sailin' as soon as ya return."

"Pennsylvania," Sean muttered, then looked his cousin in the eye. "And I be supposin' ya expect me ta ride a horse."

Dru shrugged one shoulder playfully. " 'Tis faster than walkin'."

"When do we leave?" McKenzie asked after the barmaid had given Sean a refill and gone on to her next customer.

Dru grinned openly, watching his cousin down more than half his ale in one breath.

"I can be tellin' ya that," Sean growled, slamming the mug to the table. "I be knowin' this man longer than any of ya and he be wantin' us ta leave now!" He rose irritably. "And me without a decent meal in me belly. Well, come on, Donovan or ya will be swallowin' me dust." Shoving the tricorn snugly on his head, its point shading his eyes, Sean took a step, then paused, turning back to his cousin. "The least ya can do is see us off.''

Quickly coming to his feet, Dru bowed, stretching out a hand for Sean to lead the way, and grinned at Donovan when Sean moved toward the door.

Night overtook the waterfront in an eerie blackness. It enshrouded the passage of four men on their way to the livery stable and masked the departure of two on horseback. Dru and McGuire stood in the shadows until even the sounds of the hoofbeats faded into the distance. Tapping his companion's arm with the back of his hand, Dru signaled their return to the pub, stopping abruptly when he stepped from the alleyway and nearly collided with someone. Covered with a long, flowing black cape, the stranger quickly touched a hand to his hat and stepped away, disappearing into the cloud of darkness.

''I be thinkin' by the cut of his clothes,'' John chuckled, ''that the fine gentleman doesn't want his wife ta find out where he is tonight.''

Dru smiled at the thought, but lingered a moment longer. He had heard of no brothels in this part of town.

''Darling, won't you tell me now what it is that had you so upset all evening?'' Alanna asked, neatly folding her shawl and placing it in a dresser drawer. She turned to observe her husband when she heard the clink of glass, and found him filling a goblet full of wine. ''What did Mitchell tell you?''

Beau sent her a dark scowl, one which would have made anyone else shrink away, but which only slightly affected his wife. He swallowed the wine and poured another. "Our fine scum of a jailtender let the pirate escape."

"Escape?" Alanna echoed, worry for her daughter's safety twisting the beautiful features of her face.

"Yes. And those men on the road we passed near Raven Oaks? They were his friends. I'm almost certain of it."

Alanna shook her head. "But if they were, what were they doing there?" she argued, praying her husband wrong. "Even Damon said it didn't make sense for them to be traveling away from Williamsburg."

"I don't know," he growled, slapping down his glass on a nearby table. He jerked his coat from his shoulders, tossed it to the bed, and picked up the goblet again. "And one of them was in the dining hall this evening."

"Here?" Alanna shrieked. "But how can you be certain?"

"Because I'd never seen him before."

Some of her fears vanished. "But Beau," she soothed, crossing to him. Gently, she placed a hand to his clutching the wineglass. "A lot of strangers come to Williamsburg to attend the theater."

"Yes. However, no one else caused the reaction he got from Victoria."

"What do you mean?"

"When she choked on her wine. Said she laughed when she shouldn't have. Ha!" he roared, bolting past his wife. He went to the fireplace and glared at its emptiness. "She recognized him."

"If she did, then why didn't she say something?"

His anger seemed to ebb. "That's what I wondered. It was as if—as if she protected him."

"Protected—Beau, you've let this thing get the better of you. Why would Victoria protect someone responsible for her kidnapping?"

"I don't know," he said, more calmly than before. "But I have this awful suspicion things aren't what she claims. If they were, why would these pirates still be hanging around? You'd think they'd hightail it out of here."

"But you're not truly certain the men you saw are who you think they are."

"I will be. Just as soon as Mitchell brings me the man from the dining hall." He finished his wine, set the glass on the mantel, and went to the dressing table. Pulling open a top drawer, he withdrew a gold-painted box. "Meanwhile," he added, taking out a pistol to load it, "Victoria must not be left alone. They just might have decided to take her again, since I cheated them out of their reward the first time."

"But darling, they wouldn't be foolish enough to try something in this inn. They'd never get away with it. And besides, her room is right next to ours. We'd hear something if they did try to get to her. Which they won't. They're not stupid, Beau." She hoped she sounded more confident than she felt.

"Oh? They were once."

Alanna forced a smile. "And they didn't know whom they were up against then. Now they do. And put away the gun. You know how I detest those things." She smiled sweetly at him when he made to argue, then watched contentedly while he shoved the pistol back into the box and returned it to the drawer. "When are you meeting with Henry?" she asked, purposely changing the subject.

"Tomorrow night," he sighed, crossing to the bed. He sat down and kicked off his shoes. "And promise me you won't leave Victoria alone."

Sharing the worry he felt, Alanna went to him and knelt at his feet. "I promise," she whispered. "In a while this will only be an unpleasant memory." She reached out to hold his hand, praying for the truth of her words.

"It's the third door on the left at the top of the stairs," the bright-eyed youngster told Dru.

"Was she alone?"

"Yes, sir. Said the flowers were beautiful."

"Did ya tell her what I told ya ta say?"

"Yes, sir. 'The man who sent me said to say thank you for a lovely evening,' " the boy recited.

A little premature, Dru thought with a grin, but I'm certain it will be. He pulled a coin from his pocket and gave it to the urchin, who was dressed in tattered clothes. "Be gettin' yourself somethin' ta eat."

"Thank ya, sir. And if ya need me again, ya know where to find me."

"Aye, lad, that I do," Dru smiled, patting the boy's head. He tugged his waistcoat into place as he watched the child skip away, and turned to enter the Chesterfield House, tucking his tricorn beneath his arm.

From somewhere in the exquisite lobby a clock chimed eleven, and Dru casually ascended the wide staircase on his way toward Victoria's room, the only heads turning in curiosity those of the ladies, appraising the handsome stranger. At the landing he paused, glanced briefly in both directions to find the corridor empty, and continued on. Outside the door the boy had described, a hand raised to announce his presence, Dru froze, hearing the latch click of another door somewhere near.

Sitting before her dressing table, Victoria lingeringly brushed the long, silken tresses cascading over her shoulder, her gaze fixed to the bouquet's reflection in the mirror. Bright pink flowers greeted her, and she smiled, impressed that Damon had chosen the color to match the shade of the gown she had worn to the theater. It had been a pleasant evening. Damon had filled every moment and pushed the thoughts of Sean's appearance to the back of her mind. Maybe it was what she had witnessed with the drunk earlier that gave her a sense of security. Between Damon and her father, she felt certain Dru would never be able to get close to her. And in time, he'd grow weary of trying and sail away. Her smile faded. And never return.

As if summoned by her conscience, a gentle breeze stirred outside the window of her room, idly floating in and carrying with it the fragrance of the sea. It touched her bare shoulders, caressed her neck, and she shuddered, imagining it to be the pirate captain who had stolen into her room. Shaking off the thought, she rose quickly and donned her robe, pulling its sash tightly around her waist and chasing away the illusion. Would there never be any peace for her? Would he always appear in her thoughts, day or night? No, Damon would replace the sadness in her heart.

Startled from her musings by a knock on her door, Victoria frowned, wondering who it might be at such a late hour. Picking up the candle from her dressing table, she left the bedchamber and crossed the sitting room to the door.

"Who's there?" she called.

No one answered.

"Who's there?" she said again, her voice louder.

But still she got no reply. A smile crossed her lips. Maybe Damon had come to ask if she had enjoyed his gift and feared her parents might hear if he called out. Placing the candle on the small table to one side of the door, she turned the key in the lock and lifted the latch. Only the light from the hallway flooded in, bringing a frown from her. Had she mistaken the sound? Stepping forward, she peered out into the hallway, looking to the right to find it empty. *That's odd*, she thought, *I could have sworn—* She straightened and looked the other way. Her eyes widened, her breath caught in her throat. Lounging against the wall, his arms folded over his chest, Dru smiled back at her, the dimple in his cheek heightening his devilish air.

"Oh-h-h—" she whimpered, fumbling for the door-latch behind her, her gaze frozen on his handsome, mocking face. How could she have been so stupid? She should have known he would come! Tears burned her eyes. She blinked and swallowed hard, focusing her attention on securing the door and locking him outside. Whirling, she grabbed the edge of the door, swinging it with all her might. It slammed shut. Her breath expelled in a long ragged heave. Thinking herself safe, the weary smile that touched the corner of her mouth quickly vanished when her gaze fell upon the brass key protruding from the lock.

"No-o-o—" she cried, lunging for it.

Shaky fingers twisted the key, the dull click it produced collapsing her against the door. She held her breath. Was he gone? Had she heard *his* footsteps or another's? Dear God, what should she do? She couldn't run to her father. The pirate captain might be waiting outside. Damon? No, his room was further. A tear trickled down her cheek. Would he kill her? Surely her lies weren't grave enough to warrant revenge to that degree. Then what did he intend? To take her prisoner again? To reap the profits he thought he deserved? A deadly silence enveloped her. *Had* he gone? She pressed an ear to the door. No. He only thought to trick her! He waited! He *wanted* her to open the door again so he could force his way in.

Never, her mind declared. *I'll never open the door. Stand there 'til you grow weary. I'll not be tricked!*

Slowly, she began to back away, praying the quaking of her limbs would cease. He wouldn't break down the door. It would alarm the entire inn. Then what? Did he plan to drive her mad? She pulled herself up, her lower lip trembling, and took another step. *You don't scare me, Dru Chandler,* she thought proudly, a sob betraying her.

Having absently backed across the sitting room, she reached out to brace herself against the bedchamber door, resting her brow to the coolness of its wood. Her eyes flooded with tears.

"I didn't mean for them to hurt you," she whispered. "I only wanted to even the score. You played me for a fool." *And stole my heart,* she admitted inwardly. But that he would never know. She stood erect, wiping the tears from her face, and sadly looked back at the bouquet of flowers.

Standing in the darkness of her bedchamber, she suddenly saw the open doors leading to the balcony. "Oh-h-h," she wailed, racing toward them. Frantic,

411

she hurriedly shut out the soft summer breeze, barring anyone from entering, and fell back against their security, her eyes closed as she fought to control the pounding of her heart.

What I need is a glass of wine, she thought, remembering the decanter sitting on the table in the other room. She took a deep breath, let it out in a rush, and opened her eyes. Fear paralyzed her every muscle, for, standing silhouetted in the candle's glow of the sitting room, a shadowed figure blocked her way to the front door. Feet apart, arms folded over his chest, Victoria knew in an instant she had tarried too long. She had played right into his hands, allowed him the time he needed to climb the trellis outside her room.

Dropping his swaggering stance, Dru stepped closer, stopping when she raised a hand.

"Don't come any closer," she warned, "or I'll scream."

Although she couldn't see his face, she felt certain he smiled.

"I—I mean it. Papa is right next door. You'll be taken prisoner again."

He waited, as if contemplating her threat.

Drawing courage from his stillness, she asked in a hoarse whisper, "What do you want?"

Startled when he moved again, she relaxed only a little, watching him walk toward the dressing table. Casually, he picked up her hairbrush, idly toying with it before he looked her way again. The soft yellow glow of candlelight touched his face for the first time. She had forgotten how truly handsome he was. She swallowed the knot in her throat.

"You," he said softly. "I be wantin' you."

"W-what?" she choked.

"Aye. Ya heard. If ya remember, on me ship just before I took ya to your father, I warned ya that if anythin' went wrong, I'd take the money *and* you." He tossed the brush down with a thud. "Since I be cheated of me money, I've come ta claim you."

"Y-you mean to r-rape me?" Her throat tightened, wondering how she could love a man who could take her without a care.

A smile broke the serious lines of his face. "I be thinkin' there's no need."

The fear of the moment before vanished, rage there in its stead. "Why you pompous ass, you rogue! You think I'd submit willingly?"

"Aye," he grinned, his fingers interlaced and folded in front of him.

"Ha!" she rallied. "Why? What gives you such an idea?"

Lazily, he slipped out of his jacket and laid it over the back of the chair sitting next to him, followed by the ascot. He unfastened the buttons of his waistcoat. "Me cousin and I had an enjoyable talk with a friend of yours." The finely made waistcoat found its place onto the chair.

Victoria watched its descent, blinking when she realized what he had said. "A friend—who?"

"The same who was kind enough ta bring me whiskey and food durin' me stay in your fine prison," he said, reaching for the top button of his shirt as he kicked off his shoes.

"Cinnamon?" she breathed. "You talked to Cinn— What did she tell you?"

The second button popped loose. "Now it wouldn't

413

be kind ta be repeatin' gossip," he grinned, working the next free.

"Gossip? What gossip?" Her eyes widened when he pulled the shirttail from his breeches. "Oh, God, stop that!"

"It seems the lass thinks you've fallen in love with a pompous ass, a rogue," he mimicked. He stepped nearer.

"Oh, she does, does she?" Victoria said, nervously retreating when he moved too close. "Well, she's wrong! And so are you, if you think I'll allow you to—to—" Her shoulder bumped against the armoire behind her. Her heart pounded in her ears.

"To what, Victoria? To hold ya in me arms." He whispered, taking another step. "To brush a kiss against your throat, smell the fragrance of your hair? To make love to you?"

How long had it been since the first time? And how often had she relived those moments in her daydreams, wanting to savor them, keep them forever? She closed her eyes, recalling the scent of him as he lay beside her, how safe she had felt cradled in his embrace. She relaxed, wondering if each time would be the same, or would he grow ardent in his desire and hurt her? Her eyes flew open. What did it matter? It would never happen again! Realizing she had wasted time standing so near to him, she broke for the front door, trapped when he easily reached out and grabbed her wrist.

"Don't fight it, lass," he spoke softly, pulling her close. "Ya be wantin' me as much as I be wantin' you."

"No, I don't," she barked, fighting to free the fingers held tightly to her wrist. "Let go. You're hurting

414

me.''

"Ya be causin' the pain yourself." He paused, then said, "Admit it, Victoria."

She stopped her struggles. "What?"

"That from the beginnin' I not only captured you, but your heart as well."

"You conceited fool! Do you think every woman you hold next to you falls in love?"

The dimple appeared. "Aye. But none as soft and eager as you."

Every pore of her skin tingled with rage. "Oh-h-h," she growled, raising her hand. Before she could strike the mocking grin from his face, he reached up and claimed her other wrist, twisting it in back of her to pull her to his chest.

She wiggled to break his grip, her flesh burning from the contact, but failed, instead seeming to tighten his hold. Finding it difficult to breathe, she relaxed in his arms, her head falling back. Fooled, he loosened his grip, allowing her the time to draw a deep breath, raise her foot, and bring it down hard, crushing her heel to his toe. When he set her at arms' length a moment to recover, she fleetingly praised his ability not to call out his pain and broke free of him. She raced for the door. Before she took a fourth step, his arms swooped around her, crushed her to his chest again, and, in a single leap, fell with her onto the bed.

"Ya little minx," he whispered in her ear. "I'll not be tricked so easily again."

His full weight pressing her into the softness of the feather mattress, she wonder if he intended to smother her. "I—I c-can't breathe-e-e," she moaned.

"Do ya promise not ta fight?" He did not relent an

ounce, waiting, enjoying the feel of her beneath him.

"Y-yes!"

He smiled, knowing she agreed too easily. However, since their struggles awarded him more pleasure than if they merely discussed their differences, he decided to test her, willing to endure what minor pain she might inflict in return for the touch of her rounded curves. Cautiously, he lifted from her. She rolled onto her back. But as she came around, she doubled up her fist and struck him in the stomach. Again he made no sound louder than a grunt as he clutched his belly in apparent agony, leaving Victoria free to scoot off the bed. She ran to the dresser and the bottle of perfume sitting there. She raised it high, watching him put one foot, then the other on the floor.

"One step further and I'll hit you with this," she snarled.

"Ah, but Victoria, ya not be wantin' do that. I'll only duck out of the way and its destruction will summon your father."

"Either way, he'll come. At your misfortune or mine." She smiled triumphantly.

Dru shook his dark head. "But do ya realize the price ya be payin'?"

"Me?" she exploded. "I fail to see how I'll be the one charged."

"Then be lettin' me explain," he said, taking a step, one finger raised to stress the idea. He stopped when she threatened to toss the bottle rather than hear him out. "If ya make the mistake of bringin' your father here where he's not wanted, I'll be forced ta tell him the truth of your captivity."

Her nose raised higher, not intimidated by his

words. "He wouldn't believe you. Why would he? You're nothing more than a—a pirate!"

"Aye, that I am. But a truthful one," he corrected.

"Ha!" she scorned. "You lied to me."

"Are ya meanin' our bargain?"

She nodded curtly.

"Would seem so ta you. But the truth of the matter is I sent a message to a friend of mine in New York about Miss Bensen. I would guess by now the authorities are lookin' for her."

The bottle was lowered slightly. "You did?"

Dru nodded, lounging comfortably in their temporary truce, until he noticed an angry frown appear on her face.

"The bargain was that you kill her. You still lied to me." She raised the weapon again.

"Unh-unh," he warned, wiggling a negative finger. "I'll be tellin' him the truth. *All* of it."

"Go right ahead. I'll deny it. And then how would you convince him?"

Confident now that he had won the battle, he retreated and sat down on the edge of the bed, hooking a finger to the top of his stockings to slide them off one at a time. "I'll tell him about Melissa Bensen and all she planned to do. Now how would I know about her and Dillon Gallagher if it didn't really happen? And wouldn't it be causin' ya more grief when your father finds out ya didn't tell him?"

Victoria rallied to her own defense. "But if she's to be arrested in New York and kept there as a spy, how will you prove anything if she never appears in Williamsburg? And you could have heard about her from anyone around. You must admit your story will sound

417

rather shaky.''

He reached up to scratch his chin. ''Aye. But then there's always Cinnamon.''

''Cinnamon?'' Victoria echoed, a twinge of worry gnawing at the pit of her stomach.

''Aye. I be thinkin' she's not the type ta lie ta your father.''

''That, sir, is blackmail!'' she hissed.

Dru thought about it for a moment. ''Aye, that it is.'' He stood up and dropped his shirt from his shoulders. The dimple faintly showing in his cheek, he raised his finger and motioned her near.

Her lip trembled. She lowered the bottle. She fought off the tremor rising from her knees. Vainly, knowing it to be of no use, she shook her head, denying his victory.

Dru cocked his head to one side, watching. ''Your problem be who ya fear more. Meself or your father,'' he said quietly. ''And if it be any help, ya can justify your surrender as payment for lettin' me be locked up because of your lies.'' He studied her a moment, noticing how she chewed on her lower hip, her eyes lowered to examine the bottle in her hands. He stepped closer, wondering.

Oblivious to all around her, Victoria remembered the words of her grandfather. ''Someday, my child,'' he had said, ''you will pay for your childish pranks. Someone not as understanding will trap you in your lies and not let them pass, as I do.'' Trapped! Yes, that's just what had happened. Visions of all the events of the past several weeks flashed in her mind. How could she have avoided any of it? What could she have done to change it? She had only twisted the truth to save herself. From death, from Kelsey, from the shame of giving herself to a man, the same man who stood before her now. And, without delay, she would be forced to atone for every trick, every falsehood she had played since the first. Swallowing her tears, she looked up at Dru.

"Will this be the only time?" she whispered. "Or will you return seeking payment over and over again? I am helpless to stop you, and you know it." She lowered her eyes, watching the gentle rise and fall of his muscular chest. Her hand came up to brush away a curl from her temple.

"I'll be returnin' to your bed only if ya be wantin' me there." He pressed his fingertips to her lips when she took a breath to deny the possibility. "Careful, lass. You can fool others, but not me. If ya tell me nay, I'll be honorin' your wish after this. But ya must be careful not ta thrust a knife into your heart ta spite me. Sometimes it's hard ta live the way we've said we can."

Victoria wondered at the ambiguity of his words. Thanks to Cinnamon he knew of the love she had tried to hide. But what of him? Could it mean he shared the feeling? She mentally shook off the idea. Not likely. He was a man of the sea, one who captured many hearts, only to sail away and leave them. As he planned to do with her. Don't be a fool, she told herself. He could never love you. A courage building from the desire to mask her vulnerability, she looked to him. It would give her the satisfaction to be the one who claimed no need for affection from the other, to let him remember her as the only one who had turned him away. She raised her chin higher, the pounding in her chest deafening. He stood much too near.

"I-I—" she began, choking off her words as his arms

419

came up to encircle her.

"What, me love?" he whispered against her cheek. His lips brushed her temple.

"I—I—" she breathed, closing her eyes, the scent of him intoxicating.

With a swiftness her befuddled mind could not anticipate, he stooped to sweep her into his arms, carrying her with graceful ease to the bed. His left arm slid from beneath her knees, letting her feet touch the floor again, his free hand reaching up to loosen the sash of her robe. As if to taunt her, it fell easily to the floor, unveiling the lacy transparency of her gown. Standing before her all trace of mockery disappeared from his handsome face, hands reaching up to capture the delicate line of her jaw. Gently he pulled her closer, his lips warm and soft against hers.

Victoria's mind exploded with a thousand denials; her heart longing to be his in every way, body and soul. She had thought to forget the desires he stirred in her.

His fingertips followed the long column of her neck, slipped beneath the collar of her robe, and effortlessly slid the garment from her shoulders. It pooled to the floor at her feet. He pressed closer, his lips softly nibbling at her earlobe, his hands setting her flesh afire as they moved ever so slowly down her spine to rest on the small of her back, pulling her hips to his. A kiss brushed her cheek, her temple, her brow, consuming her in their moment of passion.

Her gentle nature cried out for him to stop, to bring an end to her wanton appetite. His mouth found hers again, more ardent than before, a hand raised to the back of her head, holding her fast. His tongue sought the sweetness of their kiss, probing, searching, the fire in his loins growing.

The nightgown fell from her shoulders without any protest from her, gliding to the floor. He pulled her to him again, the strong muscles of his chest touching her round, firm breasts, their peaks aroused. Lifting the heavy ebony hair from her shoulder, he placed a soft kiss on her pale nakedness, sending shivers through her, a betraying moan coming from her lips. He nibbled gently at the tender flesh, caught up in the scent of her. His mind reeled, his long-starved passion flaring high. Cupping her face in his hands, his mouth hungrily covered hers, his tongue darting inside.

Victoria matched his moves with her own. Her hands gently glided over his shoulders, down the hard muscles of his back, his lean waist and narrow hips, unaware of the agony he endured at her touch. The warmth of him, his manly smell, aroused a hunger in her, a wicked desire to abandon all decency and sate the craving they both so obviously shared. Slipping her fingers to the buttons of his breeches, she popped them loose and let them fall from him. He eagerly kicked them away, groaning when he felt her hands touch his buttocks and pull him to her, his manly hardness pressed against her, and she felt him tremble. Her mind whirled with the newfound pleasure, the response she ignited with a simple caress, the discovery that her pirate would risk all else to have her in his arms. Had it been merely lust that drove him here? Or could it possibly be that he, too, felt something deeper, a real passion, a yearning that would live with him until his dying day? She kissed him greedily, pushing aside the fear that she might never claim his heart, satisfied to have him thus, even if it meant only this one night. She hugged him to her, needing to feel his body touching hers, to verify that the man of her dreams was really there.

Impatient to have her, he swooped her in his arms, bent a knee to the bed, and fell with her onto it. Tucking her beneath him, he covered her face, neck, and shoulder with passionate kisses, before moving to sample the fullness of her breast, his tongue teasing its nipple, his teeth gently biting. He moved lower, his hands stroking her thighs, lust devouring them. Hearing his name spoken softly, he raised up to discover the passion shining brightly in her eyes. He parted her thighs with his knee and came to her, thrusting his manhood deeply inside, a wild ecstasy exploding within him.

She clung frantically, enraptured by his nearness, the wild beating of his heart pressed against her naked breast, knowing that if he came to her bed a thousand times more, she would shamelessly, eagerly open her arms to him. She moved instinctively with him, her hips raised to greet him, to complete the melody of love their hearts sang.

Moonlight bathed the room in silvery splendor, as if it had been commissioned to silhouette the figures wrapped tightly in each other's arms, unmindful of any world except their own. They moved together as one, united in a mutual pledge to share, enjoy, love, and a long while passed before they lay content, a quiet understanding finally felt by both of them.

Stirring in the lingerings of slumber, Dru came fully awake in a rush, certain his dreams had played a grim trick on him. He moved to rise from the bed, the first hint of predawn light staining the eastern sky outside the window of the room, his breath catching once he recognized his surroundings and felt the warmth of another at his side. In undisturbed sleep, Victoria snuggled closer, content in his protection. He smiled, wishing it would never end, yet knowing it must. An emptiness filled him at the thought of leaving her, of sailing off to distant shores, to abandon the one and only woman his heart had ever known.

" 'Tis best," he whispered, leaning close to press a kiss to her brow. Quietly, he left their haven and dressed, knowing he must not tarry lest she wake and discover his true feelings for her.

The muted thuds of footsteps passing in the hallway jolted him back into reality. He must hurry. Crossing to the bouquet of flowers on the bedside table, he plucked a single bloom and laid it on the pillow next to Victoria.

"I'll be returnin', me love," he whispered softly. "Just one more time before I sail." He turned and escaped down the trellis, his parting as still as the morning air.

The petals of the rose dampened with teardrops.

TWENTY-FIVE

A disgruntled look on Sean's face kinked the scar beneath his eye as he and Donovan descended the gangplank of the ship that had sailed them from Williamsburg up Chesapeake Bay. His feet on solid ground once more, he stopped, looked back at the brigantine, and sighed.

"What's wrong, lad?" Donovan asked, having noticed his companion's unrest.

"How far ya be figurin' it is ta Chester?" Sean continued to watch the ship's crew unload their cargo.

"The captain said fourteen leagues. Maybe less, why?"

Without thought, Sean rubbed a hand to his backside. "More than half a day's ride," he muttered.

Donovan grinned. "Aye. But considerin' the distance we traveled by ship, I be thinkin' it a small amount. Besides, we be doin' it for Dru."

Sean glanced over his shoulder at him with a shake of his head. "I don't even like the smell of a horse, me friend, much less havin' ta sit on him. Even for one minute. And I wouldn't be doin' it for anyone else but Dru."

"I can't be sayin' I blame ya, lad, but it is better'n walkin'."

Sean contemplated his friend for a moment. "I might argue the point."

"Well, you go right ahead and argue, Sean, me boy, but I will be findin' meself a horse ta ride. And the sooner the better. We've already been gone a day and a half and I not be likin' the idea of Dru and McGuire left alone. Remington's a determined man, and if he thought Dru was still in town, he'd tear the place apart until he found him." He scanned the gathering of buildings surrounding them. "Over there," he pointed, starting off toward the stable.

The men spoke few words as they rode, stopping only once to eat and trade their tired horses for fresh ones. They traveled hurriedly, not wanting to waste a moment, and hoping their journey would reveal the truth about Damon Rutledge—that he was what he said. It would mean they could return to their ship and leave the colonies. Although neither of them voiced his worry, each sensed the other's desire to seek the safety of the open waters.

By midafternoon, they came upon an inn where they dismounted and tied their horses to the hitching rail to rest. Inside they could quench their thirst with a mug of ale and ask directions to Chester. But what they had thought would be a moment of relaxation was transformed instantly into one of apprehension as they entered the inn. Nearly every customer wore the uniform of the British army. Half-empty mugs left at their table, Sean and McKenzie paused only long enough to learn that the road on which they traveled led directly to their destination. Once outside again, they yanked the reins free of the post, mounted, and swiftly rode off without a backward glance or a word upon their lips.

They traveled nearly a quarter of an hour before they allowed their steeds to slow, the tension of their pilgrimage strengthening their determination to end their search in haste. Although Donovan appeared to ease with the slower pace, Sean continually glanced over his shoulder to see if they had been followed. After what seemed the hundredth time, he turned to McKenzie.

"How far did the innkeeper say?" he asked.

"An hour's ride."

Sean looked to the road behind them. "I not be likin' this, Donovan. Not one bit."

"Will ya relax?" McKenzie urged. "No one around here has reason ta be lookin' for us. Besides—" His words hung in the air like an early morning fog.

"Besides what?" Sean growled, turning to face him. Donovan sat rigid in the saddle, his gaze locked on what lay ahead of them. Slowly Sean followed McKenzie's lead, jerking his horse to a halt when he saw the fork in the road.

"Oh, fine. Now which way?"

Donovan pulled back on the reins, twisting in the saddle, one arm resting across his thigh. "Well, we could be flippin' a coin," he grinned.

Sean cast him a pleasureless smirk. "A grand idea. Or better still, why not split up?" he added sarcastically.

McKenzie shrugged. "Well, I suppose we could."

"Are ya serious?" Sean exploded. " 'Tis bad enough there's only two of us, without tryin' it on our own." He studied the landscape around them, spying a thin gray spiral of smoke rising above the treetops. "I be thinkin' we ask. If we be lucky, maybe they'll have heard of Rutledge and we can be returnin' ta Williamsburg." He spurred his horse into a trot.

"I wouldn't wager a gold coin on it," Donovan called after him.

Nestled in the middle of a clearing a few hundred feet ahead, a small stone house stood quaintly majestic amidst the surrounding greenery. Sean reined his steed to a halt, eyeing the dwelling cautiously. To all appearances the house seemed empty at the moment. The narrow path leading to the door was picked clean of weeds, the front stoop swept spotless. Crisply laundered curtains adorned the windows and flapped eratically in the gentle breeze, denoting a woman's touch. They hesitated, silently debating whether or not to travel further, when the crack of wood by a soundly placed ax greeted them from in back of the tiny house. Nodding confidently at Donovan, Sean took the lead and briskly rounded the corner in the direction from which the sound came.

In the middle of the yard behind the house a buxom woman labored with another cut of wood, standing it on end on the chopping block, her back to the new arrivals. Certain the log was steady, she raised the ax over her shoulder and swung it earthward, splitting the wood in one clean attack. Two pieces fell to the ground, and she stopped to select another and continue with her

427

work when Sean cleared his throat to announce their presence. Startled, the woman swung around to face them, the ax held threateningly in her hands.

Hurriedly retreating, Sean nearly stumbled over his own feet, caught by Donovan's aiding reach of one arm. "We be meanin' ya no harm, lass," McKenzie assured her, safely tucking Sean in back of him.

The weapon lowered slightly, but the suspicious gleam still shone in her eyes.

"Aye. 'Tis true," Sean quickly added. "We come unarmed. See?" He raised his hands for her inspection.

"Who are ya and what do ya want?" she snapped.

"We only be wantin' some directions. We didn't mean ta frighten ya," Donovan replied. "Me friend and I be lookin' for the Rutledge plantation."

"Rutledge?" she echoed. Her fists tightened around the ax handle.

"Aye. Damon Rut—"

"I know who he is. What ya lookin' for his place for?"

Feeling cocky since his instincts had so far proved right, Sean stepped out from Donovan's protection, jabbing his friend in the side. He smiled broadly. "Why, he be a friend of ours a long time ago. We came ta pay him a visit."

"A friend?" she bellowed angrily, and Sean chose to move behind Donovan again. "I didn't know he had any. Ya sure you ain't British come ta trick me?"

"British?" Sean blurted out, nearly choking on the word. "Now do we be soundin' British?"

She raised the ax again, bringing a weak but respectful smile from him.

"Well, the British killed my Arty and run Rutledge off his place near six months back. I don't trust no one no more. Figured they'd want my place next."

"Can't be sayin' I wouldn't be feelin' the same, lass," Donovan said. "But I be givin' ya me word. We only be lookin' for Damon. Might ya know where he be?"

She studied them silently for a moment. "Couldn'ta gone too far. That leg of his slowed him up a might."

Donovan and Sean traded satisfied grins.

"Too bad that fellow didn't shoot him a little higher," she continued, an evil smile twisting the woman's mouth. "Woulda served him right!"

"Ya be soundin' as if ya not liked the man," Donovan said, fighting to hide his smile.

"No, I don't," she rallied. "Never did nothin' good for his neighbors, only waited 'til they was broke so's he could buy their land out from under them. I say good riddance to him. And if you're his friends, I suggest you be on your way." She took a step closer. "I don't like nobody what likes him."

Donovan turned abruptly when it appeared she would carry out the warning and collided with Sean. "Well, lad, get movin'," he urged, "unless ya be wantin' ta test the lass."

Spinning about, the two Irishmen quickly departed the woman's company, swiftly climbed on their horses, and raced off in the direction from which they had come, never once looking back.

Charles directed Dunstan to a table near the back of the inn and sat down to wait. They ordered a bottle of brandy brought to them and waved off the young

429

maid's suggestion of food. Although nothing seemed to bother Dunstan, Charles knew that even the most tantalizing of foods set before him would simply go to waste, as his desire to eat had vanished with their near escape. If only Edwin would arrive soon.

An hour passed and Dunstan snoozed quietly in his chair while Charles's attention remained on the entrance to the inn. Each time a group of men entered the establishment, Charles would slouch down as if he had overindulged in his drink, guardedly watching their movements until they had eaten and gone. Melissa Bensen's well-thought-out plans for aiding England had not gone as devised, and Charles had the dreadful fear the high and mighty bitch had given them away by a careless slip of her tongue. It seemed everyone watched them suspiciously. Or was it only his imagination, as Edwin continually assured him?

Charles pulled his timepiece from his waistcoat pocket and took note of the hour. Where was Edwin? He should have come long ago. He snapped the lid closed and returned the watch to its place. He bowed his head, rubbing cool fingertips to his brow for what little comfort the act would give him and looked up again, spotting Edwin coming into the inn. He raised a hand to motion him near when he noticed how Edwin gasped for breath. Something had gone wrong. He knew it! Otherwise, why had Edwin been late and arrived in such a manner? He slapped the back of his hand against Dunstan's shoulder, bringing him rudely awake with a snort.

"Let's get out of here!" Edwin urged once he came to their table.

Not allowing Charles the time to question the urgency, Edwin led them through the maze of tables, out the back door, and into the alleyway. Glancing left and right, Edwin silently decided to follow the barren pathway leading between the buildings to the other end, where they could mask their passage in the busy marketplace.

The street bustled with merchants selling their wares from carts full of fresh fish, delicious pastries, and baked breads, a chorus of voices bargaining with potential customers. The three Englishmen elbowed their way through the crowds, moving swiftly, repeatedly glancing over their shoulders for anyone who posed a threat. When the sidewalk that led to the boarding-house where Melissa Bensen roomed came into view, Edwin's pace quickened. He glanced back to urge his companions on when he spotted the group of men he had tried to evade—twice as many in number as his group.

"Damn," he muttered, quickly forcing his attention elsewhere but onto the face of their leader. He thought he had lost them. And if Melissa was to be saved, he had to reach her before he was taken prisoner. How could this have happened? How could that pirate have warned the authorities? Right now it didn't matter— just escaping and seeing that his beloved Melissa fled the country with him mattered. If not, they both would be hanged.

"Stop!"

The command rang sharply in Edwin's ears. He knew who called the order and to whom it had been issued. He looked ahead, seeing the door that hid a flight of stairs behind it. At the top, she waited.

"You there. Halt!"

431

Suddenly, Edwin veered to his left, racing off down the street away from Melissa's apartment. He mustn't lead them right to her.

The crack of musket fire rang out. Edwin heard a man scream. Charles or Dunstan? It didn't matter. He couldn't stop. He must protect Melissa.

A burning fire pierced Charles between the shoulder blades. He fell to his knees, calling out his pain. Its fierceness seemed to paralyze him. The crowd around him moved away. His breath grew labored, his head spinning. He looked up for help, seeing the big, awkward shape of his friend.

"R-run, Dunstan," Charles pleaded.

"No-o-o," the hulk cried, dropping to Charles's side.

A pool of blood quickly stained the cobblestones beneath Charles. Through half-closed eyes, he looked at the man hovering over him. "G-go, Dunstan. Y-you can't help. I-I'm dead," he growled. "G-go with Edwin."

Dunstan looked up. Edwin had disappeared into the crowd. Tears brimming in his eyes, he turned back to his friend. "He's gone, Charles. I can't leave you. You're the only one who ever liked me. Please, Charles, get up. They're coming." Slipping an arm underneath Charles, Dunstan tried to lift him, stopping when Charles cried out in agony. "P-please, Charles." His face streaked with tears, Dunstan turned to the crowd surrounding them. "Please, somebody help!" No one moved. He glanced back at the dying man, seeing the pain-filled twist of his brow, the closed eyes. Suddenly Charles gasped, then fell limp in Dunstan's arms.

"No-o-o!" he wailed, pulling the lifeless form into the circle of his embrace. He rocked back and forth, tears spilling down his grief-stricken face. Then a hand touched his shoulder. Sobbing, he raised his eyes to find the group of men staring back at him.

Edwin crouched behind a rain barrel in the alleyway, certain the pounding of his heart echoed throughout the city. He had waited for darkness to veil his travels through the streets. No one must see him. He must get to Melissa. God, he hoped he wasn't too late already. If the rebels had taken Charles and Dunstan prisoner, it would only be a matter of time before one of them would tell where to find Melissa. His head fell back against the damp stone wall behind him. He closed his eyes. Charles hated Melissa, he had known that for a long while. And, given the chance, he'd sacrifice her in exchange for his own life. Dunstan, however, would never intentionally hurt anyone he liked. Bitterly, he prayed the man who had screamed had been Charles. It would insure a little more time if he was dead.

A thud at the end of the alleyway startled Edwin. He couldn't wait any longer. Carelessly, he abruptly came to his feet, hearing the voice of another call out for him to stop. Knowing it to be a patriot, he started to run, the explosion of a musket reaching his ears an instant before the lead ball ripped into his flesh and spun him around. He went crashing to the street.

No! God, no! Not yet! He must warn Melissa first. He staggered to his feet, the pain in his shoulder blinding him. He reached up, feeling the warm flow of blood dampening his jacket. Another shot rang out and Edwin found the strength to move away quickly, disappearing into the shadows.

Down the street he ran, his love for Melissa driving him on. Ahead, he could see the sidewalk leading to her apartment, but knew he must not go directly to it. He must lose the patriot first! Still running, he glanced back over his shoulder. No one had stepped from the alleyway yet. There was time, but he must hurry. Bolting through the gate of an iron fence surrounding a darkened house, he hid himself around the corner of it, his body pressed against the wall. He waited, listening to the rush of footsteps against cobblestones. His shoulder burned. He wanted to collapse, to rest, but he couldn't. This would be his only chance.

The lights of the inn sparkled brightly in the darkness, marking the way to it in a warm, friendly manner. Although the knowledge Sean and Donovan had acquired from the widow should have made their journey easier, Sean still wore a worried frown. After tying their animals to the hitching rail, Donovan started for the door, then paused when he noticed Sean lingered, glancing uneasily at the entrance.

"We have ta be sleepin', lad, and I be likin' the idea of doin' so in a bed instead of layin' on the cold ground," Donovan said. "And ya admitted yourself ya could use a mug of ale."

Sean nodded curly, his sun-darkened brow winkled. "Aye, that I could."

"Then what ya be waitin' for?"

"I be wonderin' who's inside, 'tis all."

"Soldiers?"

"Aye."

Donovan smiled reassuringly. "If there is, they be

havin' no cause ta be disturbed by our presence. But if ya stare at them the way ya are, they will wonder if ya aren't a spy."

"That's what I mean!"

Donovan straightened, a fist knotted to each hip. "And since when has Sean Rafferty been afraid?"

"Not afraid, me friend, just careful."

"Then ya sit nearest the door. But I be goin' in with or without ya. Me stomach sounds like a thunderstorm and I'm certain one mug won't quench me thirst." He turned sharply and went inside, a reluctant and troubled Sean close behind.

The candlelit room reflected a quiet peace, one which quickly soothed Sean, for of the numerous tables only one was occupied by a customer. Near the back of the room, an old man crouched over his mug, his gray head down, his attention focused on the wood graining of the table top. Both men glanced briefly at him before sitting down at a place across the room from him.

"Feelin' better?" McKenzie whispered, watching the pretty barmaid walk toward them.

"I be feelin' better when me feet are on the deck of the *Defiance*," Sean muttered, taking off his tricorn and tossing it on the empty chair next to him. He looked up and smiled at the young woman standing beside him. "Good evenin', lass."

She curtsied briskly, eyes lowered and a slight coloring on her otherwise pale complexion. "What would you like, sirs?" she asked quietly, her gaze flitting from Donovan to Sean to the knot of her apron clamped in her hands.

"Ale. And whatever ya can bring us ta eat in a hurry. We haven't had a thin' since noon," Donovan replied.

She curtsied again and turned to leave when suddenly the old man across the room slammed his mug against the table.

"Get me another!" he bellowed without lifting his eyes.

Startled by his outburst, the young girl hesitated momentarily, then hurried to retrieve the pewter tankard and fulfill his demand, hoping the newcomers would understand why she put this man ahead of them. Her task accomplished, she filled two more mugs and returned to Donovan and Sean.

"Thank ya, lass," McKenzie smiled, taking the proffered drink. Lifting the brew to his mouth, he noticed how the barmaid smiled shyly at Sean. He cleared his throat to draw her attention and asked, "Can ya be puttin' us up for the night, lass? And see someone tends ta our horses?"

"Yes, sir," she spoke softly, her attention centered on the handsome features of the second Irishman. "Only one night?"

Donovan leaned back in his chair, an elbow resting on the table, his fingertips hiding his smile. "Aye. Only one."

"I'll tell my father, and my brother will see to your horses." She continued to stare at Sean.

"And maybe water for a bath?" he asked, watching how his friend took a swallow from his mug without pulling his gaze away from the girl.

"Yes, sir," she answered, glancing to the floor, then back at Sean through lowered lashes.

Donovan grinned with a playful shake of his head, certain he could have asked for all the silver her father possessed and not been denied. "Now, lass?"

Suddenly realizing how boldly she appraised the stranger, the barmaid blinked and stiffened abruptly. "Y-yes, sir," she said, an almost fearful look twisting the fair features of her face. She turned away and went into a back room.

"For the life of me, I not be seein' what it is about ya that brings the muteness out of young lasses," Donovan chaffed, raising his mug to his lips.

"Me charm," Sean sighed lightly, his gaze studying the door behind which the maid had gone.

"Ya didn't say a word!" Donovan argued, his theory lost in the gray cylinder of the cup as he took a swallow from it.

"Then it must be me good looks."

"Ha!" Donovan exploded. " 'Tis more like she took pity on ya."

"Pity?" Sean rallied.

"Aye. The lass probably figures ya never had a woman before and out of the kindness of her heart—"

"Ya only be jealous, me bald-headed friend," Sean laughed, reaching up to smack the sun-tanned scalp.

Donovan easily ducked out of the way. "Aye, that I am," he laughed. "Must be a damned curse having women fall at your feet." He pressed back in the comfort of the chair. "Of course, I remember one ya couldn't charm inta doin' anythin'."

"Who?" Sean snapped, denying the conceivability of such a thing.

"Colleen. Ya haven't forgotten Colleen, have ya?" He watched the mirth vanish from Sean's face. "Now I wonder if she still be waitin' for ya or gone off and married Trevor," he cajoled. "Do ya suppose she lied ta ya? After all, with all your charms and good looks, she must have really loved ya, Sean, me boy.''

''I offered ta marry her,'' Sean said into his mug before downing a long swallow.

''Aye, but I not be thinkin' her father would have allowed it. Figured ya would stay only 'til the babe was born and then sail off.''

Sean sat stiffly in the chair, his gaze locked on the table's surface. Slowly a smile began to creep over his face and he raised a hand to his mouth to hide it. '' 'Tis right, he was.''

Donovan burst into laughter. ''Aye, Sean, and I'd not be surprised if half of Ireland had been fathered by ya.''

''Not that many, Donovan,'' Sean grinned. ''But give me time.''

A movement at the front door of the inn interrupted their gaiety, and they elected to sample their ale and watch the new arrivals sit down at a table just inside the entrance.

''Patience!'' one of the men sang out, the name opposing his own short temper. A moment later the young barmaid appeared before them.

''Yes, Mr. Tredway?''

''Bring us all a mug of ale,'' he growled. ''And where's your father?''

''In the back room, sir, taking count of our supplies.''

''Send him out here and be quick about it.''

''Yes, sir.'' Patience curtsied and hurriedly sought out her father.

For all of Patience's beauty, her father had none, instantly bringing about an exchange of glances between

Sean and McKenzie, their unvoiced doubt about the girl's paternity. Noticeably shorter than his daughter, the innkeeper's shirt and breeches hung from his shoulders and hips, much too large for his spindly frame. A long, thin nose supported wire-rimmed glasses and gave him an almost birdlike appearance; the only feature remotely similar to one of his daughter's was his mass of thick, dark hair, and the nervous way he wiped his hands on the white apron draped around his narrow waist. He approached the party of men hesitantly.

"Good evening, Mr. Tredway." His voice quivered.

"Finch," Tredway nodded. "I'm here to collect."

Finch's adam's apple bobbed up and down. "Yes, sir. And—and I'd like to settle the matter, but business hasn't been good."

Tredway glared up at him. "Do you really expect me to believe that?" He quickly scanned the room. "This is the slowest night you've had in a month. I've been here when I couldn't find an empty table, and all of your rooms were full. What do you spend your earnings on, those two brats of yours?" he growled, having seen Patience enter the room with a tray full of food for the two strangers. He studied the gentle sway of her hips.

"N-no, sir," Finch denied. "If you were really here—"

Tredway slammed a fist against the table top. "Are you calling me a liar?"

Finch jumped, clutching his hands up beneath his chin. "Oh, no, sir. I only meant you should have noticed that most of the customers were British soldiers. They never pay."

"Only because you don't force them, you spineless ninny."

The tray of food clattered against the table and Patience's lower lip trembled as she looked at Sean apologetically. "Forgive me, sir," she whispered, hurriedly placing the contents on the table before them.

" 'Tis all right, lass. Ya not have ta fear us." Sean glanced over at the men engaged in heated discussion. "Who might Tredway be?"

Sighing forlornly, Patience looked back at her father. "A man to whom my father owes too great a deal of money to pay off in one amount. He comes once a week, knowing father can only give him a small portion." She bowed her head when Tredway's voice grew in volume. "He only does it to shame my father."

Sean looked at Donovan with a cocked brow.

"I wish," Patience continued in a hushed whisper, "that the soldiers would claim his lands, too, as they have others'. Would serve him right to have to crawl to Father for a crumb of bread or a mug of ale." She glanced up at Sean and McKenzie. "And Father would give it to him. He's a patriot and sympathizes with anyone the British have left homeless. His biggest fault, I guess. That's why we have no money to pay. He gives away more than what he charges for."

Suddenly a loud crack resounded throughout the inn, drawing all eyes to focus on the old man sitting alone in the far corner of the room. "How can a man drink in peace with all this noise?" he clamored, slamming his cane against the table top once more. All remained quiet as they watched his twisted form slowly rise. With apparent difficulty, he started for the door, his left leg dragged grotesquely to one side, his full weight balanced on the pearl-tipped cane. Minutes seemed to lengthen unduly with each step he took, for several times it appeared he would topple and crash to the floor. Yet no one moved to aid him, his desire to be left alone made clear in the angry knot of his brow. He stopped when he reached the door of the inn and turned to the circle of men.

"Some day, Tredway," he barked, balanced on his good leg, the tip of his cane pointed at Finch, "you will grovel at his feet."

Tredway's lip curled into a sneer. "Go away, old man. If it weren't for men like you, Finch would have the money he owes me."

"And if it weren't for him, there wouldn't be men like you," the old man hissed.

"Get out, Rutledge, before I throw you out."

Sean's head shot up with announcement of the man's name. Rutledge? Crippled! A cane! He turned to Donovan to find the same suprised look on his face. Impossible! Two men of the same surname with the same physical deformities? A relative perhaps? Conceivable. But that limp! He looked back to the old man to discover the doorway empty. The group had returned to their drinks and the berating of Finch. Sean reached into his pocket, retrieved several coins and gave them to Patience.

"Thanks for your trouble, lass, but we must be speakin' with the old man," Sean said, reaching for his tricorn. Before she could reply, the two strangers had left the inn.

"Over there," Donovan said, pointing to the dark shape that hobbled further away into the shadows. A moment more and he would have disappeared into the cover of trees.

"Mr. Rutledge!" Sean called. "Please. A moment of your time."

"If ya think to rob me, you're in for a surprise. I haven't a coin to my name," he called back to them, his steps not slowing.

"No, sir. We only be wantin' ta ask ya if ya know Damon Rutledge."

The old man stopped suddenly and turned back slowly, his head tilted to one side as he looked up and down. "Who are you?"

"Doesn't matter. We just need some information on him. Do ya know him?" Sean pressed once they came within a few yards of the man.

"What kind of information?"

"Are ya related to Damon Rutledge?"

A sarcastic snicker was expelled in the darkness before them. "You could say that. Tell me. Have you ever seen Damon Rutledge?"

Sean and Donovan looked at each other. "Aye," they chorused.

"I don't think so, or you wouldn't be asking such fool questions." He turned and started to walk away. "Tell me what he looks like."

Sean and McKenzie hurriedly caught up with the old man, one on each side of him.

"He be taller than me, a little older—"

"A little?" Rutledge laughed. He stopped to face Sean. "I'm a *lot* older."

"You?"

"Yes, you idiot. *I'm* Damon Rutledge!" He started off again.

Sean shrugged helplessly at McKenzie. "But the

442

man we know came from near Chester. Owned a plantation the British took from him. He's crippled. Like you. A son. Could he be your son?''

''No. I never married. But I'll tell you what he looks like. Black hair, dark brown eyes, handsome sort, hot-tempered, and his name is Colonel Blake Kingsley of his Royal Majesty's army.''

''Colonel?'' Sean breathed. ''And how would ya be knowin' that?''

Angrily the old man grabbed the narrow trunk of a young tree to steady his balance as he twisted around to glare at them. ''Because Colonel Kingsley is the one who ordered me off my plantation. When I refused, he shot me! The Royal cur crippled me and threw me out to fend for myself without a twopence. That's how I know.''

''Saints preserve us,'' McKenzie muttered. ''We gotta be gettin' back ta Dru. He must be warnin' Miss Victoria.''

''Aye,'' Sean agreed.

With an urgency born of worry for their captain and friend, Sean and Donovan spun about and raced for their horses, a long tension-filled journey ahead of them.

TWENTY-SIX

Nervously, Melissa paced the floor of her room, glancing again at the mantel clock. Ten-thirty! Where was he? Frightened, she went to the window and pulled back the heavy draperies. A single lamplight lit the street below, a heavy mist clinging to its golden orb. No one moved about. Looking at the clock again, she decided not to wait. Going to the armoire, she pulled a cape from it, flung it around her shoulders, and crossed the room. Lifting the latch, she swung the door wide, gasping when Edwin stumbled in.

"My God, what's happened?" she choked, helping him to the bed. She knelt down beside him.

"T-they know," he moaned.

Melissa stiffened. "How?"

He took a slow, painful breath. "The Irish captain who stole back the Remington girl. He must have sent word to someone here about us." He closed his eyes, fighting off a wave of dizziness.

Melissa's breath caught in her throat, her eyes growing into wide, hate-filled circles. "What?" she roared. "How do you know that?"

He shook his head. "It doesn't matter. What does is that they have Charles and Dunstan. We must—leave here—at once."

Melissa slowly came to her feet, the fingertips of her left hand tapping her chin as she contemplated her next move. Edwin was right, of course. She mustn't stay in America. She must return to England. Maybe she could hire a coach to Quebec and there board a ship. Yes, that would do, and traveling the roads at night would grant them some secrecy for a while. But if they had Dunstan and Charles, one of them would tell, and the authorities would be looking for her. She glanced at Edwin. And he would only slow her up. Spinning about, she raced to the armoire and her satchel, stuffing as many things into it as she could.

"W-what are you doing?" Edwin asked.

Without stopping or looking his way, Melissa replied, "Packing. I'm going to see if I can hire a carriage. Then I'll come for you." The satchel full, she came to the side of the bed and smiled down at him. "You rest. It will do you good, and it will be a while before I return."

Edwin smiled. God, how he loved her. "Hurry, my darling."

"I will," she whispered, bending down to lightly kiss his brow. He burned with fever, and she smiled again, knowing that he would be dead before sunrise. Too bad. She had always liked Edwin. Flipping the hood of her cape over her blond curls, she moved to the door and looked back. "Now remember, don't answer the door for anyone. I have the key and will let myself in."

Edwin nodded, watching with loving eyes as the shapely figure cloaked in black left the room. He fell back against the pillow and closed his eyes.

Fool, she thought, descending the staircase. All men are fools! When she reached the bottom, she paused outside the door of the landlady's room, tossing the brass key in her hand. She stooped and slid it beneath the door.

Dru stood before the window of his room, catching his reflection, and readjusted the freshly laundered ascot at his neck, slightly peeved by John's insistence that he not leave this evening. How could he explain to the man that having spent the night past holding Victoria in his arms had awakened in him the need to see her again, hold her, kiss her, make love to her. He slipped into the newly pressed waistcoat and followed it with the neatly presentable jacket. He glanced quickly at John, then reached for the tricorn lying on the dresser and moved for the door.

"Dru."

His name spoken softly yet with concern halted him. He looked back at his friend.

"I can be understandin' why ya be wantin' to go to her, lad, but do ya realize the danger ya be in?"

Lowering his head, Dru studied the dark blue trim on the tricorn in his hand. "Aye. Ya told me twice already."

"But it won't be stoppin' ya."

Dru looked up and smiled gratefully. "No. Has a re-

446

ward on me head ever stopped me before? And I be thinkin' they look for a swarthy pirate, not a man dressed as finely as this.'' He swept a hand down the length of his frame.

''Aye. That they will. And only the jailer and Remington will recognize ya. But ta be walkin' right in under the man's nose is foolish. He'll have ya hanged the minute he catches ya.'' John poured himself another measure of rum from the bottle the barmaid had brought when she had returned with Dru's clean clothes.

''*If* he be catchin' me,'' Dru corrected.

Glass raised to his lips, John paused. ''Then why won't ya let me be goin' with ya? I can at least be coverin' your backside.''

''I want ya here in case Sean and Donovan return.''

'' 'Tis only an excuse!'' John bellowed, slapping the glass on the table near his elbow. ''They won't be returnin' for days.''

Dru shrugged playfully. ''Aye. Then why can't ya see you're not wanted and graciously accept the idea without forcin' me ta say it?''

John sighed heavily. ''For the same reason ya can't be understandin' why I want ta go along. I'm only one man. If you're caught, I'll be helpless. There wouldn't be time to get the crew.''

The lightness of Dru's mood vanished. ''I know,'' he half whispered. ''But 'tis a chance I must take. A foolish one—perhaps. And 'tis the reason I not be wantin' ya along. I won't be riskin' your neck as well.'' He brushed a speck of lint from the hat. ''Thank ya anyway, John.'' Without looking at him again, Dru pushed the tricorn over his brow, turned, and hurriedly left the room.

The main street of town was dotted sparingly with the dim lamplight. Dru lost himself among the crowds and easily walked the distance to the Chesterfield House, pausing briefly to check the ascot again. Satisfied, he squared his shoulders and moved toward the door, noticing that more than one man walking by stared at him curiously. Maybe John had been right. Maybe it was more dangerous than he realized. He stopped, glancing back toward the alleyway. Victoria deserved the courtesy of having a gentleman caller come to her door rather than steal into her room from the balcony, but since when was he a gentleman? And why would Victoria expect him to act like one? He grinned and started to retrace his steps when the door of the inn opened behind him.

"We'd better hurry, Damon. I'm sure they're waiting for us."

Dru's steps faltered slightly, but he managed to keep going even though he recognized Beau's voice and knew the near disaster he had just avoided. He'd have to remember to thank John. Without his forewarning, Dru felt certain he'd be on his way to the gallows at this very moment.

When he reached the alley, he ducked into the protective cover of darkness, listening to the clicks of heels pounding against the wooden sidewalk, certain Remington and his companion traveled in the opposite direction. He sucked in a deep breath to calm his jittery nerves, holding it to stillness as he witnessed the pair cross the narrow mouth of the alleyway and disappear again. Ahead of them lay very little that would interest men of their caliber—a few businesses, closed at this hour, and the waterfront. Dru frowned, quietly exhaling his long-held breath. Where were they going? And who waited for them? He glanced up at the balconies over his left shoulder, deciding his visit with Victoria would have to wait. Pulling the tricorn down to shadow his face, he cautiously stepped out to the sidewalk again.

The two men had traveled several yards, putting a safe distance between them and Dru. Their steps, confident and hurried, carried them to a darkened storefront where neither paused before Remington lifted the latch and they went inside, a tinkling bell breaking the silence. Dru looked up to the sign hanging above the doorway. The newspaper office? He frowned. What possible business could they have there at this hour? One way to find out. Looking back over his shoulder to find he stood alone, then across the street, he moved closer.

He slowed once he reached the windows of the building facing the street, then stopped as if to search his pockets for his timepiece or his pouch of pipe tobacco. Once more he checked his aloneness. No one. Guardedly, he peeked inside the newspaper office. Nothing. Total darkness reigned. Straightening, he decided the men must have gone into a back room, and if he was to learn the reason, he too would have to go inside. He moved quietly to the door, glancing hurriedly around him, and once more into the blackened room. He smiled oddly, listening to his heart pound. How many times he had fooled his cousin into thinking this sort of venture never stirred any type of emotion in him whatsoever. If he only knew—

The latch clicked with his touch. He froze. Had they heard? Concentrating on the darkness before him, he sighed when he detected no movement from inside. Reaching up, he captured the tiny bell teetering on the top of the door between his thumb and forefinger, and pushed it open enough to allow him to enter. Circling in back, he repeated the process, smiling in relief as he watched the bell sway ever so slightly in silent protest.

The huge printing press loomed out at him in the gray-black shadows of the room like some monstrous form ready to lunge. He moved past it to the counter, wondering where the men had gone, when he caught sight of a movement outside the office. Two figures stopped before the front door. Scanning the interior, the only likely place he spotted for refuge appeared to be behind the counter. Both hands pressed to its surface, he lifted himself onto it, swung his legs over, and quietly glided to the floor on the other side. He immediately ducked down.

The high-pitched, staccato tinkling of the bell rang clear, followed by an encore when one man closed the door behind them with a thud.

"Harper, is that you?" a voice funneled out from the back of the office.

"Yes, Henry. And my nephew," came the reply.

Dru held his breath. If only he could quiet the pounding in his chest.

"Will you lock the door? You're the last, and we don't want any visitors that don't belong."

A deepening of Dru's dimple went unseen.

The duet of footfalls crossed the room to a curtain covering another doorway. Light filtered in when it was

450

pulled aside, temporarily blinding Dru, but at the same time directing his awareness to the secret meeting. He waited until the gentle sway of cloth stilled gain, bringing darkness upon him once more. He moved to the end of the counter a few feet away from the entrance to the back room and listened.

"Good evening, Mr. Remington," Harper said. "I believe you know my nephew."

"Yes, of course," Remington replied. "And I'd like to introduce a friend and neighbor of mine, Damon Rutledge."

"You bought the widow Bensen's place, didn't you, Damon?" another voice asked.

"Yes. About six months ago."

"Welcome to Williamsburg," a third added.

"Thank you."

"I assume since you came here tonight with Beau that you have the same desire to see the British lose this war?" a fourth voice asked.

"Probably moreso. You see, they claimed my property near Chester, Pennsylvania as their headquarters to guard Chesapeake Bay, and ordered me off. I'd like nothing better than to claim what is rightfully mine."

"Near the bay?" another questioned.

"Yes," Remington interjected. "That's why I asked Damon to join us. I know how he hates the British, and with his knowledge of Philadelphia I decided he could be a great asset to our plans." The pungent odor of cigar smoke filled the air before Remington continued. "You see, Damon, the British outnumber us, they're better equipped for war, and have more money to back them than we do. Anything we can do will help aid our soldiers."

"Yes," Henry Wilkes agreed. "We're tired of being taxed on everything we buy or sell. Or told to whom we can trade. How can the king of England know our needs from so far away?"

"Right now General Washington and his troops are resting in Valley Forge," Beau continued. "His men are tired, cold, hungry. They need to recuperate. And we must help."

"How?" Damon asked.

"By spoiling any advance the British intend by way of Chesapeake Bay."

"How will that work?"

"We've asked for volunteers to act as couriers. If the British advance by night, we simply use lanterns to signal their approach. By day, men on horseback."

"But how can I help? You know I'm no good on a horse."

"We're not asking you to ride," Remington said. "I thought maybe you know some of the militia in Philadelphia where we could make contact and spread word to General Washington."

"But of course," Damon exclaimed, followed by a sinister laugh, "and what better way for me to settle the score?"

His legs having cramped from the position in which he crouched, Dru shifted his weight, his shoulder bumping into the counter. The slight tremor shook three books standing on end and haphazardly propped against a stack of newspapers. The bottom of the first slid out from under it and the volume thudded against the countertop. Dru froze, wondering if it had sent out the alarm of an intruder.

"Something wrong, Beau?" he heard Henry ask.

"Just nervous, I guess. I thought I heard something." The legs of a chair squealed as it was pushed across the floor. "We should be going, anyway. Don't want anyone to get suspicious. Damon and I will work out the details and get back to you."

"All right, Beau. Let me know when you're ready and we'll call another meeting," Henry said.

The curtain pulled aside, two figures stepped into the darkness of the outer office and crossed to the front door. A click echoed, followed by the tinkling of the bell. A moment later silence fell again, and Dru peeked out over the countertop to watch Remington and his companion disappear into the night. A frown creased his brow. So Remington belonged to the militia and wanted Damon to join him. A worthy endeavor. And certainly a man of his wealth would be a great aid to the cause—as long as he was not found out. The frown returned. If *he* could steal into the meeting place, stumble upon it, in fact, then maybe others had, those who could be dangerous. He must speak with Victoria. He rose to exit the building as quietly as he had come, when once again the curtain moved to flood the room with light. He stepped back into the shadows, watching six men enter the darkened cubicle. As soon as the curtain blocked out the candle's glow, he moved into the crowd walking toward the door.

"Now remember," Henry Wilkes said, leading the way, "not a word to anyone. I'll send a message when Mr. Remington wishes to meet again." He placed one hand on the doorlatch, his other on the shoulder of the man beside him.

The bell pealed loudly, more boisterous than before, it seemed to Dru as he waited to leave with the others—as if to herald the presence of one who did not belong. He prayed he would be able to leave the men before someone discovered their number had grown.

Henry now stood off to one side of the door as his guests left, gently slapping the back of each of those nearest him, a quiet gesture of encouragement for their dangerous work. Knowing even a moment's contact with the man would give him away, Dru moved to the outside of the group, pulling his tricorn further down over his brow. Two by two they filed out, and when Dru's turn came, the man at his side paused to shake Henry Wilkes's hand, giving Dru the chance to slip out unhindered. His heart pounded faster. At least now he was free to run if need be. But, since all had gone well so far, he moved into step with the others before him, sensing how the man who had lingered hurried to catch up.

"I think it's a bit of luck that Mr. Remington found Damon Rutledge. Don't you?" he asked, once he fell into the brisk pace of the group. He did not bother to look at his companion.

"Mmm," Dru replied, with as much enthusiasm as he could muster. He centered his attention on the row of darkened storefronts coming to an end at the alley before another began.

"Almost like fate threw him into our hands." The man fumbled in his left pocket for his tin of cigars, stepping off the sidewalk to cross the alley and then up the other side. Clumsily he withdrew two, popped the lid back on the container, and returned it to his pocket as he offered, "Care for a—" He stopped in the center of the walkway when he found himself alone. Looking back down the street, he saw nothing, no one moving about. He shook his head to clear his thoughts. Maybe his wife had been right when she told him that drinking was the work of the devil. It played tricks on those who partook of it. But he was sure—

"Coming Charles?" Harper called when the group paused outside the inn that was their customary place to stop after each meeting.

"Ah—yes," he managed, slipping the extra cigar into his other pocket. No sense in telling anyone. They'd just report it to Martha and she'd wag her finger under his nose and rattle on about how the Good Book never lied. He glanced once more over his shoulder, then moved to join the others.

TWENTY-SEVEN

Standing in the shadows of the alleyway, Dru looked up, quietly studying the white lace curtains adorning the french doors of Victoria's balcony turned pale yellow in the candle's glow. A shapely silhouette crossed them as the woman in the room paced back and forth. He smiled, wondering what might be going through her mind. Well, he could always ask her. Glancing left, then right, to make certain he wouldn't be discovered, he crossed to the ivy-covered trellis beneath the balcony and hoisted himself up. Noiselessly he reached the top and swung himself over the railing, landing softly outside the open doors. He paused to listen, wondering if Victoria sensed he had come. When no sound greeted him, he lifted a hand to the lace and peered into the room. Seated at her dressing table, Victoria vigorously brushed the long, dark tresses cascading over her shoulder, unaware of being watched. After one final look about the alley for safety, Dru stepped inside. He appraised the beauty sitting only a few feet away, the shiny ebony hair, narrow waistline, the rounding of her hips pressed against the small velvet cushion of the stool. The desire to explore each curve again stirred longing in his loins. He swallowed slowly, fighting the urge. He must speak with her first and then— He took off his tricorn and sailed it across the room, intent to have it land in the center of her bed.

Victoria caught its flight in the mirror's reflection long before it made its descent. Startled, she dropped her brush and spun around, nearly slipping from the bench. "Y-you," she choked. "How dare you sneak into my room?"

The dimple in his cheek appeared. He stood casually, leaning a shoulder against the door frame, his fingers interlaced in front of him. He chose not to answer, only stare, his gaze seeming to penetrate the thinness of her nightgown.

Recognizing the hunger in his eyes, Victoria quickly rose and crossed to the bed and her robe draped over the footboard. Its sash pulled tightly around her waist, she bent to retrieve his tricorn. With a flip of her wrist, she skillfully returned it to its owner in the same fashion he had disposed of it. He all but crushed it in his grasp.

"You may leave the same way you came, sir," she spat.

The flash of white teeth worried her, knowing her statement was ludicrous. This pirate captain would leave any way *he* decided to go, and he certainly wouldn't heed her request as to *when,* unless it suited him. She decided on another approach.

"Don't think you'll blackmail me anymore. I'll not

tumble into bed with you.'' Her spine stiffened in silent confirmation. "I've decided to tell my father."

One dark brow cocked doubtfully on his handsome face.

"Not the story you would tell," she answered crisply, "since you plan to sail without a care. I am not a martyr. So just turn yourself around and be gone from here."

Dru studied her a moment, then straightened, tossing the tricorn to the velvet stool. He stepped nearer.

"I mean it," she rallied nervously, her own feet frozen to their spot. God, why couldn't she move? "I—I'll scream! He'll hear!"

"I not be thinkin' so, me love," he half whispered, each word bringing him closer.

"And—and why not?" Her feet still did not carry her.

"He be too far away ta hear."

"Far away—what do you mean?" She jumped when he reached out to hook a finger in the dark curl resting lightly on her breast. Although he only touched the lock of hair, the nearness of his hand set her flesh on fire.

"He and your gentleman caller, Damon, just left the newspaper office," he said, casually examining the richness of the strands encircling his finger. "I not be thinkin' they will return here right away." His gaze shifted to the soft swell of her bosom.

Seeing where his attention lay, she jerked the ringlet from him and moved away. "I don't believe you. You only wish to trick me."

Studying his empty hand, cheated even of a moment's pleasure, he glanced briefly at her, then went into the sitting room. Curious, Victoria followed, lift-

458

ing a single lighted taper to guide her and insure a safe distance from him, if being in the same town could be considered safe. He crossed to the buffet and poured himself a glass of wine. Turning, he decided on the comfortable-looking wing chair next to the fireplace and went to it. After sitting down, he hooked a toe to the heel of his shoe and kicked it free, doing the same with the other. He stretched, then took a sip of wine.

"Ya can be relaxin', lass. I've only come ta talk. For the moment, anyway."

The warmth of his body next to hers, his passionate kiss, his gentleness of the night before burned vividly in Victoria's mind while she stared at him. She recalled her own weakness, the way she had yielded eagerly, wanting more than anything else in the world to have him hold her, kiss her, possess her. They had slept away the early hours locked in each other's embrace. Then morning had come and stoled him away. But not before the devastating truth of his feelings revealed itself in his words, a verse sung in a whisper, thought not to be heard by the one who appeared to slumber.

When she had found him standing outside her door, risking his recapture and certain death, she feared he sought revenge. But as he kissed away that fear, she had reveled in the thought that he came out of love.

Fool! she told herself. His own lips denied the fact.

"About what?" she asked, walking to the buffet where she placed the candle, its muted yellow glow creating distorted shadows on the floor.

His gray-blue eyes moved up to look at her, a hint of passion sparkling in them. He blinked, and all desire seemed to fade, hidden for the moment as the need to find some answers to his questions prevailed. "Have ya any idea why your father would meet with several other townsmen at the newspaper office this time of night?"

"What my father does is none of my business," she hissed, finding a new strength to sound indifferent. "Nor is it yours. Why don't you leave while you still have the chance? Why do you continue to stay here where you're not wanted?"

The corner of his mouth twitched upward slightly. "I stay because there's a need. And until I be satisfied things be as they should, I will be stayin' as long as it takes. Now—do you know why your father was at the newspaper office?"

She raised her nose and looked at him disdainfully.

"All right, then I'll tell you," he said, when she stubbornly refused to comply. "He and the others are members of the militia."

One delicately boned shoulder bobbed. "So? He believes in this country and will fight for it. More than I can say for you. You don't believe in anything."

Dru took another drink from the wineglass, hiding his grin. "Wouldn't ya want ta be knowin' how I found out?" he asked, once he gained control again.

"You probably spied on him. That suits your character," she said haughtily, feeling he deserved the insult.

"Aye, that I did." He watched the satisfied smile curl her lips, then added, "and if I can be findin' out such a thing, then so can those who shouldn't."

The smile vanished.

"He be in danger, Victoria. England is a powerful country and won't take kindly ta losing the war. Your father could be hanged for what he does."

Without thinking, Victoria rushed toward him and

460

knelt down, her hand covering his resting on the arm of the chair. "You won't tell, will you, Dru?"

"Now that's a fine way ta think of me. Why would I do somethin' like that?"

"Because he had you arrested and put in jail."

"Not he, lass," Dru grinned with a salute of his glass. His eyes never left hers.

She pulled back, stung by the truth. "Yes, of course." She rose and moved away, unable to look at him. "What do you want me to do?"

"Tell your father to be more discreet about the meetings and careful about who he invites to go along."

Victoria spun around. "Such as Damon?"

"Aye."

"You sound just like Cinnamon. She doesn't like Damon either, and thinks the worst of him without any proof."

"And you do like him," he stated more than asked, settling more comfortably in the chair.

A faint line showed briefly between the soft arch of her brows. In its place, a look of triumph enhanced the darkness of her eyes. "Yes, I do. He's a gentleman. And he knows how to treat a lady. Why, in fact, just a few days ago, he protected me from a drunk."

"And would have killed the man had ya not stopped him."

"Well, yes, but the man had—" Victoria stiffened. "How do you know that?"

Dru grinned. "One of McGuire's men. Sent by me ta get a good look at Mr. Rutledge."

Victoria's jaw moved up and down repeatedly, no words passing her lips. "You—you had no right spying on me," she breathed in outrage.

"Not you, lass. Mr. Rutledge."

"It's the same! What interest would you have in him, if it wasn't for me?"

Dru crossed an ankle to one knee. "Let's say I be makin' a promise I must be keepin'."

"A promise? To whom?"

"The lass—Cinnamon?—she cares a lot about you."

"So?"

"She be wantin' to be sure Mr. Rutledge is the kind of man ya should marry."

"Marry?" Victoria shrieked. "I do not intend to marry him!"

Dru cocked his head in playful disbelief. "And have ya told your father?"

"I—ah—" She lifted her nose in the air. How dare he mock her? "Who I choose to marry is my business, whether Father approves or not."

Resting both elbows on the arms of the chair, Dru half-heartedly studied the goblet balanced between his fingertips. "Even if ya chose ta marry me?"

Before she could gather her thoughts, convince herself that he only toyed with her, a gentle rapping on the door intruded, abruptly ending her tension and replacing it with worry. Frozen to her spot, she merely stared at the portal.

"Victoria, are you awake?" her father's voice called out.

Panic filled her. Frantic, she looked at Dru, finding he had already left his chair and moved to her bedchamber. She waited until he had disappeared from view and went to the door.

"Yes, Papa," she answered, her voice quivering as

462

she turned the key in the lock. "Is something wrong? I-It's so late."

Stepping inside, Remington vainly scrutinized the shadows, his eyes slow to adjust to the subdued light of her room after that of the hallway. "I thought I heard voices in here."

Her flesh tingling with guilt, she summoned a smile. "It—it was only me. I—I couldn't sleep and thought a glass of wine might help."

"Are you sure?"

"Of course. Why? What has you so upset?" she asked, purposely changing the subject.

Remington walked further into the room as he removed his tricorn and turned back to face her, running the fingers of one hand worriedly through his hair. "Just a father's foolish concern, I guess."

"About what?"

"That pirate's escape. If he sought money for your return once, I fear he may try again. *He* has the advantage now, not I."

When his gaze fell away from her to study the hat dangling from his fingertips, Victoria instinctively glanced at the chair, which only moments before had felt Dru's warmth. Her eyes widened. Carelessly tossed on the floor before it boldly lay the captain's shoes. Quickly, she covered her gasp with the back of her hand. Dear God, what should she do? She forced a smile to her lips and looked back at her father. If only she could keep his attention on her, he would not see the shoes that lay a few feet away.

"You mustn't worry, Papa. After the treatment he received in the jail, he would only wish to flee this country," she said, praying her words sounded more con-

463

vincing to her father than they did to her.

Remington looked up and smiled. "Yes, I suppose you're right."

"Of course, I am," she said, going to him. She slipped her arm into his and guided him toward the door. "And besides, I'm right next door to you and Mama. What man would be foolish enough to barge his way into my room with you so near?"

"He was foolish enough to demand money for your release," Remington pointed out.

"And he didn't know with whom he was dealing or the lengths to which you would go." She stood on tiptoes and pressed a kiss to his cheek. "Don't worry, Papa. He won't hurt me."

Remington stared at his daughter for a long while, then sighed tiredly. "Goodnight, my child," he whispered, returning the kiss before he stepped into the hallway, pulling the door closed behind him.

The key twisted in the lock, Victoria fell back against the door, her breath leaving her in a long sigh of relief. Then her gaze fell upon the shoes.

"No, Papa," she whispered, rage boiling up inside her, "he won't hurt me. I'll kill him first."

The tails of her robe flying, Victoria raced to retrieve the shoes, then stormed into her bedchamber. She stopped in the archway, her small frame rigid with fury, glaring at the man lying pompously on her bed, as if he had every right.

"Get out!" she bellowed, hurling one dark slipper at his head. He ducked out of the way. "*Out*, I say!" The second shoe sailed through the air, bouncing when it hit the bed, and slid off the other side. Before he could roll from the feather mattress, she stomped to the dressing table and the tricorn sitting on the stool. Snatching it up, she whirled and threw it his direction. She pointed a finger at the balcony. "The way you came."

A look of concern twisted his features, one hand raised in warning. "Shhh. Ya be wantin' ya father ta hear?"

"I told you before it doesn't matter. I've decided to tell him."

"Everything?"

The smile on his face suggested a deeper meaning. She hesitated before answering. "Yes."

"About last night? And of now—the way I waited here while ya talked? Let me see. What did he say? 'A father's foolish concern'?"

Victoria's chin fell in shock. "You—you wouldn't."

He moved closer, holding his voice to a whisper. "No."

"Then—then you'll go?" His nearness sent a shiver through her. How could one person affect another so?

"Aye. As soon as I be provin' somethin' ta ya."

"Prove something? To me? What?" She retreated a step, feeling her thigh touch the dressing table. She reached back to steady herself against it.

"That the words ya cry are false. That ya not truly wish me ta leave."

"I—I do so," she argued, batting away the hand that sought to touch a lock of her hair.

"Then don't be sayin' another word and let me prove ya don't." Gray-blue eyes stared warmly into hers. Her heart quickened.

"N-no."

"Are ya afraid to admit it, me love?"

"A-afraid? To admit I want you to—to leave? That's

all I want from you—just your absence."

Locking his hands behind him, he moved to within an inch of her. "Then let me kiss ya. If what ya say is true, then I'll be knowin'. And I'll be leavin'. 'Tisn't so much ta ask. One kiss ta see me off."

"All right." She gulped. "One kiss. And—and your hands stay where they are."

He nodded and Victoria felt victory near. It would be easy to fulfill his request and hide the truth at the same time. No one could tell from a simple kiss the yearnings that burned inside. She closed her eyes and stuck her chin out.

"Not like that, lass," she heard him scold.

She opened her eyes.

"I'm not your father and won't accept a kiss that belongs to him. Kiss me as a woman would."

She frowned suspiciously.

" 'Tis the only way I be knowin' the truth," he said, as if reading her thoughts.

The corner of her mouth curled scornfully. One day—one day she'd settle the score. She'd make him pay for all the insults. She stared into his eyes as he lowered his head slowly. Then the heady scent of him filled her senses. She blinked, her gaze resting on his lips, slightly parted and only a whisper away from hers. She closed her eyes again, praying her will would carry her through. He mustn't know! She mustn't weaken!

As their lips met, Victoria thought her knees would give way. She reached up to clasp the folds of his shirt front, hoping to steady her trembling limbs. But the warmth of his body so near sent her mind whirling. Oh, how she wanted him. Not just at this moment, but forever. She relaxed, then stiffened. No, it was only a

466

game to him. His mouth covered hers, his tongue teasing. Did she moan aloud? Unable to resist any longer, she raised her hands across his chest, feeling his arms surround her slim frame, pulling her closer. If he left her tomorrow, sailed away for good, would the desire he aroused in her ever fade? Could she, in time, forget him? His kiss, his touch, the scent of him? Would the fires of passion cool, or would they fan anew remembering how his warmth, his tenderness filled her? The sash of her robe came loose, the silky cloth shimmering from her to the floor. Her heart fluttered, raced, beat wildly. She shivered when his lean fingers captured the narrow straps of her nightgown and pulled them from her shoulders. It too pooled at her feet. Intoxicated with his nearness, she forgot her earlier terms for the embrace, allowing him to lift her in his arms and carry her to the bed, her own locked around his neck, as they kissed softly, passionately, lovingly.

Comforted in the feathery cushion beneath her, she watched, entranced, as he slipped from his clothes, the strong muscles of his chest, arms and thighs flexing with each move. Could another affect her in this manner? Had she turned harlot? Or fallen deeply, hopelessly in love? She studied the male hardness of him, smiling softly when she realized no modesty in her urged her to do otherwise. Her gaze traveled upward to meet his, her arms extended to welcome him. No matter what the reason, she would give herself to him now and never feel shame because of it. What she held in her heart was not lust, but a deep undying love.

Their bodies met and fused as one, moving in perfect harmony, transported with delight to heights only this common bond could achieve. They kissed, touched, loved, a unity of two never shared with any other. And when their passion ebbed, they clung to each other, silent, drinking in the bliss the other gave. He nestled her in the crook of his arm, his face buried in the mass of fragrant curls flowing about them, his fingertips tracing the smoothness of her breasts. Then suddenly he left her to don his clothes.

Snuggled in the warmth of their haven, Victoria lazily watched, savoring the sight of him and wondering when he might return—*if* he might return. Pushing herself up on one elbow, she opened her mouth to voice the question, pausing when he turned to look at her.

"Tell me, have ya ever kissed your father like that?" he teased.

A pink hue settled in her cheeks, unnoticed in the shadows of the room. "No," she admitted. "Only you."

He shook his head as if disappointed.

Alarmed, she sat up in bed, pulling the coverlet around her. "Is something wrong?"

"Aye," he said sadly. "I hate it when I'm proven wrong."

"Wrong? About what?" She saw no falsehood in her words.

He moved toward the balcony. "About your wantin' me ta stay."

"But I was the one who was wrong," she argued, rising. "I did want you to stay with me."

He raised a hand to silence her. "No, lass. No sense in lyin'. I could tell ya was only pretendin'." He slipped a leg over the railing.

A pricking of indignation stiffened her spine. "Do you think I'd do this with anyone? Just to get rid of him?"

He shrugged, the twinkle in his eye masked in the darkness. "Aye," he replied, then disappeared from view.

The warm fires of passion turned to rage. "Why you lousy, contemptible—" She scanned the room for something to hurl at him as he climbed down the trellis, deciding that the water pitcher would do nicely. Armed with her weapon, she rushed to the balcony railing and looked down, her anger dying when the alley proved dark and vacant. How could he have fled so quickly? Frustrated, she tossed the pitcher earthward, wishing him beneath it, and watched it shatter into a hundred pieces.

One tiny fragment of clay scooted over the cobblestones to stop near the toes of Dru's black shoes as he leaned comfortably in the protected area beneath her balcony. A wide smile deepened the ever mocking dimple in his cheek.

TWENTY-EIGHT

"Are ya sure the old man wasn't enjoyin' a trick?" John asked.

"Aye," Sean replied, pressing his fists to the small of his back as he stretched. He crossed to the bed and lay down, cradling his head in his arms. "After we talked with him, Donovan and I went back to see the girl at the inn. She verified everythin'."

"And bein' the type ta shoot an unarmed old man," Donovan added, glancing at Dru who stood gazing out the window, "I be thinkin' he's not the kind ta treat carelessly. He's dangerous."

"Aye," Dru agreed, absently tossing a chin in the air. "One who wouldn't stop at anything." He shoved the silver piece into his pocket and turned around. "I must be warnin' Remington."

"Remington?" Donovan contested. "Ya not be owin' the man a thing. Why would ya want ta warn

470

him? Would serve him right ta be taken in."

"I not really be doin' it for him, me friend. It's for his daughter. She's promised ta marry Rutledge and I can't be leavin' here knowin' what I do about the man."

"I agree. So tell the lass. But why worry about her father? Have ya forgotten your stay in the jail?"

A soft smile found its way to Dru's lips. "No, Donovan. 'Tis somethin' I'll never forget. But ya must be fair with the man who sent us there."

"Fair?" Donovan roared.

"Aye," Dru added, quickly raising his hand to silence any further protest. "The man only heard one side of the story, an account twisted to suit his daughter's pride. She thought she'd been lied to and sought revenge. He, like us, was an innocent victim of her pride. Had he known the truth, I be thinkin' he would have acted differently."

Donovan frowned at his captain for several moments before looking away. "Maybe," he answered quietly.

"And look at it this way, Donovan, me friend. What better way of havin' me own kind of justice than ta tell the man the one he trusted most is a spy and the one he trusted least is an ally? A cruel sort of fate, don't ya think?"

Donovan shrugged. "Aye, I be supposin' so."

"Dru," John cut in, "he'll never be believin' ya. Not without proof."

"Aye, and I be thinkin' I know a way ta do just that."

"How?" Donovan asked.

"While the two of ya were gone, I stumbled on a

471

meetin'.''

"What kind of meetin'?" Sean questioned, pushing himself up on his elbows.

"I followed Remington and Damon Rutledge—or should I be sayin' the colonel?—ta the newspaper office two nights ago. They met with several other men.''

"Why?" Sean pressed, sitting up and tossing his legs over the edge of the bed.

"Militia.''

"Beau Remington?"

"Aye. And from what I overheard, it was the first time Rutledge had been invited to attend.''

"The man must have been mighty pleased," Donovan speculated with a shake of his head, "ta finally have what he worked six months ta get.''

"Aye," Dru agreed.

"So how do ya plan ta convince Remington?" Sean posed.

"A trap.''

Dru's audience exchanged questioning glances, and he smiled in return. "The man can't be workin' alone. I'll be suggestin' ta Remington that he call another meetin' and then follow Rutledge afterward. If the meetin' reveals some very important information, the colonel will be wantin' ta pass it on as quickly as possible.''

" 'Tis a fine idea, Dru. But how will ya be gettin' Remington ta listen ta ya? One look at ya, and he'll probably shoot a hole in ya," John reminded him.

A flash of white teeth, a lift of brows, and shrug of one shoulder answered John. "Aye, he probably will. But he will listen ta his daughter.''

"Oh, that's a grand idea," Sean interjected sarcastically. "And how do ya plan ta convince her?"

The dimple in Dru's cheek deepened, a mischievous gleam sparkling in his eyes. "I have me ways."

Sean's upper lip curled. "Well, then I be suggestin' ya hurry up about it." He fell back against the bed's softness, arms crossed behind his head, one ankle draped over the other. "When Donovan and I returned the horses ta the stable, a young lad came in with instructions for the stable man ta have Remington's coach ready early tomorrow mornin'. They be returnin' home."

Dru folded his arms over his chest and leaned back against the windowframe. "Then I must be gettin' ta work. I can't be lettin' them leave town."

Sean raised up on one elbow. "And how will ya be stoppin' them?"

Dru's gaze traveled to the ceiling overhead, as if deep in thought. "We could be kidnappin' his daughter again," he finally replied, his expression played to confirm the words.

Sean's shoulders drooped, eyes rolled back as he fell to the bed again with a moan, deepening the dimple in Dru's cheek.

Thank God, we'll be going home tomorrow, Victoria thought, securing the last lock of hair into place with a pearl-tipped pin. At least then she could escape to her bedchamer, lock herself in and feel safe. She hadn't slept much in days, lying awake half the night, certain that at any moment Dru would crawl into bed with her. She stopped her labors, staring at her reflection in the mirror. A smile tugged at the corners of her mouth. You're shameless! she scolded the image looking back at her. And besides—an unflattering pout wrinkled her lip—you're just another wench where he's concerned. He'd leave you in a minute. He said so.

Her stomach knotted in hunger, and, glancing at the mantel clock, she knew her parents would be waiting for her to join them for dinner. She tucked a lace handkerchief into the sleeve of her gown and stood to examine the results of her task in the mirror, spying the open doors to the balcony.

Oh no, you won't, she scoffed silently. You'll not sneak in my room while I'm at dinner. Dropping the latch into place, she turned back to lift her shawl from the foot of the bed. The sight of Dru lounging against the brass headboard took her breath away. She fell back, grasping the thin draperies covering the french doors.

"H-How—when—"

Sitting comfortably on the feather mattress, arms cradling his head propped up against the pillows, his eyes devoured her loveliness. "Ya be lookin' grand, Victoria. Will ya be havin' your meal downstairs?"

She gulped, wondering what torture he intended for her this evening. "W-What do you want? No—no, I mean—why are you here? I—I—"

Dru grinned broadly at her nervousness, knowing if he made a sudden move she would more than likely attempt to escape down the trellis. "I've come ta warn your father."

Her anxiety disappeared, a frown knotting the soft arch of her brows. "Of what?"

He moved to leave the bed and she quickly raised a hand. "Stay where you are. This time I mean it! I'll scream and bring the place down around your ears."

He nodded defeat, if only temporary, and relaxed again. "There be a spy among ya."

"A spy? What are you talking about?"

"Several days ago I sent me cousin—you remember Sean." He fought down his laughter when she curled a lip at him. "Well, Sean and McKenzie went ta Pennsylvania."

"Whatever for?"

"Ta find out the truth."

"What truth?"

"Seems your cook was right."

Victoria sighed impatiently. "Dru Chandler, I haven't the faintest idea what you're talking about. Cinnamon was right about—" She stopped in midsentence, her eyes widening. "You can't mean Damon. You didn't spy on Damon."

He dropped his head slowly.

"What? What did they find out?" she demanded.

"That the real Damon Rutledge is an old man. He still lives near Chester. In fact, Sean and McKenzie talked ta him. It's true the British threw Rutledge off his plantation, but the man ya know who calls himself by that name is really Blake Kingsley. He's a colonel in the British army."

Victoria slowly shook her head. "You're lying. You're making that up. Papa trusts him."

"And that is why ya must tell him."

"I'll do nothing of the sort. Papa's always careful about his business partners. He'd never believe me. And besides, I don't believe it either."

"And what would I gain by lyin' ta ya?"

"And why would you not?" she challenged.

Sean knew why. So did John. And Dru suspected McKenzie had discovered the reason long ago. But it was a secret he would not, could not tell her. "I've got me reasons, Victoria. And if ya care at all about your father's safety, ya must be convincin' him that Damon Rutledge is a British officer."

Fingertips pressed to her brow, she slowly made her way to the dressing table bench and sat down. "But how *can* he be?"

Dru left the bed and came to kneel at her feet. He took her hand in his. "Think about it, Victoria. Before he bought the plantation next to yours, what did anyone know about him? And it was only luck that Sean and McKenzie found the real Damon Rutledge. How could anyone be provin' differently? A perfect cover. He assumed the identity of a real man and true events. If Sean hadn't accidentally run into the real Rutledge, I would have been satisfied with what the colonel claimed."

Victoria studied the bright lavender satin of her gown a while, then gazed upward. "Papa would never believe me. And he'd ask how and where I got my information. Then what?" She looked at him, tears shining in her eyes. "I can't just tell him you came to my room one night."

Dru remained quiet a moment. "Ya can't continue to lie to him. Not this time. Ya be playin' with his life." He reached up to spoil the path one tear made toward her chin. "I be knowin' your father still thinks we're in town. He sent a man ta look for Sean. So he'll be knowin' ya speak the truth when ya tell him I was the one who told ya. And I have a plan ta prove me story—"

A series of raps on Victoria's door interrupted. "Victoria, aren't you ready yet?" her father's voice called.

Every inch of her flesh seemed to tingle in fear and anxiety. The time for stories and pretending had come to an end. Victoria swallowed hard and looked desperately at Dru.

"Now, me love. Ya must not wait," he told her, rising. He turned and hid beside the bedchamber door.

Her lower lip trembling, she rose on shaky limbs, and looked at Dru once more for encouragement. He must be telling the truth. Why would he lie? He had never once deliberately hurt her, and although the bargain they had made so many weeks ago had not been met as agreed, he had fulfilled it in another way. And if what he said of Rutledge was true, she was the only one in the position to tell her father. It would take a lot of courage, but the time had come for her to face up to the truth and accept her punishment for all her wrongdoings.

"Yes, Papa, I'm ready," she called, quickly going to the door. She turned the key in the lock and pulled the door open. Standing alone in the hallway, her father smiled back at her.

"Good. Then let's go. I'm famished." He extended his arm for her. "Your mother's waiting downstairs with Damon."

Victoria's pulse quickened at the mention of his name. "Not yet. I'd like to tell you something first." She held out a hand, indicating her desire for their privacy in the sitting room.

A frown appeared on his face, but without a word he

477

stepped inside and waited for her to close the door behind him.

"Sit down, please, Papa."

He hesitantly obeyed, his gaze never leaving her.

"Would you care for a drink?" she asked, turning to the buffet.

"Victoria," he said, "something's wrong. What is it?"

She took a deep breath and let it out slowly, unable to meet his eyes. "I'm going to tell you something that may turn you against me for the rest of my life."

"That's absurd," he cried out.

"No, please," she interrupted, spinning about with a raised hand to silence him. "Let me say it all. Hear every word before you say another. You must." Tears choked her. She raised a quivering hand to her mouth to still her sob.

"All right. If you wish, I'll remain silent." He leaned back in the chair, his hands folded in his lap, his full attention captured by the worried look on her face.

Dear Lord, give me strength, she prayed and began to pace. "I've lied to you, Papa. For years. Just small ones to suit my need, but in the past few weeks, it's become too big to let go by. Your life is in danger, and I'm the only one who can warn you." She went to the sofa, sat down, and promptly rose again to continue pacing. "Captain Chandler never raped me. In fact he protected me from those who might have, and from Melissa Bensen." She heard his rapid intake of breath and turned to him. "She was on the island where I was taken, and when she found out who I was, she intended to blackmail you. But Dru—Captain Chandler—

478

rescued me. We found out she's in the pay of the king, and if England wins this war, she intends to claim Raven Oaks as her own.''

A frown deepened the lines of Remington's brow, but he remained silent, studying his clenched fist.

"That's not the worst of it, Papa. There's another."

An angry scowl greeted her.

"Damon Rutledge."

"Da— How do you know?"

Victoria glanced briefly at her bedchamber, then to the floor. "Captain Chandler told me."

"What?" he roared, bolting from his chair. "You've talked to him? Where? When?" His ire grew.

"Please, Papa, hear me out," she begged. "I didn't believe him at first either, but once he explained—"

"You're a fool, Victoria!" he bellowed. "He only means to get even for the treatment he received."

"No! That's not true."

"Oh?" he asked skeptically. "Then tell me why a pirate would suddenly want to warn a man who had him thrown in prison, beaten, and left there to hang? I tricked him, killed some of his men, and cheated him out of a fortune. He has every reason to hate me and seek revenge." He started for the door. "No, Victoria, I'll not believe it for a moment."

"Then let me be provin' it to ya."

Remington's broad frame stiffened at the sound of the voice. He turned back slowly, as if doubting his own ears. In the doorway of his daughter's bedchamber, the candle's glow dancing mockingly upon his face, stood Dru Chandler. "You!" he growled, the word exploding in a rush.

"Aye. And if ya will be usin' the common sense ya

have, ya will stand where ya are and listen ta what I have ta say. It could be savin' your life and those of your friends. The ones ya met with at the newspaper office."

Some of Remington's anger ebbed. "How—"

"I followed ya," Dru explained. "And if I could be findin' out ya belong ta the Militia, so can others. Now—will ya listen?"

A prickling of instinct held Remington to his spot, a sense that this man above all others would not lie. But why? He nodded, his curiosity forbidding him to do otherwise.

"I sent two of me crew ta Pennsylvania ta verify Mr. Rutledge's claim. 'Twas fact. He owned a plantation near Chester, walked with a limp, and the British stole his land."

A smile formed on Beau's face.

"However—" Dru continued, "there be one small exception. Damon Rutledge is still there, and he be an old man. The one you know is Blake Kingsley, a colonel in the British army."

"That doesn't prove anything to me. You could have made the whole thing up."

"Then ask him," Dru conceded. "But if ya find I was tellin' the truth, the man will run and you'll not be able ta stop him from tellin' the authorities or startin' up again somewhere else." Dru stared at him a while, then added, "It could be costin' ya your life."

"And what does my life mean to you? Why would you risk your own to save mine?"

Dru looked to the floor at his feet. "I not be doin' this for you."

"Then who?" Remington demanded, far from convinced. "What will you get out of this?"

Dru glanced up at Victoria, who stood in wide-eyed fear, and back at her father. "I be knowin' your daughter will not be marryin' the wrong man."

"My daughter—what has she to do with any of this?"

A faint smile played with the dimple in his cheek. " 'Tis simple, Mr. Remington. I love your daughter and will see she's happy."

Victoria stumbled to the sofa and sat down. What had he said? Had she heard correctly? No, it couldn't be. Not three nights ago, as he had left her bed, he had whispered his intention to leave her for good. If he loved her, truly loved her, why would he go? She stared at him, searching for a hint of falsity in his claim somewhere in those gray-blue eyes.

Straightening, Remington turned away with a shake of his head. "I don't believe you." But his tone denied his words.

"Then tell me why I didn't sail from here once me men freed me from prison? If ya think because I wanted ta take your daughter again and seek the ransom ya cheated me from, consider this. I had plenty of times ta do just that, but didn't. Why?"

"I don't know. I don't know!" Remington confessed irritably. He went to the buffet and poured a glass of wine.

"I can't be sayin' I wouldn't be feelin' the same as you—'tis a lot ta accept—but there be one way ta convince ya. And it might be trappin' Rutledge in his own lies."

Remington looked up at him. "How?"

"Call another meetin'. Include Rutledge. He can't

481

be workin' alone, and once the meetin' is over, we'll follow him.''

Remington stared at Dru a while, swallowed his wine in one gulp, and placed the glass on the tray again. He studied the finely cut crystal decanter. ''All right,'' he finally agreed. He glared back at Dru. ''But know I do it for only one reason. To prove you're wrong!'' He went to the door. ''I'll set it up for tonight, around eleven. Same place. You wait for me in my room. Alanna will let you in and then stay here with Victoria.'' He raised a damning finger. ''But be warned, captain. If this is some sort of trick, I'll have your head.''

Dru bowed respectfully and stood erect, glancing at Victoria, who still sat unmoving on the sofa, her mouth agape. Knowing her father watched, he failed to fight off the urge to wink playfully at her. Her mouth snapped shut and she quickly found her feet, although somewhat unsteadily.

''Come, Victoria. We must meet your mother and Damon. To give this a true test, we must not let him grow suspicious,'' Remington warned, his outstretched hand demanding her to accompany him. He glared at Dru once more. ''For your sake, captain, you better pray he doesn't.''

With his daughter held tightly by the elbow, Remington escorted her from the room, glancing back at the pirate only once.

Pausing outside the door to his room, Remington bid Damon goodnight and watched until the other had gone to his own and disappeared inside. A dark scowl hooded Remington's eyes, for he still couldn't accept the possibility that Damon wasn't one of them. When he had advised Damon of this evening's special meeting, Remington thought the anger in the man's eyes spoke of hatred for the British, and nothing else. Yet he must see the charade through to an end. If nothing more than to prove the captain a liar. He lifted the latch and went inside.

Darkness poured out to greet him, and Remington thought for an instant he had been duped, until he sensed another's presence in the room. "Captain?"

"Aye. 'Tis me. How did it go?"

Remington found a candle and touched a flame to it, flooding the room with a soft yellow hue tinged with a flickering of danger. "As I would have expected." He removed his tricorn and laid it on the side table. "So far he's given me no reason to change my way of thinking." He looked at Dru. "So what happens next?"

"I've stationed one of me men in the lobby and one in the alley below Rutledge's room. Either way he be choosin' ta go, we'll be knowin' about it. I be guessin' it won't be too long."

Remington stared at Dru for several moments, then turned and poured himself a glass of wine. He drank half of it before he turned back. "My daughter said something that bothers me. Maybe you'd care to explain."

Dru nodded consent.

"If you did indeed protect her all the while she was in your company, why did she find it necessary to say the contrary?"

Dru walked further into the room from the bedchamber where he had waited and sat down in the chair near

483

the fireplace. ''She thought I lied to her and wished ta get even.''

''About what?''

Dru traced a fingertip along the calluses of his palm, not wanting to say more. ''I'd be preferrin' she be the one ta tell ya.''

''And rightly so,'' Remington agreed. ''But you more than anyone will understand why I say I could never quite believe her.''

The dimple appeared. ''Aye. She has a way of forgettin' ta tell all the facts.''

''Then please allow me to know the whole of it.''

'' 'Tis your right. And I be more than willin' ta tell ya everythin', but not now. Once I've proven meself about Rutledge, then and only then I be knowin' ya will believe what I say. Would only be fair ta Victoria.''

Remington watched him a moment, swirled the contents of his glass, and said, ''All right. I'll wait. But it seems to me I'll never know. Rutledge is who he says he is.'' He swallowed the rest of his wine. ''What made you think he wasn't?''

Dru shrugged one shoulder. ''Somethin' your cook said.''

''My cook? When did you have the occasion to speak with her?''

Dru bowed his head and smiled, knowing he need not answer.

Remington sucked in a short breath. ''I knew it. I knew it! We did pass you on the road, didn't we?'' He waited until Dru confirmed his statement. ''And one of your men was in the dining hall the other night, wasn't he?''

"Aye. Me cousin, Sean."

Remington exploded into laughter. "Right under my nose! And I suppose you've been to see Victoria in her room more times than just tonight." He laughed again when Dru wouldn't answer. "Oh, if only you weren't a pirate."

"Sir?"

Remington returned to the wine decanter, talking more to himself than Dru. "If things were different. It would suit her just fine. You'd teach that young woman how to behave." He raised the glass, a smile still on his face. "You're not afraid of anything, are you, captain?"

Dru smiled weakly in return, knowing only one fear, the fear of fathers with single daughters they wish to see wed. He glanced toward the bedchamber doors leading to the balcony. Why hadn't someone sent the alarm? Then, as if in answer to his unspoken prayer, two raps, a pause, one rap against the door.

" 'Tis John," he said, rising. "Damon's made his move. And we better be hurryin'. He's probably shed the disguise and won't be slowed up by the limp."

"Limp?" Remington asked.

Lifting the latch, Dru looked back at Remington. " 'Aye. Tis false. Like everythin' else about him."

Remington cocked a brow. "Then let's see if you can prove it."

"He went into that buildin', capt'n," Donovan said as the group of men gathered opposite a warehouse.

"Is he alone?"

"No. They kept it dark in there so I not be knowin'

how many, but I did hear voices."

"What now?" Remington asked. "It's your move."

Dru studied their surroundings, noticing no way into the warehouse other than the front entrance and possibly one in back. "John, you stay here. If he makes a break for it, stop him. Sean and Donovan, circle around in back. No one leaves. Got it?" The two men nodded and quickly crossed the street, ducking into an alleyway that would lead them to the far side of the building where they could hide and wait. Dru turned to Remington. "I be thinkin' the only way ya will be honestly believin' this is if ya see him for yourself. You and I will be makin' an uninvited visit ta his meetin'."

Remington bowed curtly and held out a hand for Dru to lead the way. Together they started for the warehouse. Once they stepped onto the sidewalk that ran before the building, they stayed close to the protection of the shadows. One window separated them from the door, and they paused beside it to listen.

"Sergeant, you must send this information on immediately. General Wordsworth will know what to do."

"Yes, colonel. When will you know for certain?"

The dull clicks of leather heels neared the window, and Dru and Remington pressed back against the wall for safety.

"I can't say. We leave tomorrow, but since I have Remington's full trust, I'm sure he'll tell me in plenty of time."

Dru could feel the man at his side grow rigid. He started to rise, and Dru quickly touched his arm, warning him to wait.

"Colonel, since we've been friends a long time, I think you'll understand my concern when I say I've heard rumors that Remington wants you to marry his daughter. You don't plan to go through with it, do you? We could be ordered to move at any time and she'd be in the way."

The colonel smiled, staring at the dark street. "Yes, I know. I guess I'll worry about it when the time comes. *If* it comes. But somehow I feel this war will be over before then." He looked back at the sergeant. "And maybe I'll marry her, anyway. It's time I settled down, and I already own a plantation. Besides I think she's smitten with me." He went to the small table near the door, picked up his tricorn, and added, "I must get back. I wouldn't want the young lady to come to my room and find me gone. She's terribly jealous." Two voices chorused laughter, and the colonel turned to leave. "Be careful, sergeant."

"Yes, sir," the man responded as Colonel Kingsley opened the door and stepped outside.

Hugging his cape to his chin, Kingsley turned, stopping short when confronted by two figures on the sidewalk. In the shadows he could not make out who they were, but instinct warned him of danger. Slowly and unobserved, he slipped his hand inside the flowing yards of cloth to the butt of the flintlock pistol lodged in his belt. He moved to step down from the sidewalk.

"Hold it right there, colonel." The title rang with loathing.

He stopped but did not turn to face the men.

"I think I should tell you that the information you obtained this evening is false. Just as Damon Rutledge

487

is false, you lying, bloody cur,'' Remington hissed. ''If I knew the others wouldn't enjoy a piece of you, I'd beat you to death right here.'' He took a deep breath and let it out slowly. ''Instead I'm forced to take you back with me.''

''I'm afraid that's not possible,'' Kingsley disagreed, turning slowly toward the man. ''My work here may have come to an end, but I'm still of value elsewhere. And now that I know the names and faces of those who work against the Crown, *your* work has come to an end, Mr. Remington.'' In an instant, Kingsley pulled the pistol and aimed it at him.

''No!'' Dru called out, knocking Remington aside just as the powder exploded. Both went tumbling to the ground. ''John!''

Spying a movement from the sidewalk opposite him, Kingsley wasted no time in spinning about and racing off down the street, his empty weapon left behind in the dirt.

''He be unarmed, John. Take him alive!'' Dru called after his friend, watching the two men quickly disappear into the darkness. He turned to Remington, who lay grasping his shoulder, his face twisted in pain. ''Were you hit?''

''Yes,'' Remington answered through clenched teeth. ''Burns like the devil, but I don't think it's too serious.'' He struggled to sit up, clutching his left arm.

''Let me look at it,'' Dru ordered, tearing at the sleeve of Remington's jacket. ''Aye. 'Tis only a scratch. But we must be havin' a doctor look at it. Come on. Ya can lean on me.''

Supporting the older man's weight against him, Dru

quickly scanned the streets for some sign of his cousin and McKenzie, unaware of how Beau Remington watched him.

"Captain," he said softly, waiting until Dru looked at him. "I owe you a great deal. I'm not sure I'll ever be able to repay you."

The dimple appeared. "I be thinkin' of somethin'," Dru grinned.

TWENTY-NINE

Blake Kingsley longed to find a room with a soft, huge bed in it and lie down. He wanted to rest, to sleep, to not worry, to stop running. Two days had passed since he had fled Williamsburg and escaped the trio of men chasing him down the darkened streets. Dumb luck had been all that had saved him when he had spotted a hay wagon lumbering its way out of town and managed to climb onto it without the driver's knowledge. The day General Wordsworth had informed him of their plan to purchase Willow Glen as a cover for his assignment, Blake Kingsley had known it was only for a while. But, oddly enough, he had grown comfortable in the role of plantation owner, and fond of Victoria Remington. Now he was fleeing for his life. He must find General Wordsworth and advise him that the plan had failed.

Pausing outside an inn, he glanced up at the sign

hanging above the door, the place he had been told General Wordsworth and the others were staying. He must find him and soon. If the sergeant had escaped Remington and his men, the information he had forwarded to the general was false, a trap. One that could be very costly. They had to be warned. Touching a hand to the doorlatch, he went inside.

"Can I help you?" the man behind the desk asked.

"Yes," Kingsley said, approaching. "I'm Colonel Blake Kingsley and I must see General Wordsworth. Which room is he in?"

"All the generals and their staff are dining now, sir," the man replied, nodding his head in the direction of the dining hall.

Without a word, Kingsley quickly crossed the foyer and paused in the doorway, scanning the crowd for the general.

"Blake!" someone called. "Over here."

In the center of the room a man stood up and waved—Colonel Renfred, the general's advisor and Kingsley's friend.

"What are you doing here?" he asked once Kingsley reached the table.

"I'm looking for General Wordsworth. Where is he?"

"He went to Quebec two weeks ago."

"Damn," Kingsley muttered. "When do you expect him back?"

Colonel Renfred shrugged. "Hard to say. Why?"

"Did you receive any messages from Williamsburg in the last day or so?"

"Yes. Last night. Why?"

"Because it's a trap. I was found out and that message is dangerous.''

"Bloody God," Colonel Renfred exclaimed. "Everything's falling apart.''

"What do you mean?''

Renfred waved at one of the serving maids to bring a mug of ale for his friend and pulled Kingsley down to the chair next to him. "Remember Melissa Bensen?''

"Of course. She's the one who suggested her father's plantation for my cover. Without her help, things wouldn't have lasted as long as they did. What about her?''

"Well, we set her up here in New York to spy for us. Her and three of her men. Somehow they found out about her and she left here before they killed her. Stupid woman. We could have protected her. Anyway, she went to Quebec the day before yesterday, looking for General Wordsworth. She's probably there by now. She wants to return to England.''

"Can't say I blame her. I'm going to have to be reassigned myself. I've made too many enemies in Williamsburg to return there.''

"Yes, I would imagine so. Say, why not stay here? I could use the help.''

Kingsley shook his head. "I can't right now. I must find the general first and explain about the message. How long ago did you send it on?''

"Right after I got it.''

"Then I must leave right away. It will take me a couple of days to get to Quebec." He stood. "Good to see you again, Thomas. I hope the next time we can share a glass of wine and laugh about all this.''

Renfred waved off the maid with the mug of ale, his

attention centered on Kingsley hurrying from the room.

"Good morning, captain." Remington smiled with an outstretched hand, welcoming Dru into the sitting room. "Thank you for coming." He closed the door behind them and added, "May I get you a drink?"

"No, thank ya," Dru responded. He looked at Remington's bandaged shoulder, the arm bound in a sling. "How ya be feelin'?"

Remington reached up to rub his shoulder. "A little stiff, but I'll be all right in a few days." He indicated the chairs by the fireplace. "Won't you sit down?"

Dru sat in the chair on the left, Remington the other, and settled back comfortably to listen.

"I heard one of your men returned to the ship," Remington stated.

"Aye. But John is captain of his own vessel and decided he shouldn't be waitin' on the rest of us."

"Oh, I see. Then your cousin and Mr. McKenzie are members of your crew?"

"Aye. We've sailed together for a long time. They wanted me ta tell ya how sorry they be for not catchin' Rutledge or his partner."

Remington shook off the apology. "No need. He's a slippery sort. Probably had an escape route planned months ago. He'll be caught sooner or later." He reached up to scratch his chin. "Tell me. Have you ever thought of settling down?"

"If ya mean givin' up me life at sea, no. I wouldn't be knowin' what ta do with me time."

Remington smiled enthusiastically. "Well, I have an idea and a proposal."

Dru cocked a brow.

"I owe you a great deal, Captain Chandler. I had a long talk with Victoria. She told me everything, about how you protected her, rescued her from Melissa Bensen," —his tone rang with malice—"and even sent word to the authorities in New York about her plans. Then there was your help with Rutledge and the fact that you probably saved my life. Not to mention your treatment in the jail. So you see, captain, I just can't let you sail away without trying to pay you back in some way." He chuckled. "I even cheated you out of the ransom money."

"I didn't do any of it for what I might be gettin' in return," Dru pointed out.

"I never thought that for a minute," Remington assured him. "You did it for Victoria."

Dru wouldn't answer. Instead he studied the nails of one hand.

"You said you loved her. Was that the one and only lie you spoke?"

"It was a secret I meant ta carry ta me grave, sir."

"Why?"

"We be of two very different worlds. So unlike, neither of us could be sharin' the other's."

"Ah, but you're wrong," Remington contradicted. "And I've come up with a solution. Nearly everything that is raised on Raven Oaks must be shipped. For years I've thought of starting a shipping line. And what better man to run such a business than the captain of a ship? And as for your crew, your cousin, they can be the ones to sail them. That way you'll be able to settle in Williamsburg and be near Victoria." He shook his head playfully. "Though Lord knows why you'd want

494

to be after all she's done to you." His mirth disappeared. "You do know she loves you, don't you?"

A sparkling smile seemed reflected in Dru's eyes. "I've not heard it from her own lips, but I have been told. And as for your offer, I be honored ya considered me, but I be thinkin' ta turn ya down."

"I'm not asking for your answer right away. In fact I insist you think it over. Send your cousin and Mr. McKenzie back to your ship and have them sail it here to Williamsburg. They can supply it at my expense and then send word when it's ready. You will be visiting us at Raven Oaks until they do."

Dru opened his mouth to object, cut short by Remington's raised hand. "We leave tomorrow."

Melissa nervously paced the floor of her room. It had been two days since her arrival in Quebec and her conversation with General Wordsworth. Now all she had to do was wait for the docking of a ship, any ship to sail her back to England. Her work here was done, especially without the aid of her three lackeys, and the only place she would feel safe was in England. She went to the window and stared out into the bright sunlight, studying the harbor again for any sign of a frigate or brigantine. With General Wordsworth's letter, all charges of indebtedness were dropped, and she would walk the streets of London a free woman. In fact, the general had given her substantial funds to see her through until the end of the war. Then she could claim Raven Oaks and Willow Glen as her own, and live in the style to which she was accustomed. If only a ship would arrive soon.

A knock at the door of her room spun her around.

"Who's there?" she called.

"Willy, Miss Bensen. You asked me to tell you when a ship docked," a small voice responded.

Melissa glanced back outside. The smooth waters of the harbor contradicted the statement, only fishing boats disturbed its calm. "Where? I don't see it!" she barked. "You're lying!"

"It will come soon. It's been spotted up the bay. You can't see it yet," he reaffirmed. "Do ya want me to carry your things?"

Melissa pressed fingertips to her temples to still the pounding in her head. What was wrong with her? There were no patriots in Canada, only English rule, and Willy was nothing more than a child. How could she mistrust a boy?

"Yes," she answered weakly, crossing to the door to let him in.

"I'm sorry, colonel, but the General left for Nova Scotia yesterday morning."

Blake Kingsley expelled an angry sigh in a rush. "For how long?" he demanded irritably.

"If you mean when will he be back, he won't. He's to return to New York from there."

"Damn," Kingsley shouted, slamming his tricorn down on the lieutenant's desk. "I'm running around in circles. Did he sail there? Maybe I can outrun them on horseback."

"No, sir. Haven't been any ships in the harbor for weeks."

Kingsley stalked across the room to the window, glaring heatedly outside as if to study the horizon. His mind raced with solutions to his perplexing problem.

"Did he receive a message from Colonel Renfred just before he left?"

"Yes, sir. That's why he went to Nova Scotia." Fidgeting with the brass paperweight on his desk, the lieutenant hesitated, then asked, "Sir, is there something I can do?"

Kingsley glared back at him. "Only if you can make a ship appear in that harbor right now. I don't relish the thought of sitting on a horse again." His shoulders drooping in dismay, he shook his head. "But I don't see where I have any choice. This mess is my fault, and its my responsibility to see it's corrected. Before it's too late." He gazed outside again, the anger vanishing from his face. He spun around, hurried to the desk and his hat, and smiled broadly at the lieutenant. "I'll see you get a promotion for this, young man," he said lightheartedly, reaching out to shake the confused officer's hand before turning on his heel and running from the room.

"Hurry, Willy!" Melissa snapped. "We haven't a moment to waste."

"Yes'm," the boy grunted, struggling with the heavy trunk full of gowns she had acquired during her stay in Quebec. "But I think we got plenty of time. They gotta take on supplies if they're gonna sail all the way to England."

"And why do you think we must hurry? I have to find the captain of this ship and give him his orders. It takes time to reload a ship." She paused at the foot of the gangplank to survey the people bustling about the harbor and wait for Willy to catch up. "And I want to leave here as soon as possible."

"Yes'm," the boy mumbled, dragging the chest

along the wooden planks of the pier. "But I don't know why you want to hurry."

Melissa opened her mouth to sharply reprimand the boy for his insolence when she spotted a man running toward them. The pounding in her temples began again. Dear God! Surely they hadn't sent someone all the way to Canada for her. Every muscle in her thin frame knotted. It was stupid. There were none but British here. Her heart raced. They could never take her back. Not without a struggle. She reached out to grab a corner of the trunk.

"Hurry, Willy. He's coming!"

Caught off balance, the boy stumbled and dropped the chest. "Who, Miss Bensen?"

Her eyes wide with terror and filled with tears, Melissa turned to face the man while she tugged at the string of her purse. Inside she carried a small knife, and if she caught him unaware, she might be able to stab him with it, Quickly! He was much too near! In her panic, her quaking fingers seemed to tighten the knot and the bag slipped from her hands. She bent to retrieve it, hoping there still might be time—

"Allow me, madam."

She looked up to find him standing before her, smiling. Was this some sort of evil, twisted way to provoke her, to remind her that a mere woman could never carry out such a plan as she had been entrusted with? Well, they were wrong. And it didn't bother her in the least. She bit her quivering lip and nodded.

Scooping up the bag effortlessly, he held it out to her and asked, "Were you planning to sail on the ship?"

Her words failed her. She declined her head slowly.

"Then maybe you can tell me its destination."

Was this a trick? And where are the others? Surely they didn't send just one man.

"She's going to England, sir," Willy chimed in. "Sure wish I could go. Never been to England."

The man smiled down at him. "Well, maybe you can someday. Is the captain on board? I'd like to speak with him."

Willy shrugged. "Don't know. Just got here ourselves. Who are you, anyway?"

"Oh, forgive me," the man apologized with a slight bow to Melissa. "I'm Colonel Blake Kingsley. And you—"

The shocked look on her face slowly faded until the corners of her mouth turned upward and she burst into laughter.

"I'm sorry, madam, but I fail to see the humor—"

Melissa reached up to touch his arm. "Oh, it is I who should apologize, sir. But if you knew what I thought—" She reduced her laughter to only the trace of a smile. "I'm Melissa Bensen."

"Melissa—" Kingsley began, then chuckled. "I knew you were here, but I didn't expect to run into you." He covered her hand with his. "I heard about what happened. I'm glad you got away safely. I guess you could say we have a lot in common."

"Oh?"

"Yes. I was discovered too and barely escaped with my life." He glanced up at the ship. "That's why I'm here. I'm trying to catch up with General Wordsworth."

"He's in Nova Scotia."

"Yes, I know. That's why I need this ship to sail me there at once."

Melissa jerked her hand away. "It's sailing to England. Under General Wordsworth's orders."

"No problem. It's on the way."

"But—"

He looked up at the ship. "I'll talk to the captain so we can get under way immediately. If you'll excuse me," he said with a bow and started up the gangplank.

"Wait just a minute, Colonel Kingsley," Melissa snapped, following in his steps. "This ship will *not* leave immediately. It must take on supplies first. England is—"

Kingsley stopped midway up and looked back at her. "It will have to take on supplies somewhere else. It's important I reach the general as soon as possible."

"Then find another ship. This one's mine!"

Kingsley stiffened. "Must I remind you, good woman, that I'm a colonel in the British army and this ship is under British rule? Not yours!"

"Well, well, Parker, me boy. I be thinkin' the colonel has a wee bit of a problem."

A buzzing droned in Melissa's ears at the sound of a familiar voice, one she had prayed to never hear again. Slowly stepping to one side, she looked past Kingsley to the man who had spoken, her heart pounding in her chest, for standing at the top of the gangplank, feet apart, arms folded over his protruding belly, Dillon Gallagher glared down at her. Their eyes met, a hatred born of past encounters flashing in the deep blue of his stare. She shuddered, and Kingsley turned at the unspoken alarm.

"Are you the captain of this vessel?" he asked.

Only Dillon's eyes moved to acknowledge the man.

"Aye."

"Then we have business to discuss." Kingsley proceeded up the gangplank to stand before the captain and the man at his side. "I'm Colonel Blake Kingsley, and it's very important that you take me to Nova Scotia. I must speak with General Wordsworth, who's already there."

"And what if I be refusin'?" Dillon challenged with an uplifted brow.

Kingsley smiled softly. "I'm afraid you don't understand. I'm commandeering this ship and crew." He glanced up at the flag gently flapping in the breeze on the main mast. "You show English colors, which means you are subject to British rule."

Dillon grinned, his red hair gleaming in the bright sunlight. " 'Tis you who not be understandin', colonel. 'Tis me ship, and mine alone. It be sailin' where I command it."

Kingsley stiffened. "Captain, if I must, I will return with soldiers to see that you obey my orders."

Dillon glanced at Parker with a slight grin parting his lips. "Then by all means, colonel, come aboard. Parker here will see ya to your quarters, won't ya, Parker?"

The first mate nodded, stepping aside to allow Kingsley to pass, then looked to his captain again. "The hold, sir?" he asked when Kingsley moved far enough away not to hear.

"Aye," Dillon nodded. "And make sure there be enough room for another." He turned to Melissa, who stood frozen to her spot. "I believe ya came ta sail on me ship. I be interested in knowin' why."

Melissa's knees weakened, she felt faint, and the

knot in her throat threatened to strangle her. She swallowed hard. "I—I must return to England."

"England, is it? And what happened ta your grand ideas of spyin' on the colonists?" he asked, glaring down at her. " 'Twas the reason ya needed me services."

"It—it didn't work out," she replied in a small voice.

"Now I be findin' that hard ta believe, lass. I know the way ya work and can't imagine ya failed."

"I didn't fail," she snapped, her courage returning with the insult. "I was tricked."

"Tricked?"

"Yes. While I waited for you on Barbados, Dru Chandler came to see me, pretending to be one of your crew. I had no way of knowing any differently and told him of my plans. It was he who sent word to the authorities in New York about me."

Dillon cocked his head to one side. "Now why would he be doin' that? The man has no grudge against ya."

The muscles across her chest constricted. She couldn't tell him why. He hated her and had oftentimes reminded her of it. Although he had never said so, she sensed his loathing dated from their dealings years ago regarding Alanna Remington, and to admit to him now that she had planned a similar end for her daughter was sheer suicide. "It doesn't matter," she whispered, bowing her head.

"Ah, but it does, lass. If ya be wantin' ta sail on me ship, ya must be tellin' me."

Melissa lifted hopeful eyes to him. "You mean you'd take me to England?"

He shrugged. "And why not? I be growin' weary of

all this fightin' over here.''

Melissa's heart seemed to beat faster with the news. She'd tell him all he wanted to know, a little tinged perhaps, but enough to satisfy him. She motioned for Willy to follow her and moved up the wooden planks.

"Captain Chandler had kidnapped Victoria Remington, Alanna's daughter. I found out about it and stole her away. When my action threatened to take away his reward, he sought revenge.''

One bronze-colored brow lifted somewhat. "And why would ya take the lass?''

"Why to protect her, of course. Those men would have abused her.''

Dillon threw his head back and roared with laughter. Startled, Melissa retreated a step.

"Ah, such a grand lady, ya are. Ta be thinkin' of the safety of another.'' He calmed his mirth and squinted one eye at her. "Now I be tellin' ya the way I see it. When ya found out who the lass was, ya saw another evil way ta satisfy your hatred for Alanna. Ya probably planned ta kill the lass and throw the carcass on her mother's doorstep. That be more your style. Of course, ya would hire it done since ya lack the courage ta face your enemies. That be the truth of it, isn't it lass?''

Melissa shook her head vigorously. "No—no. That's not it at all.''

"Ya couldn't be satisfied with taking their land. Ya wanted ta kill their child, too.'' A strong hand shot out to seize her wrist. "Well, come on board. Ya wanted ta sail on me ship, and that's what ya will do.''

A tremor of fear overtook her when Dillon clamped onto her arms with a painful grip, hauling her up the remainder of the narrow bridge and onto the deck. He summoned one of his crew with the nod of his head and brutally shoved her into his arms.

"Take her below and put her with the colonel," he ordered with a growl, then turned on the frightened boy who stood shaking in quiet observation on the pier. "You there! Be off with ya and not a word ta anyone, unless ya like the idea of bein' me cabin boy."

Willy turned on his heel, tripped over his feet, and fell. Scrambling up again he took off in a frantic run, not once bothering to look back, the sinister laughter of the devil pirate ringing in his ears.

THIRTY

"Good morning, Dru," Remington smiled when the captain stepped out onto the mansion's wide veranda. "Come sit down and enjoy the cool morning air. I think it may turn rather warm before the day is over." He watched Dru settle in a rocker next to him. "Sleep well?"

"Aye. I must be admittin' a featherbed be more comfortable than me bunk. But I not be havin' the gentle roll of the ship ta lull me ta sleep."

Remington chuckled. "Yes, but in time I'd wager you'd get used to it."

"Still tryin' ta convince me I should stay?" Dru grinned. "It's already been nearly a week, and if me cousin doesn't send word soon, I'll be thinkin' the two of you are plottin' against me."

"Not a bad idea," Remington agreed, lifting the arm in the sling for a more comfortable position. "I've never been one to take no for an answer. Once I decide on something, nothing stops me until I've got what I want." He glanced over at Dru. "You should know that more than anyone."

Dru's dimple appeared. "Aye. That I do. I must say, I'm glad ta have ya on me side now instead of against me. I be doubtin' how many times I be comin' up the winner."

Spreading his feet apart in front of him, Remington gently set the rocker in motion. "Tell me about yourself, Dru. I know so little."

"Not much ta tell. I was born in Ireland, a small town near Dublin, and when I was thirteen, I took ta the sea."

"At thirteen?"

"Aye, as a cabin boy, until six years later."

"What happened then?"

A dark frown shaded Dru's eyes. "Somethin' odd. I came home ta visit me mother in the spring of sixty-four and found a strange ship anchored in the bay with no crew or captain on board. Then me cousin, Sean, tells me the papers of ownership were delivered ta him, in me name." Dru shook his head thoughtfully. "Fourteen years I be sailin' on the *Defiance*, and still not know who gave it to me."

"Must have been someone who cared a great deal for you."

"Aye, but the only family I had besides me mother was Sean. And his family was as poor as we. I guess I was not meant ta know."

"What about your father?"

"I don't even know if he's alive. He never married me mother, and she would never talk about him. Ta tell the truth, I not be knowin' who he was."

Remington sighed heavily, staring out across the yard at the giant black oak trees lining the drive. "I know how you feel, in a way. I was nearly your age when I found out who my real father was. And I probably wouldn't have then, if it hadn't been for Alanna." He smiled dreamily. "Dear, sweet Alanna. When I think of some of the things I did to her." He jerked his head around toward Dru. "They're alike you know, Alanna and Victoria. Except Victoria is spoiled. If she couldn't have her way, she'd lie to get it." He chuckled, looking back out at the trees. "Thought I never knew it." A moment passed in silence. "That day at the beach, when you brought her home, I suspected something was wrong. I could see it in her eyes. Why didn't you say something? Your man wanted you to."

"Would ya have believed me?" Dru asked, one corner of his mouth turned upward.

Remington laughed loudly. "No. But it took one hell of a man to keep quiet. Why did you?"

"Because I deserved her wrath. And I knew it wouldn't be long before me cousin came for me."

Remington sat forward in the rocker. "Would it be too much to ask what caused you to agree with her judgment?"

"I had promised ta kill Melissa Bensen and didn't."

"Melissa Bensen," Remington growled, falling back to rock more briskly than before. "I had thought to hear the last of her when she went to England. Someday, I'll see she pays for all the grief she's caused."

Suddenly the frantic pounding of hoofbeats from in back of the house filled the air, and Remington bolted from his retreat, wincing from the soreness in his shoulder, in time to see a blur of green velvet race across the yard on horseback and down the drive.

"What the—" he began, then recognized the skilled horsemanship of the rider. "Where in God's creation is she off to? I've told her a hundred times not to ride away from the manor. There are British soldiers about. I'm going after her," he hissed, starting past Dru only to grab his shoulder when a stab of pain shot through him.

"Ya not be up to it, sir. Ya sit here and relax. I'll get her." Dru helped Remington sit down again, turned, and placed one hand to the porch railing. In one easy movement, he swung his legs up and over the balustrade to land on the ground a few feet below.

"Dru," Remington called before he had traveled very far. "I would be eternally grateful and one hundred percent supportive if you taught that young woman a lesson. It's been a long time coming, and you're the one who can do it."

A playful smile tugged at Dru's mouth. He grinned up at Remington, clicked his heels, and saluted. "Aye, aye, sir," he said, and set off in the direction of the stable.

"And take my horse," Remington instructed, watching until Dru disappeared. He sighed, the thoughts that somehow his youth had been stolen away pushing him back in the rocker. Only yesterday he had been the one who rode out after a hot-tempered female. A smile of his own crept across his face.

Early morning kissed the hillsides with the amber shade of sunlight, sparkling in the grass's dew and warming all it touched. The sweet fragrance of wild flowers carried along in the gentle breeze filled the air, quietly disturbing the meadow's peaceful slumber, caressing it into wakefulness. A bevy of quail scurried into the thicket, started by the sudden pounding of hoofbeats racing nearer. A lone rider appeared on the horizon to break the solitude, galloping over the countryside in wild abandon.

A flash of green velvet, long, dark hair flowing unhindered in the wind, adorned the delicate figure masterfully holding the animal in rein, free enough to thunder across the high grass unrestricted yet mindful of command. The crisp morning air stung Victoria's face as she and Beldon raced across her father's land, feeling fresh and alive and free.

She slowed her horse to a trot once the river came into view, a spot her father oftentimes visited when problems troubled him and he sought the time alone to clear his mind. It seemed only natural that she would invade his private sanctuary to contemplate her own worries, for many of them concerned him. At the water's edge she dismounted, allowing Beldon to drink at his leisure while she casually strolled along the grass-covered bank.

The past several days had been a strain on her. There were so many things she wanted to discuss with Dru, but the lack of privacy forbid it. Her father constantly demanded Dru's presence and never left her a chance to speak with him alone. Each night, in her room, she waited, certain that at any moment he would come to her, an aching in her heart reborn each morning with the pale light of the eastern sky. Had his declaration of love been false? A lie to convince her father to trust him? Or had he lost the need to hold her in his arms and whisper softly to her? What had caused this change? Why did it seem he no longer cared?

Victoria stooped to pick a wild flower, its petals dew-moistened. Teardrops of the morning she often called it, now mixed with her own. She loved the fierce pirate captain and wondered at the sanity of such a situation, for until she had heard his own admission, spoken for her ears alone, she had known the hopelessness of it. One could not live a love that was not returned, and yet she now wondered if she wouldn't. Had the tricks she had played these past weeks stirred misgivings on his part, made him leery of placing his life and his heart in the hands of a woman as thoughtless and selfish as she? She would change all that if given the chance.

Sunlight stole across the meadow, its golden beacon singling out a hollowed log. Absently she went to it and sat down. When he thought she slumbered, had he not pledged to leave her? Or would he change his course if she confessed what lay hidden in her heart, if she spoke the words and laid to rest any doubt he might have?

Sighing, she stood, tossed the flower to the ground, and began to stroll along the riverbank again, pausing when a mud-darkened toad hopped across her path. She smiled. If only life were that simple. To declare undying love and devotion, to live a life of happiness without a single cloud, to forgive the wrongdoings of the past and start anew. She laughed softly. And how would she convince her father to agree to such a union? No more than one week past, he had sought revenge against the pirate. Now he offered him his home and hospitality. But would he give his daughter to the man?

Munching contentedly on the sweet grasses of the meadow, Beldon suddenly reared his head, ears twitching. Sucking in the scent, his nostrils flared and he pawed the ground, then stopped. Again his ears moved nervously, eyes widened in alarm before he wrinkled his nose in a loud whinny.

"What is it, boy?" Victoria cooed, approaching. Slowly, she reached out to grasp the steed's bridle. "Do you hear something?"

But as she voiced the question, the faint beating of hoofs against the earth reached her ears. Alarmed, for she knew the hills hid enemy soldiers, she glanced toward the grove of trees several score of yards away. A hand shading her eyes, she squinted in the day's brightness in hopes of spotting the intruder before being discovered. Then she saw him, astride her father's favorite stallion, as if he owned the world and all in it.

"Ya shouldn't be out ridin' alone, Victoria," Dru offered, reining his horse to a halt near hers. "Your father is worried about you."

Strangely enough his presence—no, his intrusion—angered her. She gave him a noncommittal look and turned away. "I'll be all right. I'm an excellent rider and can outrun even the best."

"Can ya now?" he asked with a raised brow. "And what if there were more than one ta run away from?"

She cast him a cheerless smile over her shoulder. "Well, now we'll never know, since you're here, will we?" She walked a few steps further. "Tell Papa I'm fine and I'll be home shortly."

"Ah, then ya can be tellin' him yourself. I don't plan ta return ta the house without ya."

"Then find some other place to wait. I came here to be alone."

"But I can't, love. I promised your father ta see ta

511

your safety. I'll just be sittin' here quiet as a mouse. You'll not be knowin' I'm here."

The corner of her mouth twitched. "Oh, won't I? Trying to ignore you is like trying to ignore a full chamberpot."

Laughter nearly found its way to his lips, but failed to hide the twinkle in his eyes. "I be sorry ta hear ya feel that way, me love. But it won't be for long. I'll be leavin' as soon as me cousin sends word."

Victoria's heart lurched. "And when will that be?" she asked, hoping to sound indifferent.

A wide grin stretched his lips. "Ya sound as if it matters."

"Well, you're wrong." She turned away, fighting the tears choking the very breath from her.

Dru slid from the saddle and landed noiselessly in the soft grass. He crossed his arms and gazed up at the blue, cloudless sky overhead. "I had a long talk with your father this mornin'." He stole a peek her way. She hadn't moved and did not respond to his statement. He drew a breath to try again. "He be a forgivin' sort. Says he'll not be blamin' me for all that happened."

The flesh on the back of her neck tingled. So that was his ploy, to scare her. "Oh?" she asked nonchalantly, turning around. "And exactly what did you tell him that he's so kindly forgiven you for?"

"Everythin'," he replied, looking out at the ripples and tiny whirlpools of the river.

Victoria's heart beat faster. "Every detail?" she asked calmly, a composure she little felt.

He glanced back over his shoulder at her, hesitating in an attempt to recall every word. "Almost," he finally replied and looked back at the current. "I didn't tell him about the kind of place Melissa Bensen kept ya for safekeepin'. I didn't think he would—"

"You mean you told him about—about us?" she exploded.

"About us?" he asked, looking back with a frown. "What about us?"

"You know. Our bargain?"

"Oh, that," he sighed. "No, I didn't. But I be glad ya reminded me. I be thinkin' he should know."

"Oh, Dru, you can't," she begged, hurriedly closing the distance between them. She reached out to touch his sleeve. "You mustn't! Say you won't tell him. He'd never understand. I'll do anything you ask if you just promise to keep it our secret."

The dimple in his cheek showed. "Anythin'?"

Victoria instantly released her hold as if it scorched her fingers. "I—I—" she stammered, realizing the trap he had set. She quickly turned away. "Almost," she answered weakly.

The soft bed of grass beneath his feet cushioned his step and he moved to stand behind her without her knowing. "And what is it ya not be able ta do?" He spoke quietly.

Victoria felt as if every inch of her tingled at the thought. "Y-you know," she said nervously. She walked ahead several paces, his closeness disturbing her more than his question.

Dru smiled, but she failed to see it as she stared at the horizon, wishing she could somehow disappear over it. "Be lettin' me guess," he bantered playfully. "Ya'll not be comin' ta me room should I say it is a part of the deal."

She nodded, dark curls bobbing with the movement.

"And might I be askin' why?"

"Why?" she exploded, whirling on him. "How can you honestly stand there and ask me that? We're not married! We never will be." Her voice cracked with the truth of her statement. "You've no right to expect it of me!" Tears threatened to tumble down her cheeks, and she quickly blinked them away before turning her back on him once more.

"Ya've come ta me before, Victoria—"

"A bargain!" she shouted over her shoulder. "It was a bargain!"

"Aye, and this is a deal," he teased. "A payment for a service rendered."

"Damn you!" she howled, nearly stumbling over her feet when she spun around to glare at him. "You never think of it as more than a payment! Did someone take a blade to your chest and cut out your heart? Do you ever *feel* anything?"

Dru leaned back on his heels, arms crossed and one finger raised to tap his chin. "I'm not sure," he said thoughtfully, gazing upward at the sky as though the query posed great difficulty in answering. "Do ya suppose we could be tryin' it one more time so I'll find out?" A mischievous grin creased his sun-tanned face.

Victoria's anger bubbled up, staining her cheeks scarlet. "And have you ever had a serious moment in your life?" she hissed. He opened his mouth to respond, cut short by her raised hand. "Spare me, please. I don't think I can stand another of your witty remarks." She glared at him a moment longer, then glanced around them, suddenly worried that enemy soldiers hid among the trees. "We'd better be going," she said, starting for her horse. "I wouldn't want some poor, unsuspecting Britisher to take you prisoner. I'm sure you'd talk them to death." But as she passed him, he easily reached out and caught her wrist, the contact sending a rush of emotions coursing through her.

"Then maybe a kiss, Victoria. I can be tellin' by a kiss," he said, feigning innocence.

One corner of her mouth curled disdainfully. "We've done that before, as I recall. Twice to be precise." She jerked free. "If you don't know already, then you never will."

Dru shrugged. "All right. But I think we better be takin' the time ta discuss the details of our agreement."

Victoria could feel the tremor of fury race up each knot of her spine. "There will be no deal," she spat. "Tell Papa everything. I don't care."

"Oh?" he asked, dark brows lifted slightly. "Of the times we've made love?"

She smiled sarcastically. "I've already told him as much."

"But not of the time ya offered yourself ta me."

A little of her confidence and courage faded. "He wouldn't believe you."

"A few weeks ago, I would have agreed. But since I saved his life and proved I spoke the truth about your Mr. Rutledge, I be thinkin' he'd believe almost anythin' I told him."

Victoria felt the heat rising in her cheeks.

"Ah," he grinned, crossing his arms. "I be seein' ya've changed your mind. Then be listenin' ta me and I'll tell ya me conditions ta our deal. I've no desire ta ruin the fine relationship ya have with your father, so in that respect, I can be claimin' ta feel somethin'. But I still be thinkin' ya owe me for havin' me locked up and

515

durin' me stay here on Raven Oaks I'll simply be askin' for a favor or two now and then.''

"You mean I'm to wait on you hand and foot," she chirped irritably.

He smiled broadly. "Aye. And ta seal the pact, I'll be needin' a kiss."

She glared up at him, her pretty mouth twisted in a snarl. "How about a handshake?"

The dimple reflected his amusement. "Nay, lass. A kiss."

Wondering if keeping peace in her family required so great a price, she let out a long, angry sigh and stepped closer. Standing on tiptoes, she presented him with a sisterly kiss to his cheek, grinning triumphantly when she pulled away. But the smile quickly vanished once she saw the corner of his mouth twitch into a devilish smirk, and before she could move out of reach, his hands caught both of her arms just above the elbows. He crushed her to him, his lips covering hers in a hot, demanding demonstration of his terms. She squealed, struggling to free herself, but his grip tightened, his tongue forcing her lips to part before it stole inside. It seemed every fiber of her being exploded, knowing the uncontrollable power he had over her. She knew she must break away before she weakened. Her arms still held tightly in his hands, she raised a foot and trod heavily on his instep, winning herself instant freedom. She stumbled backward, panting to catch her breath.

"Always—playing tricks—aren't you?" she seethed.

Blinking away his tears of pain, he straightened and took a step toward her. "Not anymore," he said quietly, the twinkle in his gray-blue eyes disappearing and attesting to the fact.

Victoria's chest tightened at his declaration. She backed away, one hand out in front of her. "Dru—stop this—don't come any closer." Her voice shook. He continued to advance. "I—I mean it!" Spotting Beldon from the corner of her eye, she judged the distance to reach him small enough to succeed before Dru could catch her. Spinning around, she dashed off toward the stallion, one foot raised to the stirrup when of a sudden two strong hands clamped onto her waist and jerked her from the horse.

"No!" she shrieked, arms and legs thrashing wildly. "Put me down, Dru Chandler!"

He did as she bade, but the results weren't what she had wanted, for when he let her slide to the ground one hand found her breast, his other pulling her back against his chest. He buried his face in the thick mass of dark hair drapped over one shoulder, and Victoria went livid with rage. Digging her nails into the flesh of his arms, she felt him weaken and seized her chance to break loose, running around the stallion, who pranced nervously all the while. She stopped once she had the huge beast between her and Dru.

"If you don't stop this instant, I'll tell my father what you tried to do," she snapped, bearly able to see him over the horse's wide back.

He smiled, rubbing the tender wounds she had inflicted.

"Did you hear me?" she demanded, her voice raised to stress the promise.

He continued to grin until he suddenly ducked down out of sight. The surprise of his move caught Victoria unawares and she failed to comprehend his intent until the horse snorted irritably. Looking down, she gasped when she discovered that Dru had easily stepped between the stallion's legs and was destined to grab her once more.

"No-o-o," she wailed, pivoting on her heels to race off through the meadow. But before she had traveled a dozen steps, his strong, muscular arms encircled her waist and sent them both tumbling in the tall grass. "Dru—Dru—stop!" she begged, wondering if he had a thousand hands, for it seemed he touched her everywhere. He rolled her beneath him, each wrist clamped in a steely hold and held to her sides. He had straddled her, resting back on his heels, and her strength quickly faded when she found it impossible to move. She glared up at him.

"Would you take me here—in the middle of the day—where all can see?" she demanded angrily, her dark hair tossed wildly about her face and shoulders and fanned out against the greenness of the grass.

"Nay, lass," he answered quietly. "I'm not the sort ta share. I only be meanin' ta show ya who is the strongest, and if it be what I want, I could have ya any time I decide. Now," he added, swiftly coming to his feet and bringing her with him, "I be suggestin' ya remember it. Every time I call ya, ya better come runnin' or I'll be finishin' what we started here and I'll not be carin' who's there ta watch."

Victoria's cheeks burned hotly, and once he released her wrist she hastily walked toward her horse. Gathering Beldon's reins in one hand, she hoisted herself up and bolted off for home leaving Dru to stand alone in the meadow, a wide, playful grin deepening his dimple.

"Victoria, love," Dru called from the bottom of the staircase.

A moment passed before she appeared in the doorway of her bedchamber.

"Be a sweet thin' and be bringin' me the book your father loaned me. 'Tis on the table next to me bed. I'd like ta finish readin' it."

Her gaze traveled down the length of him and up again. "That's odd," she said, her tone dripping with sarcasm, "you don't look too weak to climb the stairs. Get it yourself." She straightened and turned to reenter her room.

"Be correctin' me if I be wrong, lass," he replied, stopping her exit, "but I thought we had an understandin'." He shrugged. "Maybe not. Do ya know where your father might be?"

With her back to him, Victoria managed to hide the flare of her nostrils. "I'll get the book," she ground out between clenched teeth.

"Bring me this, my love. Bring me that," Victoria mocked, angrily crossing the foyer on her way to the parlor, tea service in hand. "And since when does a pirate like tea?"

"Victoria?"

She stopped at the sound of her name and glanced up at her mother standing at the top of the stairs.

"Why not have Daphne serve tea?" Alanna asked.

Victoria smiled as sweetly as she could. "Oh, I don't mind, Mama. It's good practice." She bit off each word. Sucking in a deep breath, she turned and stalked off to the next room, leaving her mother to stare after her in confusion.

"You really aren't interested in seeing how the mill works, are you Dru Chandler?" Victoria sneered as

519

they stepped inside.

"Of course, me darlin'. Why wouldn't I be?" He took her elbow to guide her out of the path of a man pushing a wheelbarrow full of corn.

"What possible use could such knowledge be to you?" she demanded, jerking free. "And kindly keep your hands to yourself." Haughtily lifting her nose in the air, she spun about to escape him and collided with another worker. The heavy bucket of black grease he carried slipped from his hands, plopped on the floor and splashed a thick, oozing stream in the air, seeming to purposely attack the front of Victoria's gown.

Appalled, Victoria could only stare at the sticky substance clinging to her satin gown. Her lower lip quivered, she glanced briefly at the worker who stood in silent perplexity, then slowly lifted the grease-laden skirts and in doing so managed to drip a large wad to the toes of her slippers.

"Ohhh," she howled, turning on her heel to flee the mill and race across the yard toward the house.

The side door of the manor slammed shut with such violence that it shook the pictures hanging on the wall and the figurines in the cabinet as Victoria stomped her way to her room, the hem of her soiled gown clutched in her hands. She crossed the foyer and ran up the stairs, failing to see her father lounging in the study's doorway. A moment later, Dru appeared in the hall. An innocent smile on his face and shrugging his shoulders, Dru looked at Remington, who, with a slight nod of his head Dru's direction and a wrinkle to the corner of his mouth, returned to his work without a word.

* * *

Early afternoon sunlight boldly shot in through the window and spotlighted the pair of tall, black boots sitting on the floor in the center of Victoria's bedchamber. She glared at them in disgust. Where did he get these? she wondered. He doesn't even wear boots. If I didn't know better, I'd swear they were my father's. She shook her head, stooped to retrieve one, and set about her task of polishing its rich leather to a shiny glow.

"Damn him, damn him, damn him," Victoria howled, jabbing the needle into the cloth again. "We have servants to sew on buttons, and yet he insists I do it! Ouch!"

A tiny dot of blood appeared on the tip of her finger where a careless stitch strayed from its mark.

Alanna stared worriedly through the open door of the kitchen at her daughter. "Why is she making tarts, Cinnamon?"

The robust cook shrugged. "She said she wanted to. That her father asked her to. Apparently he wants to show the captain what a fine cook she is."

"What?" Alanna asked, knowing cooking to be one of Victoria's shortcomings.

Cinnamon glanced briefly at the angry figure beating on the mound of dough and reached out to pull her friend further away from the door. "If you ask me, something funny's going on. I've offered many times to teach her how to cook and I couldn't get her near the oven. Now this. And she's obviously not thrilled with the idea."

A faint wrinkle appeared on Alanna's brow. "Well,

there's one way to find out." Lifting the many yards of cloth rustling around her feet, she turned and headed for the manor, her steps not faltering as she crossed the yard and entered the house.

Two voices raised in laughter changed Alanna's destination to the study. Without knocking, she went inside, bringing both the captain and Beau to their feet instantly.

"Why is your daughter in the kitchen making tarts?" she asked before either man had a chance to voice a greeting.

Beau stole a glance at Dru. "I would imagine because she wants to be," he replied.

One knotted fist found its way to Alanna's hip. "She hates to cook and you know it. Now what's going on?"

Remington bent to pull a cheroot from the finely carved cigar box on his desk. "Just stay out of it, Alanna," he warned softly.

One fine brow arched defiantly. "Stay out of it?" she repeated.

"Yes. It doesn't concern you, and it's best if you mind your own business." He popped the cheroot in his mouth, striking a flint to ignite it.

"Oh, really? And have you made plans how to stay warm this night?" She lifted a delicate chin in the air, eyed him challengingly, then turned and made her exit.

"I be thinkin' we pushed too far," Dru said, his attention still centered on the vacant doorway.

"Don't worry," Beau replied, a slight frown shadowing his eyes. "I can handle her." He chewed on the end of his cigar, a glimmer pricking his self-confidence.

* * *

"Victoria, I make it a practice not to pry. But I must make an exception this time," her mother began. "Something is going on between you and your father and Dru, and I want to know what it is." She stopped her pacing and stared at her daughter sitting on the bed.

Unable to meet her mother's demanding frown, Victoria played with the wrinkle in her skirt. "Don't worry yourself, Mama. I'll manage."

"Oh? And what time must you rise tomorrow morning to start breakfast? I'm sure that's what they have in mind." When Victoria failed to answer, Alanna sighed heavily and came to sit down next to her. "I only wish to help. When your father told me to mind my own business—"

Victoria's head shot up. "He did?"

Alanna nodded. "And how would you feel if your husband said that to you?"

"It would be all the more reason for me to want to find out his secret."

"Exactly. I already told him he'll sleep alone tonight and I merely want to make the sacrifice worth it."

A smile brightened Victoria's eyes. "Oh, Mama, you didn't."

"Yes, I did," she said emphatically. "And he deserves it for making you unhappy."

Victoria looked at her hands folded in her lap. "I wish I had a way to punish Dru."

"You do," her mother assured her. "And I'll help. Just tell me what it is that he's holding over you."

"I can't," she moaned, bolting from the bed. "You'd be ashamed of me."

"Why? Have you murdered someone?"

523

"No!"

"Done treasonous acts?"

"That's ridiculous."

"Stolen something?"

"Of course not!"

"Then whatever it is will not cause me shame."

Drawing courage from the need to have things said, Victoria turned to her mother, tears welling in her eyes. "Even if I told you I let Dru make love to me?"

Alanna's mouth fell open in surprise. "Oh," she whispered, taken aback.

Victoria choked on her tears, but she rushed on. "No. I didn't let him, I begged him."

"Begged him? Whatever for?"

"Mama," Victoria continued, returning to the bed. She knelt down before her mother. "At the time I thought it was the only thing I could do. Dru had found out that Melissa Bensen planned to aid England in the war and her reward would be Raven Oaks. I bartered the only thing I had in exchange for Dru's promise to see her dead."

The mere mention of the woman's name sparked the old, angry hatred that Alanna had finally laid away to rest. Twenty years had passed without the slightest curiosity about Melissa's whereabouts, and Alanna had many times secretly prayed her dead. That woman had been responsible for Radford's death as surely as if she had held the gun and shot him herself. Her actions had killed Alanna's unborn child, and now, after all this time, she planned to strike again.

"And did he?" she asked, her voice dangerously low, for in her heart she wanted the answer to put an end to all their suffering. Her instincts told her he had not.

Victoria bowed her head. "No, Mama."

"Oh, I see. Then he tricked you in order to have what you offered," Alanna said quietly.

"No. At the time I thought he had, but he wanted to see to my safety first, to return me home to you and Papa. Instead he sent word to the authorities about her. But he never told me he had, so I thought he had lied about his share of the agreement."

"Thus you told your father Dru had raped you several times."

"Yes. I sought revenge for the shame I felt."

"Oh, dear Lord. And your father put him in jail because of it."

"Yes. But I told Papa the truth the night they planned to trick Damon." She raised her head, tears streaming down her face. "I made restitution, Mama."

"And Dru wants more."

"Oh, it's nothing like that, Mama. He does this only to torment me."

"Why?" Alanna asked, failing to understand.

Victoria came to her feet and went to the french doors leading to her balcony. "Because he knows I love him," she whispered. "I have for a long time."

"Before your agreement?"

Victoria nodded. "It was just an excuse, partly. I wanted him."

Alanna smiled to herself, remembering a similar time in her life when she had let her heart rule her head. She, too, had justified her actions with love. "And does he share the feeling?"

"He said he did. To Papa, anyway, but this morning

525

he said he was returning to his ship. He's planning to leave."

"Well," Alanna grinned, bouncing to her feet, "maybe we can change his mind." She strolled playfully up behind Victoria and rested her hands on her daughter's shoulders. "At least give him something to think about. And your father. It will be a long time coming before he'll tell me what to do."

Victoria could not refrain her laughter.

"But tell me. If you admitted all this to your father, why are you allowing Dru to tell you what to do?"

"I didn't tell him everything. I mean I left out the terms of our bargain, and Dru threatened to fill him in. I couldn't take that chance. Papa isn't as understanding as you."

"Sounds to me like he already knows." She shook her head. "Those two are of the same mold, I'm afraid. But then again, so are we." She smiled brightly at Victoria and pulled her toward the bed. "So let's plan our revenge."

"But they just ate, Victoria," Cinnamon argued when the young woman appeared in the kitchen shortly after dinner had been served.

"I know. But Papa and Captain Chandler liked the cherry tarts and requested a second helping."

The buxom cook eyed Victoria closely while she placed the tray on the trestle table, crossed to the buffet, and put two tarts on a plate. After setting them on the serving dish, she went to the cupboard, opened the door and removed the container of salt. Cinnamon's brow lifted. Without hesitation, Victoria returned to the table, took the lid from the can and sprinkled a

526

heavy dose of salt over the pastry.

"What are you doing, child?"

Victoria looked up, a shining vision of purity. "I'm doing as they asked."

"They want salt on a cherry tart?"

"Oh, no, Cimmon. *I* want salt on it."

She snapped the lid on the container, lifted the tray from the table, and walked from the kitchen.

A smile crimped the corner of Victoria's mouth as she strode across the yard and entered the house. In the next few minutes they would learn who was the master of such games.

"Where will you go from here, Dru?" Victoria heard her mother ask as she crossed the foyer, silver tray in hand, and stepped into the parlor.

"South America, maybe," he answered, watching the slim figure glide across the floor and place one dessert plate on a table next to him. She failed to look at him, instead quietly handed the second tart to her father before she returned to her spot on the sofa next to her mother.

"That's so far away. It will be a long time before you come to visit again. Have you ever thought of settling down?" Alanna took a dainty sip of tea, her eyes watching Dru as he reached for the pastry.

"Alanna," Beau interjected, "what the man plans to do in the future is none of our business."

"Oh, forgive me, dear. That was rude of me, wasn't it?" she asked innocently, causing a suspicious frown to form on her husband's brow and Victoria to suddenly clear her throat. He glanced from one to the other, sensing they shared a secret. He picked up the tart.

Dru studied the two women sitting across from him,

527

amazed by their similarity. Had he not known they were in fact mother and daughter, he thought how easily they could pass for sisters. Her mother's beauty made Dru realize that Victoria would remain just as alluring as the older Remington woman and not grow lumpy and wrinkled with the passing of years. It would be an honor for any man to have her at his side. He took a bite of the tart, instantly tasting the overabundance of salt. His eyes watered. He held the mouthful without swallowing, not daring to look at anyone.

"You know, Dru," Alanna said, looking at him over the rim of her teacup, "I'm so glad Beau suggested that Victoria make the dessert tonight. It gives you an idea what she's capable of. Don't you agree?" She smiled demurely at him, returning the cup to its saucer.

"Mmm," he replied with a forced smile, and swallowed the lump in one gulp. He leaned in to retrieve his cup of tea.

Looking back at her husband, Alanna nodded a silent suggestion that he share in the treat. He obeyed immediately, sinking his teeth into the feathery lightness of the crust. His eyes widened, and, out of sheer politeness, he arduously swallowed the awful-tasting pastry. Quickly he reached for his teacup, washed away the lingering of bitterness in his mouth, and glanced up at his wife, tears moistening his eyes.

"Now, dear husband," Alanna said with a raised brow, "what was it you said about minding my own business?"

The two men exchanged glances and burst into laughter.

"See why I married her, Dru?" Remington chuckled. "Never a dull moment." He took another sip of tea. "God, that was awful. And before you decide to poison us, I suggest a truce. Don't you agree, Dru?"

"Aye," he grinned. "Somehow I be thinkin' we be outnumbered if we don't."

"Good," Alanna nodded, placing her cup and saucer on the table. She reached over and patted Victoria's hand, adding, "Why don't we all go out on the porch where it's cooler, and watch the sunset?"

"An excellent idea," Beau replied, coming to his feet. He looked at Dru. "Captain?"

Victoria and her mother taking the lead, the group made their way across the foyer and out onto the veranda. They had just settled themselves into the chairs, Dru leaning against the porch railing, when the clatter of hoofbeats greeted them. Rising, Remington went to the top of the porch steps to wait for the young courier galloping down the lane toward the house.

"Good evening, Mr. Remington," the lad said, dismounting.

"Harold," Remington nodded.

"I have a message for Captain Chandler. His cousin sent me to tell him the *Defiance* is loaded and awaiting his command."

Sharing the porch swing, Alanna could feel her daughter tense. Without looking at her, Alanna gently covered Victoria's hand with hers. Both remained silent.

"Thank you, Harold. Why don't you go around back to the kitchen?" Remington offered. "I'm sure Cinnamon can find you something to eat."

"Thank *you*, Mr. Remington," the boy exclaimed, starting off.

Remington returned to the rocker and said, "Well,

Dru, I guess the decision is up to you now."

"What decision?" Alanna interrupted.

"I offered the management of my new shipping lines to Dru."

"Why that's wonderful," Alanna cried out excitedly. "You can stay right here in Williamsburg." She laughed. "And come for dinner as often as you wish. We have plenty of tarts."

Three voices chorused laughter. But Victoria couldn't find it in her heart to join them. She knew that in the morning Dru would leave for good.

Moonlight hugged the night within her silvery arms, a quiet peace encasing all within its embrace. The sweet chorus of crickets filled the air and lulled the creatures of the earth to blissful slumber, warm breezes playing softly with the branches of the willow, the fragrance of jasmine intoxicating. The world seemed content, at rest, save for the lone figure standing in the gardens near the manor, drinking in the splendor of the scene. Tears glistened in her eyes and trailed moist paths to her chin, long, dark curls cascading over her shoulder to rest against the white silk of her robe.

Victoria had sought the privacy of her room hours before, to be driven out again from her solitude when she thought the confinement would rob her sanity. At morning's light she would see her pirate board a carriage to travel to Williamsburg, knowing he would sail away without a care. Her heart thumped heavily in her chest, the agony of their parting kindled by the visions her mind created. Would he mock her? Would he promise to return if his travels brought him near? Or would he present her with a deep bow, the wink of an eye, and a kiss to her brow? She couldn't bear the thoughts, when all she truly wanted was to hear him say, "I love you, Victoria."

Barefoot, she strolled aimlessly among the flower beds, pausing to smell a delicate blossom and wondering if she would live through the day. Yet, what of her? Could she walk him to the buggy, smile politely, and simply wave good-bye? Could she stop the words of her heart from spilling forth? Would she cry? Would she beg him not to go? Her lips quivering, Victoria brushed away her tears with the back of her hand. No, she would not, for something deep inside her filled her with the doubt that he really cared, and to be denied by him would only further destroy the shattered remnants of her pride.

Looking skyward, she studied the twinkling of the stars, small glittering diamonds cushioned on black velvet, and suddenly felt a strange desire. She wished to carry his child in her womb, to keep a part of him with her for the rest of her life. *I do love him,* she thought, *and if it be his wish to leave me, I will not stop him.* Her gaze drifted back to the manor, dark and serene, and she looked upon the window of the room where he slept. Did his dreams trouble him? Or did he sleep contentedly? As if guided by angelic hands, Victoria did not fight the need to go to him, to watch him unobserved in slumber, to burn his image into her mind for all eternity. She left the gardens, entered the house, and climbed the stairs, pausing only briefly before she lifted the latch and stepped into the room.

Moonlight flooded in through the window, platinum streams falling softly on the wide bed, and without hesitation she crossed to stand beside it. Several moments passed as she gazed down lovingly on the still form, the quilt draped enticingly over his hips, the bare muscles of his shoulders and chest illuminated in the silver glow of the room. He stirred, and Victoria's breath caught in her throat, not wanting to awaken him. When he quieted once more, she slowly fell to her knees, resting back on her heels to study him more closely. With his face turned to the light, she felt drawn to reach out and trace her fingertip along his brow, the thin, straight nose and silky, dark lashes pressed against his suntanned face. Her lips tingled with the need to touch them to his, to kiss his mouth, his cheek, to have him hold her in his arms. Tears filled her eyes. Her gaze languidly traveled the length of him, vividly recalling the strength of his muscles, the manly shape of him, and her heart fluttered with the memory of him pressed against her, his touch, his caress, his gentleness. Could she ever erase the vision from her mind?

Worry that he would awake brought her to her feet, yet in her heart she prayed he would, that he would call to her, open his arms, and draw her to him. Her lip trembled and she pressed shaky fingertips to her mouth. *Good-bye, my Irish rogue,* she thought, *my pirate, my love.* She turned to leave, a gasp escaping her when she felt a warm hand upon her own, and she glanced back to find him watching, the steel-blueness of his eyes reflecting the ashen light of the room. Her tears blurred her vision of him, and for a moment she wondered if it had all been a cruel dream, that in reality she still walked the path of the gardens. She blinked, a silvery droplet tumbling down her cheek, and she bit her lower lip to stop its quiver.

''Dru—'' she whispered with a sob, yearning, needing to say the words in her heart, pausing when he raised up on one elbow and pressed a finger to his lips to still her words. He released her hand to fold back the covers of his bed, in silent understanding of her desire.

Filled with unbounded joy, her tears fell freely, and she stood unmoving before him, all shame for her act vanishing. She loved him, and though they spoke not the bonds of wedlock, she knew that even God would bless them.

The silk robe slipped from her shoulders and glided gently to the floor at her feet, her gaze feasting on the handsome face staring back at her. No smile curled his lips or twinkled in his eyes, and Victoria knew then that his time for playing with her had come to an end. Whether he truly loved her as he had claimed or merely desired her, mattered to no degree, for on this night he would be hers alone to have, to hold, to love. She slid the gown from her tiny figure, letting it float to the floor and pool out around her. Lifting the heavy mass of her long black hair, she draped it over one shoulder, smiling happily when she saw his gaze roam freely, his body tremble from the pleasure.

Without a word, she moved to the bed, pressed a knee against it and fell gently into his open arms. Their lips met softly at first, as if testing the illusion of their dreams before they clung frantically, deliriously, wanting to be as one, united in the rapture of their love. He showered her with kisses, to her mouth, nose, cheek, each eyelid, bringing a delighted giggle from her, and she returned his ardor, leaving them both panting. His hands moved against the white, smooth flesh of her back to rest intimately on her buttocks, his face buried in the ebony locks of her hair, drinking in the scent of her. He rolled her beneath him, his mouth hungrily tasting the silken skin of her neck, playfully biting a creamy white shoulder before he sought the fullness of her breast, his tongue teasing its nipple. Victoria moaned, caught up in the delicious splendor of his moves, fingers entwined within the dark curls at the nape of his neck, guiding him, silently urging him to continue, to sample again the treasure she could offer.

His mouth found her other breast, nibbling gently, sucking greedily, his hands exploring every curve before he claimed her lips once more in a demanding kiss, his heart pounding wildly. His manhood throbbed against her thigh, and, unwilling to wait a moment longer, Victoria moved to welcome him, whispering his name over and over again as he raised above her, her nails digging into the muscles of his shoulders. He slid an arm beneath her narrow waist, held her tightly and gently pressed his manly hardness in her, waiting, savoring, never wanting the time to end.

Victoria clung desperately, clawing at his back when he thrust deeper, faster, their bodies surrendering to passion's embrace. A wild magic exploded within them, soaring them on widespread wings to heights beyond their imaginings, floating endlessly, then gliding earthward to lie cradled in each other's arms, breathless, sated, complete.

A long while passed before Dru raised up to look at her, a soft smile on his lips, a tenderness in his eyes. He leaned to gently kiss her, then pull her to him within the circle of his arms, her cheek pressed against his chest, and Victoria lay content, listening to the steady rhythm of his heartbeat. She closed her eyes, forbidding sleep to come, cherishing the final moments she would spend with him. Then morning light stained the eastern sky and Victoria slipped from the warmth of his bed to dress, gazing down at his sleeping face before she quietly stole from the room.

Steel-blue eyes filled with tears watched her departure.

THIRTY-ONE

Victoria stared worriedly at her father sitting across from her in the carriage. In a short while they would reach Williamsburg. At first when her mother had suggested they go along with her father and Dru to see Dru off, Victoria had said no, that seeing him board his ship and sail away would be more than she could bear. If he simply walked out the door and rode down the drive of Raven Oaks, she could tell herself it was only for a while, that next week he'd return. There was something so final about a ship's sailing, something with which she felt certain she could not cope. But Alanna had argued the point, that once Dru was faced with the actual farewell, maybe then he'd realize he couldn't do it. And now there was the note.

She watched her father absently fold and unfold the piece of paper time and time again, a troubled expression wrinkling his brow. A messenger had found them at the inn the night past just as they had sat down to eat the evening meal. A sudden rush of damp, crisp air had flooded into the room when the young man sought the inn for protection against the driving rain, calling everyone's attention to him. He looked about the room with an apology for his intrusion upon his lips, and spied her father sitting at a far table. He hurried forward, raindrops dripping from his hat and mud caked on his clothes, offering the message.

"I'm glad I stopped, sir," he said. "It saved me a trip all the way to Raven Oaks. And I apologize about the note, but I was thrown from my horse a way back. It got muddy, I'm afraid."

Remington waved off the apology and gave the young man a piece of silver for his trouble. He waited until the youth had left them, then turned his attention to the paper in his hand.

"What is it, Beau?" Alanna asked.

Everyone watched him pull apart the seal of the tattered letter, a confused look on his face once he had read it in its entirety.

"I'm not certain," he said slowly.

"Well, read it aloud. Maybe we can help," Alanna urged.

Remington held the note before him, tilted a little to better catch the light. " 'I have something you might be interested in. Let's say it's my way of making up for an injustice I caused many years ago. Meet me as soon as you can at the vacant warehouse near the pier in Williamsburg. Bring someone with you if you wish.' "

"Who's it from?" Alanna asked uneasily.

He squinted his eyes, staring at the bottom of the page. Finally, he shook his head. "I can't make it out.

It's torn here and spotted with dirt. Can you?'' He handed the message to Dru.

''Looks like a 'C', then a space and maybe 'P-a-r,' '' Dru said, after a while.

''Par, Par,'' Remington repeated, searching his memory for any hint of recognition. ''Does it bring anyone to mind, Alanna?''

''No. No one,'' she admitted. ''What will you do?''

Remington had remained quiet for several minutes before he had said, ''I guess I'll be going to the warehouse. Will you come with me, Dru?''

And Dru had agreed.

No one spoke of the message after that, for although her father had been told to bring someone with him, the entire situation boded danger. Victoria glanced at her father again. Did he really not know who had sent the invitation, or had he lied? Could he, in fact, know exactly who had sent it, and only wished to save his family worry? One corner of her mouth twitched in an understanding smile. They called her actions lies, her father's wisdom. But in reality they both hid the truth when they thought it best. She relaxed and stared out the window, spying the distant rooftops that announced their arrival in Williamsburg. Whether given permission or not, she would be going to the meeting place.

''Beau, at least have dinner before you go,'' Alanna argued as they stood at the bottom of the staircase in the Chesterfield House.

''This won't take long,'' he replied with a smile. ''Dru and I will be back before you know it.''

''I just don't like the idea of your carrying a pistol.''

''Would you rather I went without it?''

538

She frowned, surrendering.

Beau reached out to encircle his wife's slim frame in his arm and pulled her toward the door. "If it's any consolation, Dru is on his way to his ship now to get his cousin and Mr. McKenzie. We won't be alone. In fact, Dru intends to ask his cousin if he's heard anything about a man wanting to meet with me. He'll make certain it isn't a trap." He sighed, glancing back over his shoulder at the stairway leading to their rooms. "I only wish I could have convinced him to stay. He's what Victoria needs."

"And wants," Alanna added. "Beau, why is Dru leaving if he loves Victoria and knows she loves him?"

"We must admire him for it, Alanna, my sweet. He doesn't feel either of them would be happy for very long living in a way to which they're not accustomed."

"That's foolish," Alanna snapped. "Does he think she'll be happier without him?"

Beau pulled her close. "Give him time, my love. I've gotten to know that young man quite well in the past week, and I find he and I are a lot alike. Remember how long it took me to realize I couldn't live without you?"

Alanna laughed softly. "Almost a year."

"Right. And a ship is capable of sailing into port as well as out."

"You're right, of course." She glanced up toward Victoria's room. "I just hope I can convince her and ease the waiting."

"I have no doubt but what you can. Now run along and dress for dinner. We'll be back within the hour." He hugged his wife, then stood aside to watch her gracefully ascend the stairs.

539

As Remington neared the newspaper office, the place where they had agreed to meet, he spotted Dru, his cousin, and McKenzie walking toward him.

"Good evening, gentlemen," he nodded.

"Mr. Remington," Sean and McKenzie chorused.

"Has Dru explained everything?"

"Aye, sir," Sean replied. "As we be tellin' him, tis the first we heard of it. We did notice one ship has stayed anchored offshore since before we sailed in, but we not be knowin' who commanded her."

"Well, then I guess there's nothing more we can do. Shall we proceed?"

With Dru and Remington leading the way, the others followed closely behind as they set off toward the pier.

Dying streams of sunlight cast long, distorted shadows on the ground across the remnants of golden light on the path the men followed toward the waterfront. When they came to the end of the sidewalk, they paused, studying the only vacant building in the lot. Dru motioned his friends to wait outside. Another, similar time flashing in their minds, Dru and Beau Remington crossed the street and approached the single entrance to the warehouse.

"They'll be expectin' ya, not me," Dru whispered, "so be lettin' me go in first. I'll signal if it is all clear."

"No," Remington said firmly. "I asked you to come along, not fight my battles. We go in together, or you don't go."

Dru grinned at him. "Just like your daughter," he said, and Remington nodded, smiling in return.

The door proved unlocked when Dru touched a hand to it and it squealed briefly on its hinges before it opened onto a full view of the room inside. Tension prickled the hair on the back of Dru's neck when they found no one waiting. He was certain they hid somewhere in anticipation to their coming. They moved further in and closed the door quietly, hoping to allow them a moment more to study their surroundings.

The two windows of the warehouse permitted the fading sunlight to steal in, painting golden rectangles on the dirt-covered floor. Particles of dust floating in the air were all the cubicle provided, no boxes or crates or furniture of any kind. Opposite them, they spotted a door, closed and barring further inspection of the room beyond. Motioning for Remington to stay where he was, Dru stepped forward, intent on investigating, when the latch clicked, freezing them where they stood, pistols drawn.

Victoria waited until she heard the door to her mother's room close before opening her own to peek out into the hallway. She had only a half hour until her mother would return, expecting to find Victoria ready to go down to the dining hall. She would have to hurry if she wished to catch up with her father and Dru, and she decided it best to travel through the alleyways, where she would be less likely to be seen. She quickly descended the wide staircase, walked across the entry-hall, and out onto the sidewalk. Hastily, she rounded the corner of the Chesterfield House and started off toward the pier. If only she knew for certain which warehouse.

In the hushed stillness of early evening, no other's

presence felt, she listened to the gentle slaps of water breaking against the ships anchored in the harbor and smelled the fresh salt air, urging her to hurry. She must arrive before anything happened. *Dear God, don't let them hurt Dru or my father,* she prayed. At the end of the row of buildings, she faced several darkened storefronts. Which one? The first? The second? Glancing left, then right, she decided the only way to find out would be to look in each window. She stepped from the sidewalk, sensing someone in the shadows next to her. She spun around, sucking in a breath to scream when she spied the figure, and instantly felt the two strong hands of another come up from in back to clamp onto her and stifle her outcry.

"Mr. Remington?" the man in the doorway asked, his face shadowed in the absence of candlelight.

"Yes," Remington answered.

"We intend you no harm." He raised his hands and stepped forward. "I'm unarmed. Although I don't blame you for being careful, I must ask you to put away your weapons. Otherwise I shall keep what I offer."

"Which is?"

"The pistols first, sir."

Remington looked at Dru and saw him nod in the muted amber of the setting sun.

"Just lay them on the floor in front of you while we talk."

"Who are you?" Remington demanded, stooping to do as instructed.

"My name is Clayton Parker."

"Parker. Par—" Remington repeated, glancing at Dru and back to the man again. "You sent the message?''

"I signed it. But the words were recited to me by my captain.''

"Who is?'' Remington frowned.

The man stepped aside and Beau fought the urge to retrieve his firearm when another figure more than filled the doorway.

"What in the devil are ya doin' here?'' Sean demanded.

Victoria struggled free and spun around, planting the instep of her slipper to his shin. "How dare you frighten me!'' she barked, watching him bounce about on one foot, his other ankle held in his hand.

"We couldn't be letting ya walk in one them, lass,'' Donovan explained. "It could be dangerous.''

She flashed him an angry glare. "Then why are you standing out here? You should have gone with them.''

"Because Dru ordered us ta stay,'' Sean added, his voice tinged with pain.

"Hang his orders!''

"Aye. And 'tis what he would do ta us if we disobeyed, lass,'' Donovan pointed out. "If ya want ta help them, ya will stay with us.''

"And do what?'' she demanded.

"Wait,'' Donovan answered quietly.

"I thought you said no weapons,'' Remington hissed once he spotted the pistol in the second man's hand.

" 'Tis only ta be makin' sure ya will listen ta me and not try ta blow me head off,'' the huge pirate maintained.

"And why would I want to do that?''

His round belly shook when he chuckled. "Maybe I should be tellin' ya me name. 'Tis Dillon Gallagher, Captain of the *Sea Falcon*." He stepped from the shadows, his red hair set aglow in the remaining faded sunlight.

Remington's mind whirled with memories of years gone by, the torment he had felt when this man had kidnapped Alanna, the grief and pain that had torn at him while he held his dying friend in his arms, murdered by the man who stood before him now. Twenty years had passed since that day, and it had all eased only to be reborn again now in his need to see justice done for Radford Chamberlain's death. His hatred ruling him, blinding him to all else, he made to lunge for the pistol lying at his feet, finding his arms pinned to his sides when Dru threw himself at Beau, firmly holding the man in a grip of steel.

"Hear him out, Beau," Dru urged. "He has no reason ta see ya dead, but he will if ya try somethin' so foolish as this."

Remington struggled briefly, finding his captor's strength greater than his. "You don't understand," he choked.

"Ah, but I do. Victoria told me everythin'. Think about it, man. Why would he put himself before ya, knowin' the hatred ya carry? His message said he be havin' somethin' ta give in return for an injustice of years ago. He be askin' your pardon."

"Never! Never!" Beau screamed. "He killed my friend."

"Aye, that I did," Dillon said softly, lowering his pistol. "But it wouldn't have happened if a certain lass hadn't filled me head with lies."

Remington glared silently at him.

"Just like you, Alanna, and your friend, I had been tricked, too. We were given a note that was supposed ta have come from her betrothed, tellin' Alanna he not be wantin' ta marry her. It near killed the lass inside. And when I found you two standin' before me that day, all I could be thinkin' of was how the man rejected her for someone else."

"Wait a minute," Remington interrupted. "If all you had was the note, how did you find out it was a lie?"

The long scar on Dillon's cheek wrinkled with his smile. "The same way I be knowin' the man left his plantation ta Alanna in his will." He waved a hand. " 'Tisn't important anyway. Only that I do know."

"All right," Remington agreed, shaking lose of Dru, "then what do you have that you could possibly think would justify killing Alanna's betrothed and my closed friend?"

"I be havin' two things I be thinkin' ya could use."

"Use?"

"Aye." Dillon nodded to his first mate. Tucking the pistol into his breeches, Dillon turned to follow Clayton into the adjoining room, where he struck a flint to the single candle sitting on a crate. A golden hue settled over the area, and out of curiosity Beau and Dru cautiously followed. "Come," Dillon urged when the men ventured no further than the doorway. "I be wantin' ya ta get a good view."

Crossing to another door beside which Clayton stood, he motioned the first mate to open it and waited while the man went inside. A moment later, a third figure catapulted from within the darkened recesses to stumble and fall at Remington's feet.

"Kingsley!" Remington bellowed.

Hands bound behind him, the colonel struggled to rise, kept there when Dru stepped closer and pushed him back with the heel of his shoe firmly planted to the space between his shoulder blades.

"Where did you find him?" Remington asked.

A satisfied grin spread over Dillon's face. "I be thinkin' ya would like me present. He came ta me tellin' me ta sail him to Nova Scotia. Now, not bein' the sort ta take orders from anyone, I threw him in the hold and left him there until he would tell me why. Did ya know how he came ta be ownin' Willow Glen?"

"He purchased it," Remington said.

"Aye. But how would he be knowin' it was for sale?"

Remington's eyes slowly widened, his lips parting in silent understanding.

"Aye, Beau Remington," Dillon smiled. He looked at Parker with a jerk of his head toward the door. Again Clayton disappeared inside, but when he returned he held Melissa Bensen by the arm. Her eyes unaccustomed to the light, she squinted, blinked, then glared at Beau.

" 'Tis me second gift ta ya, Beau Remington. Now ya can be seein' her hanged, and no one will be stoppin' ya. This be me real way of makin' up for killin' your friend. And me way of tellin' Alanna how sorry I be for bein' the one who kidnapped her."

Remington frowned, recalling how Alanna had declared that her safety on Gallagher's ship had come only from his protection. "From what she told me, captain, had it not been you who took her, she might not be alive today. I don't think she'll expect your apology,

546

nor think there was a need." He sighed. "As for me, I accept your gifts eagerly and pray that, at last, the memory of how Radford died will fade, knowing his murderer will pay." He glared at Melissa, who returned him an equally hate-filled stare. "Take Kingsley outside," he said to Dru. "It will be my pleasure to see to this one."

When Dru bent to haul the colonel to his feet, he caught Melissa's attention. Her eyes widened, her nostrils flared, and she jerked free of Parker as she hissed Dru's name.

"Dru Chandler?" Dillon questioned, staring at the young man before him.

"Yes," she spat. "I wouldn't be here now if it weren't for him."

Frantically looking about her, she spied the pistol stuck in Dillon's belt. Too quickly to be noticed, she lunged for the weapon, turned, and aimed it at Dru.

"No!" Dillon screamed, swinging a huge fist.

The blow struck her across the temple, instantly ripping open a wide gash in the soft flesh of her cheek, the firearm discharging as it flew from her hand. The power behind the blow hurled her blindly into the wall, smashing her delicate torso against the unrelenting barrier, the crack of snapping bones sharply piercing the unearthly quiet. Eyes glazed, neck twisted grotesquely, the lifeless form of Melissa Bensen slithered to the floor.

"But I heard a shot!" Victoria sobbed, fighting desperately to break free of Sean.

"Ya are ta stay here," he ordered. "We'll go."

"No," she cried, twisting from his hold. Skirts lifted to clear her step, Victoria raced off in the direction of the shot, Sean and Donovan running after her.

She cleared the sidewalk easily, lifted the latch of the warehouse door, and bolted inside, tears streaming down her face, nearly blinding her. But the worry that harm had befallen her loved ones urged her carelessly forward, rushing her through the darkened room to the second one where yellow candlelight flickered. She stopped in the doorway, her companions catching up to crowd in around her. In an instant, her gaze took in the scene before her. Across the room from her stood her father, gazing down upon the unmoving form of a woman, her body limp, her face bloody, her eyes unseeing. Near him, Dru knelt on the floor, Damon Rutledge held in Dru's arms, a bright red stain marring the man's shirt front. Two other men stood away, observing in silence.

"What happened?" Sean demanded, stepping past Victoria.

Dru looked up. "An accident. He took a bullet meant for me."

Sean's eyes flashed dangerously at the two strangers, his hand slipping to the butt of his pistol lodged in his belt.

"Not them, cousin," Dru quickly said. "Her." He nodded toward the dead woman.

"Who was she?"

"Melissa Bensen," Remington offered.

Sean's chin fell in surprise. "Melissa Bensen?"

"Aye," Dru replied.

"How did she—"

"I'll be explainin' later. You and Donovan take the colonel to the doctor. He's hurt badly and I be thinkin' Mr. Remington doesn't want ta see him die before his

548

trial."

The two men did as instructed, lifting the unconscious Englishman in their arms. Dru waited until they had gone before settling his gaze on Victoria.

"What are ya doin' here, lass?" he asked, his tone hinting disapproval.

A flood of emotions washed over her, pent up for so many weeks that when he asked the question they became jumbled in her mind, preventing a single word from passing her lips. Her tears renewing in a steadier stream, she rushed toward him, threw her arms around his neck, and sobbed uncontrollably.

"Take it easy, lass," he chuckled. "Ya be makin' me think ya care."

"I do, you fool," she choked out. "I love you."

Setting her at arms' length, he asked, "What did ya say?"

"I said I love you, you hard-headed Irishman. Oh, Dru, when I heard gunfire, I was so scared you'd been killed." She fell against him again.

"He would have been if it hadn't been for Captain Gallagher," her father offered.

"Aye," Dru agreed, holding Victoria close. His expression changed to wonder, and he turned to face Dillon, Victoria held in the circle of his arm. "Why did ya stop her from killin' me?"

Dillon glanced briefly at Parker, then walked a few steps to bend and retrieve his pistol from the floor. He shrugged, studying the weapon in his hand. "I be thinkin' there's been enough killin'."

Clayton stepped forward. "If you don't tell him, I will, Dillon."

The fire in the man's eyes matched the color of his

hair. "Tell him what?" Dillon growled.

"How long have I known you, Dillon? Thirty? Thirty-five years? I know what you're thinking before you do. And I know you've hidden an ache in your heart all that time. We're getting too old to sail anymore. You said so yourself. And if you're to spend the rest of your days in peace, you must clear your conscience."

"What makes ya think ya be knowin' what ails me?" Gallagher hissed.

"I knew it the day we left the *Defiance* anchored in the bay. No man without a secret would give away a ship to a total stranger without just cause."

"You gave me that ship?" Dru asked.

Dillon looked at him, his mouth opened to respond, then glanced at Remington, Parker and the floor, heaving a sigh. "Aye."

"But why?"

Dillon refused to answer.

"Tell him, or I will," Clayton threatened.

Dillon shifted the flintlock from one hand to the other. "Ya be testin' our friendship, Clayton," he warned.

"No, captain, only strengthening it."

Dillon's gray-blue eyes moved up to stare at the man, his anger slowly fading. He smiled. "Aye, that ya are." He turned to face Dru. "I be owin' Katherine Chandler, that's why."

"Me mother?"

"Aye."

"For what?"

"For not forcin' her ta marry me when she carried me child."

Dru's face paled in the yellow light. "What?"

"Aye, ladie. Ya be me son."

The gentle breeze of morning filled with the fragrance of the sea floated up to Victoria, brushing against the tears on her cheeks as she stood on the balcony of her room. Gazing out at the tall masts of the ships anchored in the bay, she pictured the crew of the *Defiance* making ready to set sail filling the hold with supplies enough to see them to Ireland. Before the heat of day had reached its fullest, Dru would be on that ship, commanding his men to weigh anchor and set course, to briskly cut the ocean's surface on its way home, the *Sea Falcon* just off port.

It's what he must do, she told herself. *I won't stand in his way.* Her lower lip quivered and she bit it to still the return of a flood of tears. It was his decision alone to make. And she understood, she truly did. He lived his life the way he chose, full, except for the constant void a second parent's guidance could have brought. They had a lifetime of catching up to do, he and his father, tears, joy, a sharing. She turned away from the day's brightness. *And I will not complicate their reunion with my presence. To say farewell will be my destiny.*

EPILOGUE

September, 1778

The bright, vivid colors of fall set the hillsides on fire in oranges, golds, and reds. The days grew shorter, the night air chilly, the mornings more difficult to greet. Four months had slipped away, and, although Victoria busied herself with many tasks, her mind and heart carried only one memory.

Since the British attack on Chesapeake Bay, her father stayed away from Raven Oaks more often and for longer periods of time, pledging to help the struggling young rebels as best he could. In his absence, Victoria assumed the role of master of the great plantation, issuing orders and seeing that the crops were harvested. To those who praised her, she seemed an unselfish child, freeing her father to do another work, while in truth, her purpose was to fill her days and fall exhausted into a dreamless sleep.

"Victoria."

She glanced up from the papers spread over the surface of her father's desk and smiled. "Hello, Mother."

Dressed in her nightclothes, Alanna walked further into the study. "It's after midnight, Victoria. You'll do no one any good by making yourself sick."

Returning the quill to the well, Victoria leaned back and stretched, an unexpected yawn escaping her. "I guess I am a little tired. You go on to bed, Mama. I'll finish this and do the same."

"Promise?"

She nodded. "Only ten more minutes, I promise." She raised a quizzical brow when her mother did not move.

"Your father will be very proud of you. You've selflessly taken on a job you needn't have."

"And who would have done it if I hadn't?" she asked, not remembering how her mother had once run her own plantation. "No, Mama. I had to do it. Don't give me praise where it's not deserved."

"Maybe. But I'm sure he'll still be very proud, no matter what your reason. Goodnight, my child."

"Goodnight, Mama," she said, watching the slim figure turn and seem to glide from the room. She leaned forward, extinguished the flames in the candelabrum, and settled back in her father's chair once more, the desire to complete the row of figures in the ledger gone. The firelight from the hearth danced warmly about the room, pulling her gaze to its source. Would she ever have cause to be happy again? she wondered. She doubted it, for with Dru's sailing something had seemed to die inside her. She sighed, knowing if she sat there much longer tears would burn her eyes and morning would come to find her weeping, as it so often had. She rose, went to the fireplace, and took a taper from the mantel. Igniting its wick, she placed the candle in the holder and started for her room.

The only sound that filled the manor that of her footfalls against the stairs, Victoria sadly climbed the steps, somehow wishing she never would again. After all, hadn't she truly died a long time ago? She passed her mother's room and traveled further down the hall to her own. Inside, she closed the door and went directly to her dressing table where she set the candle and absently slipped from her muslin gown, letting it lie where it fell. A warm fire in the hearth took away any chill, and she sat down on the bench clothed only in her camisole, to brush out her hair, studying the somber reflection staring back at her. Then her gaze looked past the figure in the mirror to fall upon the image of the pillow on her bed. She frowned, leaning in to get a better view. Unable to distinguish the tiny item lying there, she turned around, the frown disappearing in a look of surprise. Slowly rising, she went to the bed and lifted the single rose from its cushion.

"Ya must be learnin' ta lock your doors, me love. No tellin' what kind of rogue ya be findin' in your room."

Victoria closed her eyes, one hand pressed to her mouth to still her sobs. Had her mind played tricks? If she opened her eyes again to look, would she find the room empty? The sweet fragrance of the flower filled her senses. No. It was real. He was here.

"Dru," she choked, opening her eyes. She glanced over her shoulder to see him step from the shadows, a flood of joyful tears streaming down her face. "Oh, Dru. You came back."

"Aye, me love. I had ta return. I forgot somethin'."

"What?" she whispered hopefully.

"The woman I be meanin' ta marry."

A smile broke free, and, dropping the rose to the floor, Victoria ran into his outstretched arms.

THE BEST IN HISTORICAL ROMANCE
by Penelope Neri

HEARTS ENCHANTED (1432, $3.75)
When Lord Brian Fitzwarren saw the saucy, slender wench bathing in the river, her fresh, sun-warmed skin beckoned for his touch. That she was his enemy's daughter no longer mattered. The masterful lord vowed that somehow he would claim the irresistible beauty as his own . . .

BELOVED SCOUNDREL (1259, $3.75)
When the handsome sea captain James Mallory was robbed by the scruffy street urchin, his fury flared into hot-blooded desire upon discovering the thief was really curvaceous Christianne. The golden-haired beauty fought off her captor with all of her strength — until her blows became caresses and her struggles an embrace . . .

PASSION'S RAPTURE (1433, $3.75)
Through a series of misfortunes, an English beauty becomes the captive of the very man who ruined her life. By day she rages against her imprisonment — but by night, she's in passion's thrall!

JASMINE PARADISE (1170, $3.75)
When Heath sets his eyes on the lovely Sarah, the beauty of the tropics pales in comparison. And he's soon intoxicated with the honeyed nectar of her full lips. Together, they explore the paradise . . . of love.

SENSATIONAL SAGAS!

MORE RAPTUROUS READING

HISTORICAL ROMANCE AT ITS BEST!
by KATHLEEN DRYMON

SAVAGE DAWN   (1436, $3.75)
Lisa should have been terrified of the awesome Indian who attacked her carriage and took her captive. Instead Silver Fox's touch made her melt into wild reckless rapture . . . until the SAVAGE DAWN.

TEXAS BLOSSOM   (1305, $3.75)
When Sorrel's luscious curves silhouetted the firelight, Mathew felt lust and desire like he never felt before. Soon, he was enmeshed in her silvery web of love — their passion flowering like a wild TEXAS BLOSSOM!

WILD DESIRES   (1103, $3.50)
The tempestuous saga of three generations of women, set in the back streets of London, glamorous New Orleans and the sultry tropics — where each finds passion in a stranger's arms!

TENDER PASSIONS   (1032, $3.50)
While countless men professed their adoration for Katherine, she tossed her head in rejection. But when she's pirated away by a man whose object is lust, she finds herself willing!

by BRENNA McCARTNEY

REBEL BRIDE   (1442, $3.50)
When Southern Major Brant Faulkner suggested Amber warm his bed to save her life, she was ready to hang for being a Union spy. But when his demanding lips closed over hers, the curvaceous beauty forgot dying and felt she'd gone straight to heaven!

PASSION'S BLOSSOM   (1109, $3.50)
Lovely, innocent Catherine's fantasies were shattered when her aunts promised her in marriage to a rich, leering old man. When she met dashing, handsome Cameron she vowed that — married or not — only he would lead her to the garden of love.

Available wherever paperbacks are sold, or order direct from the Publisher. Send cover price plus 50¢ per copy for mailing and handling to Zebra Books, 475 Park Avenue South, New York, N.Y. 10016. DO NOT SEND CASH.